Beauty from Ashes

Suzie Waltner

Beauty from Ashes

ISBN-13: 978-1500736132

ISBN-10: 1500736139

Suzie Waltner

This novel is a work of fiction. Names, characters, places, and incidents are either
products of the author's imagination or used fictitiously. All characters are fictional,
and any similarity to people living or dead is purely coincidental.

DEDICATION

To Him who is able to do immeasurably more than I can ask or imagine. Thank you, Lord, for the gift of stories.

Suzie Waltner

ACKNOWLEDGMENTS

My writing journey has taught me a lot. Mostly that it takes a great group of people around you to help create a good book.

Many thanks to my first readers, Denise Covell and Allison Jones. From there, this book made its way through my first ever critique group. I learned a lot from the other ACFW scribes who took the time to read my story and give me feedback. Special thanks to Audrey Appenzeller, Michael Blaylock, Jim Robar, and Janet Teitsort who stuck with me until the end. My beta readers and proofreaders are indispensable. Thank you Jessica Dumoulin, Janet O'Hare, Sherry Rozell, Chalene Waltner, Emily Waltner, and Wendy Waltner.

Suzie Waltner

ONE

Libby James stuffed papers into her carrier bag and glanced around her desk to make sure she hadn't left anything. When the phone rang, she cringed as her boss's extension filled the display. The last thing she wanted to do tonight was talk to her demanding employer. She took a deep breath and lifted the handset.

"Libby, please come in here for a minute." It was a demand, not a request. Linda Taylor was only a few years older than Libby but spoke to her as if she were a disobedient child.

She always hated when Linda asked her to come by her office. Nothing good ever happened in that room. In her fourth year at Taylor Designs, Libby was the most senior staff member, but only because no one else lasted more than six months. Even Libby had entertained the idea of resigning at least half a dozen times when Linda took credit for her work—something that occurred on a regular basis. Pausing outside the door, she inhaled a deep breath and stepped into view.

"Please sit down." Linda waved her hand in the general direction of the matching armchairs on the other side of the desk. "How are things going at the Patterson home?"

"Everything's right on schedule." Libby pressed her hand against her knee to stop her leg from bouncing. "Mrs. Patterson is pleased, and we should finish by the end of the month."

"You're from Perry, aren't you?"

The rapid subject change unnerved her. She gave up on keeping her legs still. Why did Linda care where she was from? "Yes, I grew up there but I've lived in Raleigh for the past seven years."

Linda's perfectly manicured fingernails tapped on the desk. With each click, Libby's control slipped a little more. "I need you to drive down for a consultation next Wednesday. I'll take over at the Patterson home."

Libby bit the inside of her cheek to keep from saying something that would anger her boss. These were the times she hated her job. After two months of working on Mrs. Patterson's living room, she wouldn't get to finish the project. The woman had praised Libby's work but now—when she was close to completion—Linda would swoop in and receive all of the accolades. She couldn't keep quiet. "Even with the drive, a consultation will only take a few hours. I can still finish the Patterson job."

With a raised eyebrow, Linda scowled, somehow managing to convey menace with her expression. "This client is extremely important. You'll need to get started right away."

"Stacy or Janet should take the consult since I'm going on vacation next month."

"I hoped you might consider rescheduling that. This is a busy time for us."

She couldn't believe her ears. Linda had approved her vacation six months ago. The plane tickets were purchased, the rooms were reserved, and Libby's sister and friend were counting on her to help with the kids. She would not back out on her family. "I'm sorry but I can't do that. My family is expecting my help."

"You're valuable to this firm, Libby." Linda's voice was cold. "Many people compliment you and your work. I would hate for you to throw everything away. Think about it over the weekend. We'll discuss this again on Monday." She wiggled the tips of her French manicure at Libby in dismissal.

Had Linda just threatened to fire her? Libby refused to get worked up over the conversation. She'd put a lot of hours into Taylor Designs over the past few years, many without compensation. Her vacation was overdue, and she wouldn't cancel her trip. No longer caring if she had everything, she snatched up her bag and hurried to her car. She needed to talk to Emily.

Em? You here?" Libby entered the front door, and the oasis she'd created in the apartment immediately soothed her frazzled nerves.

"Be out in a minute," her roommate called from the back.

Libby dropped onto the blue couch and ran her hand over the soft microfiber. The piece was comfortable and functional, not to mention one of her favorite Craigslist finds. The couch had been the inspiration for the rest of the room. The soft blues and yellows were reminiscent of the ocean on a summer day.

"How was your day?" Emily plopped on the other end of the sofa.

Libby repeated the exchange with her boss.

"That's ridiculous, Lib. She can't threaten you like that. You deserve a vacation more than anyone there."

"I agree. Neither Janet nor Stacy is working on projects right now, so it makes more sense for them to handle this new one." She leaned her head on the back of the couch and closed her eyes. "Am I crazy to stay at Taylor Designs, Em? Should I suck it up and find another job?"

"How do you feel about leaving?"

"Starting somewhere new scares me. There's always uncertainty when entering a new situation, but maybe it would give me more freedom with my own designs."

"You should consider it. You did a terrific job with this place, and your nieces loved how you fixed up their rooms."

"I didn't do much for Charity and Hope. We only added a few accents in their favorite colors and painted the walls."

"Learn to accept a compliment." Emily elbowed her in the ribs.

"It's the truth. I hardly did anything." She stood. "I'm starving. Want to order dinner?"

"What a surprise." Emily rolled her eyes, but her smile suggested she wasn't against the idea. "What are you in the mood for?"

"Fajitas?"

"You're killing me." She groaned. "If we eat Mexican for dinner, I have to go to the gym this weekend."

"I don't understand why you pay for a membership. You're

gorgeous and don't need to work out."

"Are you kidding me? This takes work." She waved her hand at her stomach and legs. "Not all of us are blessed with your metabolism."

True. Libby ate all day long and lost weight. Most of her girlfriends griped about it while guys were impressed by the amount of food she could put away. She would eat most of them under the table and go back for seconds.

Libby ordered from their favorite Mexican place. When she hung up the phone, she looked back at her best friend and roommate. "Hey, didn't you have a date tonight?"

Emily twisted toward the kitchen and made a face. "Jeff canceled. Again. He's so not worth all of this trouble. We've tried to schedule this date for two months now, and every time, something comes up."

"There are plenty of other guys lined up to ask you out." Libby was invisible whenever she went anywhere with her gorgeous friend. Men couldn't resist Emily's exotic beauty.

"Maybe it's time to move on," Emily said with a sigh and brushed her long black hair over her shoulder. "What about you?"

"What about me what?"

"When's the last time you went on a date? Are you interested in anyone?"

Libby snorted. "Nope. I have enough on my plate without adding a relationship to the mix."

"Oh, come on. There are several good looking guys in the singles' class at church."

5

"And every one of them is waiting for an opportunity to ask you out."

"Give me a break, Libby. Those guys don't even talk to me but they fall all over themselves to hang out with you."

"Yeah, because I'm the girl they hang out with. I'm never the girl they date. And they don't talk to you because they're intimidated."

Libby glanced at the clock hanging on the blue accent wall in the dining room. "I'll pick up dinner and swing by the store for ice cream. Do you need anything else?"

"No." Emily jerked her head up and narrowed her eyes. "And don't you dare come home with a bunch of junk food, Libby James. I don't need the temptation."

On Saturday afternoon, Libby called her sister. She wanted to talk to someone else about her job situation, and Callie usually offered good insight. She was quite a bit older than Libby, but the two of them had become close over the past several years.

When her brother-in-law answered the phone, Libby asked for Callie and waited several minutes.

"Hi, Lib. What's up?"

"Linda threatened me yesterday," she blurted. "It wasn't overt, but she hinted I might lose my job if I take my vacation. I don't know how she keeps her clients, Callie."

"We'll understand if you can't come next month, but I don't

think it's fair to suggest you change your vacation."

"I agree. And I'm not bailing on you and Becca. I need this getaway as much as you guys do. It's been months since I've had a day off. What should I do, Cal? Is it time to find something else, even if it means leaving interior design for a while? The non-compete clause in my contract states that I can't work for a competitor for six months if I leave." A little detail she'd remembered last night that had kept her up later than she'd planned.

"E-mail it. I'll ask Alex to look it over."

"Thanks. I'll pay him for his time."

Callie laughed. "I'll mention it, but he won't accept your money." The teasing tone left her voice. "Any idea what you would do if you left Taylor Designs?"

"Emily said she would ask her boss about bringing me on for the summer. It sounds like they could use the help. They get pretty busy, and this would allow me to keep working with some of my vendors as well as provide a paycheck."

"Would you enjoy event planning?"

"Possibly. It will only be for a few months, so I'm not too concerned about liking it. At this point, anything is looking better than continuing at Taylor Designs, even going back to retail. I might be able to build some new business relationships. They host a lot of weddings but manage some company parties and dinners as well."

"I've attended a couple of their events," Callie said. "They do an excellent job. What about pay?"

"I don't know any details. If it's not even a possibility, I don't want to get my hopes up. I can always live like a starving college student and pick up some part-time shifts at Target again." She winced at the thought of going back to her high school job.

"Chris and I can help you out."

Libby gritted her teeth. She hated when her family tried to solve her problems for her. They seemed to forget she was an adult sometimes. "No, Cal. I'll figure this out."

"We're praying for you. Call me this week and let me know what you decide."

"I will. Thanks for listening."

"I'm here anytime, Lib. We miss you and love you. I'm glad we get to spend some time together and catch up next month."

"Looking forward to it myself. Give Charity and Hope hugs for me. Tell them I love them and I'll see them soon."

Libby ended the call. *Okay, Lord, I need guidance. Leaving my job is scary, but I can't go on like this any longer. Please show me where you want me.*

TWO

Jack Price hated weddings. Thirteen years ago, he had a front row seat to his parents' ugly divorce. He would never understand the point of spending thousands of dollars on something with a fifty percent chance of failing. Some of his friends from school were divorced before the age of thirty. He was perfectly content pouring his time and energy into his business. Too bad the most popular and well-paying events for that business were weddings. Avoiding them was not a viable option since sixty percent of the company's income came from those affairs.

He'd earned his degree in hospitality management. When he received an inheritance after his grandmother passed away four years ago, he used it to start his own business. He understood how rare this kind of success was for a twenty-eight year old. And his event planning company, An Affair to Remember, was gaining a name in the community.

"Hey, Jack, when things slow down, I need to talk to you." Emily Duncan passed him with an armload of table linens. Hiring her had been one of the wisest decisions he'd made. She could talk almost anyone into a deal. Men fell over themselves to give the beautiful woman whatever she wanted, but she also managed not to alienate the women.

"What's wrong?" He resisted the urge to run his fingers through his hair. They still had a couple of hours left of work, and he needed to remain professional, not appear like some crazed madman.

"Nothing." Her tone was soft, soothing as if talking to a hyperactive child or pet. "I'll find you when we've wrapped up."

Please don't quit. His small staff was stretched thin, and a full calendar meant he couldn't afford to lose anyone. In fact, he'd considered hiring a couple more people to ease the workload for the others.

This afternoon's wedding was a small affair, and the reception ended late afternoon. Jack looked forward to spending an evening at home. He found Emily talking with the caterers as they were packing everything and waited for them to finish. His curiosity as to what Emily wanted to discuss had consumed his thoughts.

Once she'd released the caterers, she joined him. "I'm glad we're done early tonight. I planned to go to the gym tomorrow, but maybe I'll stop on the way home instead."

"A free Saturday evening is rare for us." He gave her a fake scowl. "Don't get used to it. Once we hit May, our schedule's filled. What did you want to talk about?"

"I should've known better than to say anything earlier." She chuckled under her breath. "You always assume the worst. Did you fret about this all afternoon?"

He smiled wryly. "Maybe a little."

"It's not a big deal, Jack. I wanted to ask whether you'd consider hiring someone else for the summer. My roommate might need a job for a few months. She'd be a great asset. Her eye for décor and floral arrangements is impeccable." She turned her smile on him. "And I'm not just saying that because she's my friend. She's an interior designer."

"I've thought about hiring some additional help, but this

10

would probably be a step down for your friend."

Emily nodded. "It is, if she leaves her current position, she can't work for a competitor for six months due to her contract. A friend of ours is reviewing it to figure out whether she can even work with us. Will you at least meet with her?"

"Sure." What could it hurt to talk to the woman? "I'm free Tuesday after the staff meeting."

"We'll be at church tomorrow. I'll introduce you after the second service. You two can work out a time for an interview then."

"Okay. I'll meet you in the café when I'm done greeting people."

"Perfect." She beamed. "Thanks, Jack."

On Sunday morning, Jack dropped his nametag in the basket behind the welcome desk and went to find Emily. They'd had a lot of first-time visitors this morning, and he'd had a difficult time getting away. It was a good problem to have, but people were getting lost in the crowd when they visited. The church had been considering adding a third service to accommodate everyone, and after this morning, he understood the need.

He rounded the corner into the small café the youth group ran. Emily stood alone near the coffee urns, eyeing a group of guys sitting at one of the tables. When he drew a closer, he noticed a young woman in the middle of the group. Her light brown, chin-length hair had a lot of texture. What did his mom call that?

11

Layers? Man, Mom would be disappointed if she realized how little attention he'd paid to her stories about her salon clients.

When the woman leaned her head back and laughed, Jack couldn't stop his grin. The sound was infectious, loud but feminine at the same time.

"Sorry I'm late." He moved alongside Emily.

"No problem. Libby's been entertaining some of the guys from the class." She jutted her chin toward the table. The young woman glanced at them and held up two fingers.

"Would you two like to go to lunch?" he asked. "My treat."

"That sounds great." Emily peered at the table again. "But don't tell Libby you're buying."

His brow wrinkled at the odd request. Maybe her friend was one of those modern women who didn't let guys pay for anything. "Sure. What sounds good?"

"How about PF Chang's?" She brushed her hair back over her shoulder. "I'm craving Chinese food."

"No objections here."

When Libby joined them, Emily waved between them. "Libby, this is my boss, Jack Price. Jack, meet my roommate and best friend, Libby James."

"I'm glad to meet you," Jack said and held out his hand. She took his hand in a firm grip, not the limp fish thing women often did. Surprised by the heat of her touch, he released the grip first.

She smiled. "You too. When Emily mentioned we attend the same church, I was surprised we haven't met before now."

"Someone asks me if I'm new almost every week," he

answered. "And I've attended for six years." *Not to mention I greet people once a month.*

"It's not a bad problem for a church." Libby's statement echoed his earlier thoughts.

"Jack invited us to lunch, Lib." Emily grinned at her friend. "Are you okay with PF Chang's?"

Her entire face lit up. "Do you even have to ask?"

"I didn't think you'd complain." Emily spun back to him. "We'll meet you there."

Jack drove to the restaurant and put his name on the wait list. When the hostess led them to a table, the women discussed whether to order an appetizer. Libby waffled between two options.

"Get both," Emily said. "I'll share with you. Jack will eat some too."

Libby gave Emily an odd look. "I guess I should splurge while I can still afford it."

When the waitress returned to the table with their drinks, Jack ordered the appetizers. She left to put the order in, and he focused his attention on Libby. "I understand you may be searching for a job soon."

"I'm not sure yet. Everything hinges on my boss's reaction tomorrow." She lifted her gaze to the ceiling and sighed. "I may turn in my resignation. Before we discuss anything, I should warn you I'm going on vacation for two weeks."

"When?"

"End of April. I'll be back May first. She doesn't want me to take the time off even though she approved my vacation months ago."

"Nothing is ever enough for her." Emily cut into the conversation. "I'm glad you're my boss, Jack. If you were anything like Libby's, I wouldn't stick around."

His scrutiny shifted back to the other young woman after Emily's interruption. "Tell me about what you do."

Libby lifted her left shoulder in a small shrug. "A little bit of everything. I meet with potential clients to get a sense of what they want before drawing up some ideas. Once we establish a good foundation and a game plan, I purchase the materials and go to their homes to create a new space. I do everything from choosing the wall colors and hiring the painters to buying and placing the décor that brings the room together."

Jack saw her passion as she talked about her job. She was practically glowing with excitement. He shook his head at the thought. "If I asked you to design a new living room for me, what would you suggest?"

Her stare bored into him. The way the gold flecks in her hazel eyes brightened was mesmerizing. "The first step is getting into the space. From there, I'd learn your likes and dislikes, favorite colors, what the room will be used for, and so on. I'd determine which existing items in the room I might repurpose then take some time to draw up three or four ideas. We would work together to make any changes to the design you choose."

The waitress dropped off their appetizers, and they stopped talking while they loaded small plates with the food.

After Jack had said a quick prayer, his attention returned to Libby. "Do you have a portfolio?"

"Yes. I can bring it to your office sometime this week."

"Tuesday? Around eleven?"

"Works for me," she said.

"We're hosting a small event at Oakwood a week from Saturday—an open house for a restored home. Could you help out? It would give you an idea of what's involved."

Surprise crossed her face. "The house on Polk Street?"

"Yes." His brow furrowed. How did she know that? "Why?"

"My sister's company did the restorations." She whipped her head toward Emily. "Why didn't you mention you were doing Cal's open house?"

"I didn't realize it was one of hers." Emily smiled. "This is great. I haven't seen Callie in a while."

Jack's mouth slackened as he listened to the women. "Callie Graham is your sister? You've got to be ten years younger than her."

"Twelve." Libby's answer came with no hesitation as if she repeated it often.

He stared at Emily. "Why didn't you mention you know Callie Graham?"

Emily rolled her eyes. "Jack, you've seen me talking to her and her husband. We've hosted some events where she's received awards for her work."

"You talk to everybody at those dinners. I didn't think anything of it."

Libby snickered. "He's got you there, Em. You do make the

rounds at a party."

"You're one to talk," she shot back.

When they'd finished their meal, Jack asked the waitress for the bill.

Libby looked chagrined. "You don't have to pay for us. We can get our own."

"I told Emily lunch was on me."

Libby glowered at her friend. Emily held her gaze and smiled unapologetically. "He did. Did I forget to mention it?"

"You did this on purpose." A blush crept into her face. Whether it was from anger or embarrassment, he couldn't tell.

"Yep, I couldn't decide whether to tell Jack what he was getting himself into or let him figure it out for himself."

"It's my pleasure." He didn't understand why this was an issue. "I enjoyed the company."

"If I realized you were buying, we would have skipped the appetizers," Libby said. "Can I at least pay for those?"

"No, I ate them as well." And his mother would have his hide if she found out he'd allowed any woman to pay for any portion of a meal.

"Be glad she didn't order dessert," Emily said. "If you do hire her, you'll need to double your employee food budget."

"I guess the secret's out." Libby smiled sheepishly.

"I'm glad you enjoyed everything," he assured her. The amount of food she ate was almost humorous, but it didn't offend him. He would enjoy cooking a meal for her. He frowned at the errant thought. Where had that come from?

THREE

I can't believe you didn't tell me he was buying lunch," Libby said as Emily drove home. She had already been under a microscope with the impromptu interview and sitting between Jack and Emily had been uncomfortable. The two of them looked like models. With his short, dark brown hair, brown eyes, and wide shoulders, she struggled not to stare at him.

Libby always felt frumpy next to Emily but even more so today. Her hair was shorter than it had been in years thanks to an accident with Callie's youngest daughter at Christmastime. All of the blond had disappeared after a gloomy and gray winter. Not only that, but she hadn't dressed up for church today because she wanted to be comfortable instead of stylish in case she got roped into helping in one of the children's Sunday school classes again. She glanced down at the pilled sweater and sighed.

She'd only planned to meet Emily's boss after church and set up an interview, not go to lunch and talk to him. He'd asked a lot of questions but never mentioned what he expected of her if she worked for him. One thing was certain; she needed to make a better second impression on Tuesday morning.

"Don't worry, Lib." Emily patted her shoulder. "He liked you."

"How can you tell? All he did was ask questions."

"Jack's a pessimist," Emily said. "You'll understand what I mean the first time you work an event with us. He was cool today, though. He listened to what you said and didn't add anything negative. I'm sure he'll give you the job."

"I guess I'll find out whether or not I need it after meeting with Linda tomorrow. I'm so jealous you have Mondays off."

"It's a tradeoff. I work Saturdays. And sometimes Friday nights. My love life suffers because of it."

Hardly. Libby shook her head.

Libby grabbed the pillow from her bed, buried her face, and screamed her frustration into the soft cushion. This morning had not started well. After waking up late, she dressed for work only to find a tear in her skirt. Now she'd changed but couldn't find the boots that went with her new outfit.

Completely frazzled by the time she walked out the front door of the apartment, Libby took several calming breaths. After speaking with her mom last night, she knew what she had to do today. She would confront Linda as soon as she got to the office despite her nerves.

The drive to work was too short. Once she'd dropped her bag off at her desk, she squared her shoulders and strode to Linda's office. She knocked and peeked in the vertical rectangular window to the side of the door. *Empty.* At least she wouldn't be reprimanded for arriving a few minutes late. After asking both of her co-workers if they'd heard from their boss and receiving negative answers, she returned to her desk. It wasn't unusual for Linda to come in late even though she gave others a hard time for the same behavior. Libby wanted this conversation out of the way before she met with Mrs. Patterson.

Lord, please give me the words to talk to Linda. Help me stay calm and not back down. Open a door for me to keep doing what I love. My future's in your hands.

When Linda showed up, Libby was on the phone. Her boss stood outside her cubicle, waiting for her to finish the call.

"Who were you talking to?" she asked when Libby hung up.

"The furniture store, setting up a delivery for the chair and ottoman Mrs. Patterson chose."

"Shouldn't you have cleared that with me?"

Libby bit her tongue and counted to ten. "I need to talk to you. Can we go to your office?"

Linda nodded her head once, walked across the room, and entered her office without a backward glance to see whether Libby followed. She sat behind her desk, folded her hands on top, and waited.

"I'll finish the Patterson job, then I'm leaving," Libby blurted and handed Linda the resignation letter she'd agonized over last night. "I appreciate the experience you've provided over the past four years, but it's time for me to move on."

The other woman stared at the letter for several seconds without touching it. When she looked up, her lips pursed and her cheeks grew red. After several uncomfortable seconds of silence, she said, "You can't work for anyone else."

"I understand. No one has approached me with an offer or anything. But I don't have any room to grow here. I never get to complete my projects because I'm pulled away to handle another client before I've finished with the previous one. It's been more than eight months since I've had a day off. It's time for a change."

"Well, if you're determined to leave, you can go ahead and do it today." Linda waved her hand toward the door in dismissal.

"What about the Pattersons?" Was this one more job she wouldn't get to finish?

"I'll complete the project." Her hard stare made Libby squirm. "You are not to contact them." She squinted and held out her hand, palm up. "I need your key."

Libby clenched her hands into fists to control their shaking. "It's in my bag. I'll drop it by on my way out." She went to the back room and found a box to put her things in. When she returned to her desk, Linda stood there. "I want to make sure you don't take anything belonging to the company."

As Libby loaded her personal items into the box, she blinked back tears. After all she'd given this company, her boss treated her like a criminal who couldn't be trusted. She pulled her messenger bag out from under the desk and dug around the bottom until her fingers closed around her keychain. After fighting to get a key off the ring, she handed it to Linda.

"I'll find out if you're working for someone else, Libby."

She swallowed a nasty retort and nodded. "I'll adhere to the non-compete clause. Someone is reviewing my contract in order to clarify what I can and can't do. Please apologize to Mrs. Patterson for my absence."

"Good-bye." Linda ushered her out the front door with her box of belongings.

It was humiliating. She didn't even get an opportunity to tell her co-workers she was leaving.

Once settled in her car, she drove to a park a few miles away, parked, took out her cell phone, and called home. Her mom lifted her spirits a little and suggested she visit her family this week. After her meeting with Jack Price tomorrow morning, she'd drive to Perry and spend some time with them.

Because she needed something to cheer her up, she stopped by the store and bought some flowers before heading to her apartment.

When she walked in the front door, Emily glanced up. A bowl of cereal and a magazine sat on the small dining table in front of her. "What are you doing home?"

Libby blew her bangs out of her eyes and went to the kitchen to find a vase for the daisies. "I gave Linda my letter of resignation. She told me to go ahead and leave."

"Oh, Lib, I'm sorry." Emily entered the kitchen and gave her a hug.

"I'm okay—or I will be. I talked to Mom, and I'm going home after my meeting with Jack. You get the place to yourself this week."

"What a fantastic idea. How about I for some time off so I can come with you? I haven't been home since Christmas. We could go to church next Sunday and catch up with everyone."

"I'd love some company." She'd be less likely to dwell on her situation with Emily tagging along.

"Let's do it. I'll call Jack now. We can pack and load everything in the car today so we can leave right after your interview."

"Looks like I may be coming to work with you, Em." *If Jack's interest in hiring me.*

FOUR

An Affair to Remember. Jack Price speaking. How may I help you?" He gave his staff Mondays off but usually spent the day in the office while things were quiet. It was the perfect time to prepare for the staff meeting, pay bills, and send out invoices.

"Jack, it's Emily. I was hoping to catch you."

He took his eyes from the computer screen. "What's wrong?"

"Nothing's wrong." She huffed out a breath. "You are such a Negative Nellie. Have we booked anything this weekend?"

"Nothing until the open house in two weeks. Why?"

"Libby's going to visit her family after she meets with you. I thought I'd go with her and see my parents. I'll come in for the staff meeting, but there's not much I have to do this week—a few calls. I can make those from anywhere, right? Can I have the rest of the week off?"

He considered the request. Opportunities like this would be rare once the summer season started. "I don't mind as long as I can reach you if something comes up."

"Absolutely. I'm only an hour away if I need to come back for anything."

"It's fine." He wouldn't make her drive back for something any of them could handle efficiently. "Enjoy your vacation."

"Thank you, thank you, thank you." As she squealed, he pulled the phone away from his ear. "We'll see you tomorrow. Libby resigned this morning."

He hung up the phone and thought about Emily's friend. The young woman was personable. And cute. He'd enjoyed talking with her yesterday but purposely avoided asking why she was leaving her current position. What if her boss didn't want her around because she didn't work? Shaking his head, he dismissed the thought. She wouldn't leave if she was getting paid for doing nothing. At the same time, his business couldn't handle someone who didn't pull their weight. It wouldn't be fair to his other employees to bring someone in who didn't benefit everyone.

If no one has anything else to share, I've got an appointment." During the meeting, Jack made no mention of interviewing a possible staff member. It would be best to surprise everyone—with the exception of Emily—when, or if, everything was cemented. No need to get their hopes up if he decided not to hire Libby James.

He strode out of the kitchen and halted at the sight of the woman herself. When she noticed him and stood, he checked his watch. *Pretty and punctual.* He cleared his throat. No need to go any farther down that path. "Have you been here long?"

"Only a few minutes," she said. "I'm a little early. If you have something pressing to take care of, I don't mind waiting."

"Come on in." He led the way to his office, cleared a stack of papers from a chair, and motioned for her to sit.

Libby placed her large bag on the floor and took the seat he'd indicated. Her eyes met his without wavering. "I know Emily told you I resigned, but I wanted to explain my decision to leave."

Her directness saved him from asking some uncomfortable questions. He nodded, leaned his elbows on his desk, and nudged her to continue. "Go ahead."

She took a deep breath and plunged ahead. "I worked for my boss—former boss, I guess—almost four years. She never appreciated anything I did.

"When she not so subtly hinted I should reschedule my vacation, which she approved months ago, I started to seriously consider leaving. It wasn't the first time I'd thought about it. After spending the weekend in prayer and discussing my options with people I trust, I felt like resigning was the right thing to do. When I turned in my resignation yesterday and assured her I'd finish with my current client, I was told me not to bother."

"Thank you for sharing all of this with me." Her confession eased his doubts. "Did you bring your portfolio?"

She picked up her bag, pulled out a leather-bound eleven-by-seventeen case, and passed it across the desk. He scanned a few pages. He wasn't sure what he'd been expecting, perhaps some ultra-modern or trendy rooms. What he found drew him in. Everything she had done was comfortable and inviting yet functional. "This is beautiful work, Libby. You designed all of these?"

"Yes." Her lips curved upward in a slight smile. "My dad says improving homes runs in my blood."

"Are you able to work with us?"

Any traces of a smile disappeared. "I'm not sure yet. Working for another design firm is out of the question, but that's all I'm certain of right now. A friend of the family is reviewing my contract. I hope to talk to him this week."

"How do you feel about the change to event planning?"

"I honestly don't know," she said. "Emily loves her job, and some of it sounds interesting. I enjoy meeting new people and building business relationships and connections, so that aspect is appealing. Plus I could continue to work with some of my favorite vendors."

Every new vendor meant more opportunities for clients in his business. She bit her bottom lip, and her gaze drifted behind him. It was the first time she'd broken eye contact.

"What concerns you?" he asked.

"I love coming up with an idea or a vision and executing it. From what Em has shared about her job, you contract everything to vendors. I'll miss the creative outlet."

"We do contract out most of our work because no one on my staff can take on more responsibilities. If you see something you could handle efficiently, I'm willing to work with you."

He'd already decided to offer her the job but didn't want her to accept if she'd be miserable. "If you're still interested, we can give this a trial run at the Oakwood open house a week from Saturday. It's a smaller event and, to be perfectly honest, I'd love to add you to the team since you're related to Callie Graham. Then we can both decide whether or not we're a good fit for each other."

When Libby smiled, her eyes lightened. "That sounds fair."

"Good. Come in with Emily next Tuesday. She'll show you around and introduce you to everyone." He returned her portfolio.

She stood and held out her hand. "Thank you, Mr. Price. I appreciate the opportunity."

"Please call me Jack."

As she walked out the door, he squeezed his hand into a tight fist. The heat from her hand ignited and warmth burned up his arm and across his chest.

FIVE

As soon as Libby's oldest sister, Amy, learned she'd be in town for the week, she suggested the James sisters meet for lunch on Wednesday. "It's been way too long since we've done this," she said as they sat around a table in the middle of the restaurant.

So far they'd discussed Callie's business, Callie's and Amy's kids, and Libby's job situation. She'd talked with Alex Newsome the day before and learned while she couldn't work for any design firms or use any of the businesses Linda Taylor had contracts with, event planning wouldn't be an issue. Alex also pointed out she wouldn't be violating the clause if she provided her interior design services independently. He suggested she print some business cards to hand out to potential clients.

"I'm glad this worked out." Callie sipped her iced tea. "I hoped to share some news with both of you without little ears around. Lib, it's something you should know before we go on vacation."

"Okay?" She waited for her to continue.

"Becca lost her baby last week."

"Oh, no." Libby's hand covered her mouth. Becca had been four months pregnant with her sixth child. "Alex didn't mention anything yesterday."

"I'm not surprised." Callie shook her head slowly. "He's grieving alongside her. When I talked to her last night and told her

I was having lunch with you two, she said I could tell you."

"How is she doing?" Having lost a child to miscarriage, Amy could empathize with their friend the most. "What does she need?"

"Time," Callie answered. "She's heartbroken but talking about it, which is a huge step for her. They went in for a routine appointment. When the doctor couldn't find the baby's heartbeat, she did an ultrasound. The baby was gone.

"Alex called the next day. He took the morning off to stay home with Becca but had a meeting he wasn't able to reschedule that afternoon. I went over, so she wasn't alone. We had a good talk. I just didn't want either of you to ask about the baby next time you see her." They discussed Becca and her kids until the conversation ran its course.

"When are you headed back, Lib?" Amy pushed her plate closer her.

Libby didn't object and picked up a French fry. "We're leaving right after church on Sunday. Emily wants to go into work on Monday so she can show me around before the Tuesday morning staff meeting."

"I'm glad you'll be at the open house," Callie said. "I'm going to leave the girls with Chris. Dad's coming with me instead."

Libby smiled. "Good. It will be a relief to have your support at my first event. You and Dad can stay at our place if you don't want to drive back that night."

"We might take you up on the offer. Maybe we can all go to dinner. Jon's covering for the first two hours of the party, and I'll relieve him for the second half."

"Have you met the new youth pastor at the church?" Amy changed the subject abruptly.

Libby and Callie exchanged a knowing glance. Their big sister had always hated being left out of a conversation.

"He's single," Amy continued, either not noticing or ignoring the exchange between her younger sisters.

"Amy, don't start," Libby said. "I don't have time for a relationship right now, especially with someone who doesn't even live in the same city."

"He is pretty cute in an unassuming sort of way." Callie grinned. "And you're only an hour away. I make the drive a few times a week."

"I want to see the girls." Libby attempted to shift the subject again.

"Come over for dinner tonight," Callie said.

"Okay," Libby agreed and looked at Amy. "What about you?"

"What about me?"

Libby rolled her eyes and spoke slowly. "When can I come hang out with my nephews and my other niece?"

"Anytime. You're always welcome. If you want time with Cindy, you'd better plan to come after six. She's got a crazy schedule right now with soccer practices."

"Would Saturday evening work?"

"Yep, and I guess since Callie's feeding you tonight, I'll need to make up for it."

The three of them laughed. Callie did not cook. That hadn't changed in the eight years she'd been married.

The week with her family allowed Libby a time of rest and rejuvenation. Emily had managed to get a few friends from high school together for lunch on Friday. They had a blast catching up with the other girls. The time had flown by, and it was time to get back to reality.

Emily arrived to pick her up. They both wanted to get to the church early to visit since they planned to drive back to Raleigh immediately after service.

"Jack called me freaking out Friday afternoon." Emily vented her frustration as she backed out of the driveway.

"Was he upset you took the week off?"

"No." Emily waved a hand in the air between them. "I was serious when I told you he's pessimistic. When anything goes wrong, he blows it way out of proportion."

"Oh, no. What happened?"

"The florist he hired for next weekend canceled." Emily turned left onto the road that led out of town. "He's convinced they had a better-paying gig. I called and talked to them, and the other party scheduled a month before us. It was an honest mistake on their part."

"Maybe so, but now Jack's in a bind." Libby could commiserate with the guy. "It'll be hard to find someone else with only a week's notice."

"That's the same thing he said. Thankfully, I know someone who will take care of the flowers."

Libby turned her head toward the driver's seat. Emily had

never mentioned she knew a florist. "Who?"

She grinned and glanced over. "You."

"Me?"

"Why not? You're perfect. On Monday, I'll show you some pictures of the house and what the other florist put together for us. You'll come up with something even better."

"What about Jack?" Libby clutched her hands in her lap.

"What about him? When he sees how good you are, he'll quit hiring florists, especially once he realizes how much money you're saving him."

"I'll agree to this on one condition." She'd been friends with Emily too long for her to not clarify this point. "We tell Jack the plan. Don't keep this from him to prove a point."

"Deal," Emily said. "I'll have to tell him so he'll give you the company credit card anyway." She pulled into the church parking lot and found an empty spot.

"Look, there's Mark." Libby pointed across the parking lot at the man who had volunteered with the youth group when they were teenagers. "Let's go say hi."

Emily slid her sunglasses to the top of her head. "Who's the hot guy he's talking to?"

Libby stared at her friend incredulously. Was she serious? She didn't consider that guy hot. Jack Price on the other hand.... She shook her head. There was no need to go there. "That's Adam."

"Adam?" Emily swung her head back around. "Why didn't you tell me he's gorgeous now?"

"Since he's worked with Chris for eight years, he's practically family. It's like calling my brother hot. Gross."

Emily laughed. "You don't have a brother."

"Yes, I do. His name is Adam." Libby drew out the two syllables of his name out as they climbed from the car.

Mark grinned and waved them over when he noticed them, finishing his conversation with Adam as they approached. When they stopped in front of him, he gave each of them a hug. "Hi, ladies. This is a pleasant surprise. Leah will be thrilled to see you."

"Chris didn't tell you I was in town?" Libby asked. Mark was her brother-in-law's brother. Yes, it got confusing.

"No. We haven't seen Chris for a while. He and Callie stay busy."

"Where is Leah?" Emily asked. "I want to talk to her before church."

Mark glanced around the parking lot as if expecting to see his wife. "She's probably still downstairs. She and Elizabeth were showing Randi the changes to the building."

"Randi's here?" both girls asked at the same time before rushing across the parking lot to find their friend. Mark's laughter followed them inside.

Emily beat Libby to the bottom of the stairs and squealed.

The pastor's daughter, their good friend, ran over to hug them. "Lib! Em! I didn't know you guys were here."

"No one told us you were either," Emily said. "How's Nashville?"

"Good." Randi wrinkled her nose. "We're working on a Christmas album this year."

"Now?" It was March, hard to get into the Christmas spirit this time of year.

"Yeah." Their friend laughed. "We have to start early, so it's ready to sell in November."

"I can't wait to hear it," Libby said. "Your last CD is still in my car." Randi had moved right out of high school and was now the lead singer of an all-female Christian band.

Randi's mom and Leah joined them for another round of hugs. The women visited until Sunday school let out, and people streamed into the multi-purpose room. Libby had fond memories of this place. She and her parents began attending the church when she was thirteen.

"This brings back memories, doesn't it?" Leah smiled at the three young women. "I sure miss you girls."

"We miss you too," Randi said. "You were the best role model. I think about you all the time."

Leah hugged her again. "That's sweet. Thank you, Randi. I still pray for every one of you."

Adam came by, said hello again, and introduced the guy with him. "This is Brandon. Brandon, this is Emily, Libby, and Randi. We were all in the youth group together. I won't mention how many years ago that was since there are ladies present."

"Brandon's our new youth pastor," Randi's mom explained.

He shook his head but smiled. "Elizabeth, I don't understand why everyone calls new. I've been here three years now."

"You're the newest out of every person standing right here." She circled her hand around the group. "Come on, we should get to church. I don't think John would appreciate his wife and daughter coming in late."

Emily linked arms with Libby and Randi as they followed the others up the stairs. She stopped them at the top. "Why weren't the guys this good looking when we attended here?"

Libby shook her head. "You're hopeless, Em. Let's get to church."

SIX

"Mom?" Jack stepped inside his childhood home after unlocking the front door with the key she insisted he keep. Today was their monthly Sunday lunch. Still stressed over the whole florist situation, the comfort of his mom's place beckoned him. Emily had assured him she could get someone to take care of the problem, but it would take a miracle to find anyone available on such short notice.

"In the kitchen." His mom's voice carried from the right side of the house.

Rachel Price stood in front of the stove in a frilly floral apron, her dark hair mixed with some gray, styled short, not a strand out of place.

Jack scooted around the counter and bent to give her a hug and a kiss on the cheek before he pulled dishes from the cupboard to set the table. "How are you, Mom?"

"I'm fine. No need to worry."

"I can't help it." He winked at her. "You're my favorite girl."

She rolled her brown eyes at him. While his height and build came from his father, he'd inherited her hair and eye color. "Humph. You need to find a nice girl to marry and worry about her. What about Emily?"

Jack shook his head. His mom was forever trying to set him up. "I'm not interested in Emily that way. Besides, she works for

35

me."

"She's pretty."

"She's beautiful." No need for him to argue that point. "But I won't date an employee, especially one as valuable as Emily Duncan. It would only complicate matters."

"All right." She patted his chest with her palm. "I can respect that. What about someone else? I bet there are some nice girls at your church."

The image of Libby James laughing at the table in the little café flashed in his mind for a second. He blinked the image away. She was about to become another employee. "Why bother? I'm never getting married, so there's no point in leading some poor woman on."

"You're going to eat those words one day, Jack. It's your duty to give me grandchildren."

He barked a laugh. "This isn't about me at all. You just want some little ones around so you can spoil them."

"Pretty much." She grinned at him. "Gary has six grandkids and another one on the way."

Jack frowned. *Is Mom dating someone?* He should be thrilled she was moving on. It had been years since his father left and, as far as he knew, she'd never even gone to dinner with another man. "Who's Gary?"

"He lives across the street. You met him last year."

The muscles in his shoulders and across his back relaxed. "Is he the guy who hosted the neighborhood cookout?" He remembered meeting the man—and his wife.

"Yes, Peggy and Gary throw one every year. You're always welcome to come."

Most likely he'd be working, so he didn't commit to anything.

They sat down to eat, and Jack told her about church that morning. She talked about her clients at an upscale salon in the area, and he shared details about the events they had coming up this month.

"You work too much," she said. "You need to take some time for yourself once in a while."

"Can't do it, Mom. We're about to start our busiest summer yet." He got up and ran hot water in the sink.

She waited until he shut the faucet off. "Hire more people. You can afford an extra person or two. There are more important things in life, Jack."

He made certain his back was to her when he answered. "I may have found someone to come in for the summer. We're giving it a trial run this week to see what we each think of the arrangement."

"Wonderful. Who is she?"

How does she know it's a woman? "A friend of Emily's. She left her interior design job and needs something for the next few months."

"Is she any good?"

"How should I know?" He didn't want to talk about Libby. The spark of interest disconcerted him, and if his mom got any inkling, she would fan the spark into a bonfire. "She hasn't started working for me yet."

His mom picked up a towel and dried the dishes as he placed them in the dish rack. "I meant as an interior designer."

"Her portfolio was impressive." His eyes narrowed as he looked at his mom. She had an agenda. "Why?"

"I wouldn't turn down advice on updating this place." She glanced toward the living room.

Jack pulled the plug to drain the sink and spun around to face her. "Seriously, Mom? You tell me I need to hire help and in the next breath try to steal the person I've lined up?"

"You're right." She patted him on the chest again. "You can send her my way when you run her off."

"Mom! I don't plan to run her off. She can't do any interior design work for six months, anyway. Someone's looking over her contract to determine whether she can even work for me."

"I thought you said you were testing out the arrangement. Now you sound like you've already decided to keep her."

He gave her a wry grin. "I may have but don't want to count on this only to lose her before she's started."

"Everything will work out, son. Why do you always assume the worst? God is in control." She ran her fingers through his hair. "Let's go outside so I can trim this."

They'd set this routine years ago. They ate lunch, did the dishes together, and Mom cut his hair. An afternoon spent sharing what was happening in their lives. Jack enjoyed this time with his mother—the one parent who had stuck around and invested in him. Rachel Price was indeed a special woman.

When he sat in the chair, she wrapped a cape around his neck. "Did you talk to your dad yet?"

His head jerked up. He was lucky she hadn't started cutting yet, or he'd be missing a large chunk of hair. His dad had called and left a message on Wednesday asking Jack to call him back. It was the first time he'd heard from the man in more than five years.

"Did you?" He answered her question with one of his own.

"Yes, he called me last week. You should talk to him."

"I'd rather not." He grimaced.

"Don't hold on to bitterness, honey," she said. "You won't have a meaningful relationship until you forgive your dad. Read the end of Ephesians 4."

"Have you? Forgiven him?"

Her answer was so quiet, he strained to hear it. "Years ago. I had to for your sake."

"How, Mom? He hurt you. Us."

"It wasn't always easy and took time, but I refused to let bitterness rule our lives. You were my number one priority, and I couldn't dwell on what went wrong. We were too young and rushed into marriage before learning about each other. I carry some responsibility for things not working out."

"But you stayed. He left and never looked back."

"That's not true." She moved to stand in front of him. "He regrets not being in your life. Pray about this, Jack. I think it will do you good to talk to him."

"I'll pray, Mom, but I can't promise anything."

As far as Jack was concerned, his dad deserved the same cold shoulder he'd received from the man all these years.

SEVEN

Let's stop and get coffee and donuts," Emily said as she drove toward the office Monday morning.

Libby peeked at her friend. Her request raised suspicions. "You never eat donuts."

"They sound good, okay? And why are you complaining?"

"I'm not. I'm just surprised you suggested it." The true reason for Emily's sugar and carb craving hit her. "You're nervous."

"Maybe a little bit. I'm sure Jack will be fine with you doing the flowers." Emily turned her head and batted her eyelashes. "Once I convince him."

"We did discuss this when we met last week," Libby said. "He told me if I found something I wanted to do, to let him know."

"Why didn't you tell me? I've been fretting over this since Friday."

She shrugged. "I didn't think an opportunity would come up this soon." A smile split her face. "Besides, this way I get breakfast."

After a quick stop to pick up the food, Emily continued to the office. Once there, Libby asked her to explain everything about her job. In addition to Jack and Emily, two others worked at An Affair to Remember. Her friend explained everyone's roles in the company—different areas of the events handled by each of them.

"You'll probably work with whoever needs you most each week." Emily took the final bite of the half a donut she'd cut and put on her plate. "They won't be in until tomorrow. Today I'll show you everything without interruption. I'm glad you're here, Lib. This summer's going to be crazy busy. We've already got most Saturdays booked until Labor Day and have a couple weekends with both Friday and Saturday booked."

"You guys are doing something right if you're in such high demand."

"Oh yeah, it's terrific for the business, but not so much for those of us working sixty hours a week. Or for those of us who might want to go out on a date once in a while." She scanned the room. "What time is it, anyway? I thought Jack would beat us here this morning."

Libby checked her cell phone. "Almost ten."

"Oh, well. He probably had a meeting or something." Emily shrugged and circled her hand in front of her. "We use this room for Tuesday morning staff meetings and to drop off food. Anything left in here without a note on it is fair game. Come on, I'll show you the rest of the place."

Libby grabbed a second donut and held out the box to Emily, who shook her head. "Seriously, Em? You bought a dozen donuts and you're not even going to eat a whole one?"

"I'll eat the other half later and if not, I'm sure you'll take care of it. Grab your coffee and let's get going."

After she had topped off her drink, Libby hiked her bag onto her shoulder and followed Emily from the kitchen.

There were seven doors total spaced around an open area and a short hallway Emily said led to the bathrooms. To Libby's eyes, the dingy white area was a blank canvas. The tour began in Emily's office where they dropped off their bags. Her friend pointed out the other offices before heading to the two rooms Emily said were used for client meetings.

"Other than Tuesday morning staff meetings, we're rarely all here at the same time," Emily explained as they returned to her office. "A lot of our consultations and meetings are held offsite with vendors and clients. We can share my office, or you can use one of the conference rooms whenever they're empty—which is most of the time."

"They're kind of stark, aren't they?" Libby sank onto one of the chairs across from Emily's desk. "A little color would cheer them up and make them more inviting."

"I doubt Jack's even thought of painting. Talk to him, he might consider updating them."

"Updating what?"

They both turned toward the door. Libby sank lower in her seat. She did not know this man well and here she was criticizing his office. Jack hadn't even agreed to give her a job yet.

"Good morning, Jack." Emily smiled at him. "You're late."

His eyebrows lifted. "I didn't realize I was supposed to be here by a certain time today. The Olsons wanted to approve the final menu for the wedding, so I met with them and the caterer."

"Uh-oh," Emily said. "You can thank me for bringing caffeine and sugar. Donuts and coffee are in the break room. Help yourself."

"Are you trying to butter me up for something?"

Libby hoped he was kidding, but his expression gave nothing

away.

"Maybe." Emily waved her fingers to shoo him off. "Go get some breakfast then come talk with us." Once he left the room, Emily looked at Libby and lowered her voice even though Jack was now across the building. "He hates weddings so he's grumpy. Don't let him scare you."

"Don't forget who I used to work for. Jack's not going to scare me." Give her a healthy guilt complex, yes. Scare her? Not a chance.

"Good." She leaned back in her chair and pulled her hair over her shoulder. "Did Callie show you pictures of the Oakwood house?"

"She asked me to help her choose which ones to add to her website."

"Then you have a good idea of what the house is like. I'll show you what else we're doing for the party when we're done with Jack."

"Sounds good. I'd like to go by the wholesale florist this afternoon and check out what's in stock, maybe put together some ideas."

"Please tell me you found someone to replace the florist." Jack dropped onto the empty chair next to Libby. She tried to scoot away from him a pinch without drawing attention to her actions.

"I found someone to replace the florist." Emily smirked.

"I still can't believe they dropped us for a bigger sale." He continued as if he hadn't heard her. "We're never using them again."

Emily leveled her gaze at him. "They double booked. I talked to the manager. It was an honest mistake, and the other party had made arrangements a month before us. You should have called me to take the meeting with the caterer this morning."

"No." He looked at Libby and she froze. "I knew Libby was coming with you today, and you'd do a better job of going over everything than I would. Who did you find to do the flowers?"

Emily peeked at Libby before giving Jack a huge grin. "You're sitting right next to her."

"Libby?" He stared at her, dumbfounded. "Are you sure that's a good idea?"

He may as well have slapped her in the face. If he didn't trust her with a few simple centerpieces, perhaps this arrangement wouldn't work out.

"She hasn't seen the house," Jack continued. "It's too much to take on for her first week."

After inhaling and counting to five, she addressed his concerns. "Callie showed me pictures of the house, and this is a pretty small-scale event. I don't mind doing the flowers."

"Take her with you tomorrow," Emily encouraged. "She can take some examples of what she can do and meet the Millers."

Jack shook his head. The movement so small, she almost missed it. "I'd like to see what she comes up with first."

Ignoring the fact he was talking as if she weren't in the room, she spoke. "I was planning to pick up a few items this afternoon and put together some centerpieces." She loved arranging fresh flowers and enjoyed adding them to her designs. Not everyone wanted to change those out on a regular basis, though. This project was simple, and she could easily handle it.

"What were you talking about updating before?" Jack changed the subject.

Libby looked at Emily, her eyes pleading with her to forget

the whole thing. She felt like she was on Jack's bad side already and didn't want him to dismiss her before she had an opportunity to prove herself. Emily ignored her. "Libby thinks the conference rooms would be more inviting if they weren't so stark. Her word, by the way."

"Thanks a lot, Em," Libby muttered under her breath.

"We don't have time right now." Jack scowled. Or perhaps brooded was more accurate.

"It wouldn't take much." Libby bit her tongue. Why couldn't she keep her mouth shut?

He scrutinized her for several uncomfortable seconds. "What would you do, and how much will it cost me?"

"Painting the walls would make a huge difference, but some pictures would make it more inviting. I suggest using photographs from your events and framing them. They would add some atmosphere to the room as well as advertise your services."

"How much?" The scowl eased up but remained.

"If you kept the existing furniture, both rooms could be done for less than seven hundred."

He seemed to be considering what she said. Without answering, he jumped up. "Let me know what you come up with for the Millers by the end of the day." And with that, he left the office.

Libby tucked her hair behind her ear and stared at her friend. "What did I say?"

"Don't worry about it." Emily waved her hand toward the empty doorway. "That's Jack."

"I don't think he likes me, Em. You might not get the help you wanted this summer."

"Oh, I'll get my help." She glanced at the empty space Jack had just vacated. "Let's get to work. The sooner we can put his mind at ease, the better."

EIGHT

Jack entered his office and leaned against the door once it was closed behind him. He'd been in a bad mood when he arrived and took it out on Libby. The poor girl probably wouldn't stick around through the weekend if he kept this up. *Lord, I'm sorry. I didn't make Libby feel welcome. I don't take criticism well, and the call from Dad put me on edge.*

He never did read those verses his mom suggested yesterday. He went online and looked up Ephesians 4. Verses 29-31 were meant for him. *"Do not let any unwholesome talk come out of your mouths, but only what is helpful for building others up according to their needs, that it may benefit those who listen. And do not grieve the Holy Spirit of God, with whom you were sealed for the day of redemption. Get rid of all bitterness, rage and anger, brawling and slander, along with every form of malice. Be kind and compassionate to one another, forgiving each other, just as in Christ God forgave you."*

He felt convicted about the way he'd treated Libby. While needing to apologize, for now, he'd focus on getting some work finished. Determined to speak with her later, he buried himself in billing invoices.

What in the world, Jack?" Emily burst into his office. With her hands resting on her hips, she glared at him.

"I'm sorry, Emily. I've had a rough few days."

She held up her hand, palm out. "I'm not the one you should be apologizing to, and that's a horrible excuse for the way you treated Libby. We need her. She's excellent at everything she puts her mind to. If you just give her a chance, you'll love her."

"I want to give her a chance." He let out a deep sigh and rubbed the back of his neck with his hand. "A part of me is concerned about her doing too good a job and us becoming dependent on her. She's only wanting something temporary; she won't stay."

"No, she won't." Emily shook her head emphatically. "You shouldn't expect her to, either. But why not use her while she's here? We can all learn from her, and she'll improve our business. Everyone who meets her loves her." She pointed at him. "And you could use her connections."

Jack glanced out the open door behind Emily. "You're right, of course. Where is she? I'll go apologize."

"She's reviewing everything we're doing for the Millers. You frightened her so much, she's putting triple effort into impressing you. Her suggestions about the conference rooms were valid too. This place should be comfortable for people who come in for meetings and consultations. A place we're proud to show off to potential clients."

"You're right, and I'm considering it."

"Good." She reached for the door knob but stopped and twisted back around. "The best way to apologize to Lib is with food. Go get her a burger with everything and bring me a salad."

Jack fought a grin. "Anything else?"

"Dessert wouldn't hurt. Something chocolate." She spun on

her heel and left without another word.

Jack returned forty-five minutes later with a couple of burgers, fries, salad, and half a dozen cupcakes for which he'd made an additional stop.

Emily joined him as he set everything out in the break room and pulled paper plates and plastic utensils from one of the cupboards. "She's in the large conference room. Tell her lunch is here. I'll find drinks."

Libby was bent over a sketchpad as she worked, her chin-length bangs falling forward to hide her face. She didn't look up when he sat down across from her. "Is it lunch time yet? I'm starving and I smell burgers." When she didn't receive an answer, her head lifted. Surprise lit her hazel eyes. "Oh. Sorry, Jack, I thought you were Emily."

"I get that all the time." He laughed at his lame joke. "I picked up lunch. Why don't you take a break and eat?"

"Thanks." Her smile didn't reach her eyes. What happened to the confident woman he'd seen laughing at the church a week ago?

It bothered him she doubted herself because of his words. "Libby, I owe you an apology. I'm struggling with a couple things right now and took it out on you this morning. I'm sorry."

"Me too. I didn't intend to come in and criticize your business my first morning here. You're doing me a huge favor, and I shouldn't have said anything."

"I suspect I'll get more out of this arrangement than you will. Can we forget about this morning and start over?"

"Done." The full force of her smile hit him in the gut, and the gold flecks in her eyes brightened. "You brought food."

As the three of them ate, Libby shared her ideas for the centerpieces. She turned to Emily. "Can I use your car after lunch? I want to run by the wholesalers and a craft store to get a few things for the arrangements."

"I'll take you," Jack said. Both women gaped at him. "I'd like to check out this flower wholesaler. They may come in handy in the future."

"If I tell you all of my secrets now, you might not want to keep me around all summer." Libby's teasing indicated forgiveness of his earlier sour attitude.

"No, Lib. Jack needs me to stick around so he'll keep his word and hire the help I requested."

He laughed. "My worst fear is losing you, Emily. You should use that fact more often to get your way." The girls' laughter joined his. "Libby's experience will fill in some gaps. I'm looking for one more person to join the team. Our own photographer would be ideal. We could offer a photo package with every one of our events."

"I know someone who might be interested." Libby straightened in her seat. "He's taken a few family portraits for me."

Emily gawked at her friend. "Can you work with him every day?"

She shrugged. "I don't see why not. We've done stuff together several times since college."

There seemed to be some history between Libby and this other person, but the unspoken communication between the women confused Jack. Maybe an ex-boyfriend or something?

"Logan's a terrific guy and dependable," Libby said. "His

portfolio is amazing. He's got a good eye for great shots."

"Ask him if he'd be interested in coming to talk to me next week." He would ask Emily more about her concerns later. "There are cupcakes." He inclined his head toward the box on the counter.

"You don't have to keep feeding me." Libby's smile belied her objection to dessert. "Thank you again for lunch."

"Why don't you like weddings?" Libby asked as Jack drove them downtown.

He glanced at her for a second before returning his attention to the road. "Emily's been talking about me, huh?"

"Yes, but she doesn't know why. Her theory is you were married, and your wife left. I don't think that's it, though."

A short bark of laughter escaped him. "You're right. I don't have a secret ex-wife. I never want to get married."

"Why not?"

This was something he only talked about with his mother and a couple of close friends, but he told Libby about his parents' divorce and his dad's absence from their lives since he was fourteen. He told her how much his mom struggled with raising him alone while trying to make ends meet—picking up every extra shift she could get at the salon and cleaning houses in the evenings and on her days off.

"You're mom sounds like a special woman."

Libby was a good listener.

"She is. I'm lucky she's in my life."

"I feel the same way about my mom. My parents lived in Peru for a year in order to supervise the building of a church when I was seventeen. My sister—Callie—moved back home to run Dad's business and stay with me. I missed Mom every day. Don't get me wrong, I wouldn't trade my time with Callie for anything. We grew closer, and she became a Christian, but she wasn't mom."

He nodded. "I understand what you mean. You've mentioned your mom, your dad, and your sister in the short time I've known you. Your family seems close."

"We are. We love each other and help out whenever we're needed. It's the main reason I wouldn't cancel my vacation next month. I promised Callie and her best friend I'd watch the kids so they can enjoy their vacation. Becca has five kids under the age of seven, and Callie has two."

"Doesn't sound like much of a vacation."

"It will be a blast. I love those kids." She was quiet for a few minutes before returning to their original conversation. "Do you ever talk to your dad?"

"No." He didn't mention his dad had left a couple of messages over the past two weeks. "The last time I saw my dad was at my grandmother's funeral, and we didn't speak to each other that day."

"I'm sorry, Jack." Libby placed her hand on his forearm. Like a branding iron, her touch burned into him.

NINE

Libby wanted to comfort Jack after he shared about his strained relationship with his father. He didn't grow up watching a partnership between a man and woman like she had. Instead, he saw anger and manipulation. No wonder he was cynical about weddings.

"Why are you apologizing?" His deep voice broke into her thoughts. "It's not your fault."

"There's a spot." She ignored the question and pointed to an empty parking space on the street. When he pulled into the spot, she picked up her bag from under her feet. "It's a few blocks. Do you mind walking?"

"Not at all. It's a beautiful spring day."

They could have parked closer, but she loved walking around the buildings in this area. When she entered the front door of the converted warehouse, she closed her eyes and inhaled through her nose. The scent of the flowers permeated this place. The mixture of dirt, flowers, and other plants calmed her. When she opened her eyes, she saw Jack staring at her and gave him a sheepish smile. "Sorry. I love the earthy scent of the plants."

"Don't apologize for enjoying yourself."

"Libby James." A young woman wearing a green apron hurried to them. "I'm glad you're here. Stacy came in last week. She said Linda fired you."

"What?" Her breath caught in her lungs. *Linda's telling people she fired me? How embarrassing. Jack probably thinks I lied about resigning.* She forced a shaky smile onto her face. "I resigned, Pam. Linda told me not to stay my final two weeks."

"Oh, thank goodness. Stacy suspected there was more to the story than what they'd been told. She said three people canceled their consultations when they learned you weren't there anymore."

"That's unfortunate. I don't want them to lose business because I decided to leave." Although, there was a little justification for her decision.

"You're too modest, Libby. Stacy said Linda was terrified of you leaving Taylor Designs and competing with her. Why do you think she pulled you out of every job before you finished?"

She hadn't considered that reason. Gossiping about her former boss didn't make any difference, so she got to the point of her visit. "Pam, this is Jack Price. He owns An Affair to Remember. I'm helping him out."

"Oh, I've heard about you guys." Pam looked Jack up and down before shaking the hand he offered. Libby's brows drew together when she held on longer than necessary.

At least Jack had the decency to direct the conversation back to her. "What did you need today, Libby?"

Pam returned her attention to the sale and once again became a professional sales associate. "We got a shipment in this morning. Everything's fresh."

"Are you getting another one this week? I'm working on some sample arrangements today but once we decide on something, I'll need to pick up more flowers Thursday or Friday."

"You're in luck. The truck's coming again Friday morning. Call us when you decide what you want, and we'll keep your order in the cooler."

Libby gave the woman a side hug. "You're the best."

"It's our pleasure. We love working with you. What are you looking for today?"

"I need some miniature sunflowers, gerbera daisies, and tulips. Can I look around and see if anything else catches my eye?"

"Of course. How many of the others do you want?"

"Let's go with a dozen each of daisies and tulips. Only reds, oranges, and a few yellows. And half a dozen of the sunflowers."

"I'll get those started for you. If you're looking for some other options in those shades, check out the snapdragons."

"The stems are too long for the small centerpieces I have in mind. Any suggestions for a good contrasting flower? Not white."

"How about some freesia?" Pam's mouth formed an O. "No, the cornflowers would go perfectly with these colors. They're an astounding blue."

"Show me." In Libby's excitement, she completely forgot about Jack as she wandered around and examined the plants. When she went back up front to check out, he was sitting in one of the chairs near the front desk.

"Did you find everything you needed?" His expression held humor.

"I'm sorry, Jack. I tend to get tunnel vision when I'm shopping for a project."

"No need to apologize. Your passion for this place is obvious."

"Do you need anything else?" Pam moved behind the counter.

"No, this will do. Thanks for your help. The cornflowers were a fantastic suggestion."

"Bring in pictures of your arrangements. We love what you do with our flowers."

"I will," Libby promised.

"Should I put this on the account?" Pam's face fell. "Oh, I'm so sorry. I forgot you no longer have one."

The weight on her lungs prevented Libby from taking a breath for a moment. "I'm sure you won't be the last person to ask."

Jack stepped beside her. "Can I open an account?"

His kindness touched Libby, but she didn't want him to go through the trouble of opening an account only she would use. "You don't need to do that."

"I would like to. I didn't even know this place existed, and the prices are better than any florist we've used." He winked at Pam, who blushed. "What do you need from me to open an account for An Affair to Remember?"

"A company credit card, business card, and the names of everyone authorized to use it." Pam ticked the three items off on her fingers.

He pulled out his wallet and removed a credit card and business card. He flipped over the business card and wrote Libby's name at the top followed by his other employees. "What's your billing cycle?" He passed the two cards across the counter and pulled one of the wholesaler's cards from the stack on the counter.

"We invoice the first of the month and charge your card on the tenth." As Pam explained everything and entered his information in the computer, he took notes. "Your total today is thirty-two dollars."

"Go ahead and put it on the account, and when Libby calls to tell you what she needs on Friday, add that as well."

Pam wrapped the flowers and handed them to Libby with a grin. "I'm glad someone appreciates your talent."

Libby started to object and explain she hadn't done anything yet, but Jack took her elbow, and all coherent thought flew from her mind. He held open the door and lifted the flowers out of her arms, carrying them as they returned to the car.

"I can't believe this only cost me thirty-two dollars. You are going to save me a lot of money, Libby James."

"Don't count on it. We've got one more stop, and it's the store where I tend to do the most damage." She gave him a big smile and skipped ahead like a little girl. Shopping was her favorite pastime. "Let's go to the craft store."

Sometimes she would spend hours there. Thankfully, she had a pretty good idea of what she was looking for today—vases for her floral arrangements and a couple white tablecloths. Emily mentioned they'd planned to use black ones, but they would only darken the entire room.

Jack drove to the store and followed her inside despite her insistence he wait in the car. Guys didn't enjoy shopping with her. She was looking over some choices for vases when someone called her name.

"Libby? Libby James?"

She lifted her head and squinted at a woman three feet in front of her.

"I almost didn't recognize you," the woman said. "Your short hair is adorable."

Libby fingered her shoulder-length strands. "Thank you. I had an unfortunate accident with one of my nieces, chewing gum, and a pair of scissors at Christmas."

The woman laughed. "Oh, that brings back some memories. At my house, Josie was the one who got the haircut."

Libby designed the girl's bedroom last summer. "Is she still liking her room?"

"She never wants to leave. You did such a wonderful job listening to her. She thinks it's perfect."

"I'm glad."

The woman paused a moment. "Maybe you could help me? I'm looking for something to go on the wall in the hallway between the kids' rooms. It's too bare."

Libby turned to Jack standing a little behind her. He nodded his assent.

"Do you have anything particular in mind?"

"Not really. I just know whatever I get should be about three feet wide and two feet high."

"What about a family photo?"

She shook her head. "No, I want something unique."

"What about a framed piece of artwork? Or a saying about family?"

"I'm horrible at this, Libby. Would you mind?"

When Jack cleared his throat, Libby cringed. How rude of her not to introduce him. "Oh, I'm sorry. Mrs. Whitman, this is Jack Price. I'm helping him out with an open house."

"You're not with Taylor Designs any longer?"

Why, oh why, did this continue to come up today? And in front of Jack. "No, I left a week ago."

Her eyebrows shot up into her hairline. "Please tell me you struck out on your own."

"Right now I'm working for Jack at An Affair to Remember, an event planning company."

"Go ahead and find her artwork," Jack said. "We've got time."

"Are you sure?" She tried to gauge his true opinion about the interruption. He was a busy man with plenty to do, and this was the second time someone stopped to visit with her this afternoon.

"Positive."

"Thank you," Mrs. Whitman said with relief. "Do you do birthday parties for children? My daughter's turning ten this fall, and we want to do something special for her."

"We've done a few." He pulled another business card out of his wallet. "Give me a call and tell me what you're looking for."

Libby led the woman to the section of the store with the prints. She found the perfect one for Mrs. Whitman's home, but it needed to be matted and framed. "Is your hallway still the mint green?"

"I can't believe you remember."

She opened her bag, pulled out her sketch book, and wrote down the name and address of a local business. Lowering her voice, she said, "Call this guy. He's the best. Tell him I sent you and suggest a light coral matte with a charcoal gray frame. I'll write it down for you. If he has any questions, tell him to call me."

Mrs. Whitman squeezed her hand. "You're the best. Thank you for your help." When they headed toward the front of the store, Jack stood watching them with an amused expression.

"You're lucky to have her," Mrs. Whitman said.

"I'm beginning to agree." He smiled and winked at the

woman, causing her to blush.

Did he charm everyone like this? Mrs. Whitman wasn't the only one with color in her cheeks.

TEN

Does that happen often?" Jack loaded the bags in the back of his SUV. He had spent forty dollars on the vases and a couple other small items Libby needed. It would've been more, but she'd pulled out a coupon when they were at the checkout counter, reducing the total by twenty percent.

Libby laughed. "All.The.Time. I don't mind, though. Thanks for being patient with us."

"You're welcome. Have you considered going freelance with your interior design?"

"I never gave it any thought until I talked to Alex last week." She peeked over at him once they settled in the car. "He's the person who reviewed my contract. He said the non-compete clause only prohibits me from getting a job with a competitor or a vendor Taylor Designs has a contract with. The second part won't ever be an issue since her tastes run on the expensive side, and I prefer to save people money. Anyway, Alex suggested I print some business cards and spend the summer networking."

She grew quiet before adding, "Don't worry, though. If I decide to work for you, I'll stay through the summer."

"I appreciate that, but it won't bother me if you pass out business cards to anyone who shows an interest. You could let them know you're not available until fall." He wanted her to consider the possibility. Running your own business was hard work, but the rewards were worth the effort.

"I'll think about it." She occupied herself with digging through her bag.

Sensing she didn't want to discuss it any longer, he changed the topic. "Since you're used to giving people design advice, tell me what you would do to my conference rooms."

She shared her ideas. The more she talked, the more animated she became, but he got the impression she was holding back. Her suggestion of making the larger conference room more formal for company and corporate meetings appealed to him. The smaller room would be more intimate where they could discuss weddings and smaller parties.

"How long would you need to complete both rooms?"

"Not long," she said. "Probably a month at most. Painting will take the most time."

"Would you like to decorate them?" From the corner of his eye, he saw her shake her head. "Why not?"

"It will take time away from what you're hiring me for—to ease the workload for the rest of your staff."

"What if we came to a compromise? I'll put some more thought into it, and we'll talk again tomorrow."

"If I agree, I have one condition."

He glanced over at her. "O-kay?"

"Once the paint is on the walls, everyone stays out until I'm finished. I'll work on one room at a time, so the other stays free for meetings."

"You've got a deal, Libby James." He pulled into the parking lot behind the office and shut off the car.

"Can I use one of the conference rooms today?" She came around to the back of the car and took the flowers when Jack lifted the gate. "I want to spread out so I can see what I'm working with."

"Sure. Use whatever space you need."

After grabbing the other bags, he followed her inside and deposited them with her before he went to check in with Emily.

"Hey, you were gone a while," she said as he sat in a chair across from her desk.

"We would have been back an hour ago, but someone stopped us and asked for Libby's assistance."

She gave him a wry smile. "I should have warned you. That happens all the time. She says it's a compliment when people ask for her opinion when she's out and about. Linda hated that she helped people off the clock, claimed it took away business. I'm pretty sure Lib's generosity did the opposite."

"The girl at the flower shop mentioned one of Libby's former co-workers thought she'd been fired."

Emily's eyes widened with surprise. "How did she react to the news?"

"Better than I would have." She'd impressed him with the way she'd handled the situation. "Libby told the girl she resigned and changed the subject. I think she was trying not to say anything bad about her former boss."

"That's exactly what she was doing. She hates gossip and either changes the subject or leaves the conversation."

Something else to admire about Libby James. "She's very genuine. There are no pretenses with her."

"You're going to hire her." Emily's face lit with excitement.

"Yes, I would like to. She shared some of her ideas for the conference rooms. I asked if she wanted to work on them."

Emily's smile fell. She stood to peek out the door and spun back around. "She won't do it, Jack. She'll think she's disappointing us by not giving herself fully to our events."

"She told me as much, but I have an idea. She's going on vacation in five weeks, and we're covered on everything through then. Libby said painting the walls would be the most time consuming. What if we all came in and painted over the next couple Mondays? I'll give anyone who comes in overtime."

"I like the thought of doing the painting ourselves, but you shouldn't pay us. Well, except for Libby since she'll be doing most of the work. Make it voluntary for the rest of us. You can buy lunch and provide snacks. Everyone will be on board since redecorating will improve this place."

"This is why I keep you around." He stood. "You know what motivates people." He returned to his seat when he remembered something else. "What's your concern about the photographer she brought up at lunch?"

Emily rolled her eyes. "Libby dated him for a year when we were in college. They broke up because she wasn't really attracted to him. She claimed he was more like a brother than a boyfriend. Logan's still in love with her. She won't acknowledge it, but he drops everything when she asks for a favor."

"So you would advise against hiring him?"

"Not necessarily." She was quiet for a minute, lost in thought. "Libby didn't exaggerate about his work. He's a talented photographer, excellent when it comes to portraits. You'd have the added benefit of him wanting to impress Libby. He's dependable. My biggest concern is how he'll react if she starts dating someone or if another guy flirts with her. Guys like her. She puts them at ease, and they like spending time with her."

He had experienced that with her a couple of hours ago when he opened up about his dad. The idea of someone dating her or flirting with her bothered him a little. He chastised himself. She was about to become his employee. He didn't need to concern himself with her love life. "Should I meet with him?"

"Probably, since Libby recommended him. I'll put out the word so we can find a few more candidates as well."

"Thank you. I appreciate the input. I'll mention it to Julie and Kevin too."

"Anytime, Jack. Hiring an in-house photographer will be a smart move."

He went to the kitchen and poured himself a cup of coffee before heading back to his office. He'd gotten little done so far but wasn't too bothered by the fact. Having the ladies around was nice. He sat at his desk and found the paperwork Libby would need to fill out, prepared to offer her the job.

Libby's ready to show us what she's got." Emily stopped by his office a little before five.

"Excellent. I'm interested to see what she's come up with." He had no doubt she'd impress him.

"Be kind, Jack." Under her breath, Emily added, "She's going to surprise you."

After his behavior this morning, he deserved the warning. "I'm serious, Emily. I watched her in that flower shop today. She was in her element."

65

He wasn't disappointed. After spending less than a hundred dollars on supplies, Libby had created five centerpieces. Every single one of them better than the arrangements the florist had put together at three times the price.

"Which do you like best?" Libby's gaze bounced from Emily to Jack.

"The daisies," Emily answered.

"I'm shocked." Libby laughed, her comment laced with sarcasm. "What about you, Jack?"

"They're all great."

"That's not what I asked. Which is your favorite?"

"If you're going to make me choose *one*...the sunflowers mixed with the blue flowers."

She beamed. "That one's my favorite too." Her forehead wrinkled as she studied the flowers. "But it's missing something."

"Like what?" It looked great to him.

"I'm not sure." Libby shrugged. "Maybe it will come to me tonight. Can I leave these here?"

"That's fine. You can ask Julie and Kevin for their opinions tomorrow morning. For now, you two should call it a day and go home."

"You don't have to tell me twice," Emily said. "I'm glad we came in today, though. I got a lot done."

Jack waited at the back door as the ladies walked to the car and heard Libby ask about dinner before she climbed in. He held back a grin. Emily wasn't kidding; he'd have to increase the food budget. If it meant keeping Libby James around, he would do it without complaint.

ELEVEN

What did you think?"

Libby took her time chewing a bite of her sandwich before answering Emily. She needed to stop eating out. If she took the job at An Affair to Remember, it meant less pay than interior design. Not to mention she wouldn't start until she got back from vacation. She justified tonight's purchase by using a two-for-one coupon.

"I had fun. Things were a little strained this morning, but it got better after lunch."

"Jack wasn't rude this afternoon, was he?" Emily wrapped up half of her sandwich.

"Not at all. In fact, he was very accommodating. He opened an account at the wholesale florist and didn't complain when Mrs. Whitman asked for some assistance at the craft store. I should've realized I would run into someone there."

"He's ready to hire you, Lib."

"After one day?" She hadn't decided whether she would accept the job if he offered. "I haven't even done an event yet."

"Jack might be grouchy and pessimistic but he knows a good thing when she's standing in front of him. You handled yourself well in several different situations today and impressed him. He said you were genuine."

"That was kind of him." Libby tried not to read more into the compliment.

"Do you think you'll accept the job?"

"I want to meet Kevin and Julie before I make up my mind." It was a valid concern and would hopefully satisfy Emily for the time being.

"You'll like them. Now, as your best friend, it's my duty to warn you about something."

"You can tell me anything, Em."

"Jack wants you to redo the conference rooms."

This wasn't a surprise. "We talked about the possibility today."

"He's going to bring it up tomorrow during the staff meeting."

Libby's stomach dipped, and she set the rest of her sandwich on the table, her appetite gone. Why would he do that without discussing it with her first? "He said we'd talk more. I didn't realize he meant in front of everyone else."

"I thought that might be the case." Emily leaned forward. "He plans to discuss it in front of the group because we'll support the idea. You should do this, Lib."

"What about helping with the events? Isn't that why you wanted me to work with you—to ease your workload?"

"Jack hopes you'll redecorate before you leave for vacation. Think about it, okay? You weren't going to start until May, anyway. This will provide a paycheck for the next few weeks."

"A project would keep me busy. Do you promise you'll tell me if you need me for anything event related?"

"Promise." Emily hooked her pinky with Libby's. "I can't wait to see what you do with the place. When you're finished, we'll actually enjoy spending time in those rooms instead of being embarrassed to invite people to the office."

"I've got a few ideas but want to look at some pictures from past events."

"You can use my computer after the staff meeting tomorrow—which starts at nine, by the way. Jack provides breakfast."

Libby frowned. "He shouldn't keep buying me food."

"It's how he shows his appreciation, Lib. Besides, this isn't out of the ordinary. He always brings breakfast to the meeting. And I told him to buy lunch today. It was the least he could do after his poor attitude this morning."

"Emily, you didn't!" She was horrified to learn Emily pulled this on her. Again.

"I did." She nodded once, indicating the argument was over and waved her hands in a shooing motion. "You're dying to get your ideas down on paper. Go."

"Can we leave a little early tomorrow and stop by the grocery store? I figured out what's missing in my centerpiece."

"Sure. How much extra time do you need?"

"Fifteen minutes should be plenty," Libby said.

"Okay. Let's plan to leave at eight."

"I can drive."

"No, I need my car for a couple of meetings tomorrow afternoon. Jack reimburses me for gas, so it's not a big deal."

Libby caught her bottom lip between her teeth. "He's a good

boss, isn't he?"

"He's the perfect boss when he's not working weddings. For the most part, he leaves us alone to do our jobs but he's available when we need him."

"If he dislikes weddings so much, why does he agree to do them?"

"They're more than half of our business," Emily explained. "Julie and I love them. I've even gotten some ideas for my wedding from some of our events."

"Maybe he'll change his mind someday."

Emily shook her head adamantly. "No way. He's a perpetual bachelor."

The disappointment that engulfed her at the statement took her by surprise. "Good night, Em."

"Night, Lib. Don't stay up too late."

She went to her room and worked on design ideas for a couple of hours before she put her sketchpad away. After pulling her Bible onto her lap, she opened it to where the bookmark rested. She was currently reading through I John. Tonight she read and re-read I John 4:7-12. *"Dear friends, let us love one another, for love comes from God. Everyone who loves has been born of God and knows God. Whoever does not love does not know God, because God is love. This is how God showed his love among us: He sent his one and only son into the world that we might live through him. This is love: not that we loved God, but that he loved us and sent his son as an atoning sacrifice for our sins. Dear friends, since God so loved us, we also ought to love one another. No one has ever seen God; but if we love one another, God lives in us and his love is made complete in us."*

Libby closed her Bible, lay back on her bed, and stared at the ceiling. *Lord, help me love people like that, even those who aren't kind to me. Be with Jack and show him the love of a father. Thank you for a job and the opportunity to try something new. Help me learn and grow from it and be a light to everyone I meet. Give me wisdom about my future with interior design. I'm still unsure about soliciting clients. Thank you for Emily's friendship and thoughtfulness. Direct her path. Continue to grow my future husband into the man I need when I meet him. Amen.*

When Libby entered the living room Tuesday morning, Emily eyed her outfit. "That shirt is adorable. Julie will love it. She's really into polka dots."

"Thanks. I never asked what to wear to work." Today she chose black slacks and a white blouse with large, black polka dots. A red sweater and black half-inch heels completed the ensemble.

"This is perfect. During the week, we dress down unless we're meeting with clients. If you're meeting someone, wear what you did when you consulted at Taylor Designs. Since you're going to the Millers' today, you're good. For non-wedding events, we wear black slacks and white shirts. Make sure you get comfortable shoes. I prefer my ballet flats. If we're working a wedding, we dress according to the style the bride has chosen for her day. You might want to buy a couple of formal dresses. Julie and I usually change at the venue about an hour before the ceremony begins. It's too hard to get everything done in those fancy dresses."

Overwhelmed by all the details Emily had thrown at her, she concentrated on the last one. "Maybe I can talk Becca into shopping with me on vacation."

"That's a fantastic idea. Becca's got a good eye."

As Emily backed out of her parking spot, Libby asked another question—this one not related to the job. "Remember how Leah encouraged us to pray for our spouses at camp that one time? Do you still pray for your future husband?"

Emily glanced over at her. "Sometimes. Why?"

"I still pray for mine every night." She shrugged. "I wondered if anyone else did."

"God answered Leah's prayers in the husband department. I should pray for mine more often."

They rode in silence, each lost in their own thoughts. When they reached the grocery store, Libby hopped out of the car, then leaned back in. "Need anything?"

"Yes, actually. A couple twelve packs of soda for the office—one diet and one regular. We drank the last of our stock yesterday."

"Got it. I'll be quick." She ran into the store, found the drinks, and picked up a bottle of her favorite coconut coffee creamer. In the produce section, she selected three ripened limes. Less than ten minutes later, she was outside again.

Once she'd loaded everything in the back seat, Libby buckled herself in the passenger seat. Emily gave her an odd expression.

"What?"

"You know, it's funny you mentioned praying for our future husbands. Guess who called me last night."

"I didn't realize you already had your husband picked out," Libby teased. "Did Jeff call again?"

"No, not Jeff. Adam. He and Brandon are coming to town this Friday and asked if they could take us to dinner."

"Are you serious, Em?" Her teasing mood quickly disappeared. "That sounds like a double date."

"It *is* a double date. Please, Libby?"

She winced at the whiny tone of Emily's voice.

"I haven't been on a date in forever, and Adam is gorgeous." Her friend was prone to exaggerate from time to time.

"I've only met Brandon once. It'll be weird." A weak argument but true, nonetheless.

"Only if you let it be." Emily shrugged. "Guys like hanging out with you."

"I hate when people say that—it will only be weird if I let it. All the pressure's on *me*."

Emily grinned. "You'll go?"

"Dinner only." She'd go because her best friend asked, not because she wanted to. "Nothing more."

"Thank you, thank you, thank you!" Emily's squeals filled the car. "I'll call Adam tonight and tell him the good news."

How did she get dragged into this? She didn't even see it coming. Emily and Adam could go to dinner without her. She gazed out the window and prayed it wouldn't be a mistake.

TWELVE

Good morning, ladies. You're here early." Jack carried breakfast into the kitchen.

"Hey, Jack." Emily lifted her mug. "Coffee's ready."

"Morning," Libby said and left the room without glancing in his direction.

He stared after her. She seemed…off. "Is something wrong?"

"She's upset with me," Emily said. "I sprang something on her this morning, and she's trying to decide if she gave the right answer."

"Did you tell her about redecorating the office?" He'd questioned whether bringing it up during the meeting was the right thing to do. But if she saw everyone's enthusiasm, maybe she wouldn't be so hesitant. At the same time, he didn't want to embarrass her.

"No, it's not work related." Emily patted his back twice. "I did mention your plan to her and think she's on board. But for future reference, you might want to talk to her about this stuff first."

"Okay, I will. What was she doing?" She had a plate of sliced limes in her hand when she left the room.

Emily shrugged. "Working on the centerpieces, said she figured out what was missing. She's a perfectionist when it comes to a project."

"Good morning, Emily. Jack." Julie joined them.

He turned around. "Good morning. How was your day off?"

"Perfect. I'm refreshed and ready to get back to work." She bumped hips with Emily. "Is your friend here? I want to meet her. Jack told us last Friday he's considering hiring her."

Emily grinned. "She's in the conference room working on the flowers for the open house. Come see what she put together. She'll want your opinion." The women started toward the conference room.

"Are you coming, Jack?" Julie called from the open area.

"In a minute." He finished setting out the food and went to find out what else Libby had done.

"I like all of them." Julie's response reached him before he entered the room.

"You must like one more than the others."

Jack smiled to himself. She definitely valued honest opinions.

"The one with the sunflowers and daisies would be my first choice," Julie said. "But the one with the sunflowers and limes is a close second."

He glanced at the flowers lined up on the table. Libby had placed several slices of lime in the glass vase of the sunflower arrangement.

"Hello?" Kevin called.

Jack poked his head out the door. "In here."

The last member of his staff arrived, and Emily handled introductions. "She's doing the centerpieces for Saturday. Which one do you like?"

"Um…" Kevin hesitated as if she'd asked a trick question. "All of them?"

"I hate to break this up," Jack said, taking pity on the man, "but breakfast is getting cold."

Libby stood from her chair, and the group filed to the kitchen. Kevin waved the women in front of him. "Ladies first."

Emily brushed past. "I give you two weeks, Kevin."

"For what?"

"Before you quit letting Libby go in front of you when food's involved."

"Why?" He eyed Libby as if sizing her up.

Jack knew what his friend saw—five foot four, small waist, perhaps a few extra pounds in her hips and stomach, but they accentuated her hourglass figure. She came away from the counter with a plate piled with food, and Kevin's eyes grew round.

Emily laughed at his expression. "That's why. Libby's always hungry."

"Thanks a lot, Em." She sat down at the table and bowed her head.

The movement was natural, something Jack could tell she did regularly. This young woman continued to surprise him, and the more he learned, the more he wanted to know about her.

When she looked up and met his gaze, he cleared his throat. "Would you like something to drink?"

"I'll get something in a minute. You should eat."

As soon as everyone sat at the table, Jack began the meeting. He verified everything was ready for Saturday's event. They had weddings the following two Saturdays and an employee appreciation luncheon the weekend after that. No one expressed any concerns about the upcoming events.

"Anything else?" When Libby raised her hand, he hid a grin. "Yes, Libby?"

"I have a suggestion. Emily mentioned you rent your table linens if the venue doesn't provide them. You should purchase your own. Just buy black and white for now. The investment will pay for itself within three months if you rent more than twice a month."

"What about cleaning them?" Was she trying to tell him how to run his business? He'd done fine without her input. Renting was convenient. Perhaps she hadn't considered all the costs and time involved. "And who will drop them off and pick them up?"

Her gaze didn't waver from his. "Still better to have your own. My dry cleaner gives discounts to repeat customers. I'm sure others do too. And several cleaners offer pick-up and delivery."

This wasn't a discussion he had time for today. After running her around yesterday, he had plenty of work to catch up on. "Get me some hard figures, and I'll make a decision."

"One more thing."

Jack clenched his jaw. It seemed adding Libby to his staff meant he'd be pulling out the company checkbook. Perhaps his excitement over her saving him money yesterday had been premature. One day, and he was already handing her money to redecorate his office.

"If anyone needs help with anything, please find me. I'm here to make your lives easier."

He let out a breath he didn't realize he'd been holding.

"Where are we going to put you?" Julie asked.

"We'll share my office." Emily laid an arm across Libby's shoulders. "Can we use the table from your office? We'll need the extra workspace."

"It's yours. I rarely use it, and getting it out of there will give me more room. Come get it anytime."

"I'll move it for you," Kevin offered.

Jack cleared his throat. "Before everyone starts rearranging the furniture, there's one more thing I'd like to discuss." He explained about Libby redecorating the conference rooms and asked for volunteers. "I'll provide snacks and lunch for anyone who comes to paint."

"I'm available while the girls are in school," Julie said.

"I'll have to check with Amber but don't think it'll be a problem," Kevin added. "Maybe she'll come too."

"Great. Let's meet next Monday at nine." He closed his laptop. "Now, everyone get to work."

Kevin followed him to his office and shut the door behind them. "I like her."

"Me too." *Too much.* He'd been short with her in the meeting in an attempt to stem his growing attraction.

Jack and Kevin had met during their freshman year of college. After rooming together the following three years, Kevin had become Jack's closest friend.

"I'm surprised you asked her to redo the rooms." Kevin folded his arms across his chest.

"Why?"

"You don't like to spend money, Jack. Steam almost came out of your ears when she suggested we purchase our own table linens—which is a solid suggestion, by the way."

Jack sighed and sank onto his chair. "I agree. And I'm sure any other suggestion Libby James makes will be excellent as well. She just tends to blindside me with these things."

"I'm glad someone can knock you off your game." Kevin sat down and leaned back in the chair. "Is something else going on? You're more uptight than usual. Did you take that meeting yesterday morning or give it to Emily like I told you to?"

"I took it, but this stress isn't about work. My dad has left a few messages." Another one this morning. Hence his defensiveness during the meeting.

"Why?"

"No idea," Jack said. "I haven't returned any of the calls."

"What do you have going on Friday? Amber wants to invite you to dinner. We can talk about this more."

"Is this another setup?" Jack was immediately suspicious. Kevin's wife had arranged for a fourth person—always a single woman—to join them for dinner a few too many times in the past.

"Not this time." Kevin chuckled.

"Okay, I'll be there."

"You'll make her day. I need to go move that table."

"I'll help you." At this rate, he wouldn't get much work done today either.

THIRTEEN

Libby followed Julie into her office to make sure she'd cleared enough space for the table. "This room is so cute." She turned in a circle and examined Julie's space. The walls were painted a bright pink, and large black polka dots were spread around the room at random.

Julie smiled. "Thanks. I got the idea from Pinterest."

"Oh, don't you love it? I use Pinterest for inspiration often." She ran her hand over one of the polka dots and paused. "Is this construction paper?"

"Yeah. It was faster than painting them on, but they don't stay up. I need to come in one afternoon with some paint and finish the job."

"I can help if you like."

"You don't have to do that."

"It would be my pleasure. Some framed black and white pictures would look great in here as well. I'll find some for you while I'm looking through photographs for the conference rooms." Libby moved to the bookshelves and studied the framed photos then pointed at one. "Are these your daughters?"

"They are." Julie moved beside her. "Mandy is ten and Amy is eight."

"Is Mandy short for Amanda?"

"Yes. Why do you ask?"

"My mom is Amanda," Libby explained, "and my oldest sister is Amy. You and I are going to get along fine."

"I hope so. I adore Emily, and she's always had good things to say about you."

"You might not want to believe everything she says." Libby stepped away from the bookshelf and took in the room again. "If we paint those polka dots on your wall, bring your girls. They can help."

"They would love that."

"Let me know what day works best, and I'll be here."

The women visited for a while. Julie was five years older than her. The oldest person in the office, she said. She'd met Jack in the restaurant where he'd worked as a line cook during college. Julie was one of their vendors at the time but jumped at the opportunity to branch out. Jack recruited her and put her in charge of food for all their events. The hours were better, and she didn't have to work overtime, allowed her to spend more time with her family.

"I'm excited you're going to do the conference rooms." Julie ended her short history and moved on. "How did you convince Jack to let you redecorate?"

"That was all Emily. He overheard us talking and got kind of upset. I was a little worried, but Em said it was because of some appointment he'd had with a caterer for one of the weddings."

"Yeah, that would do it. You should talk to him about doing the common area between the offices as well." She grimaced. "It's so ugly out there."

"The area could be functional." Libby couldn't keep from sharing the ideas she'd had upon seeing the space when she'd come in for her interview last week. "You could add a couple chairs and a small table to display brochures and business cards."

"Anything would be better than how it looks now. Talk to Jack."

"No, I won't ask him to spend more money. He didn't take my suggestion about the linens well."

"It was a smart recommendation, and he'll come to agree," Julie said. "I'll talk to him about the entry."

"What about the entry?" Kevin filled the doorway. He was tall and had a little paunch around his middle—a sign of a well-fed husband.

Jack stood behind him, and Libby wished the floor would swallow her up. She ducked her head to hide her flush of embarrassment.

"Jack, Libby has some good ideas—"

"It's not important." Her head lifted, and she gave Julie a pleading expression before turning toward the men. "Do you need us for something?"

Confusion filled Kevin's face. "We were coming to move the table for you."

Libby was relieved for a project to take their minds off the conversation they'd walked in on. "Great. Emily and I already cleared a spot." She followed the men as they carried the table across the office.

Jack shook his head upon seeing the empty area in Emily's office, and his gaze landed on Emily. "Who moved your desk?"

She pointed to Libby and then back to herself. "We did."

"You should have asked Kevin or me to do that."

"Why?" The question slipped out without thought. Libby moved furniture all of the time. It wasn't as if she were useless when it came to this stuff. Why did he care if she moved the desk?

"Because it's heavy." He answered both her asked and unasked questions. "You could have injured yourselves."

"It's not a big deal," Libby said. For the second day in a row, she'd unintentionally upset him. Hopefully, this wasn't an indication of the working relationship to come.

"Libby arranges furniture for a living, Jack." Emily attempted to diffuse the tension hanging between them. "We brought some of those coaster things for moving furniture with us today."

"Em and I have a system." Libby moved two chairs to the table.

Jack opened his mouth like he wanted to say more, but shut it when Kevin shook his head. When they left, Libby set up her makeshift desk.

Once she was settled, Emily set a laptop in front of her. "Here are the photos you wanted to look through. They're grouped by type of event, and each event has its own folder. I'll talk to Jack about getting you a computer."

Libby grabbed her hand to stop her. "Please don't, Em. I don't want him any more upset with me."

"You can't do your job without a computer. All our events are listed on a shared calendar. If he hasn't already ordered you one, he needs to get on it."

"I won't need it until I get back from vacation. Please, Emily?"

She pulled her hand out of Libby's. "Okay, I'll let this go for now because I don't need my computer. Bu if sharing becomes an issue, I'm talking to him."

"Thank you."

"You're welcome. I guess I owe you one for Friday night."

Ugh. She'd managed to forget about their double date. Maybe she should use it to her advantage this week.

Libby immersed herself in the photographs and was surprised when someone knocked on the door.

"How's everything going in here?"

Sucking in a breath at Jack's reappearance, she concentrated on the computer screen.

"Fabulous," Emily answered for them. "I have several meetings lined up for the fall calendar, and Libby's been furiously working over there."

Looking up from the computer, Libby met Jack's brown-eyed gaze. "These are beautiful pictures. I'm going to have a tough time choosing which to use."

"I ordered you a computer," Jack said. "It should be ready next week. Will you be ready to go in about thirty minutes?"

"What time is it?" She turned to Emily for the answer.

"I thought your stomach would tell you it was late," she said. "Want to get some lunch before you leave?"

Libby gathered her things.

"I could eat." Jack leaned against the doorframe. "We can go now and stop for something on our way." He glanced at Emily. "Unless you wanted lunch."

She waved her hand in dismissal. "I'm still full from breakfast. You guys go. I'll pick up something between my meetings."

Libby flung her bag over her shoulder and stepped toward the door—and Jack. "If we stop for lunch, I'm paying. You brought breakfast." *And paid for lunch yesterday.* She passed him and threw over her shoulder, "I need to get the centerpieces."

He followed her to the conference room. She'd already packed the flowers in a box, so they were ready to go.

When she bent to pick it up, Jack stooped alongside her. "Let me take that."

She inhaled. The fresh scents of soap and fabric softener assaulted her. After taking a large step back, she scurried to open the door. "We should get going." Mentally slapping herself on the forehead, she wondered if she could sound any more like an idiot.

After a quick lunch at Chick-Fil-A, Jack drove to Oakwood.

"I hope she likes the flowers." Libby's nervousness increased the closer they got to the house.

"You sound concerned. Everyone liked them."

"I know, but Callie told me Mrs. Miller is kind of particular."

Jack laughed. "That's one way to describe her. You have no reason to worry, though. She'll have several options to choose from, and when I tell her you're saving her money, she's bound to love one of them."

Libby relaxed in her seat. "Thanks, Jack."

"Julie mentioned your ideas about the entryway."

Every muscle in her body tensed again. So much for being at

ease. "I asked her not to."

"She said as much."

"I'm sorry. When people ask my opinion about a room, I can't keep my mouth shut."

"You're apologizing again." He shook his head at her as if she'd done something wrong. "If you did the entry, would you still be able to finish everything before your vacation?"

"With everybody helping paint? Absolutely."

"Okay. Do it. I'll start you with fifteen hundred for all three rooms. Let me know if you need more."

"That's too much, Jack."

"And I want you to use all of it." He continued as if he hadn't heard her objection. "Don't cut something out because you don't want to spend the money." He parked in front of a house and shut off the car but made no attempt to get out. "I apologize for my reaction to your suggestion during the meeting. If it's cost efficient, I'm on board."

"It is." She had no doubt the table linens would save the company money in the long run.

"Ready?" He rested his hand on the door handle.

She nodded once and gave him a cheesy smile. "Let's go." Oh, good grief, now she sounded like a cheerleader. All she needed were some pompoms.

FOURTEEN

When Mrs. Miller opened the door, her eyes took in Jack then Libby, who was standing beside and slightly behind him. The homeowner's gaze returned to him. "Jack Price. Is everything ready for Saturday?"

"Almost, Mrs. Miller. We had a little hiccup with the flowers."

"Oh no, what happened?"

"The florist double booked and canceled on us."

She wrung her hands together. "What are we going to do?"

Jack gently nudged Libby forward. "This is Libby James. She's working with us this summer and has put together some centerpieces for you."

Libby smiled at the woman. "I brought some arrangements for you to choose from. If you don't like them, we'll find something you're happy with."

Jack picked up the box at his feet and followed the ladies to the kitchen. Libby lined the centerpieces up on the counter.

"Oh, my goodness," Mrs. Miller exclaimed. "I don't know how I'm going to decide between these."

Jack's chest filled with pride. Libby's earlier nervousness had been unfounded. He knew she'd impress their client.

"Which do you like the least?" Libby's focus remained on the customer.

"Well, I'm not overly fond of tulips."

"Okay, let's take those arrangements out of the running." She put the three arrangements that included tulips back in the box and motioned toward the counter with her hand. "Which of these is your favorite?"

"I don't know," Mrs. Miller said. "Is it tacky to use both?"

"Not at all." Libby grasped the woman's hand. "This is the perfect setting to mix and match, and it will add originality. I'll make three of each arrangement and add some cornflowers to the daisies to tie them all together."

She pulled the blue flowers out of one of the arrangements in the box and added them to the one on the counter. Jack was impressed with how easily she'd met the request.

"It's beautiful," the homeowner said, "but I like the square vases better than the round ones."

Libby nodded. "I can do everything in the square vases." She picked up the round vase of the arrangement she'd just been working with. "And for this one, I'll use lemons instead of limes to add more balance."

"Thank you." Mrs. Miller squeezed Libby's arm. "You're a life saver."

"I've got more good news." Jack jumped in with his trump card. "Since Libby's doing the flowers, we'll refund you a hundred dollars."

"Ralph will like that," she said before returning her attention to Libby. "Would you like a tour of the house?"

"I'd love one." She glanced at Jack. "Do we have time?"

He nodded. "I'd like to look around again and make sure everything's ready for Saturday."

As they went through the house, Jack noted how Libby complimented something in every room; even the ones he thought were over the top.

"Have we met before, Libby?" Mrs. Miller asked during the tour. "Your name seems so familiar."

"We haven't, but if you spent any time with Callie while she worked on your restoration, I'm sure she mentioned me."

"You're her sister!" The woman's eyes sparkled with recognition. "She speaks highly of you, but she said you're an interior designer."

A brief shadow crossed Libby's face. Jack didn't miss the disappointment in her eyes. She would rather be decorating a room. "I'm taking a break for the summer."

"Can I ask your opinion about my sitting room? I don't know what to do with it. There's something missing."

Libby perked right back up. "Lead the way."

"You don't look anything like Callie." Mrs. Miller apprised her before turning toward the back of the house.

"I know." Libby exhaled a half laugh, half sigh. "Callie's gorgeous."

"I didn't mean that." The woman's hands covered her own cheeks in a move Jack considered embarrassment. "You're a pretty girl. Don't you agree?" She looked pointedly at him.

"I do," he said. Libby wasn't beautiful like Emily but was pretty in her own way. Her hazel eyes had fascinated him since the

89

day they met. But what made her most attractive was her approachability. You *wanted* to spend time in her presence.

"What I meant was you don't favor her." Mrs. Miller pursed her lips and squinted at the younger woman. "She's got red hair."

"And green eyes and she's tall," Libby added. "Her mom was, too. Tall, I mean. Callie and our oldest sister are adopted. Their parents—my aunt and uncle—died when Callie was a baby. Mom and Dad adopted them, and I came along years later. After they'd given up on having kids of their own."

"Callie's your cousin?"

Libby laughed—her real laugh. The one that enveloped others in her joy. "I never considered it. She's always been my sister, but you're right."

Everything in the sitting room was white or tan. It felt sterile to him. If he lived here, Jack would avoid this room for fear of tracking in dirt.

"What do you think?" Mrs. Miller gazed at Libby expectantly.

She walked around the room, studying it. "You've got a good foundation with the white. My only suggestion is to add some color in several places—some throw pillows, a vase, maybe a couple items on the bookshelves. What you want to do is add depth to the muted tones."

"What colors would you suggest?"

"Use the same color throughout, but anything will work with white—red, purple, burgundy, dark green—"

"Ralph's favorite color is green."

"Green it is," Libby said. "If you like, I can find a few things and bring them on Saturday."

"Oh, would you?" Mrs. Miller clasped her hands in front of her. "I would appreciate it."

Libby smiled. "It's my pleasure. I'll come an hour early, and we'll put everything together."

"Thank you." The elderly woman pinned Jack with her gaze. "Give my refund to Libby so she can buy whatever she needs."

Resisting the urge to call her ma'am and salute her, Jack nodded. "I will, Mrs. Miller. We'll see you Saturday morning. Call if you need anything before then."

They returned to the kitchen, and Libby packed up the remaining centerpieces. Jack took the box again, and they left the house. After placing the flowers in the back of his SUV, he hurried around to the side and opened Libby's door. "You did a great job in there, Libby James."

When he scooted behind the wheel, he added, "Is there anyone who doesn't like you two minutes after meeting you?"

She shrugged. "I can think of a couple people. My former boss never liked me."

"That's because she was jealous." He didn't give her a chance to object. "Are you sure you have enough time to help Mrs. Miller with her room?"

"I do. It'll only take a couple hours to find what she needs."

"No one has a set schedule at the office. If you want to take some time this week to shop for her, you're welcome to do so."

"Thank you, Jack. I might take you up on that. I need to go back to the craft store and pick up more vases. There's a home décor place nearby. I'll combine the two errands."

"Okay. I don't want you to stretch yourself too thin trying to please everyone."

"This won't take long," she said. "Besides, shopping is like therapy for me.

"If you say so." He'd reached his limit for the next several months when they were out and about yesterday. "I put together some paperwork for you to fill out if you decide to work with us. I hope you'll stick around." They could all learn a thing or two from her.

FIFTEEN

Friday morning, Libby searched through more photos when someone let out a low whistle. She looked up and smiled at Julie.

"Wow, you two look fantastic. What's the occasion?"

Emily beamed and almost bounced out of her seat with excitement. "We're going out tonight. It's been so long since a guy took me to dinner." She let out a dreamy sigh.

Libby resisted the urge to roll her eyes. It wasn't like Emily couldn't get a date anytime she wanted. All she had to do was smile at a man—or breathe. She was choosy and turned down a lot of offers.

At her friend's insistence, Libby wore a dress today. Since they were meeting the guys right after work, she'd be stuck in it all day. At least it was comfortable, and she liked the turquoise A-line dress with the wide brown belt. Brown leggings, knee-high boots, and a knit sweater completed the outfit.

When she'd first put it on this morning, she'd felt pretty. Until she saw Emily in a red sweater dress and black heels, both of which showcased her long legs—an asset Libby didn't have. No one would pay her any attention with the raven-haired beauty at the table.

"Turn around, Libby." Julie circled her index finger in the air.

Libby spun around slowly then sat down again.

"Your waist is so tiny." Julie cocked her head. "I've seen you eat. What's your secret?"

Libby shrugged. She answered the question often. "No secret. I'm blessed with a fast metabolism. I'm always hungry and eat a lot, but everything burns right off."

"We're going to double team the guys at the limo place and try to talk them into giving us a discount." Emily waggled her eyebrows. "Wanna come? We can get lunch afterward."

"Lunch sounds great," Julie said, "but I'll wait in the car while you discuss the deal with the limo guys. Let me grab my purse."

"I'll come with you." Libby stood up again. "I have a question for you."

Once they were in Julie's office, Libby asked who designed Jack's business cards.

Julie eyed her dubiously. "I think it was a college buddy of his, but I'm not sure. Ask him."

"He's not here." Libby lifted her shoulder in a slight shrug. "He's taking me to get the flowers after lunch. I'll ask then."

"What did you really want to talk about, Libby? I don't believe for a second you need a graphic designer."

She took a seat in one of the chairs. "I do need some brochures made, but you're right, there's more. And I can't talk to Emily. She's so excited about tonight while I'm kind of dreading this date."

"Is it a blind date?"

"Not really. Adam—Em's date—has worked for my brother-in-law for years, and the three of us went to high school together. But I've met Brandon once. He's the new youth pastor at the church we used to attend back home."

"Sounds like someone with potential," Julie said. "What's the problem?"

Libby chewed the inside of her cheek. This sounded so petty. What did it matter? This was one date. She didn't plan on going out with Brandon again. "Emily's beautiful. I don't want to feel like an afterthought at dinner."

"First of all, you're gorgeous. Any guy who doesn't realize it is blind. Second, you have a huge advantage over Emily. She's almost too beautiful. It intimidates men to the point they steer clear of her. I've seen how guys react around her. Odds are the limo guys give us a deal today because *you* put them at ease around her. People like you, Libby."

Struggling to accept the compliments, she shifted the topic. "Sometimes I just wish I could be the girlfriend instead of the friend who happens to be a girl."

Julie tucked a brown curl behind her ear and sat beside Libby. "Your time will come. Enjoy tonight. Think of it as hanging out with a new friend with good food thrown in. Doesn't it sound like a pleasant evening?"

Libby giggled. "When you put it that way, it's not so bad. Thank you." She gave Julie an awkward seated hug before standing up. "We'd better get out of here. I need to get back in time to meet Jack."

"I almost feel sorry for these guys." Julie retrieved her purse from her bottom desk drawer.

"Me too." Libby grinned. "I love negotiating a good deal."

Two hours later, Emily was laughing so hard she couldn't speak when she climbed in the car. Julie glanced at Libby in the rearview mirror. "I take it she got what she wanted?"

Libby nodded. "And then some. Once they picked their jaws up off the floor, they offered us a one-year contract with a twenty percent discount and priority status."

"Jack will be over the moon." Julie patted Emily's knee. "Good job."

She sobered. "Oh, it wasn't me. They offered me a ten percent cut before Libby pulled out the big guns. She told them we handle a lot of weddings and formal events, and they could become our exclusive car service if they gave us a better discount as well as their assurance they wouldn't back out on us. Then she told them we'd go somewhere else if they didn't want that opportunity."

"Wow, Libby." Julie chuckled. "Remind me never to negotiate with you. Where would you like to celebrate?"

"How about the little lunch place by the office?" Libby rested her elbows on the back of the front seats and leaned forward. "I've been hoping to check it out."

"Sounds good to me. How about you, Emily?"

"Sure. I'm only going to get a salad so I can save all of my calories for tonight."

Julie parked the car at the office, and the trio strolled to the café.

"Libby, are we still on for Sunday afternoon?" Julie asked as they made their way down the street. "The girls are excited to paint."

"You bet." Libby scooted closer to Julie to let a couple coming from the other direction pass. "I can't wait to meet them. Does two o'clock sound good?"

"Yes. Will three hours give us enough time?"

"Plenty, but I'd rather have too much time than too little. I bought all the paint and supplies for the office yesterday."

"Are you really not going to let us in the conference rooms after we paint?" Emily crossed her arms in front of her and poked her lower lip out.

Libby knew this was her way of pouting, but it had no effect on her after years of friendship. "Nope, unless I need a hand with something. If I do, I promise to come to you first."

"I can't wait to see what colors you chose," Julie said.

"I can't wait for tonight," Emily added.

"I can't wait for lunch." When Libby opened the door, they all entered the restaurant laughing. Having another close female friend was nice. She could always call and talk with Callie or Amy, but someone sitting across from you beat a conversation over the phone.

And speaking of conversations…"Em, I forgot to tell you I talked to Stacy yesterday." Libby included Julie. "I worked with Stacy at my last job."

"What did she say?" Emily scooted her chair closer to Libby's.

"I asked if we could get coffee but she didn't want to risk Linda finding out. Mrs. Patterson fired Linda and demanded a refund because Linda said the project was less than halfway completed. But then she only refunded Mrs. Patterson the money for the work I hadn't finished."

"How could she do that when she claimed the project was nowhere near complete?" Julie asked.

"I have no idea, but Mrs. Patterson has been telling everyone not to use Taylor Designs." She looked at Emily. "Do you think I should call her?"

"I'm sure no one explained your disappearance," she said. "Since Linda's no longer involved, you can talk to her. Maybe you could finish the job. Do you think that's legal?"

"Her husband's a lawyer. I bet he could find out if she wanted him to. Although, if I took her shopping, she could purchase the few things she still needs and won't be paying me for any services. I'll call her when we get back to the office."

After lunch, Libby made some phone calls, the first to Mrs. Patterson.

"Oh, Libby, I can't tell you how relieved I am to hear from you."

"I'm sorry I didn't call sooner. When Stacy mentioned you'd cut ties with Taylor Designs, I thought it would be okay."

"Don't you worry about a thing, dear. If Linda Taylor throws a fit, I'll sic Harold on her," she said, speaking of her husband—the lawyer. "But are you all right? Do you need anything?"

Mrs. Patterson's concern brought a smile to her lips. "I'm fine. My friend found me a temporary position for the summer while I decide what's next for me. I've only been here a week but I'm enjoying it so far." This wasn't why she'd called, so she got to the point. "Did you finish the living room?"

A sigh carried over the line. "No. We were almost done too."

"I have an idea. Would you like to meet me one afternoon for a little shopping? I can point out a few things you might consider adding to the room to finish it up."

"That sounds wonderful," Mrs. Patterson said. "How much do you charge?"

"You don't have to pay me," Libby said. "In fact, I can't accept any compensation because it would be in direct violation of my contract with Taylor Designs. This is just two friends spending an afternoon shopping."

After deciding on a date and time, Mrs. Patterson ended the conversation. "I'm so glad you called me. We've been praying for you. Keep in touch, okay?"

"I will, Mrs. Patterson. Thank you."

"We're friends, Libby. Call me Gina."

Libby had a couple more calls to make before picking up the flowers. Once she had those, the remainder of the afternoon would consist of putting together the six centerpieces for the open house.

She had found some beautiful pieces for Mrs. Miller's sitting room, and the flowers were a hit, but she most looked forward to seeing Callie and her dad. Spending time with her family was something she cherished. Raleigh was only an hour away, but she stayed so busy, they didn't get together as often as she would like.

Suzie Waltner

SIXTEEN

Jack spent most of the morning running errands. His arms were full when he finally arrived at the office a little past eleven. After dropping everything at his desk, he went to check in with the others to find out if he could assist with anything. Julie's car wasn't outside, so he skipped her office. Emily's office stood empty as well.

"They went to talk to the limo guys." Kevin exited the kitchen with a cup of coffee in hand. "Emily said something about double-teaming them."

Jack shook his head. "They won't know what hit them."

"They didn't even stand a chance *before* those two got all dolled up. I'm not sure it's entirely fair."

"What do you mean?" Did he want to hear the answer?

"I overheard Emily telling Julie she and Libby have a double date tonight. They're both dressed to kill. I bet the limo guys are still trying to get their eyeballs back in their sockets."

"Emily does leave an impression."

"Libby too," Kevin said over his shoulder as he continued toward his office. When he reached the door, he paused and looked back at Jack. "You still coming to dinner?"

"Planning on it."

"Good. I'll call and let Amber know."

Jack returned to his office and shut the door, his mind going several different directions. This week had put him severely behind. Hopefully, the girls would come back with a decent deal from the limo place. Thankfully, Kevin hadn't asked where he'd been. His entire morning had been centered on Libby. He'd picked up her computer from their IT guy, made copies of the keys to the building, and stopped by Ben's for her business cards. She hadn't completed the paperwork yet, so maybe all of this was premature. But he trusted this was where God wanted her.

Determined to wrap up a few things before he and Libby went to get the flowers, he logged on his computer. Emily had offered Libby the use of her car, but he'd insisted on taking her himself, with the excuse it would be easier to load and unload everything in his SUV. Only to himself did he admit he enjoyed running errands with her. At the office, he had to share her with the others. But when he drove her somewhere, he got her all to himself. Something he found himself looking forward to.

Someone knocked on his door, and he called for them to come in. Emily opened it and handed him several sheets of paper. She was stunning in a red dress with a black belt and black heels, her shiny hair hanging almost to her waist. Her beauty had shocked him when they'd first met, even to the point of speechlessness once or twice.

"What's this?" He shook off the thought and scanned the papers she'd given him.

"Our new contract with Raleigh-Durham Limo, including a twenty percent discount and VIP priority for the next year."

His eyebrows shot up, and his lips curled up in a grin. The offer was much better than he'd anticipated. "I'm impressed, Emily."

"I only got them to ten percent. Libby talked them into the

rest. Hire her already."

Libby did this? Did that mean she was staying? "I'm trying. She has the paperwork. This is all for her." He waved toward the chair where he'd moved the business cards, keys, and computer. "I'm not the person who needs convincing here."

Emily opened the box of cards and pulled one out. "Cool. Can I give these to her?"

"Sure. Take all of it. Tell her I'll be ready to go to the florist in an hour."

"Okay. She's on the phone with Logan making arrangements to meet this Sunday." Emily rolled her eyes. "I don't know why she wants to get together with him when two perfectly wonderful guys are taking us to dinner."

Something pinched in Jack's gut when she confirmed the date. "Be careful, Emily. Not everyone's as great as they might appear at first."

"Don't worry, Jack. We've known Adam since we were fourteen, and Brandon's the youth pastor at our old church. I think we're safe." She picked up Libby's things and sashayed from the room.

He wasn't sure which he disliked more—the idea of Libby with a youth pastor who would adore her or the thought of her with someone who already knew what a treasure she was. *Get a grip, Jack. She's practically an employee, and you don't want to get involved. She deserves someone who's willing to be a husband and a father, something you can't offer.*

He finished his tasks then picked up his keys and wallet before striding to Emily's office. Libby sat at the table with her new laptop open in front of her and her phone to her ear. She smiled at him, held up two fingers to indicate she'd be a couple more minutes, and motioned to the chair across from her.

"Hi, Kay," she said. "Can you help Ty with a matte color? He's clueless. I sent someone in there with a picture that needs a light coral matte. You wore a sweater about a month ago with some pearl embellishments on the collar." She listened and nodded. "Yes, that's the one. That color. Would you put Ty back on the phone?"

She held the phone against her shoulder. "Sorry, this won't take long."

He shrugged. "We've got time." A couple more minutes wouldn't hurt anything.

She returned the phone to her ear. "Ty, what kind of deal will you give me on framing sixteen photos? Ten of them are large—thirty by twenty. The others are eleven-by-seventeen or eight-by-ten…Knock another fifty off and you've got a deal." She shook her head and laughed at whatever the person said. "You're the best. I'll bring everything by next week."

When she hung up, she dropped the phone in her bag. "Sorry again, Jack. I didn't realize it was so late."

"It's fine. We're not locked into a schedule." Jack's shirt collar shrank around his neck when Libby was in full view. She'd been hidden behind the table and her computer. Everything but Libby faded away the moment she stood. Overwhelmed by the sudden urge to pull her to him, he fisted his hands.

"Have fun." Emily's voice pulled him back from the line he'd almost crossed.

"Shall we?" He let Libby lead the way. Big mistake. The view from the back tempted him again. Her belt hugged her small waist. She was typically a few inches shorter than him, but her heeled boots made them almost the same height. Jack closed his hand around his car keys to stop himself from taking her hand. Once they were outside, he opened the car door for her. If he couldn't touch her, at least he could be a gentleman.

"Thanks for the computer and business cards." She clicked her seatbelt into place. "I guess this makes everything official."

"Nothing's official until you sign the paperwork. I hope you decide to stay, though."

"I finished the paperwork, but you weren't here this morning."

"Great. I'll get it from you later. Congratulations on the limo contract, by the way. Emily told me you're to thank for the outstanding offer."

"It's not a big deal." Libby ducked her head like she was embarrassed. "Most businesses will work with you if it leads to repeat customers."

"Don't downplay your role in this. Most people would have been content with the ten percent they offered Emily."

She didn't respond. Why was it difficult for her to accept a compliment? He wouldn't press the issue. "Are you looking forward to your date tonight?"

"Emily told you, huh?"

He recalled her exuberance. "She's excited."

"Yes, she is."

"And you?" *Say no.*

"Not even for the food."

He released the breath he'd been holding. "Why not?"

She glanced at him for a second before focusing on the passing scenery out the front window. "I love Emily to death, but a double date with her is a nightmare. She's beautiful, and guys fight for her attention. It doesn't usually bother me, and most of the time I'm content being the friend, the person guys hang out with. But when someone asks you out, you want their attention to remain on you. You want to be the only girl in the room for that guy. With Emily at the table, that won't happen." She blew out a breath after her confession.

Did Libby not realize how beautiful she was? Men stared at her. He'd seen it a few times now. A few hours ago, she'd gone to a car service and landed the biggest contract his office had ever negotiated. He started to tell her all of that, but she spoke first.

"I'm sorry. That was awful for me to unload on you, and I'm sure I sound like a horrible, whiny friend. They're my insecurities. God says I'm made in his image." A humorless laugh escaped her lips. "And who am I to complain about his creation?"

Leave it to her to view things that way. He could learn a lesson or two in humility from this young woman. "You have an interesting way of looking at the world, Libby James. It's refreshing."

He found a parking spot downtown and came around to open her door. Libby took his proffered hand as she stepped from the SUV, and he reveled in the few seconds of contact. As they walked, he couldn't help but notice how men turned around for a second glance at her. Others openly stared. He stood taller because he was with her. No one knew their relationship was strictly professional.

"Libby?" Pam approached as soon as they were inside the door and squealed. "You look amazing. Who's the lucky guy?"

Libby peeked at him, eyes wide. Intervening wasn't wise for either of them. He shook his head slightly and sat on a chair near the front counter.

"I'm meeting someone for dinner," she said. "Do you have my flowers?"

"We've got everything ready to go. Did you bring pictures?"

Jack watched Libby pull a digital camera from her bag and show the women at the counter photos of her arrangements. They praised her work and asked about the open house. Content where he was, Jack let her enjoy the spotlight for a while. This little reminder that she was special and unique was a blessing for her today.

SEVENTEEN

Libby felt Jack's eyes on her as she visited with the employees at the front counter. She shouldn't have expressed her concerns about her date on the ride over. In fact, she rarely let anyone glimpse her insecurities but she'd unloaded them on Jack.

Was it because of the way he had looked at her earlier? With interest, and perhaps a bit of desire?

Before they'd left the office, a little tremor of excitement shot through her when he stared at her instead of Emily. And fifteen minutes ago, when she'd taken his hand as she got out of the car, a pleasant current ran up her arm. He was handsome, successful, an excellent listener, and thoughtful. Stifling a sigh, she tried to focus on the conversation. Why was she attracted to the one guy who was off limits? Her boss. A man who didn't believe in marriage—something she longed for.

Lord, help me out here. I can't get involved with my boss, a man who doesn't want anything to do with marriage. Help me keep an open mind tonight and show me your will for my future.

She charged the flowers to the business account, took the box Pam set on the counter, and twist around to tell Jack she was ready to go. He stood right behind her, and she took a small step back, stopped by the counter.

"Let me get those." He lifted the box out her arms.

"I can carry them." She snapped her mouth shut and released

her grip at his stern expression.

Once they were outside, she punched him in the arm playfully. "Why didn't you help me out when Pam made the comment about the lucky guy?" She could do this. Bantering with Jack like she did with her other guy friends would keep her from crossing the friendship line.

"You work for me, so we probably shouldn't discuss your personal life. And no one in there," he jerked his head backward, "needed to know we talked about your date."

Of course, he was right. The gossip about her and Linda had spread fast enough. She'd managed fine without his assistance in the end.

Jack drove them back to the office, carried the flowers to the conference room, and left her alone. For all the conversation on the way to the flower shop, there was almost none on the drive back. Had she done something else to upset him? No use dwelling on it. She had work to do.

She focused on the centerpieces instead. Emily would come find her when it was time to leave for dinner. The grimace and eye roll came instantly when she thought about tonight. Her best friend owed her big time for this.

A little after four, she placed the last flower arrangement in the box, stood, and stretched her shoulders and back. *Time to spare.*

Julie poked her head inside. "How's everything going in here?"

"I'm done. Did I hear you say you're stopping by the office in the morning?"

"Yeah, I want to take care of a couple of things since we're not starting until ten. Why?"

"Would you mind bringing the flowers to the open house? I don't want to leave them in Em's car all evening. And mine's loaded with the stuff for Mrs. Miller's sitting room."

"Don't worry about it. I'll bring them," Julie said. "It's silly for you to drive out of the way when I'm already here."

Libby pointed at the vases, floral foam, and other tools scattered across the table. "I guess I should find a place to store all of this stuff."

"There are a couple of empty cupboards in the break room. We'll use those for now."

They made short work of cleaning up. Libby could organize the kitchen later. "We might need more room by the end of the summer." She thought about the painting supplies, table linens, and several items she would like to have on hand to do more floral arrangements.

"There's a small storage room in Jack's office. We can ask him about it next week."

She'd noticed the door. "I thought that was a closet."

"It could be converted to a walk-in, but right now there are shelves lining two of the walls."

Perfect for storing everything. "Thanks for helping, Jules." She scrunched her nose. "Guess it's time for the big date."

Julie chuckled. "It's not the end of the world. Enjoy yourself. I expect a glowing report tomorrow."

The closer they got to one of her favorite restaurants, the tighter the knot in Libby's stomach grew. Emily chattered. It didn't happen often, but Libby's appetite disappeared.

Emily, who hadn't stopped talking since they left the office, whipped her car into the first empty spot she saw. After turning off the ignition and dropping her keys in her purse, she twisted in her seat. "I know you're scared, but—"

"I'm not scared."

"Okay, nervous then, but thank you. It means the world you agreed to do this as a favor to me. If you want, we'll leave right after dinner." A small smile lifted her lips. "Unless, of course, you decide to order dessert."

Libby's eyes narrowed as Emily's cunning registered. "You suggested The Cheesecake Factory." She never turned down dessert here, a fact her best friend knew without a doubt.

"Maybe." Her gaze shifted over Libby's shoulder and out the window. "Promise you'll keep an open mind and give this a chance."

"I promise." Hadn't she given Julie the same assurance?

"Good." Emily's smile was brilliant. "The guys are waiting."

Jerking her head around, Libby scanned the front of the restaurant. Sure enough, Adam stood to the side of the front doors with another guy. Truth be told, she barely remembered Brandon. Their introduction was brief, and her mind had been on so many other things that day—the flowers, Randi's visit, her family, her new job. Jack.

She took a deep breath and yanked the door handle. As she exited the car, she chastised herself for thinking about Jack. Again. She refused to spend the evening comparing him and Brandon. It wasn't fair to her date, or to herself.

Appreciation lit Adam's eyes when Emily approached him. They dimmed a little when they shifted to Libby, but it didn't bother her. Much.

"You're right on time." He held up the pager. "They just buzzed us."

Libby peeked at Brandon. He smiled and waved his hand in front of him to indicate the girls should go first. "Shall we?"

He held the door as they entered, as much a gentleman as Jack. *Stop it! You're not on a date with Jack.*

The waitress led them to a booth, and Libby hesitated. Why hadn't she considered this? She assumed they'd sit at a table, each in their own chair. On their own side. Instead, they had a booth. A cramped and cozy booth.

"Why don't you and Emily sit together?" Brandon solved her dilemma. "You'll have more room."

It was sweet of him. Sacrificial, even, since neither guy was scrawny. Adam had more going for him in the muscle department thanks to his career in construction.

After scooting onto the bench, Libby snuck another peek at Brandon as he settled across from her. Dirty blond hair, blue eyes, toned but not overly muscular. She'd noted he was several inches taller than her—right around the six-foot mark she guessed. And then he smiled at her. His eyes lightened a shade, and a dimple appeared on his right cheek, and Libby relaxed. The friendly expression put her at ease, assured her everything would be all right. It held the comfort of a friend. Odd how one gesture calmed her nerves. She smiled back and picked up her menu. Now she could eat.

"Let's start with a couple of appetizers." Adam's suggestion touched her. Libby's appetite was a running joke in her family, and he was well aware of the volume of food she could consume. "Any requests?"

111

"Avocado egg rolls." Emily tucked her hair behind her ear and stared at her menu. Libby noted the small concession for her sake. Em preferred the spinach dip.

"Great." Adam's gaze remained on Emily. "Anyone object to the spinach and cheese dip?"

They all shook their heads. Libby wondered if he and Emily had that in common or if he'd done some research. She kind of hoped he'd asked around. Several people back home knew about Em's weakness for cheesy appetizers—Callie and Chris included.

"How's the new job, Lib?" Adam's question pulled her back to the present.

"It's good so far, but this is only my first week."

"Jack asked her to redecorate some of the office," Emily said. "The plan is to get it done before she leaves for Hawaii."

The foursome spent the next couple hours talking about vacations, jobs, families, and mutual friends punctuated with periodic interruptions from the waitress. When their dinner plates had been removed, Libby thought about the evening. It had been pleasant, and she enjoyed talking to Brandon. He was sweet.

He caught her staring at him. "Dessert?"

She bit the inside of her cheek. Yes, she wanted dessert, but he didn't know her as well as Emily or Adam. Would he think she was a pig? And why did it matter?

Brandon nodded at the waitress. "Go ahead and bring us some menus, and we'll make a decision. I, for one, want something."

Libby stole a peek at Emily to find her eyebrows furrowed. Her expression indicated she wasn't ready to call it a night, and Libby couldn't deny her a little more time with Adam. There were sparks between those two she couldn't deny.

"We could split something," Adam suggested.

"Or each order a slice and share them," Brandon said, causing Libby to consider the possibility he'd done his own research.

Emily shook her head. "I can't eat that much. You three order, and I'll try a bite of each of yours."

"You can have more than one bite of mine." Adam's eyes found hers, something that had happened often tonight. It was as if Adam and Emily were unable to resist some magnetic pull between them. Sweet in a sappy, sickening kind of way.

Brandon cleared this throat. "Libby, your sister mentioned she'll be at your open house tomorrow."

It was more Callie's open house—or Jack's—but she didn't correct him. "She will. Dad too. I saw them last week, but it's a relief to have their support during my first official event."

"They're proud of you," he said. "I've heard so much about you over the past three years, I feel like we're already friends."

While she didn't have the same knowledge of him, she felt the same way. *Friends* being the key word in the sentiment. "Me too."

"Maybe we could get together again." The request took her by surprise. He didn't live here. "I mean, if you're not busy," he quickly amended.

She sensed Emily's glee and pretended not to notice. "I can't make any promises. This new job will take up a lot of my time."

"Why don't you give me your number, and we'll see if something works out."

There was no way to bow out of the request gracefully. She recited her number, and he punched it into his phone. The fact he'd asked her for the information rather than get it from her family or friends should have been a relief. Instead an air of expectation she wasn't prepared for almost suffocated her.

EIGHTEEN

After work, Jack ran home to change. Kevin and Amber lived closer to the office than he did. His place was out of his way, but the extra time to collect himself was necessary. Amber could be tenacious, and Jack wanted to be certain his interest in Libby was buried deep enough she wouldn't dig it out. Besides, he was still half-convinced a fourth person would be at the dinner table tonight.

Despite all the conversations they'd had over the years—him expressing disdain and unbelief in marriage and Amber supporting it—she hadn't given up hope someone out there would change his mind. Until two weeks ago, he'd been positive no such woman existed. No, he would not go down this road. No matter how often a pair of bright hazel eyes haunted him.

Jack drove back across town, promising himself he would not think of Libby tonight. She was out with another man. Perhaps a fourth at dinner wasn't such a bad idea. He snorted at his twisted thoughts. Amber's choice of women was questionable—sometimes embarrassing, sometimes humorous. Those dinners always ended up awkward and stilted. Why would he wish that on himself?

He groaned at the back of his throat as he pulled into the driveway and saw Kevin in the garage. His friend was watching for him, waiting to warn him about something. A quick survey of the cars in the driveway and on the street confirmed there was not another guest. Unless they hadn't driven here.

As Kevin approached the SUV, he fought the urge to put it in reverse and peel out of the driveway. Before he'd made up his mind, his friend leaned down to peer in Jack's open window. "Hey, Jack."

"What's wrong? Did Amber set me up after all?"

Kevin's laughter held relief. "No blind date tonight. She had someone in mind, but I talked her out of it."

A small miracle. Jack would take it. He got out of the car. "So why are you out here?"

"Well, I…" Kevin took a step back, squared his shoulders, and blurted, "Amber knows about your dad's phone calls."

Something he'd assumed since they were supposed to discuss it tonight. He narrowed his eyes at Kevin. "And?"

"She's convinced you need to talk to him."

It wasn't her decision. He thought Amber would take his dad's side. Wait a minute. He looked up and down the street again as heaviness settled in his stomach. "Please tell me she didn't do something stupid." Like find his dad and invite him to dinner.

With his palms up, Kevin shook his head. "No, nothing to do with your dad. He's not inside or anything. I wanted to warn you because she's got her teeth in this one."

Jack released a breath. *This* he could handle, or avoid, or distract her from. "Duly noted. Let's go eat. I'm starving."

"Me too." His friend chuckled. "Libby's appetite must be contagious."

His step faltered, but he caught himself and kept moving. So much for not thinking about *her* tonight. He should have realized Amber would want details about his newest employee. At least he had his distraction if she tried to engage in a long, drawn out discussion about his dad.

Upon entering the kitchen, Jack snuck behind the cute redhead and covered her eyes with his hands. Her ponytail slapped his cheek when she twisted her head around, but her smile made up for it.

"Hi, Jack. Dinner's almost ready."

He released her and inhaled. "It smells delicious. Lasagna?" Her specialty.

"Flattery will get you everywhere." She rolled her eyes. "It's nothing special, but I know you like it."

Yes, he did, and he anticipated her next request. "What can I do?"

"Will you make your cheesy bread?" Her blue eyes grew wide. "Mine never turns out as tasty as yours."

Probably because she was too impatient to mix the ingredients for the full three minutes. Jack wisely held his tongue and washed his hands. After finding a bowl in the cupboard, he set to work. Spending time in Amber's kitchen was therapeutic, and he began to relax.

"Talked to your dad yet?"

His spine stiffened at the question. "No, Amber."

She stood next to him, her hip resting against the counter. "Why not?"

"I'm not ready." He didn't think he'd ever be.

"You have to do it sometime. Why not get it over with? You've held onto this hurt long enough."

Jack concentrated on the cheese, butter, and garlic mixture and inhaled the aromas in the kitchen—tomato, onion, cheese, garlic. "I can't."

"Jack…" Amber leaned closer.

"Let's not do this right now." He dipped his finger in the mixture and put a dollop on the tip of her nose. "I came over to enjoy dinner with friends and don't want to insult you by leaving before we sit down at the table."

He watched her internal debate. Her expression changed from one of stubbornness to defeat in a matter of seconds before she nodded.

"Thank you."

Her whispered response sounded suspiciously like "This isn't over."

They finished preparing dinner in relative silence. Once the food was on the table, they gathered around, and Kevin said grace. After the murmurs of appreciation for the food had subsided, Kevin broke the silence. "Amber's coming to paint with us on Monday."

There was no question in the statement, no doubt of whether Jack would allow it. The decision was made. Jack lifted a brow at Amber.

"I want to meet Libby." She studied her plate and added, "And get some decorating tips."

Their home was almost as sparse as Jack's. At least they had several framed photographs around the house, a couple colorful pillows on the couch, and matching kitchen towels and potholders. Jack had none of those things. Well, maybe the kitchen towels.

"I told Amber how much Libby ate Tuesday." Kevin said it like it explained everything.

Jack smirked at the impression Libby made on him. Amber ate like a bird.

"It's all he's talked about," she said. "All I know about this woman is she eats a lot, is an interior designer, and is working at An Affair to Remember for the summer." She tipped her head toward her husband. "He won't even tell me what she looks like."

"Not making that mistake again," Kevin muttered.

Ah, the joys of marriage. Jack choked back a laugh with a large bite of his lasagna.

"What do you think of her?" Amber's blue eyes met his.

Slowly chewing his food, Jack formulated an acceptable answer. One that would satisfy Amber's curiosity without revealing the depth of his own internal struggle. "She's...different."

Amber's forehead creased. "Different good or different bad?"

"Good. She's friendly and open. Easy to talk to. Talented." He stopped himself, fearing he'd said too much.

Setting her fork on her plate, Amber leaned forward and glanced between Jack and Kevin. "I want a yes or no answer. Is she pretty?"

"Yes," Kevin said.

"No," Jack answered at the same time.

Kevin stilled and gaped at Jack. He guessed Kevin only said yes because he was sure Jack would as well. At Amber's laugh, the two men broke eye contact.

"Good grief, Kevin. Don't act like I'm going to make you sleep on the couch because you finally admitted you have another pretty coworker. I suspected as much when you refused to answer my questions. Don't forget I've met Emily and Julie."

"Julie's married."

Jack chuckled. "And Emily's way out of his league."

"Okay, describe Libby to me." Her gaze landed on him.

"Uh…" How would he get himself out of this? Stick with the facts, show no emotion. "She has short, light brown hair and hazel eyes." Beautiful eyes. "And despite how much she eats, she's trim." Small enough, he felt protective of her. "What makes Libby beautiful is her character." He snapped his mouth shut. Large foot officially inserted.

Amber grinned. "Is she single?"

"She's on a date tonight," Kevin said.

"Doesn't mean anything." She waggled her eyebrows at her husband. "You have no idea how many dates I went on before I found you."

He winked at her. "Saved the best for last, did you?"

She stood and gathered the plates. "No, just gave up on the search." Her laughter floated behind her as she walked into the kitchen.

"See what I have to put up with?" Kevin's grin indicated there was no hardship. "I'll assist with the dishes."

Jack stayed in his seat and gave his friends some privacy, certain dishes and kisses were somewhat synonymous in this household. They had been married three years. It was astounding how each of their strengths complemented the other's weaknesses. He'd seen it a few times and prayed their marriage would last. Of course, it had taken fifteen years before his mom and dad grew to despise each other.

NINETEEN

Libby sang along with the song playing on the radio as she parked her blue Altima in front of the Millers' home early Saturday morning. When it ended, she turned off the ignition, got out of the car, and circled around to the trunk. She'd park elsewhere before the open house. Arms full, she hurried to the front door.

Mrs. Miller answered when Libby knocked, took a couple of the bags from her, and led the way to the sitting room.

"I picked up more than you'll actually need, so you have plenty of options." Libby pulled items out of the bags. "You have several options, and I'll return whatever you don't want to use." She unwrapped two vases, a lamp, a couple of picture frames, and three throw pillows. The green Pothos plant she'd transplanted into a ceramic planter was the final item.

Mrs. Miller eyed the plant with appreciation, causing Libby to smile. "I noticed you had several in your home and hoped you wouldn't mind one more."

"This is wonderful. I can't wait to see how it comes together."

Libby visited with Mrs. Miller as she placed her finds on shelves, tables, and chairs. "I found a green wingback chair that would go well in here. It's on hold under your name if you're interested."

"Where would I put it?" Mrs. Miller scanned the room.

Tilting her head toward the far wall, Libby said, "Shift the table in the corner to the left and you have plenty of room."

Mrs. Miller studied the area for several seconds. "Okay, give me the information, and I'll send Ralph to pick it up. Thank you, Libby. You were right; this room needed color."

"It was an easy adjustment. You did a beautiful job in here."

"Do you have a card? My friends will ask who did this."

She dug in her bag and pulled out one of the cards Jack had given her. She wrote her cell number on the back and handed it to Mrs. Miller. "This is where you can reach me until September. After that, you can call my cell. I'm committed through the summer and can't take on any jobs until this fall."

When Mrs. Miller gave her stamp of approval on the room, Libby packed up the unused décor, loaded it in her car, and parked two blocks away. No sense in taking up a prime parking spot during the open house.

The rest of the crew showed up when Libby returned to the house. Until the caterers arrived in an hour, she couldn't set up the centerpieces, so she pitched in wherever she could.

The men moved furniture, and Libby walked through the house, making sure nothing breakable remained in the path of the guests. Everything came together smoothly, but this party was simpler than most of the upcoming events. She'd get a better feel how things ran at the wedding next weekend. She wasn't in charge of any specific area but had agreed to work all of the events until she left for vacation. Jack wouldn't turn down an extra set of hands, especially at a wedding.

She returned to the kitchen to find Julie and Emily deep in conversation. From the dreamy expression on Emily's face, Libby guessed they were talking about last night. Julie's eyes locked on Libby when she entered the room. "Emily told me how much fun she had at dinner. What did you think?"

After their date, the two of them had talked late into the night, and Libby agreed to give Brandon a fair chance. If he called and invited her out, she'd accept.

"It was better than I imagined it would be." She smiled. "Brandon's sweet. And funny. He asked for my number, and if he calls and asks me out, I'll go."

Julie's own smile widened. "I'm glad you had a good time."

Someone cleared his throat, and they all turned to find Jack. Libby's stomach dropped like she was coming down from the top of a rollercoaster. The man made a habit of walking in on conversations she'd prefer he didn't hear. Embarrassed about the girl talk, she asked, "Can I help with anything?"

"The caterers are here. Let's finish setting up."

Was that disappointment in his eyes or did she imagine it?

They finished fifteen minutes later as the first guests arrived. The open house was a drop-in event, but Libby knew Callie and her business partner, Jon Spencer, planned to stay two hours each. They wanted a representative from New Life Restorations available all afternoon to answer questions or set up interviews and appointments. Callie's company had made quite a name for itself over the past few years.

When Jon Spencer and his wife arrived, Jen gave Libby a hug. "I didn't realize you'd be here today. Did Callie invite you?"

"I'm actually working." She introduced her co-workers and explained her plans for the summer.

Libby received another hug when Jon joined them. "Callie said you'd be here today. I'm glad we get to see you."

"Thank you. It's been a while." Libby didn't like to interrupt Jon and Callie when they came to Raleigh for work, even though her sister insisted it wasn't a bother. The Spencers visited with her until Mrs. Miller pulled Jon away to introduce him to her other visitors.

Libby tried to remain in the background and anticipate any needs, but Mrs. Miller had taken a liking to her and kept dragging her away. Jon and Jen were leaving when she found Jack in the kitchen. She stood in the doorway. "I'm sorry, Jack. Please find me if you need anything."

He peered at her. "It's fine, Libby. You're meeting people— potential clients—and they like you. I've heard several of them comment on the sitting room."

She stared at him in disbelief. "Really?"

"Yes. In fact—"

"Libby!"

She turned around as Callie crossed the living room and squeezed her in a warm embrace. The show of affection might embarrass some people, but not her. She loved her sister. "Where's Dad?" Leaning around Callie, Libby scanned the room behind her.

"He got sidetracked talking to Jon. Give him a few minutes."

As Jack shuffled past them, Libby grabbed his arm. "Cal, this is my new boss, Jack Price." She released him and waved her hand between the two of them. "Jack, this is my sister, Callie Graham."

"We've met a couple of times." Callie shook his hand. "Thank you for giving our Libby a job."

His gaze connected with Libby's, and he winked at her. "I'd

say I'm the one getting the most out of the arrangement."

Her face heated at the compliment. Too bad he was only speaking about work. Callie eyed her closely as Libby brushed the errant thoughts from her mind.

"Excuse me, ladies. I need to check on the others." Jack left them alone.

Callie tilted her head a smidge. "How was the big date last night?"

Libby sighed. Of course Callie knew. Adam had probably told them all about it. "Fine."

"Just fine?"

"Callie, you're here." Mrs. Miller saved her. "Come see what your sister did. She's got a gift."

Resisting the urge to hug the woman for her impeccable timing, Libby watched her drag Callie across the room.

"I agree." Callie grinned at Libby before Mrs. Miller swept her from the room.

TWENTY

"I'm sorry. Again." Libby caught up with him when Jack returned to the living room after checking on the guests out back. "What were you trying to say earlier?"

"If you want to—"

"Libby!" An older man entered the house.

Her face lit up, and she beamed at the man Jack assumed was her father. "Dad." She moved toward him, wrapped her arms around his torso and rested her cheek on his shoulder. "I'm glad you're here."

The man laughed. "You were home last week, Libby girl."

"I know. It's been a long week." She glanced over her shoulder. "Not in a bad way."

"David James." Libby's dad held out his hand behind Libby while simultaneously keeping her nestled against him.

He shook it. "Jack Price."

"Oh, I'm sorry. How rude of me." She stepped out of her dad's embrace. "Dad, Jack's my new boss. Jack, this is my dad."

"It's great to meet you," David said. "Emily speaks highly of you. Thank you for helping out our girl."

Libby rolled her eyes. "I'm not a girl."

"You'll always be my girl, Lib." He pinched her cheek, and she blushed scarlet.

Jack watched the exchange between Libby and her father with a twinge of envy. It was apparent they were close, something he'd never experience with his own dad. Two more calls this week, but Jack still hadn't spoken to him—wouldn't speak to him.

"I'm definitely getting the better end of the deal," he said.

Libby blushed again at his compliment. Did it embarrass her? Most of the time she shrugged them off.

"If you'll excuse me, I need to check on a couple of things." Jack pivoted away from them.

"I'll do it." Libby made a move toward the kitchen.

"Wait, Libby. Why don't you find Mrs. Miller and introduce your dad?" Jack smiled at David James. "She's been singing the praises of both your daughters all morning."

"Doesn't surprise me one bit," he said. "God gave me three talented and beautiful girls."

Before he could respond, Libby laid her hand on his arm, stealing the words from his mouth. "Are you sure?"

Jack nodded. "Go ahead." Her bright smile confirmed he'd made the right decision. They could handle everything with only two members of his staff. Before her family arrived, he was about to suggest she mingle. Mrs. Miller was enamored and shared how she'd helped with the flowers and her sitting room with anyone who would listen. No surprise since he was enamored with Libby James himself.

He'd never been drawn to a woman so quickly and thoroughly. The few girls he'd dated in college understood he wasn't serious, so the relationships ended after a handful of dates. He was always upfront with them, refusing to get attached or lead someone on knowing he wouldn't marry. But with Libby, he wanted to be near her, talk to her, and listen to her laugh. He almost wished for more. In a few short months, she'd be out of his life again. Maybe not completely considering they attended the same church and both had connections to Emily, but not immersed in it like she had been this week.

You're an idiot, Jack. She's not interested in you. She gave her number to that other guy. A youth pastor, no less. Someone who would marry her.

The thought left a hollow pit in his stomach. He reminded himself once again that Libby worked for him. Anything more than a professional relationship, and perhaps friendship, was out of the question. He needed to stop considering a future beyond September.

The kitchen was running smoothly. Julie and the caterers had the food handled, so Jack made another pass through the house, stopping to chat with a couple guests.

A while later, Bradford Jackson—the son of one of the wealthiest businessmen in the area—walked in with a tall brunette. Emily, Julie, and Jack were discussing the clean up when the big man entered. He filled the room, hard to miss.

Bradford laughed at Libby's surprise when he lifted her off the floor in a bear hug. "How are you doing, kid?"

What was up with everyone touching and hugging her? It made him envious of how comfortable these people were around her.

"What are you doing here?" Libby wiggled in his arms until he set her feet back on the floor.

"When Bec mentioned you'd be here today, I finagled Dad's invite. It's been a while."

Libby's neck had to hurt from looking up at the guy. "I live in town, you know. How's married life?"

"Better than I ever imagined." He let go of Libby and wrapped his arm around the brunette's shoulders.

Jack elbowed Emily. "Libby knows the Jacksons?"

"Callie's best friend is Becca Jackson. Lib's going on vacation with her."

"Seriously?" His mind worked on ways he might use the advantageous connection. Jackson Enterprises would be a huge account, one that would elevate his company in the business world.

Emily leaned close and hissed in his ear. "Don't even think about it. Libby thinks of Becca as another sister and wouldn't dream of exploiting their relationship."

Sunday after church and a quick lunch, Jack drove to the office with plans to catch up on some work. Since they were painting tomorrow, he needed to find a pocket of time for the accounts, already behind because he'd spent so much time with Libby the past week. Focusing on his own responsibilities for the next few weeks while she redecorated would tame his attraction. At least he hoped it would.

He pulled into the parking lot behind the office and parked beside Julie's car. After unlocking the back door, he entered the building. Laughter erupted in Julie's office. He debated whether to investigate and decided to make his presence known so he didn't scare her. "Hello?"

She stuck her head out of her door. "Hey, Jack. What are you doing here?"

"I was about to ask you the same thing. I wanted to work on the accounts this afternoon."

"We're painting," she said. "Come say hi to the girls. You remember Mandy and Amy?"

He moved to the doorway and smiled at Julie's daughters. "Sure do. How are you girls doing?"

"Awesome!" Julie's youngest had black paint all over her shirt. "Libby's helping us paint Mom's office."

He glanced around the room, but Libby wasn't there.

"She went to pick up someone." Julie must have seen his confusion. "We're making the polka dots permanent."

"Have fun. I'll be in my office."

"Thanks. Holler if we're disturbing you."

He waved his hand over his shoulder. "I'll shut my door. Knock if you need me."

Someone did knock twenty minutes later. "Come in, Julie."

The door opened to reveal Libby instead. "Hey, Jack. Julie said you were working today. How's it going?"

"I'm just getting started, but everything's fine so far. How's the painting?"

"Almost done. I'll get the high areas later. There are too many people in the room to bring in a ladder right now." She hesitated for a second, and her gaze collided with his. "Logan's here. I asked him to take some photos of Julie's girls."

"That's thoughtful. I'm sure she'll love that."

Libby smiled. "I hope so. I'd like a couple shots I can frame and hang in her office. Logan mentioned he has an interview on Wednesday, but would you like to meet him?"

His curiosity about what kind of guy Libby once dated overrode his good sense. "Sure. I'll be there in a minute." He took the time to prepare himself. He saw a tall, lanky guy talking with Julie's girls when he joined them.

"Logan?" Libby waited until the girls finished talking. "This is Jack Price. Jack, meet Logan Griffin."

The guy stretched his arm forward, and his blond bangs fell into his eyes. He looked young but had to be at least twenty-five. Jack didn't think Libby would date a younger man. It surprised him she had dated this laid back, nondescript guy. "It's good to meet you." Jack shook the proffered hand.

"You too. I'm excited for the opportunity to sit down with you on Wednesday."

"Thank you. I understand you're taking some pictures today. Maybe Libby can give me a preview of your work before the interview." Where had that come from? Hadn't he been telling himself he needed distance from her? He was like a dog marking his territory, waiting to observe the guy's reaction when he mentioned Libby.

Logan looked at her with an expression of pure adoration. "I hope she will. Libby's my biggest cheerleader."

"You have a gift." At her compliment, Logan's grin grew so large Jack wondered if his cheeks would cramp.

"We need to get out of here." Libby lifted her bag onto her shoulder. "Julie needs to be home by five, and I want photos from two different places."

"Let's get going, then." Julie pulled her purse out of her desk drawer. "Come on, girls. See you tomorrow, Jack."

Libby lowered her voice as she passed. "At least you'll get some peace and quiet."

"You weren't bothering me." He pulled his gaze from her and acknowledged Julie and Logan. "Have a good afternoon."

As the group walked toward the back door, he didn't miss the move Logan made to grasp Libby's hand. Or the way she tactfully took the option away by digging in her bag.

He'd never set any type of policy regarding employee relationships in the office, but if Logan came on board, it might be time. If nothing else, it would be a good reminder for himself.

TWENTY-ONE

When Libby drove into the empty parking lot, disappointment stabbed at her. She let out a short huff. After the long conversation with Logan, she felt like a hypocrite considering her huge crush on the boss.

Logan had tried to convince her to go to dinner and talk, but she turned him down flat. The entire time they were with Julie and the girls, he tried to put his arm around her shoulders or hold her hand. Exhausted from dodging his advances, she refused to encourage him further.

During the drive back to Logan's place, she mentally prepared to tell him everything. As they sat in her car in front of his house, she talked. If they were going to work together, he couldn't continue to flirt with her. He needed to remain professional and treat her like any other coworker. Then she told him about Brandon. His dejected expression pinched her conscience, but he needed to accept the truth. They were not getting back together.

Perhaps she should've ended the friendship when she broke up with him, but she hated hurting him more. When he asked if they could still be friends, she agreed. She wasn't as blind to his interest as Emily believed. Instead, she chose to ignore it. Now she realized her mistake.

After finishing up in Julie's office, she prepared the large conference and front rooms for painting. She piled the paint cans, rollers, brushes, and trays in the back corner of the kitchen and taped the walls. The entire evening her thoughts waffled from

Logan to Brandon to Jack. Hopefully, Brandon would call. Logan was her past, and it was pointless to dwell on Jack. Might Brandon be her future? There wasn't that spark of attraction she felt with Jack, but friendship was a good starting point.

The clock read a quarter to ten when she climbed back in her car to go home, both emotionally and physically spent. *Lord, give me guidance. I'm unsure where to go from here and don't want to pursue something that will hurt my heart. Please show me the man you've chosen for me. If it's Brandon, make it clear to me. If it's someone I've yet to meet, give me peace.*

Trust me, Jack. You'll change your mind when you see the entire room." The others had already left to get drinks and snacks from the kitchen. Libby had waited to paint the accent wall last. Jack had teased her from the moment she opened the first can of white paint now covering three of the four walls in the conference room. She *was* the one who said the room needed color.

And now it had color with the addition of the icy blue wall—the focal point of the room. She'd chosen photographs from some of the more elegant parties and designed the room around them. It had taken several hours to narrow them down to only four. The colors in the pictures made her think of ice and frost. The reason she chose this particular color for the wall. The arctic blue would complement the photos and tie them together.

"I trust you," Jack said, "but will you paint over it if I hate it?"

Libby laughed. Emily was right. Pessimistic described him well. "I'll agree if you promise to keep an open mind. Don't form an opinion until you see the finished product."

"You've got a deal, Libby James."

Everyone else shortened her name, but Jack drew it out like a line from a favorite song. "Thank you. If you and Kevin will finish in here, the rest of us can get started in the lobby. At this rate, we'll get done before Julie has to pick up her girls."

They'd made quick progress in the conference room. The common area had more trim and angles so it would take longer. With her, Emily, Julie, and Kevin's wife, Amber—who came to help—working on the space, they should finish by mid-afternoon.

"If that's the case, we should go ahead and paint the small conference room too." Jack leaned against the table now covered with a drop cloth. "Everyone would probably prefer to spend the time today instead of giving up another Monday."

"I don't want anyone to feel like they have to stay."

Jack crossed his arms in front of his broad chest, drawing her attention down. "How about we present the options and take a vote?"

"What if it's a tie?"

"I'm the boss; I get the tie breaker."

"Bet this isn't the first time you've used that." She glanced at the door. "I'm hungry. Let's go eat."

At Jack's grin, she rolled her eyes, a little annoyed her stupid stomach amused him.

When he took a vote a few minutes later, the decision was unanimous. Julie even offered to come back with her girls. After the group got some nourishment, the four ladies set up in the lobby. Libby assigned each of the other three women to a wall while she painted the trim. Amber seemed to fit naturally in the group. Emily and Julie had met her before but hadn't spent much time getting to know her.

"We should get together for a girls' lunch once a month."

Libby voiced the idea she'd been mulling over since meeting Amber that morning.

"Count me in," Julie said. "I miss meaningful conversations with grown women. It's nice having you and Emily here, but some things you can't talk about at work."

"Let's do it." Emily wiped the back of her hand across her forehead. "What day works best for everyone?"

They discussed their options with Mondays winning out. Two weeks from today, they'd meet for lunch.

When the guys finished in the large conference room, they left to pick up food.

"Would you like a sneak peek?" Libby couldn't contain her excitement. While she wanted them to wait to see the completed room, she was bursting to show someone the photos she'd found for the space.

"Yes!" Julie laid her paintbrush on the edge of her tray and spun around.

Libby asked them to wait in the large conference room and ran to get her computer from her office.

"I love this color." Amber pointed to the blue wall.

"Jack asked if I would agree to paint over it if he doesn't like it."

Emily shook her head. "He's a man, what does he know? Besides, it's Jack. He'll hate any color."

Libby set her computer on the table. "These are the photos I'm going to blow up and frame."

"They're perfect with the blue, Lib." Emily looked at the accent wall.

"Exactly why I chose that color."

"What about the other room?" Amber asked.

"The only hint I'll give for that one is that the photos are from weddings, baby showers, and birthday parties."

"What about the lobby?" Emily asked.

"The company name will go on the longest wall with a table centered under it. Everyone can leave their business cards out there, and I'm getting some brochures printed. The photos on the walls are smaller because of the way the space is set up. They're pictures of area landmarks—the skyline, Pullen Park, and Duke University."

"I can't wait to see everything completed." Amber clapped her hands together like an excited child at Christmas. "I'll have to make sure Kevin tells me when you're finished."

"What's your phone number?" Libby jotted it down. "I'll call and let you know when I'm done so you can come to the reveal. Since I can't keep the main room a secret, I'm going to finish it first."

The guys returned with lunch. Amber giggled when they reached the kitchen. All four women had returned to painting, leaving no hint of their short interlude. The aroma of Italian food wafted into the lobby.

"Man, it smells good." Libby's stomach growled loudly. Emily and Julie snickered, and she smiled sheepishly. "Okay, you don't have to make such a big deal about it."

Julie started to explain their sudden humor to Amber, but the woman held up her hand. "All Kevin's talked about for the past week is how much Libby ate at the staff meeting. I want to witness this for myself."

"Oh, you will." Emily set down her paintbrush and propped an arm on Libby's shoulder. "Prepare to be amazed."

Kevin stuck his head out of the kitchen. "Food's ready. Ladies first. I hope I don't regret that," he added under his breath as Libby passed by.

"I picked up extra," Jack said. "We'll leave any leftovers in the fridge."

After lunch, Libby moved Jack, Kevin, and Amber into the small conference room. She held her breath as she opened the first can of the cement gray paint she'd chosen for this space. It wasn't until Jack expressed his approval that she released it.

A short while after they'd returned to painting, someone knocked on the front door. Emily, Julie, and Libby stared at the man peering through the glass door.

Emily was the first to act. "Flowers! Do either of you have your keys?"

The office was older, so the front door could only be unlocked with a key. They left it locked when the office was closed. Julie and Libby both shook their heads.

"Is someone at the door?" Jack strode from the conference room.

"Yes." Emily's head pumped up and down. "Where are your keys?"

He dug them out of his pocket and opened the door.

"Is there a Libby James here?" the delivery guy asked.

She stepped beside Jack and forced her gaze to remain on the man in front of her instead of the one next to her. "I'm Libby James."

"These are for you." He handed her a vase filled with a dozen assorted roses. "Have a nice day."

"Thank you." Libby watched him walk to his van. She spun around and carried the flowers to her office, leaving Jack to shut and lock the door.

"Are they from Brandon?" Emily followed on her heels like a yapping puppy. "I bet they're from him."

She set the vase on the table and found the card.

In her excitement, Emily shifted from one foot to the other. "So?"

"They're from Brandon. He says he enjoyed Friday night and hopes we can do it again soon."

"How romantic." She sighed. "I hope Adam sends flowers."

Libby wished these were for her friend. It was thoughtful of Brandon, but as someone who worked with flowers, generic bouquets didn't impress her. If someone was going to send her flowers—which weren't her first choice—she wanted something unique, something that wasn't overpriced on a dozen internet websites. It would be rude not to thank him, but she hoped this wouldn't become a habit.

TWENTY-TWO

Jack's gaze followed Libby as she walked to her office with Emily trailing close behind her. "I wouldn't have bought her flowers." He grunted and returned to the conference room.

Kevin glanced up. "Who was it?"

"Delivery. Flowers for Libby. Emily thinks they're from the guy she went to dinner with on Friday."

Amber twisted around from where she painted. "Who would send flowers to a woman who arranges them?"

"She's not a florist." Kevin waved his hand around the room to emphasize his point.

"Still, she doesn't seem the type to get all mushy over a bouquet of flowers. Chocolate seems more fitting."

Kevin snorted. "She does not need more food. Did you see how much she put away at lunch?"

Ignoring her husband, Amber focused on Jack. "What do you think?" Her raised eyebrows punctuated the question.

He picked up his roller and resumed painting. "I think what she'd most appreciate is for us to finish painting." Amber had been watching him closely all day, and he refused to have this discussion with someone who could read him so well.

"Chicken." Her taunt was just loud enough for him to hear.

They spent the rest of the afternoon painting and wrapped up a little before five. Libby rinsed everything in the sink while the rest of the group sat around the table. They'd offered to help, but Libby declined, insisting she was particular about cleanup. Jack figured she'd reached her limit of accepting assistance when she said something about not expecting them to do any more of her work.

"Anyone interested in going to dinner?" Emily asked. "Lib and I are going to grab a quick bite at the deli a couple blocks over."

Jack watched Kevin and Amber silently communicate before Kevin agreed. This wasn't the first time he'd observed this kind of exchange between them.

"What about you, Jack?" Emily's attention shifted to him.

"Sorry, can't. I have some errands to run tonight." None of them was pressing, but once again he wanted some distance from Libby James. A long summer stretched in front of him.

"Is there someplace I can keep this stuff?" Libby twisted away from the sink, and her gaze collided with his. Was she disappointed he said no to dinner?

"You can use the storage room in my office."

"You're not using it for anything?"

"No. I think there may be a couple boxes in there. I've intended to sort through them for months."

"Oohh…can I?" Libby's eyes shone with more excitement than they had over the flowers.

Jack hid his grin, grateful he could give her something that made her happy. "Sure. It's mostly junk, things people didn't want to hold onto after their parties."

"You never know, Jack." Libby plopped onto the chair beside

him and lowered her voice. "Sometimes the junk one person leaves behind can turn into a treasure someone else will cherish."

He liked the sound of that. Despite the messiness of his past, he wanted Libby James to see him as someone to cherish.

On Tuesday morning, Jack carried breakfast into the office. When he'd left last night—after showing Libby the storage room and warning her to keep the door propped open—he decided to make breakfast for this week's staff meeting. Cooking relaxed him and allowed him to think clearly. He didn't do it often enough. Picking up the groceries and preparing the food had kept him occupied until late, but he spent the time talking to God about his growing attraction toward his newest employee.

He reminded himself she'd only be working for him through Labor Day. If she was still single at the end of the summer (a big if), and if he still felt the same way about her (no question), he would ask her on a date. Maybe by then he would be able figure out whether or not she was interested in him at all.

"Wow, something smells delicious." Libby entered the break room with an empty mug in her hand.

"Did you cook?" Emily eyed the food as she followed Libby. "It's been a while since you made something for us."

"I agree." Jack arranged the food on the counter. "A homemade breakfast sounded good after all the takeout we've been eating."

Spinach quiche, baked French toast, and a breakfast casserole loaded with potatoes, eggs, and cheese lined the counter. There was also a large bowl of fresh fruit. Amber's comment yesterday about giving Libby food instead of flowers had inspired him. He'd gone a little overboard. This would last them the entire week.

"You two can go ahead and eat while we wait for the others."

"I'm here." Julie rushed into the kitchen. "Kevin's right behind me."

Once everyone was seated with their food, Jack began the meeting. They went over the details for the Hanson wedding on Saturday. Libby said she was available every day but Thursday if anyone wanted her assistance. Jack announced he had lined up interviews with three potential staff photographers, which led to a discussion of where they could put another person.

"I can share my office," Kevin said. "It's bigger than Emily's, and she and Libby seem to be doing okay in there."

"Em and I are friends and live together. You and Lo—" Libby caught herself. "You and the photographer don't know anything about each other. We don't even know who it is yet."

"Do we have another option?" Kevin glanced at Jack.

"We don't." He shook his head. "I want to keep the conference rooms free for meetings."

Libby peered at him. "Can I draw up some ideas of how to make Kevin's office functional for two people?"

Jack's brows drew together. "You have enough to do."

"I'm waiting on several things before I can proceed with the conference rooms. Plus, my sister offered to help if I need her."

"I guess it wouldn't hurt." He didn't have the heart to squash her enthusiasm. "Go ahead and put your ideas on paper. If you can give me estimates, I'd appreciate it." If he thought she was taking on too much, he'd hire someone else to take care of Kevin's office.

Her smile was bright, and the golden flecks in her eyes became more pronounced. "I'll have them to you by Friday."

"No rush. The soonest we'll need the space is the end of May."

They finished the meeting by reviewing the calendar for the upcoming month, confirming a couple consultations, and discussing some concerns, all of them minor.

Logan Griffith, Jack's first interview for a photographer, arrived right on time. He'd browsed the work of the other two candidates online. Their work was mediocre. He wanted someone who would help his company stand out and give them an advantage over the competition. As he thumbed through Logan's portfolio, he confirmed what he'd seen in the pictures of Julie's girls, which Libby had shown him. The guy had an excellent eye for detail. His photos were crisp and vibrant, overall quite impressive.

They discussed his experience and career goals. Logan hoped to make a living with photography but waited tables to supplement his income. Studios didn't interest him because he preferred shooting on location to using static backgrounds. Jack explained he wouldn't have much for Logan to do for several months. They had already hired photographers for the summer weddings, but could use him at their less formal events.

Logan assured him the arrangement worked for him. He needed to give notice at the restaurant, which confirmed he was responsible. When he took the portfolio back from Jack, he hesitated a moment.

"Any questions?" Jack gave him an opening to say what was on his mind.

"Is it okay if I do some side work? Like what I did last weekend for Libby? I have a few regulars I'd like to keep."

"As long as you're available during events and for the Tuesday morning staff meetings, I don't foresee a problem," he said.

Logan moved to get up.

"Before you go, I'd like to discuss one more thing." Libby. "Is working with Libby going to be a problem? It's my understanding you two have a bit of history, and I don't want things to become awkward for either of you."

"No, it's not a problem." Logan deflated as he leaned back in his chair. "I hoped Libby would change her mind about me, but she told me she's dating someone else. We had a long talk about working together last Sunday. Well, she talked. I listened."

Jack resisted the urge to roll his eyes. Since when did dinner and flowers equal dating? He focused on Logan. "Good. I have a couple more interviews, but will make a decision in the next two weeks. I'll let you know either way."

"Thank you, Mr. Price." Logan stood and shook his hand.

"Call me Jack."

Logan nodded, picked up his portfolio, and exited the office. Jack eavesdropped as the guy begged Libby to go to dinner. Even though the guy claimed working with her wouldn't be an issue, Jack had his doubts. She was hard to resist.

TWENTY-THREE

On Thursday morning, Libby arrived at the office two hours early. She'd accomplished a lot thus far this week. The photographs were enlarged and in Ty's possession. She had gone through the boxes from Jack's office and found a few things she could use, drawn several sketches for Kevin's office, and emailed Jack the figures for purchasing their own table linens. She'd even included long-term projections for that last one.

Chris was coming by today with Callie's truck, so she could buy the crown molding for all the rooms. He'd even offered to install it when she explained why she wanted to borrow the truck. Yesterday, Libby had found a table on Craigslist she wanted to use in the front room. If she told her brother-in-law about it, he would insist on taking her.

She was using the time before everyone arrived to choose the pictures for the brochures and load them onto a thumb drive. Jack had given her the name and contact information of the friend who designed his business cards, and Libby set up a meeting with him tomorrow morning.

When Jack stopped by and asked if she had a minute to talk, she was finishing up. As she followed him to his office, she wondered what she'd done now. She slid into one of the chairs across from his desk, clasped her hands in her lap, and waited, squirming under his scrutiny.

He startled her when he finally spoke. "Will working with Logan be an issue?"

She released the breath trapped in her lungs. Okay, not something she'd done wrong. "Not at all. We talked last week about setting professional boundaries."

"Emily thinks he might have trouble with you dating someone."

Why did he care? Was this about Logan or her date last Friday? "He knows about Brandon if that's what you're hinting at."

"Good." His stare burned into her. "Will you tell me if things get uneasy between you two?"

"Are you going to give him the job?" She held his gaze, refusing to break eye contact first.

Jack's eyes shifted to the left. "I have two more interviews, but judging from my research, his photographs are better than those of the other candidates. He's also excited about the opportunity."

"He is talented; and yes, if things become weird or uncomfortable, I'll talk to him." She held up a palm when he opened his mouth. "If that doesn't solve the issue, I'll bring my concerns to you. Logan and I have worked together several times over the past five years, so I don't foresee any problems." At least not after last Sunday's conversation.

"Thank you." He folded his hands on his desk and leaned forward. "Now, let's talk table linens."

Her jaw slackened in surprise before she remembered the information she'd sent last night. "You read my email."

"I did. You're thorough. And you were correct. It makes more sense to purchase our own rather than continue to rent. Go ahead and order enough to cover twenty round and twenty rectangular tables. Both the black and the white."

Libby spent a few minutes updating him on the progress with the decorating. He told her where he thought she'd be the most help at Saturday's wedding. Someone rapped on the door, and Libby twisted in her seat to see Kevin.

"Sorry to interrupt, but some guy's out here asking for you, Libby." He smiled at her.

"Chris!" She jumped from her chair to go greet her brother-in-law. Before she rushed out of the room, she remembered she was meeting with her boss and sat back down. Heat filled her face. "Did you need anything else?"

Something flitted across his face. Anger? Annoyance? Was he upset she'd tried to rush out to see Chris before he dismissed her?

He opened his mouth then snapped it shut and shook his head. "That's all for now. Thanks for your time, Libby."

She hurried into the lobby and lunged into Chris's outstretched arms. "Thank you so much for coming today. I know you're busy."

"Anything for you, Lib." He chuckled and released her. "Spending the day with you is a treat. And I'm under strict orders to make sure you're happy."

"Whose orders?" She squinted up at him. "Never mind. It's either Callie or Dad."

"Both."

Figured. She batted her eyelashes playfully. "I'll be happier if we can pick up the table I found on Craigslist. I told the woman I'd stop by around ten."

He glanced at his watch. "We should get going."

"Let me grab my bag and the directions."

"Where's Em?" Chris asked when she returned.

"At a meeting. She'll be here this afternoon. I'll introduce you to everyone later."

"Okay. Let's get your errands out of the way, and I'll take you to lunch before you put me to work."

"I was going to buy lunch." Libby gave him a mock scowl that didn't stay through her laughter.

"Come on, you can argue with me about it in the truck." They walked out the front door. "What's the table for?"

"It's a console table for the lobby. It needs sanding and staining, but otherwise it's perfect. If Jack lets me redo Kevin's office, I'll have to find a desk. Maybe two desks. I might try to find one for myself. The table is okay, but a desk with drawers would be nice. Although, I don't expect Jack to pay for it." She was rambling, but her brother-in-law knew her well. He didn't mind when she got lost in the world of design, so she continued her monolog.

"It's cool of Jack to let you redecorate so much of the office," Chris said when Libby took a breath.

"Yes, it is. He wasn't thrilled with the idea at first. The rest of the group convinced him this would be good for business."

"Don't worry, Lib." He winked at her. "He'll agree when he sees how much better you've made the place."

"Aw. Thanks for the compliment."

"I've seen your work; it's well-deserved."

They arrived at the address on Libby's notes. An elderly woman answered the door and invited them inside. Since the table needed some TLC, she only wanted thirty dollars. This purchase almost bested her couch. When she factored in the sanding and staining, the couch won.

The next stop was The Home Depot. Libby pulled the measurements out of her bag and passed them to Chris.

He glanced at the paper. "This is a lot, Lib. Want me to pay for it?"

She thought this might come up today. Both Callie and her mom had offered her money again, but she refused to accept it. Her family's concern was sometimes smothering. She understood they only wanted to help, but she wasn't little Libby any longer. She was capable of doing this on her own.

Besides, this wasn't coming out of her pocket. "No, Jack gave me the company credit card. It's covered."

They separated. Chris went to get the wood cut while Libby shopped for stain, a shelving unit, and a few other items on her list. Once they'd checked out and loaded everything into the back of the truck, Chris drove to a restaurant.

After lunch, Libby grew nervous. The day was more than halfway over, and they hadn't gotten any work done at the office. "Do you think we can get everything done today?"

"If not, Callie and I will come back when she gets off and finish up."

"What about the girls?"

"They're spending the night with your parents. I'm sure Charity and Hope are enjoying themselves so much, they don't even miss us." She laughed at his phony sad face. "Cal and I are staying in town tonight."

"You're welcome to crash at our place."

"Thanks, but we hoped to spend some one-on-one time together."

Libby peeked over at him. "Then you shouldn't waste your

evening with me."

"Libby." He huffed out a breath. "We don't mind. Call your sister and discuss this with her, okay?"

"Fine." She directed him to the back of the office building. "Come inside. I'll introduce you to everyone and recruit them to unload the truck."

They stopped at her office so she could drop off her bag. Emily jumped up from behind the desk and rushed around to give Chris a hug. "I hoped to catch you before I left for my other meetings."

"How are you, Emily?" Chris grinned when he noticed the roses on the table. "Who gave you the flowers?"

She looked at Libby in confusion. He must think Adam sent them.

"Those are mine, Chris." She should have taken them home.

"Who's giving you flowers?" His expression shifted from amusement to disapproval.

Libby rolled her eyes. Sure, he was happy when he believed they belonged to Emily but overprotective when someone showed an interest in her. "Brandon."

"Brandon?" Recognition lit his face, and his smile returned. "The date went well?"

She tugged on his arm. "It's not a big deal. Come meet everyone else."

"Jack's not here." Emily's words caused Libby's step to falter. "I don't know where he went, but he was in a bad mood when he left."

"Cut him some slack, Em." Her defense of Jack was

automatic. "He's got a lot to do."

She detoured to Julie's office and tapped on the open door. The woman's head lifted, and Libby waved Chris into the room. "Julie, this is my brother-in-law, Chris Graham. He's here to work for me today."

"*With* you," he corrected. "I came to work *with* you today."

Julie laughed. "I met Callie last weekend. Her restoration work is impressive. She's so sweet and humble, you can't help but like her."

"One of the many reasons I asked her to marry me." Chris wrapped a muscled arm around Libby's shoulders. "I have a soft spot for the members of the James family right here." He tapped his chest over his heart.

Kevin came to investigate the commotion. Libby made the introductions and asked who had time to help unload the truck. Everyone made quick work of hauling the wood inside. When they unloaded her table, Chris asked, "Where should we put this, Lib?"

"Right there." She pointed to the back wall of the building. "I'll sand and stain out here."

Kevin nodded, and the two men carried the table to where she directed. Chris ran a hand over the tabletop. "My sander's in the truck if you want to use it. You can drop it off with Callie when you're done."

"Thanks. I'm sure yours is much better quality than mine." She circled her hands around his forearm and tugged. "Let's get to work. You need to get out of here at a decent time."

"Don't worry about me. Can I set up my saw before you start bossing me around?"

In addition to the crown molding, Libby wanted him to install the shelving on the blue accent wall. Time moved faster than she'd anticipated, and she was determined to give Chris and Callie some spare time tonight. They deserved it.

TWENTY-FOUR

The dark mood hovering over Jack hadn't dissipated. The way Libby talked to that guy this morning made it evident they knew each other well. Exactly how many men were willing to do Libby James a favor? He'd made an excuse and left before he said something he'd regret.

When he returned a little after two, Emily stopped him. "Jack, you're here. You have to meet Chris!"

He rubbed the back of his neck as Emily sauntered to the conference room. It seemed she approved of this guy.

Libby's laughter filled the air when the door opened but ended abruptly. "Emily, no peeking."

"Give me a break, Lib. We unloaded the truck, remember? I know what you're doing in here."

"Fine, but this is the last time."

Emily's back stiffened. "Fine." She mimicked Libby's tone. "I came to tell you Jack's back, but if you'd rather not—"

"Thanks, Em." Her voice lightened. "Chris, let's take a break and talk to Jack."

He closed his eyes and clenched and relaxed his fists. *Be civil.*

Libby and Emily dragged a tall blond guy out of the room. He laughed. This reaction from women must not be new for him.

When she saw Jack, Libby grinned. She was excited this guy was here. Someone should tell her he was too old.

"Jack, this is my brother-in-law, Chris Graham."

Upon hearing the guy's name, relief flooded him. "You're Callie's husband." He shook the man's hand.

"That's me. I rode up with her so I could spend the day with Lib." He rested an arm on her shoulders and tucked her against his side.

"We appreciate your time," Jack said.

Chris glanced at the top of Libby's head. A protective move she didn't see. "And we appreciate you giving Lib a job while she's in transition."

"It's my pleasure. She's proven herself invaluable. I'm already dreading losing her this fall." In more ways than one.

"Enough." Libby stepped between them. "I'm standing right here. Chris, if we don't get back to work, we won't finish before Callie calls."

His heavy sigh indicated this was not the first time they'd discussed it. "I told you we'll come back. We can pick up a pizza for dinner."

"Why don't I buy the pizza?" Jack ignored Libby's glare and spoke directly to Chris. "I'd like to do something to express my appreciation."

"I won't turn you down." He winked at his sister-in-law. "I fed her once today."

"Hey, I offered to buy." She punched him in the arm, much like she'd done with Jack last week. Then she hugged him. "Thank you for lunch."

Chris knuckled the top of her head. "You're welcome. Callie would have my hide if I didn't feed you." He laughed again when she stuck her tongue out at him.

Envious of their playful banter, Jack wondered if he'd ever become that comfortable or free with Libby. He wished he could tease her, hug her, or hold her like this.

"Get back to work." She pointed toward the conference room.

Chris turned when Emily coughed. "It was great to see you again, Em. Stop by the house next time you're in town."

"I will. It's getting late, and I need to get going." She gave him a hug. "Call if you're going to be later than ten, Lib."

"We'll be done by then, but I'll call before I leave."

Libby and Chris returned to the conference room, and Jack shut himself in his office. He planned to return some phone calls before another interview with a photographer at four. Three people from the open house had left messages this week. But before any of that, he had a confession to make.

Okay, God, I jumped to conclusions earlier and made myself miserable for no reason. Help me become more discerning and patient. Show me what to do about Libby. Keep my jealousy where she's concerned in check. Give me wisdom about the photographer position. Thank you for bringing in enough business that it's become necessary to enlarge my staff.

The interview with the second photographer was short. The woman's portfolio convinced Jack she was not an ideal candidate. Most of her photographs leaned toward the abstract, with random objects the focus instead of the people. Not how his customers would want to commemorate their special occasions. In addition, she was blunt to the point of rudeness. The image of her bringing a bride to tears on her wedding day made Jack cringe. Of the two, Logan won in regards to both talent and personality.

A light knock on the door pulled him from his thoughts.

"Hey, Jack. How'd the interview go?"

He answered with a grimace, and Libby laughed. "I won't ask. Chris and I are going to pick up Callie from work. We'll be back in about forty-five minutes. Oh, and here's the credit card and receipt from this morning."

"Thanks." He took the card and set it on the desk. "What kind of pizza should I order?"

"You don't have to buy dinner." She glanced over her shoulder. "I don't mind paying for it."

"Let me do this, Libby. Chris and Callie are volunteering their time to help me out."

"No, they're doing this for me."

"Yes, but I'm benefiting from it as well. Besides, I'd like to visit with your family."

She tilted her head and studied him for several seconds. "If you're sure."

"Positive. What does everyone like?"

"Chris and I will eat any type of meat lovers, and Callie likes veggies." She spun to leave but stopped herself and moved around his desk. "Is everything okay?"

"Yes. Why do you ask?"

She shrugged. "Emily said you were out of sorts earlier."

"Slight misunderstanding. It's been cleared up." No way would he elaborate on those vague statements.

"Good." Her smile stole his breath. "Thank you for getting

dinner. We'll be back shortly."

When she left, Jack went to find out whether anyone else planned to work late. Julie said she was on her way out, and he ended up in Kevin's office.

"Have a seat." He nodded toward an empty chair and scrutinized Jack as he sat. "What's up?"

"Are you sticking around tonight? Libby and Chris went to pick up her sister, and they're coming back to do some more work. I'm supplying the pizza."

"Are you sure that's a good idea?"

"Of course it's a good idea. They're giving us free labor. The least I can do is provide dinner."

"Let me rephrase the question." Kevin leaned his elbows on the desk and lowered his voice. "Are you sure it's a good idea for *you* to hang around and eat dinner with them?"

"What do you mean?"

"You're either rearranging your schedule to run errands with Libby or avoiding her. You get upset with her when she presents valid suggestions, then offer to buy dinner for her and her family. Be careful, Jack. I would hate for you to run her off before the summer even begins."

"I'm not trying to run her off."

"No, you're not, but if you keep heading down this road, you will."

"And what road is that exactly?" He wasn't sure whether he wanted to hear the answer. On the one hand, he would like someone to talk to, someone who'd keep him accountable. On the other, he didn't need Kevin—or anyone—reminding him of his opinion about marriage.

"You like her. As more than a competent employee. But she *is* an employee, and you need to remember that. Relationships among co-workers complicate matters for everyone, even more-so when a superior's involved."

Jack sucked in a breath and let it out slowly. "You're right. I was just telling myself the same thing Monday night. Look, I'm not going to do anything to jeopardize the business. She's only with us until September. I can wait until then to pursue something if I'm still interested."

Kevin raised an eyebrow. "You shouldn't spend time alone with her. I've never seen you this taken with a woman."

"I don't know what it is about her." He raked a hand through his hair. "I'll admit I *am* attracted. She's easy to talk to and makes fast friends with everyone she meets." He dropped his forehead into his palm. "This consuming attraction scares me, Kev."

"I'm sure it does. Amber said you'd fight it."

"Amber knows?" Jack's head jerked up.

Kevin chuckled. "She figured it out first. When you came to dinner last Friday, she suspected something. After we painted, she insisted I keep an eye on you. And when I told her you made breakfast on Tuesday morning, she said you're in love."

"Wh-what? I'm n-not in l-love with Libby. I only met the girl three weeks ago."

"Yeah, that was convincing. Deny it all you want, Jack. You can't help who you fall in love with. You don't want to admit your feelings to yourself because you can't figure out where she stands in regards to you."

"This conversation is over." He hoped.

"One more thing." His index finger lifted in the air. "If you cross a line with her, I won't hesitate to call you on the carpet. I like Libby and won't let you hurt her."

"I wouldn't ever hurt her."

"Not intentionally, but let's not forget your solemn oath never to marry. How long will a relationship last with that hanging over it?"

His words came back to haunt him. "Okay, I get it." He stood. "I'm not good enough for her."

"I didn't say that."

"You implied plenty. Nothing will happen between Libby and me, but if you think I'm out of line, feel free to talk to me."

"I will. And Jack?"

"Yeah?"

"Amber and I are praying for you. I'm right here if you want to talk."

TWENTY-FIVE

We only have the lobby left, Cal." Libby sat in the back of the extended cab as Chris drove back to the office. "Two hours max."

Callie reached back and laid her hand on Libby's bouncing knee. "Stop. The girls are thrilled they get to sleep at Mom and Dad's tonight, and we have no plans. Maybe we can do something else while we're here."

"At least we're getting dinner out of the deal." Chris stretched his arm across the back of the seat and squeezed Callie's shoulder.

"It was thoughtful of Jack to buy dinner," she said. "The man has already figured out the way to Libby's heart."

Libby bit her tongue. No way would she respond to that comment. She appreciated Jack's willingness to buy her food but wished it wasn't out of a sense of obligation. Every time she was around him, she fought the urge to stare at him like a schoolgirl with a crush on her teacher. Why were her emotions so unsettled around him?

Ugh, Callie will suspect something if I'm not careful. I need to watch how I act around Jack tonight.

"Speaking of making Libby happy," Chris paused for effect, "Brandon sent her flowers."

Callie's eyebrows pinched together when she looked at her. "Did you tell him you work with flowers?"

"I did."

"That's lame, Lib."

"Thank you!" She threw her hands in the air like she'd scored a goal in a game. "No one else gets it."

"What's wrong with flowers?"

Callie patted her husband's hand. "It's cute how clueless you are sometimes."

"I thought girls liked flowers." He flipped his hand over, grasped Callie's hand, and pulled it down on the seat between them.

"Girls who don't work with flowers for a living do," Callie explained. "If you're going to send flowers to someone who handles them often, they'd better be spectacular." She twisted around again. "Were they spectacular?"

She bit her lip. Her mom's voice rang through her mind with that *if you can't say anything nice* mantra.

"Well, that answers my question," Callie said. They did have the same mother, after all.

"What do you want instead of flowers?" Chris looked at Libby in the rearview mirror.

"Oh no, I'm not giving you any ideas to pass on to Brandon. He'll have to figure out how to impress me all by himself."

"Did he call?" Callie must have decided to take the heat off him.

Libby nodded before realizing her sister couldn't see her. "Yeah. We talked for an hour Tuesday evening. He's coming to Raleigh next Monday and asked if I can meet him for lunch."

"I'm glad someone's finally taken notice what an incredible woman you are."

They returned to the office as Jack paid the delivery man for the pizza. He wrestled with the boxes in one hand while struggling to find the right key for the front door lock with his other.

Libby took pity on him. "I'll get it, Jack." She took the keys from him.

"Thanks." He moved out of her way. "Your timing is impeccable."

Chris approached and took the boxes from him. "Why don't we get dinner set out and let Libby give Cal the grand tour."

Callie lowered her voice so the men couldn't hear her. "If you ever tell Chris this, I'll deny I said it. Your boss is handsome."

She ducked her head so Callie couldn't see the blush on her face. "Yeah, he is." She hurried into her office. When Callie followed, she waved her hand at the desk and table. "This is where Emily and I work."

"You're not going to distract me that easily." Callie closed the door and pivoted to face her. "You like Jack? You're attracted to him?"

She wouldn't lie to her sister. "I am, Cal. He's not only handsome, but kind, hardworking, and smart. Oh, and he cooks. I almost melted into a puddle when he made breakfast last week. But he's my boss, so nothing can come of it."

"He's only your boss for a few months."

"He doesn't want to get married." She covered her mouth with her hand. Why had she let that tidbit slip?

"Callie's green eyes widened. "I'm not sure whether to ask how you know that or why."

"Em mentioned he hated weddings, so I asked him about it. He told me about his parents' nasty divorce, then said he'd never get married and put someone through that."

"The right girl could change his mind."

She'd considered it but… "I don't want to put my heart out there only to find I'm not the right girl, Cal." She sighed. "I want to get married someday—to have what you do with Chris."

"You will, Libby. I've prayed for your future husband for years." Callie pulled her into a crushing hug.

"Thank you." She slipped out of the embrace. "Let's finish the tour and eat. I'm starving."

Callie's hands found her hips in what Libby called her mom stance. "I thought Chris took you to lunch."

"That was hours ago, and he bossed me around all afternoon."

"I'm certain it was the other way around." Callie snickered.

Jack had ordered three pizzas and a deep dish chocolate chip cookie. Chris and Callie answered his questions about their jobs and the kids while they ate. When Chris mentioned he sometimes worked with Callie and her crew, Jack's line of questioning grew more specific.

Guess he meant it when he said he wanted to talk to my family. His interest seems genuine.

Chris was telling Jack about his current building project, so Libby turned to Callie. "How's Becca?" She glanced over at the sudden silence.

"Are you talking about Becca Jackson?" Jack looked directly at her.

Libby's spine stiffened, and she glared at him. She'd

specifically avoided mentioning Becca's name around him. "I never told you her name, which is Newsome, by the way."

"Emily said you knew her."

I'm going to kill Emily.

Callie laid a hand on her arm. "Hold on. Before you get upset with Em, you'd better listen to the whole story. We both talked to Brad at the open house, and his face is well-known."

Libby stared at Jack, waiting for an explanation.

"I saw you talking to him on Saturday," he confirmed. "He gave you a huge hug, so I assumed he knew you well. Emily said Becca and Callie are friends."

Best friends, but no point in correcting him. "Is that all she said?"

"No." He rolled his lips inward as if he was trying to remember her exact words. "She also told me not to bother asking you about her because she's like another sister."

"I don't think Bec will care," Callie said. "She's more relaxed about people knowing since she married Alex. I'll talk to her."

"No need, Cal." Libby held Jack's gaze. "We can trust Jack."

"You can." His earnest brown eyes didn't waver.

"We should get back to work." Chris stood, breaking the tension in the room.

"Need any help?" Jack followed his lead.

Chris shook his head. "I was about to suggest Libby sand the table while Callie and I finish the crown molding. Three people and a ladder in that space is too much."

Jack turned to her. "Are you going to sand outside?"

"Yeah," she said. "There's enough light out there to get it done."

"Want some company?"

"That's okay." She wanted some time alone. "I'll leave the back door open so Chris and Callie can hear me. Go home, Jack. I'll put the leftovers away." Perhaps sanding the table would keep her hands occupied while she processed her thoughts.

"I enjoyed visiting with you," he said to Chris and Callie.

"Us too." Callie gathered the paper plates and threw them away. "I'm sure we'll run into you again. Thanks for dinner."

"You're welcome. Good night." Jack hesitated when he glanced at Libby again. "Call if you need anything. I'll see you tomorrow."

"I'm meeting your graphic designer in the morning, so I'll be late."

Callie and Chris finished the crown molding within the hour, and Libby prepared the table for staining. She'd do that Friday evening and let it dry over the weekend.

"Looking good, Lib." Callie stood next to Chris as Libby locked the back door. "I'll have to come back when you're done."

"Anytime, Cal."

"Call us if you need anything else or want to borrow the truck." Chris slid his arm around Callie's shoulders. "Your sister's gotten soft since she became a mom."

Libby laughed. Callie used to hate loaning her truck to anyone. Now she offered before you asked.

"I wouldn't want it any other way." Callie smiled at him.

He dropped a tender kiss on her forehead. "Me either, honey."

Libby watched them with longing. They'd been married almost eight years, and Chris showed Callie he loved her in small ways like this. She shook off the melancholy. "Love you guys. Thanks again for helping today."

"You're welcome. Dad said to tell you he's available too."

"I'll give him a call this week."

They got into their cars, and Chris waved for her to leave ahead of them.

I want a man like Chris, Lord. Someone who's my partner and protector. A man who shows me how much he loves me every day. Give me the patience to wait for him.

TWENTY-SIX

"Good morning, Jack." Libby stood beside her table outside the building.

He shook his head. How did she manage to beat him here every day? "Good morning."

"You're right on time." She swiped at her forehead with the back of her hand. "Will you help me carry this inside?"

"Sure. Give me one minute." He set his briefcase inside the door before moving to the opposite end of the table. "This doesn't look like the same table you put out here last week."

"Isn't it amazing how a little sanding and polishing can make something new again?"

"Are we still talking about the table?" Jack's eyes found hers.

She scrunched her lips and lifted her shoulders. "*I* was talking about it, but if you got more out of the statement, go with it." She lifted her end and maneuvered around so she led the way, backward. All he could do was follow her to the longest wall in the lobby.

When she was satisfied with the placement, he released the table and surveyed the room. "How long have you been here?"

"A couple of hours. I want to finish out here today."

"Did you come in yesterday?"

"No." His doubt must have showed on his face because she quickly added, "Em and I went shopping after church."

"Good. You work too much."

"Then you'll be happy to hear I'm taking a couple hours off this afternoon. Brandon's meeting me for lunch before I pick up some pictures from Ty."

The emotion churning through him at the mention of Brandon was not happiness.

"What do you think so far?" She held both arms out at her sides.

The table now sat under the company name painted on the wall in black scroll. The black crown molding contrasted elegantly with the blue-gray walls.

"Wait." She stopped him before he answered. "I don't want to know until it's done. Tell me this afternoon."

Her nervousness was adorable, and he couldn't resist teasing her. "Are you sure? I can give you my opinion now."

"I am." She stepped away from him. "I'll be in the conference room if you need me."

"Okay, let me know if you need my muscles again."

Libby spun around. "Nice try, Jack. You're not getting a sneak peek before everyone else." She slipped into the room. "And I could have gotten the table inside by myself but didn't want to scratch it."

He chuckled. "Have a productive day, Libby James."

"You too." She shut the door, and he heard the click of the lock. She took the "no peeking" stipulation seriously.

He shook his head. When she had a mission, Libby was unstoppable. The lobby looked fantastic. The space was rich, warm, and inviting—a complete transformation from the dingy white room furnished with two metal folding chairs.

For the next few hours, Jack immersed himself in the event calendar. All but two Saturdays between now and Labor Day were booked. In addition, three weekends held two events. Cancelations were sometimes a concern, but less so with the brimming calendar. Time to hire a photographer.

Digging the resumés out from under a stack of papers, he dialed the number at the top of one.

"Hello?"

"Logan Griffin?"

"Yes?"

"This is Jack Price. I'm calling to offer you the photographer position."

Several seconds of silence greeted him before Logan's breathy reply reached Jack's ear. "Really?"

"Yes. Your talent is what we'd like to add here at An Affair to Remember. As we discussed, I don't have much for you to do until May. My photographers are already contracted for the weddings over the summer, but we're happy to use you for less formal events. There are a handful of birthday parties and a couple of family reunions."

"Cool," Logan said. "I need to give notice at the restaurant, anyway."

His response proved Jack had made the right choice. "We're working on getting a desk set up for you. You'll share an office, but Libby's drawing up some plans to give you and Kevin your own work areas."

"Sharing's cool. Whatever Lib comes up with is fine. Thank you so much for this opportunity. I'm excited to work with you."

"You're welcome. Are you available tomorrow morning? I'd like to introduce you to the rest of the staff. We start at nine, and I provide breakfast."

"I'll be there. My shift at the restaurant doesn't start until two. See you tomorrow, Mr. Price."

"Please call me Jack and bring your portfolio. Welcome to the team, Logan."

Jack heard Libby return from her lunch date but remained in his office. If she stopped to pick up her pictures as planned, their lunch hadn't lasted long.

When Libby spoke to someone else, his curiosity drove him to investigate. He saw Amber King and tried to return to his office unnoticed.

"Hi, Jack." She waved at him.

He gave up and moved into the lobby. "What's up, Amber? Is Kevin here?"

"No." She grabbed Libby's arm. "Libby here called and asked if I wanted to help her this afternoon. I couldn't say no."

Libby gawked at her. "You could have told me no."

"Absolutely not! I want a look at this room before Kevin. It will give me something to hold over his head tonight."

"Poor guy." Jack sympathized with the man. Amber got an

odd sort of excitement out of knowing a secret.

"I apologize ahead of time for the noise, Jack." Libby pulled her arm from Amber's grasp. "We'll try not to disturb you too much."

"I'm heading out for a couple hours. After my meeting, I'll run by the store to restock the fridge. Do you ladies need anything?"

They both shook their heads.

"Okay, call me if you change your minds."

When he turned to leave, he remembered something else. "I talked to Logan earlier."

"And?"

"He'll start full-time at the end of May. I asked him to sit in on the meeting tomorrow."

"That's wonderful. He hoped to get the job." Her attention returned to Amber. "Would you like to see some of his work? He took some pictures of Julie and her girls last week. I got two of them enlarged and picked them up from my frame guy this afternoon."

Amber grinned. "Of course!"

"Give me a minute. We can hang them in Julie's office and surprise her." She hesitated for a moment then glanced at Jack. "Wait here."

He'd already seen the pictures but remained where he was as instructed.

Several minutes later, she returned with two eleven-by-seventeen framed photos. She flipped the first one around. Both of Julie's girls lay on their stomachs and sniffed a flower while smiling up at the camera.

Amber brought both hands to her chest. "Oh, this is perfect for her office. I love the black-and-white with the pop of color in the pink flower."

The other photo had no color accent. Julie held both girls' hands as they walked down a path, their backs to the viewer.

"These are my favorites, but I'm going to put a few of the others in smaller frames." A soft smile graced her face. "Logan's a master at capturing the perfect shot."

"Can we put these up first?" Amber took one of the frames from her.

"Sure. Let me get my tools and the stepladder."

"Be careful." Jack instantly regretted the comment. Libby did this for a living. She wasn't going to smash her thumb with a hammer or fall off the ladder.

Amber's eyebrows shot up while Libby's scrunched together. The expression on her face indicated an argument lurked near the surface.

"I better go," he said in an effort to distract her. Before either of the women could say more, he walked out the back door.

TWENTY-SEVEN

Do you like working here?" Amber's question hung in the air between them.

Libby set up the laser level her father had given her when she graduated college. "I do, but I feel guilty for not doing more with the events. When these rooms are done, I can concentrate on what Jack hired me for."

"How's Jack as a boss?"

She took a moment to gather her thoughts before answering. "He has his moments but he's fair. Even if he doesn't like a suggestion, he gives it thoughtful consideration when provided with facts and figures. The first day I came in with Emily, he overheard us talking about the conference rooms. His reaction concerned me, and I had some doubts about the position. After Em talked to him, he apologized."

"He would have without Emily's prompting," Amber said. "We've been friends for years. He hates conflict. It's why he hasn't called his dad back."

Libby almost dropped the picture in her hands. Once it was secured to the wall, she turned and gaped at Amber. "He told me he doesn't talk to his dad, hasn't seen him since his grandmother's funeral."

"Jack talked to you about his dad?" Amber sank onto a chair.

"Yes. He explained what happened with his parents when I

asked why he doesn't like weddings. My heart aches for him. I can't imagine life without my dad." She lifted the final framed photo—a close-up of a wedding cake with white fondant and intricate black scrollwork. She hung it up and stepped back to admire the room.

"These are gorgeous." Amber twisted in her seat. "I wouldn't have thought to use black-and-white photos. Thank goodness Kevin doesn't care about decor. Our house is boring."

"I'm sure it reflects your tastes, and that's what matters."

They moved to the lobby. Amber studied the framed pictures Libby set out for the space. "I'm glad you called. This is fun."

"It is, and I'm enjoying the company." Libby chose the photo of Pullen Park. "Ty surprised me and finished framing all my pictures early."

"This room looks a hundred times better already." Amber ran her hand over the table. "This is a perfect fit."

"I know. When I found it on Craigslist, I called right away. It took some elbow grease to refurbish. At thirty dollars, I couldn't pass it up." She set the level. "There are only four pictures for this space, then we'll move to the conference room."

"Oh, I can't wait to see what all you've done in there." She glanced over Libby's shoulder at the closed door. "Let's get to work."

When the pictures were up, Libby put out the office supplies she'd purchased—a black penholder, business card stand, and brochure stands. A black cylindrical vase she'd found in the boxes in the storage room joined the other items on the table. After work, she'd get some flowers. White and light blue would brighten things up. Perhaps white peonies and blue hydrangeas if they were available.

"Please tell me you're getting different chairs." Amber

wrinkled her nose at the metal folding chairs.

"I'm searching for a couple the perfect ones." She'd eliminate the seating entirely if she couldn't find anything. Those metal chairs were uncomfortable and ugly.

When the women finished out front, Libby got her keys from her office. "I left the larger pictures in the car."

Libby slid three thirty-by-twenty frames from her backseat and showed them to Amber. The first photograph was taken at twilight. The dark blue sky, framed in the window behind the table, made an astounding background for the crystal chandeliers and white china place settings. The next picture was from a Christmas party at a local lounge. The lighting against the white decorations gave them a light purple hue. The final one was from a small, formal rehearsal dinner. Silver tablecloths covered five tables with elaborate centerpieces on each one. The baby grand piano at the center of the photo added to the elegance of the scene.

Ty had used black frames and no mattes per Libby's instructions. They would stand out against the white walls.

They set the artwork on the table, and Amber examined everything. Five-and-a-half inch white scalloped crown molding topped the entire room. Three white shelves, six-feet long, anchored the blue wall. Libby had neglected to inform Jack of her plan for the accent wall when he complained about the color. The shelves now housed a dozen photos in silver or black frames of people, food, and flowers from different events. Five small silk floral arrangements in black and silver vases rested strategically among the pictures.

"What's going here?" Amber pointed to the empty section on the bottom shelf.

"Coffee mugs. They're black with the company name printed on them in silver. I'm keeping my fingers crossed they're here by the end of the week."

The final focal piece in the room, a coffee service Libby put together, sat in the center of the large table. She hadn't found what she wanted in a set, so she pieced her own together using a tray, black and silver coffee carafe, and silver sugar and creamer set.

Once she'd prepared to hang the first picture, Amber helped her lift it into place. "This room is beautiful, Libby."

"Let's get the rest of the artwork up so you can see it put together."

They had just secured the second frame to the wall when Jack knocked. "Libby? You in there?"

"Give us two minutes." She gave Amber a nervous smile and inhaled. "Judgment time."

"He'll love it."

They entered the lobby to find Jack wandering around. He carried a box as he examined the photos. At their arrival, he grinned at Libby. His chocolate brown eyes shone with warmth, and her breath caught in her chest.

"I'm speechless. When you asked earlier what I thought, I was going to say it was nice. This is…astounding."

Her cheeks heated at his praise. "Thank you. Logan gave me most of these photographs." A shadow crossed Jack's eyes, but she pressed on, unable to decipher what it meant. "I'm not quite done. The brochures won't be here until Friday, and everyone needs to put their business cards out. There are eight sections in the holder. A couple people can double up."

"Or you could put some interior design cards out. I'm sure we'll get a lot of compliments. People will want to know who redid the office."

She shook her head from side to side. "I don't have any."

"You should get some and start to line up clients for the fall."

"Until I meet with the first one and determine the timeframe, I couldn't schedule anything else. *If* that's what I decide to do. I'm here to work for you, not search out future business for myself."

"You can do both." He rested the box against his hip. "Use your days off to meet with people. I won't push if you don't feel comfortable, but think about this."

"I will." Eager to change the subject, she pointed to the package. "What's that?"

He peered down as if he'd forgotten he was holding it. "I was going to ask you. It's addressed to Libby James."

She let out a little squeal of excitement and bounced on her toes. Her order had arrived sooner than expected. "Oh. I'll take it to the kitchen."

"It's heavy. I'll carry it for you."

As he set the box on the table, Amber dug around in the drawers to find something to open the package. She handed Libby a knife. She would finish the larger conference room today and could now start on the smaller one.

Libby's muscles strained in her attempt to hold back her excitement. She glanced at Jack before sliding the knife between the flaps of the box. "I only need sixteen of these, but the minimum order was thirty. Each staff member can keep one, and we'll use the rest as backups."

"Now I'm curious." He remained beside her. "Show us what's in the box."

When she lifted the flaps, Libby gasped. "Oh, I didn't realize these would come too." She pulled out a bag of black click pens with the company name printed on them. They'd go in the penholder on the table out front. After passing them to Jack, she pulled out two of the large coffee mugs and handed one to Amber.

She gripped the handle and lifted the cup up and down a couple of inches. "These are nice and sturdy."

"No sense spending less for smaller, weaker mugs only to replace them in two months." She peeked at Jack, and her heart fell as he scowled at the mug in his hand. "You don't like them."

Judging from his expression, he hated them.

"I should have asked before I placed the order."

His head came up, and his gaze collided with hers. "No, these are fine. I do like them." He turned his attention to the 250 pens he'd set on the table.

She sensed he wanted to say more. "But?"

"Why did you buy these? They're advertising. I should have purchased them."

"I'm way under my budget, Jack."

"If you didn't buy these, what else could you add to the rooms?"

She hesitated because she still needed chairs for the lobby.

He didn't miss the pause. "I thought so. Let me know what this cost, and I'll put it back into your decorating account."

"If you're going to be stubborn about this, I won't argue."

His eyebrows hiked up his forehead. "I'm stubborn?"

She ignored the question, took the mugs back, and stuffed them in the box. The pens followed. "Amber and I are going back to work." No need to continue the conversation with the frustrating man.

She marched to the sanctity of the conference room. Amber followed several minutes later. Without a word between them, they finished hanging the pictures.

Libby stepped back and admired the room. "All that's left to do is wash the mugs and put them on the shelf." It was bittersweet whenever she finished a project. The end result thrilled her but so did the process of putting it all together.

Amber laid a hand on Libby's shoulder. "Come on. I'll help with the mugs before I go home."

"I won't argue with that offer." She hugged her new friend. "Thanks for coming today."

"Are you kidding? I should be thanking you. This was fun, and I got to see how talented you are."

She smiled at the compliment. "I hope everyone else feels the same when I reveal the room tomorrow." And by everyone, she meant Jack.

TWENTY-EIGHT

When Jack arrived Tuesday morning, the first thing he noticed was Libby's car. Did the woman ever take a break? He exhaled a heavy sigh. Once again, they'd be the only people in the office.

After the warning look Amber gave him yesterday, he expected another lecture from Kevin. Should he wait for someone else to show up or go in? This was insane. He and Libby were professionals.

The sun glinted off Julie's windshield as she turned into the parking lot, and Jack silenced his internal argument as he climbed out of his vehicle.

"Need some help?" She locked her car and walked over to him.

"Can you get the door?"

She unlocked the back door and held it open while he carried the breakfast trays inside. He slowed his pace, waiting for her reaction to the lobby.

Once Libby finished with the conference rooms, she'd work on Kevin's office. Her touch would be reflected in more than half the building. He considered asking her to decorate the other two offices as well.

"Holy cow!" Julie turned in a slow circle. "This is gorgeous, Libby."

"Thank you." Libby's voice followed him into the kitchen. "I'm still waiting on a couple more things for the table and need to find some chairs. The ones I like are way out of my budget, so I'm keeping an eye out for a good deal."

He shook his head. Was she so concerned with offending him she wouldn't ask for more money than what he'd allotted? *It's your own fault. You haven't exactly given her suggestions a warm welcome.*

Emily arrived and gushed over every detail. Libby remained gracious, always saying thank you, but she was also modest. Jack smiled as he imagined the blush spreading across her cheeks at this moment.

Someone shrieked, and he rushed to the lobby. He hadn't heard Kevin come in, but he stood staring at Julie's office.

"I love them! They're perfect!" Julie rushed from the other room and threw her arms around Libby.

"What?" Emily eyed the two women with a mixture of curiosity and concern.

Julie grabbed her arm. "Come see." She pulled Emily along.

At Emily's screech, Jack exchanged a glance with Kevin. They went to find out what caused the commotion.

"Look what Libby did." Julie pointed at the pictures of her girls now hanging on the walls.

Once again, Libby's talent surprised and pleased him. He turned to see her standing in the doorway watching them contentedly.

Kevin patted her shoulder as he left the room. "Good job."

"I only hung the pictures. Julie did the rest." Something behind her drew her attention, and a smile split her face. "Logan!"

Jack's stomach knotted. How could he handle that reaction every day? *Down, Jack. She's not yours.*

"You're right on time." Jack crossed to him. Logan's arrival gave him an excuse to usher everyone into the break room. "Breakfast is getting cold."

The excitement ramped up again at the discovery of the new coffee cups. When everyone got their food and sat down, Jack began the meeting by introducing Logan. Some sort of silent exchange passed between Emily and Libby, and he made a mental note to talk to Emily later.

"Logan brought his portfolio," he said. "I thought Julie and Kevin would like to see some of his work."

"We got a preview in my office." Julie turned to him. "The photographs of my girls are gorgeous."

"Thanks." The corners of his mouth tipped up.

Jack cleared his throat. "Let's get down to business."

They discussed Saturday's wedding. It was formal, with the ceremony and reception in two different locations. Emily, Julie, and Libby would go to the church and handle everything for the wedding before meeting him and Kevin at the reception. The day promised to be hectic.

"I'm returning calls to three potential clients this afternoon to set up consultations," Jack said. "Anyone available to sit in?"

Libby raised her hand. "I am."

"I can come if they're in the afternoon," Emily said.

"You should hold those here," Libby added.

Emily laughed. "I don't think we'll have enough privacy out front, Lib."

Jack was mesmerized by Libby's shining eyes. Was it his imagination, or did the gold in her eyes stand out more when something excited her?

"Not the lobby." Her smile grew radiant, and she looked at him. "Do you have anything else to go over?"

Since he couldn't form any words with her gaze on him, he shook his head.

She didn't break eye contact but addressed the entire group. "I finished the large conference room ahead of schedule. It's done and ready for use."

He found his voice. "Already?"

Still grinning, she nodded. "Ty finished the artwork sooner than I expected. The other room will be done by Friday, and I can start on Kevin's office next week."

"Can we see it?" Emily asked, and all eyes turned to Libby.

Her gaze still locked with his, she tilted her head. "What do you think?"

"I'm as anxious as everyone else."

She blew out a breath. "Okay, go."

The group stood and hurried from the room. When Libby remained in her seat, Jack stopped. "You coming?"

"In a minute."

He reached the room last and couldn't keep from gawking in amazement at the transformation. It was sophisticated now, an appropriate setting to meet any company or corporation and discuss their event planning needs. As he and the others walked around the room, they marveled at the change. Even the blue wall got his stamp of approval.

From behind him, Libby whispered, "I hope you like it because I'm *not* painting over that wall."

Julie spoke up. "This is beautiful, Libby."

"I won't be embarrassed to bring clients here for meetings anymore." Emily hugged her.

"Good job." A man of few words, Kevin repeated the compliment he'd given earlier.

Libby's embarrassment at the sudden attention showed in her rouged cheeks and the hunch of her shoulders.

Jack jumped in to take the spotlight off her for the moment. "Logan, why don't you bring your portfolio in here?"

Libby gave him a grateful smile as Logan left the room.

When he returned and sat at the table, Julie and Kevin joined him while Jack slipped out.

As he cleaned up breakfast, Libby entered the kitchen. "You never answered me. Do you like it?"

He set the tray of fruit aside and pivoted to face her. "I more than like it. It's better than anything I imagined." The same thing could be said of the woman standing in front of him. Before he let his mind wander any further, he asked, "Did you get enough to eat?"

"I'm good. I had a cinnamon roll with my coffee on the way in."

He noted the slight shadows under her eyes. "Are you working too much? You need to take some time for yourself. I don't want you to burn out before the summer gets here."

"I'm going on vacation in two weeks, Jack."

"Didn't you say you're taking care of seven kids? That's not relaxing."

She crossed her arms in front of her and raised her chin. "I won't be watching them the entire time."

"Okay." He held his palms out in surrender. "When you come back, I want you to stay away from the office on your days off."

"Fine, I will."

"Thank you." He doubted she'd stay true to her word, but it was worth a try.

On Thursday morning, Jack found an opportunity to talk with Emily and knocked on her open door. "Got a minute?"

"Sure, Jack. What's up?" When he glanced toward the table, she added, "Libby's shopping."

He dragged a chair in front of the desk and sat. "Are you all right with my hiring Logan? I'm sorry I didn't ask before he came in to meet everyone."

She shrugged. "It's fine. Libby said they talked, and she told him about Brandon. I just worry about her. He's convinced he'll win her back."

"Before I offered the job, I spoke with both of them. They assured me working together wouldn't be an issue."

"Libby won't say anything if there is one." She fiddled with her pen.

"Which is why I'm asking you to let me know if something

arises."

"I will."

He had one more concern on his mind. "Is she working too much?"

"This is nothing compared to the hours she used to put in." Emily dropped her pen and folded her arms on the desk. "You're allowing Lib to do what she loves. If she weren't here, she'd be at home sketching or scouring the internet for deals. It's how she relaxes."

"Maybe, but she needs to take a day or two off from the office."

Emily bit her bottom lip and dropped her gaze.

"What's wrong?" he asked.

"We talked about decorating in here. She'd only agree with two conditions." As she spoke, Emily ticked them off on her fingers. "One, we don't ask you for money and two, we use our free time to do it."

"That's ridiculous." He brought a hand to his neck and kneaded the muscles. "She's worked on everyone else's offices; why would I care if she wants to improve her own space?"

"That's Libby." Her head jerked back. "And don't you dare tell her I said any of this. She'll think I went behind her back."

"What if I ask her to decorate the rest of the office? Since she's done so much already, it makes sense for her to update everything else."

"That might work. Let me drop a few hints and get back to you on Tuesday."

"Okay. Let me know." He stood up. "Thanks, Emily."

A smile spread across her face. "Hopefully, I'll be the one thanking you."

TWENTY-NINE

On Saturday morning, Libby spread her dress across the backseat of Emily's car with care, admiring it once more. They'd gone shopping Monday evening, and she'd found the emerald green halter dress for today's wedding and reception. The chiffon was airy while flattering her figure. The floor length gown with an A-line silhouette had thin straps at her shoulders, so she wouldn't be worrying about it falling open as she worked. The sunburst pattern made of silver and green beading shimmered, and she'd pair it with black kitten heels and her vintage silver and enamel choker.

"Ready?" Em slid on her sunglasses with a smirk. "You'll be sick of that dress by the end of the night."

"I doubt it." She'd never tire of it. "Let's go." She hopped into the passenger seat. Emily got in beside her and started the car.

From the moment they arrived at the church, a flurry of activity surrounded them. Libby spoke to the florist and assisted with the placement of the flowers. Julie set the bridal party up with the hairstylists and cosmetician while Emily met with the musicians and photographer.

They strove to keep everything running smoothly and on schedule. They'd clean up the church before making their way over to the reception once the ceremony ended. Thankfully, most of the décor for that was handled by the hotel, and the florist would take care of the rest. The guys would be there in case a problem arose but wouldn't have a lot to do until guests arrived.

An hour before the wedding, the women took turns changing

into their dresses.

Libby asked two of the ushers to move the gift table to the side, so it didn't obstruct anyone's path as they entered the sanctuary. They continued to follow her around once they'd completed the small task. When Julie came through the foyer, she suggested the men assist the guests in finding their seats.

Libby waited until they were out of hearing. "Thank you. I kept dropping hints about how busy we are, but they went right over their heads. I guess I encouraged them by chatting when they moved the table."

"They're infatuated, Libby." Julie gave her hand a brief squeeze. "You're stunning in that dress. Of course they soaked up the attention. But today isn't about them, so let's focus on the bride and groom."

"Sometimes it's hard when guys just want to hang out with me. I need to figure out how to deal with things like this during events."

"You're a beautiful woman, and men will always be drawn to you."

"Guys are attracted to Emily." She waved her hand at herself. "Not this."

"You're wrong, but we'll table this discussion since I need to check on the bridal party." Julie hurried away.

Emily returned to the foyer after delivering the bouquets and boutonnieres. Libby peeked at the ushers who'd moved the table for her earlier. Both of them openly stared at her friend. *Yeah, right. I'll never compare.*

But she knew Emily hated it—hated never being able to talk to a guy when she first met him because he was so tongue tied or not forming close friendships with men without them expecting more from the relationship. Libby shook her head and walked out of the foyer. Everyone had their own burdens to bear.

A few minutes before the ceremony, the three women slipped into the back pew. Julie passed out tissues.

Emily leaned closer to Libby but hadn't perfected the art of whispering. "She always cries at weddings."

"Like I'm the only one." Julie elbowed her.

"I know." Emily sighed dreamily. "It's just so romantic. My favorite part is when they say their vows, especially when they write their own. I told Adam I want to write my vows when I get married."

Libby swallowed the lump in her throat. Emily and Adam had talked about getting married? They'd called each other almost every night since their double date and had gone to dinner a few times. It had only been a few weeks. Surely, she wasn't about to lose her best friend.

As if sensing her turmoil, Emily laid a hand on her arm. "He asked what I like most about my job. We're not there yet, Lib."

Yet.

The word hung in the air between them. Libby promised herself she'd spend some time with her best friend this week. Most of their recent conversations involved either work or Logan.

The wedding was beautiful. Libby enjoyed the secret smiles passed between the bride and groom. *I want this someday, Lord. Help me be patient and wait for the man you've chosen for me.*

Jack's face flashed in her mind, and she quickly dismissed it. With his disdain for marriage, he wasn't the one God had chosen for her. Still, why she was so attracted to the man perplexed her. She found herself working on a sketch or looking at something in a store and wondering whether he'd approve. An astonishing amount of her thoughts wandered to him.

His compliments on Monday and Tuesday had bolstered her confidence. She'd been concerned about his reaction to the other conference room since she used photographs from weddings and baby showers. When she revealed the smaller meeting room yesterday morning, she'd blossomed under his praise.

Pulling her attention back to the present, she heard the minister announce the new couple as husband and wife. They kissed and were introduced to the guests as Mr. and Mrs. before they led the bridal party from the room. The minister told everyone about the reception at the hotel and explained the bride and groom would arrive after photographs.

As the guests exited the sanctuary, Emily took charge. "Libby, you load the gifts in the car." She handed over her keys. "Julie and I will straighten the changing rooms and make sure nothing is left behind. The photographer should be done by the time we're finished, and we'll all clean up in here."

Libby carried a couple small presents outside with her and popped open Emily's trunk with the remote. After she tucked the packages inside and turned to go back into the church, a voice slowed her steps.

"Hey, Libby." The usher with curly black hair leaned against a car parked a couple spaces from Emily's. "Do you need a hand?"

"No, thanks. I can manage."

"You're all dressed up, and it's warm out here. Let us help you. Come on, Jason." He jerked his head toward the church, and his friend followed his instructions.

She sighed. It wasn't worth the argument. Once they finished, she'd send them on their way.

When she slammed the trunk shut, she smiled at them. "Thank you for helping."

"We'll unload them for you at the reception." Jason pressed

close enough to Libby to cause her alarm.

She took a step backward. "Our coworkers are there and will take care of everything. You guys enjoy the party."

"We're heading over now." Rob's gaze raked over her. "We'll keep an eye out for you."

Libby shuddered at the way he ogled her and rubbed the goosebumps spreading over her arms. "Don't worry about me. Have fun." Her legs strained against the desire to run as she hurried inside.

"We saw you pull up." Rob appeared the instant Libby stepped from the car, his friend right behind him.

Were they watching for us? She could smell the alcohol on his breath.

Emily opened the trunk, pulled some gifts out, and divided them between the two guys. "One trip. Once we're inside, we'll find our boss, and he'll get the rest." Her tone left no room for argument.

Libby lifted a couple packages out, and Emily tucked the guest book into the basket of cards and snatched it up. When they reached the reception hall, Emily passed the basket over and said, "I'll find Jack or Kevin."

Watching as her friend made her way to the far side of the room, Libby's eyes skimmed over her head, and her stomach fluttered as she met Jack's gaze. *Oh my, he looks fantastic in a suit.* He smiled at her then ducked his head toward Emily as she said something to her. Shaking her head at herself, Libby rearranged the gifts on the table to make room for the remainder of the packages in the car. An arm settled over her shoulders, and her spine went rigid.

"Are you sure you don't need any more assistance?" Rob pressed his mouth to her ear.

His arm fell away when she jumped back. Desperate, she searched the room and saw both Jack and Kevin striding out the door. Struggling to control her panic, she gave Rob a tight smile that felt more like a grimace. "No, thank you. There's my boss and another co-worker." She pointed at their retreating backs. "They'll get the rest."

She hurried outside and tried to calm her racing heart. Rob and Jason were getting too friendly, and the alcohol would only lower their inhibitions. Deep in thought, strategizing how best to avoid them, she shuffled outside. When someone placed a hand on her arm, Libby jerked away.

Jack's eyebrows drew together. "Are you all right?"

Trying to focus, she looked into his searching brown eyes. "Yeah. Sorry, I was thinking of everything we have to do." It was sort of true.

He dipped his head a fraction and forced her to hold eye contact. "You sure?"

"Yes," she snapped and took a step back. Her irritation disappeared as her gaze traveled from his gelled hair to the tips of his oxford dress shoes and back to his face. "You look handsome today, Jack. This is the first time I've seen you in a suit and tie." Did she imagine him standing taller?

"Thank you. And you're beautiful as always."

"Thanks." She gave him a half-hearted smile. Why did he have to use *that* word?

"I mean it, Libby." He winked before continuing inside.

Butterflies took flight in her stomach. Her body responded in a different way to Jack's flirtations than Rob's. The corners of her mouth turned down as her thoughts returned to the two ushers.

"What's wrong?" Emily stood beside the car and put her hands on her hips when she saw Libby's expression. "What did Jack say to you?"

"Nothing." She wished he would've used any other word to compliment her. She wasn't beautiful. Cute, yes. Pretty, perhaps. But never beautiful. Tears started to build behind her eyes, and she blinked rapidly. She refused to cry over Jack's kindness. He'd probably told Emily the same thing.

And she hated herself for testing her theory. "Did Jack or Kevin say anything about your dress?" Libby hoped the question wasn't too obvious since Emily had purchased it when they went shopping last week.

"Kevin whistled, and Jack gave me his standard compliment." She deepened her voice in a lame attempt to sound like Jack. "'You look nice.'"

Libby gulped down air and forced a chuckle. Something was wrong—and oddly exciting—when a man told Emily she looked nice and Libby she was beautiful. Had he meant it? Her mind told her not to hope, but her heart refused to listen.

Your first long event." Julie leaned against the wall beside her. "What do you think?"

"My feet are killing me," Libby admitted.

Julie glanced down at the heels and nodded. "You'll get used to it. There's a bench in the hallway near the bathrooms. Go sit for fifteen minutes. I'll find you if you're needed."

"You're an angel." Libby squeezed her hand. Getting off her feet for a few minutes sounded like bliss, even if it would be torture to get back up.

When she found the bench, she sank onto it, leaned her head back, and closed her eyes. It would take no time to fall asleep tonight. Today had worn her out. She was trying to convince herself to return when someone approached. Her eyes flew open, and her heart rate increased.

"You didn't say good-bye," Rob said. Jason moved beside him, forming a wall in front of her.

Libby forgot about her sore feet and jumped up. "It's been a busy night. I should get back before someone misses me." She took a step toward escape. A large hand circled her wrist and stopped her progress.

Rob laid his other hand on her hip and pulled her to him until she felt his chest against her back. "The night's not over yet." His breath heated her cheek as he moved his head closer. "We've got plenty of time for a proper send off."

Squeezing her eyelids shut, Libby said a desperate prayer. Why had she been so careless? She'd avoided them all evening. Anytime she went near the guys, she'd made sure someone came along. Now they were alone in a secluded hallway.

Rob spun her around and pushed her up against the wall. His body pressed into hers, pinning her in place. She jerked her head away from the nauseating mixture of alcohol and overpowering cologne. Her stomach rolled. Would they leave her alone if she got sick?

Jason leered at her and held up a keycard. "Let's make this party private."

"Please," Libby pleaded. "My friends are going to notice I haven't come back any minute now."

"What? You think you're better than us?" He trailed the keycard down her neck and shoulder. Sliding it under the strap of her dress, he added, "You're the help."

"Please don't do this." Her voice sounded weak in her ears, and her knees shook so badly she didn't know how she still stood. There was no escape.

THIRTY

Jack berated himself all evening. From the first time Libby walked into the reception hall, he couldn't take his eyes off her. Soft curls framed her face, and her dress emphasized her femininity. When she'd told him he looked handsome, she'd given him a gift. Wanting to return the favor, he said the thing that had run through his mind from the moment he saw her. It was the wrong compliment. Her entire countenance fell when he told her she was beautiful.

It wasn't until later he remembered their conversation the afternoon of her double date. He could have used any other adjective to describe her but chose the one she refused to believe about herself.

The reception was running smoothly. Dinner had been served, and most of the guests were now dancing. It would still be a couple hours before they could take down the room and call it a night. Jack found Kevin and told him he was going outside to get some air. Voices carried to him as he passed a hallway.

"You think you're better than us? You're the help."

His paced slowed. What was going on?

A woman's voice followed. "Please don't do this." The words were shaky and uncertain.

Unwilling to leave any woman in a compromising situation, he went to investigate. "Is everything okay back here?" He called out a warning as he stepped into the corridor. Two men stood side by side, their backs to him as they trapped a woman against the wall.

White heat shot through Jack's veins when she lifted huge hazel eyes to him. Eyes full of pain and fear.

"Jack?" she whispered.

His pulse pounded in his ears as he fought the urge to haul both of these guys outside and teach them a lesson. He spoke through a clenched jaw. "It's time for you two to go back to the reception."

"We're more interested in private parties." The redhead pressed closer to Libby.

These punks were young, early twenties maybe, and scrawny. Jack pulled himself to his full height, expanded his chest chiseled by his daily weightlifting regime, and inclined his head toward Libby. "She's not."

He moved behind the guy who held her and yanked his shoulder. Libby scrambled away and moved behind him, close enough where Jack could feel her tremors.

"You can't do this," the black-haired guy said. "I'm a guest."

"And that gives you permission to force yourself on a woman?"

He sneered at Jack. "I didn't force myself on anyone. She asked for this."

Libby's gasp almost undid his control. He fisted his hands and struggled to control his rage. "I'll say this one more time. Go back to the party. If I find you near anyone on my staff, I'll report you for harassment."

The red-haired guy's gaze darted down the hallway and back

as he shifted from one foot to the other, but the other guy stood his ground. "They wouldn't do anything."

"Maybe not," Jack said, "but you'll spend the rest of the weekend explaining to your friends and family why the police wanted to question you."

"She's not worth it, anyway." The dark haired guy called Jack a few off-color names and stormed away.

Once he was certain they were gone, Jack turned his attention to a trembling Libby. Tempted to hold her in his arms, he rejected the thought, knowing it might be too much for her right now.

Instead, he settled her on the bench and knelt in front of her. "Are you okay? Did they hurt you?" *Please let her be okay.*

She shook her head, eyes still wide and shadowed.

"I'll get Emily or Julie." He started to get up, but she grabbed his hand.

"D-d-don't leave m-me." Her whispered voice caught on a sob.

He should find one of the ladies, but when she looked at him with that expression of vulnerability, there was no question of what to do. Folding her hand in his, he sat beside her.

"I'm sorry, Jack. I tried to stay away from them all night." She cried softly, releasing tears that tore him to shreds.

"Libby, you back there?"

Jack lifted his head and peered toward the end of the carpeted hallway. "We're here, Julie."

She rounded the corner. "Jack? What are you...?" The question died on her lips when she noticed Libby's tears.

Julie glared at him for several seconds before her expression softened, and she approached. "Libby, honey, what's wrong? What happened?"

Jack stood and gestured for Julie to take his place. "I'm going back inside. Take as long as you need."

Did Julie think he made Libby cry? Trusting Libby to explain, he found Kevin to tell him what had happened and point out the two guys. They'd make sure those two didn't go anywhere near the ladies again.

Now the part he dreaded. He quietly spoke with Emily. She gaped at him as he finished, her eyes full of fire. "Who was it?" When he nodded toward the guys, her expression grew tight. "I knew they'd be trouble. They waited for us to get here and offered to carry the gifts inside. I told them one trip. They were flirting with Libby at the church before the wedding, and I'm sure they hoped to keep it going."

"What?" The muscles in his shoulders and back grew taut. How did he miss them? He thought he'd kept an eye on Libby all night, aware of where she was most of the time.

"It happens all the time, Jack. She doesn't realize guys are flirting." Her eyes widened, and her mouth went slack. "She'll blame herself for what those jerks did. Where is she?"

"She and Julie are in the hallway past the kitchen. Take her home, Emily. She shouldn't stay here."

"You're okay with losing both of us for the night?" Her hands rested on her hips. "Because I'm not leaving her alone."

"We can handle everything here. The hotel staff will help."

"Good. I'll get her."

"Text me and let me know you both got home safely."

She glanced at him. "It might take a while to convince her to leave, though."

"You and Julie can talk her into it."

He kept himself busy for the next hour, trying not to worry about Libby. When Julie finally returned, the party was breaking up.

"Did they hurt her?" He prayed for strength when he heard the answer.

"No, thank the Lord. They scared her pretty badly. If you hadn't stopped them..." Julie didn't finish the thought as if it was too horrifying to even consider. "She and Emily just left."

"How hard did she argue to stay?"

Julie chuckled. "She objected to leaving us with all the work, but we convinced her we'd work faster without fretting over her."

"Thank you, Julie."

"What's going on, Jack?" She studied him.

"What do you mean?"

"You're awfully concerned about Libby."

"I'd be if this happened to you or Emily as well."

"Yeah, I suppose so. But would you sit with us and hold our hands while we cried?" She didn't allow him time to defend himself before she added, "Be careful. Libby's my friend, and I don't want to see her heart get broken."

His brow furrowed. He wanted to deny his feelings, to tell her she had nothing to worry about. That's not what came out of his mouth. "Why do you assume I'll break her heart?"

She fixed her gaze on him. "Have you changed your mind about marriage?"

"No."

"Every girl longs to find love with someone who will offer her happily ever after. And you can't if you're not willing to marry her."

"Why does it have to go straight to marriage?"

"Because if that's not even a possibility, it doesn't need to go anywhere. Don't start something you can't finish well, Jack."

"I'm not going to start anything." No matter how much he longed to. "She's my employee. How would that look?"

"Like you're human and realize what a wonderful woman Libby is. Like you're not a total idiot for letting her slip through your fingers."

"Now you're encouraging me?" His mind spun at her change of opinion. Women were so confusing. "We need to get to work or we'll be here all night."

"You're the boss." She flashed a quick, saucy grin before her expression fell. "I'll check on Libby tomorrow afternoon, and we're having lunch with Amber on Monday. She'll be okay. We'll get her through this."

As they returned the room to normal, Julie's admonishment played on repeat in his head. Libby deserved her happily ever after. No matter how much he liked her, he couldn't steal that away from her.

It was after eleven when they left the reception. They'd worked twelve hours, and with the extra adrenaline running through him, exhaustion weighed him down. He climbed in his car and reached for his phone. Emily had texted and told him she'd call tomorrow.

He also had a voicemail from a number he didn't recognize. Expecting the message to concern an event, he pulled a small notebook and pen out of the center console and played the voicemail, poised to jot down any pertinent information.

"Jack? It's your father again. You haven't returned any of my calls, and I understand. I wasn't available for you or your mother so I shouldn't expect you to be available now, but I want to talk to you, to apologize. I'm leaving town at the end of the week and would like to talk before then if possible. Please call me."

After disconnecting the call, Jack threw the phone onto the passenger seat. His dad would have to wait a lot longer than the end of the week to hear from him. He had nothing to say to the man who chose to leave. These issues with his dad emphasized the reasons he couldn't get involved with anyone, why he refused to pursue a long-term relationship. He wouldn't put anyone through the pain, especially not Libby. He loved her too much.

His hand stilled as he reached for the keys in the ignition. Did he love her? Where had that thought come from? He'd known her a month—hadn't even kissed her—but did he love her? *What have I gotten myself into, God? Help me do what's best for Libby and let go of any selfish desires.*

THIRTY-ONE

Sunday evening, Libby shut herself in her bedroom. Emily had called Callie the night before and told her what happened. Libby had spent most of the day convincing her family not to drive up to Raleigh. She couldn't deal with her well-meaning family coddling her right now. When she'd spoken to Callie this morning, her sister wouldn't let her off the phone until she promised to meet for dinner.

Embarrassed and ashamed by the entire situation, Libby swore she'd never allow herself to be put herself in that kind of compromising situation again. She cringed when the phone rang. Who could be calling now? In addition to Callie, she'd also talked to her parents and her oldest sister. Julie had stopped by the apartment as well. They spent the hour avoiding any talk of the night before.

When Libby saw Becca's number on the screen, she sat up on the bed and answered. Her friend would understand how Libby felt since she'd been through much worse several years ago.

"How are you doing, Lib? And don't tell me fine."

Tears she'd stuffed down all day sprang to her eyes. "I was stupid, Bec. I avoided those guys all night then forgot about them because I wanted to get off my feet for a few minutes."

"This isn't your fault. I know you don't believe me, but the more you hear it, the more the truth will sink in. Callie said they were drinking. Those guys would've harassed someone else if they hadn't sought you out."

"I encouraged them when I allowed them to keep talking to me. I wish I'd just moved the table myself."

"Stop." Becca's voice was stern. "You've always made fast friends and people like you. It's why you're an excellent interior designer. Don't let this change who you are, Lib. I learned the hard way. Don't follow my example."

"Did you feel guilty about what happened? I can't shake the idea this was somehow my fault."

"Yes, I did." Becca sighed. "It was therapeutic when I talked about everything. Not only the details of Martin's actions but how selfish I'd been during the months leading up to the kidnapping. I spoke with a psychologist during my hospital stay and met with her for several months afterward. Alex even came a few times."

"When I think of what could have happened if Jack hadn't come by when he did..." She shuddered and swept aside the images that once again tried to invade her mind.

"Don't dwell on it. God sent Jack at exactly the right time. Callie mentioned he's a good-looking guy. And a Christian."

"He is."

"Which one?"

Libby smiled. "Both."

"He came to your rescue."

"Pretty pathetic, huh?"

"It's romantic," Becca said.

"He's my boss. Nothing romantic about it."

"Alex was my boss."

"It's not the same." Libby rolled her eyes. "You and Alex were friends long before you worked together. Plus, you didn't need your job like I do."

"You're right, but I can tell you're smiling when you talk about him. You're interested."

"It's a little crush, but Brandon and I are sort of dating."

"Brandon? The guy from Callie's church?"

"Yes, their youth pastor." Libby hugged a pillow against her stomach. What if someone told him about the incident, and he called? Could she talk to him about this?

"He's not right for you. Don't drag it out to spare his feelings. Tell him now if you're not interested."

"Why do you say he's not right for me?" Even if she disagreed, Becca's opinion mattered to Libby.

"He's too young."

"He's a year older than me," Libby said in his defense.

"Maybe he seems young because he makes a living hanging out with teenagers." Becca clicked her tongue. "I always pictured you with someone more serious and mature."

Someone like Jack. "Well, if you meet this mystery man, send him my way."

Becca laughed. "Maybe you'll meet him in Hawaii."

"Oh, then I could live there."

"Never mind, you won't meet him on vacation." Becca's firm tone brought another smile to Libby's lips. "One week until vacation. You ready?"

"I need to pack."

"Then get off the phone and get to it." Motherhood had made Becca more demanding.

"Okay, Bec. I won't argue with you. Thanks for calling."

"You're welcome. I love you, Lib. Call anytime."

"Love you too. See you next Sunday. Give Alex and the kids my love and hugs."

"Will do. Rest up this week. We've got a long day of travel."

Libby took solace in the quiet of the office. She arrived early with plans to paint until lunch. A distraction would give her something to focus on. Besides, with her vacation looming, getting as much as possible done with Kevin's office was her top priority this week.

Sage green paint covered an entire wall when someone opened the back door. Her heart hammered in her chest. She told herself it was Jack, but her body refused to listen to her mind and froze.

"Libby?"

She relaxed at Jack's voice. "In here."

"You okay?" Pity filled his eyes as he stood in the doorway.

"Yeah." Her weak answer didn't sound convincing to her. "You spooked me. It's not a big deal."

"I'm sorry. I considered knocking but thought better of it."

"Probably a wise decision. Loud noises would have been worse." She gave him a sardonic smile. "It's okay, Jack. Go work."

"I brought breakfast. Come eat with me."

"No thanks. I'm not hungry." She pushed the roller through the paint pan and returned to her task.

She hadn't eaten since Saturday morning, but Emily would force her to today. Her friend had commented on her loss of appetite yesterday, and Libby held no illusions about her keeping that information to herself.

"Are you sure? There's plenty for both of us."

"Positive. I'm meeting Emily, Julie, and Amber for lunch in a while and want to save room." Anyone who knew her would see right through the lame excuse.

"If you say so." He didn't look convinced. "I'll leave my door open in case you need anything."

"Thanks."

She'd ruined everything. After the incident, she dreaded seeing her coworkers. Libby should to thank Jack for saving her, but she hated the strain between them.

Was it ridiculous that when he told those guys not to go near anyone on his staff she'd felt disappointment? She longed for him to defend her honor. His comment only drove home the fact he saw her as nothing more than an employee. After his compliments, she'd begun to hope he might view her as more.

One twenty-minute pep talk later, she worked up the courage to speak to him.

He looked up from his computer at her rap on the door and smiled. "Change your mind about breakfast?"

"No." Why was he so insistent she eat? Realization flowed through her. "You talked to Emily."

"She called yesterday. We're concerned about you."

"It'll take some time to process, but I'll be okay, Jack."

His expression clouded. "I'm sorry this happened to you."

"It wasn't your fault," she said.

"It wasn't yours either." He pressed his palms against the top of his desk. "You know that, right?"

"I'm getting there. It's hard not to blame myself." This wasn't the conversation she'd prepared for. "I wanted to thank you. If you hadn't stopped..." She couldn't continue around the lump in her throat.

"I wish I had come by sooner. I wanted to teach those two a lesson the second I saw you."

"It's best you didn't. If you'd over-reacted, your business could've suffered."

"My business?" He scowled at his hands. Strong, capable hands. "You're more important than a few bookings. I could handle a few canceled events. I don't know what I'd have done if they'd hurt you."

Libby dropped her gaze to the floor. She couldn't figure him out. One minute he was aloof and taciturn and the next he said something like that.

He stood and moved in front of her, forcing her eyes up to his. "I'm telling you the truth."

She searched his face and found only sincerity. "Thank you for staying with me and letting Emily take me home. I'm sorry it made more work for the rest of you."

"The hotel staff helped. It didn't take us long."

With nothing more to say, she made her escape. "I'm going to paint some more before lunch."

"I'm free this afternoon if you'd like some assistance."

"I was wavering about coming back, but if you're willing to help, I'll be here. Can I bring you some lunch? We're going to Torero's."

"No, thank you. I ate a big breakfast." He grinned and winked at her.

Libby laughed at his attempt to make light of the fact she didn't want to eat. Another piece of herself clicked back into place. She'd get past this.

THIRTY-TWO

The corners of Jack's mouth lifted as Libby left his office, her laughter floating in the air. When he didn't find either of the girls at church Sunday morning, he'd grown concerned. Emily called later that evening and explained they'd stayed home. The fact Libby wasn't eating concerned her. According to her, Libby had been on the phone with her family throughout the day.

He hoped she'd come to the office today, wanting to determine for himself how she was coping. When he'd arrived and found her in Kevin's office and saw her pale face, he realized he'd frightened her. Causing her discomfort slammed him in the gut.

The offer to paint came out of the blue. He hadn't planned to spend the afternoon with her, but his desire to put her at ease won out. They forced conversation right now. She was leaving in a week, and business would get insanely busy when she returned. He wanted to everything returned to normal before she left.

He was immersed in paying and sending out invoices when Libby returned from lunch, taking him by surprise. "Still interested in painting?"

He pulled his attention from the computer. "You bet. Give me twenty minutes."

She blew out a breath and hesitated as if she was about to say something unpleasant. "Before I forget, Callie would like you to dinner with us Wednesday night if you're not busy. Chris is coming too."

"You eat out a lot, Libby."

"I know. I should marry a man who can cook." Her face flushed, and she lowered her lashes, shielding her eyes from him.

He wanted to point out the obvious—he cooked—but changed the subject instead. "Let me finish this up." He pointed at his computer. "I'm sure you plan to get this project finished early."

"You're learning, Jack. What about dinner?"

"I'd love to go. We'll meet them at the restaurant."

"Thanks. I'll tell Callie you plan to come."

He wrapped up the paperwork, shut down his computer, and crossed to Kevin's office, sure to make plenty of noise on his way. After filling the tray with light green paint, he grabbed a roller and slicked some on the wall opposite Libby. Racking his brain for a neutral topic, Jack finally asked about lunch.

"It was fun. I had the fajitas and some of Emily's enchiladas."

Relief flowed through him at her proclamation. She'd not only eaten, but eaten more than one serving. As he let her talk, the stress of the past two days dissipated.

"Amber might drop by to check out the other conference room later," Libby said.

"She'll love it. I'm surprised she hasn't recruited you to decorate her house yet."

"She promised me lunch."

"I take it that means she asked."

"No, I offered."

Jack shook his head. "Do you ever take time off to do

something for yourself?"

"Do you?" she shot back. "You're here as much as I am."

"True, but I don't spend my days off working for friends."

"It's relaxing for me. Making someone's surroundings fresh and new is rewarding. The shopping is a bonus."

"Good." He turned to look at her. Emily might be upset he pushed forward without talking to her but... "I'd like you to decorate my office. And you can't do that without upsetting Emily so you'd better do hers too."

"What about—?"

"And if you redecorate our offices, the ugly kitchen will stand out, so you may as well work on it too."

Libby peered over her shoulder. "What about the bathrooms?"

By the tone of her voice, Jack couldn't tell if she was annoyed, and she'd turned back around, so he couldn't see her face. "I honestly hadn't thought about them. What do you think? Will you do it?"

"Can I have until the end of the summer to complete everything? The events need to come first. You hired me to ease the workload, not redecorate."

"That's fine. I'm sure you'll finish long before then."

"Under promise and over deliver, Jack. It's good business sense."

"Yes, it is. You'll be wonderful on your own, Libby James."

The paint roller stilled on the wall. "I haven't decided to go independent."

"You should. I'll help you get set up."

"*If* I decide to go that route, I know someone who will get me up and running. He used to do it for a living."

Jack wasn't surprised to hear yet another man would lend her a hand. Slivers of disappointment poked under his skin when she dismissed his offer so quickly. "Well, I'm here if you change your mind."

"I appreciate it," she said.

"You never answered my question about the decorating."

Her shoulders rose to her ears and fell away, but her tone held a hint of amusement when she answered. "You never gave me a budget."

"Why don't you draw up a few ideas and give me an estimate. Be sure to include the cost of the chairs you want for the lobby."

She spun around. "Really?"

"Yes." He blinked at her radiant smile.

"You've got a deal, Jack. Emily and I already talked about her office, so I'm ahead of schedule." Her enthusiasm was palpable as she resumed painting and thought out loud. "And I'm still going to make her work in there. The kitchen won't need much. Neither will the bathrooms. Your office is the biggest challenge. What's your favorite color? What do you like to do when you're not here?"

"Dark blue or green, and I read a lot when I'm home."

"What do you read?"

A little of everything, but one genre more than the others. "Mostly mysteries."

Her roller paused in its path along the wall.

"Does that surprise you?" he asked.

"It shouldn't. We haven't known each other long. It's just…"

"What?"

After shaking her head as if to clear her thoughts, her arm moved again, up and down on a slight diagonal. "In some ways, it feels like we've known each other longer than a month. Your answer reminded me there's a lot I don't know about you."

I should warn you," Libby said as they drove to meet Callie Wednesday evening.

Jack noticed her silence on the drive over. The tremor in her voice made him wonder if she was nervous. He parked the car at Olive Garden and twisted in his seat to focus his full attention on her. "About what?"

"Callie made me agree to this dinner so she can make sure I'm okay. I bet you're here so she can thank you."

The temptation to reach over and touch the soft skin of her cheek pulled at him. He clenched his hand into a fist to keep from acting on the impulse. "I'll assure her you are more than okay, and there's no need to thank me." He winked at her. "At least we're getting dinner out of the deal."

Libby laughed. "I knew I liked you for a reason."

He leaned forward until their noses were a centimeter apart and gazed into those hazel eyes. "Only one?"

"No." The word came out on a breath. "Not just one."

Could she hear the loud thump of his heart right now? He cleared his throat. "Wait there. I'll get your door."

After hurrying around the car, he took her hand as exited the SUV. Giving it a gentle squeeze, he released it after too short a time.

As she led the way to the front of the restaurant, Jack kept his eyes on her. The teal blouse she wore complemented her skin tone. Her black slacks allowed him to admire her backside. When she stopped suddenly, he almost walked into her. With a hop and a squeal, she hugged a short woman with long, curly, dark blonde hair.

The other sister?

"Surprise!" The woman held onto Libby for several seconds.

"Callie didn't tell me you were coming. Where are the kids?" She pulled away from her sister.

"They're with Brad and Sarah. She wanted the practice, but I bet Brad's regretting it already."

"Is Alex here?" Libby scanned the area behind them.

Jack shifted until he could see face.

"He's inside." The older blond grinned at him, her bright blue eyes glistening. "Are you going to introduce us, Lib?"

She gave the woman an odd look he couldn't decipher before speaking. "Becca, this is my boss, Jack Price. Jack, this is Becca Newsome."

Not her sister. The hair color was the only trait Becca *Jackson* Newsome shared with her brother. This petite woman was related to Bradford Jackson? The man the press had nicknamed Bear? Jack held out his hand, but Becca bypassed it and hugged him instead.

"Anyone who rescues our Libby gets a hug."

"Becca," Libby hissed. "Don't embarrass the poor man."

"I'm not embarrassing him." Becca eyed him with a challenge.

He was wrong. Her no-nonsense, *I'll get my way* expression was pure Jackson.

"Am I?" she asked.

"No, you're not." Jack chuckled. "It's a pleasure to meet you. Libby's mentioned you a few times."

"I hear Emily has too."

"Becca!" Libby cried. "Take me to Alex. He'll keep you in line."

The other woman laughed loudly—a laugh almost as endearing as Libby's. Jack shook his head in amusement and followed as she linked her arm with Libby's and dragged her inside. They reached the table, and everyone stood to welcome them. Callie kept a close eye on her sister.

Libby hugged her. "Why didn't you tell me Becca and Alex would be here?"

"Bec wanted to surprise you."

"I needed to get out of the house." Becca straightened her pink blouse and grasped the arm of the blond man Jack hadn't met yet. "We've got free babysitting in Raleigh. If Brad and Sarah hadn't taken the kids, I would've split them up between Mom and Abby."

"Abby's my sister," the man said and reached his hand across the table. "Alex Newsome."

"Jack Price."

"Oh, I'm sorry, Jack," Libby said. "You'll get used to the chaos."

Once they settled around the table, everyone began talking at once. Jack sat beside Libby on one side of the table with Becca and Alex across from them. The waitress approached and took their drink orders, promising to return shortly with breadsticks and salad.

Seated on the other side of Libby, Callie grew serious. "How are you doing, Lib?"

When she didn't answer for several seconds, Jack peeked at her and noticed the grip she had on the edge of her chair. He gently loosened her fingers and enveloped them in his hand, squeezing in reassurance. His desire to offer support became something entirely different the moment her small, smooth hand rested in his.

As if it were a lifeline, she clung to him. "I'm doing all right, Cal. A lot of people are speaking truth into the situation, and I'm trying to listen."

Callie's gaze shifted past Libby to him. He nodded his confirmation, and she visibly relaxed.

"Glad we got that out of the way." Becca clapped her hands once before rubbing them together. "Why don't you tell us about yourself, Jack?"

Until she was ready, Jack didn't plan to release Libby's hand. To his delight, she didn't seem in any hurry to sever the connection. He answered Becca's questions about work and his mom. When the food arrived, he was forced to either let go of Libby or reveal their little secret.

THIRTY-THREE

When Jack grasped her hand, Libby struggled not to react. A pleasant current ran up her arm as his strong and solid fingers enveloped hers. What did Callie just ask? Oh yeah. Libby told her sister the truth. She was doing better, and the people around her had been encouraging. Hopefully, when Callie saw she had her appetite back, she'd be satisfied enough to quit watching Libby's every move.

Like a good sport, Jack endured Becca's interrogation. Libby knew why she'd come tonight, and surprising her had nothing to do with it. Curiosity had gotten the better of her friend.

The salad and breadsticks arrived, and Libby swallowed the sad sigh that tried to escape when Jack let go of her. She'd never had this kind of reaction to a man's touch in any of her previous relationships.

"Let me pray for dinner." Alex removed his glasses, and everyone bowed their heads. "Thank you, God, for a night with friends. Thank you for your protection over Libby. Continue to bless her in all areas of her life. May our conversation be pleasing to you. Thank you for the food you've provided. Amen."

A chorus of amens echoed around the table.

Chris passed the salad to Libby. "Ladies first."

"You might regret that," Jack said. "Her appetite's back."

She smiled wryly. "Why do you think I asked to come here? Unlimited salad and breadsticks."

"She did choose the place." Callie squeezed Libby's shoulder. "I'm glad you're eating again."

Dinner was a blast. Libby didn't feel like a fifth wheel with Jack beside her. Even though he was ten years younger than them, Chris and Callie liked him, and Becca and Alex welcomed him into the group.

When they'd finished their meals, Becca dug through her black leather tote. "I have something for you, Lib. I needed a project."

Libby had been so focused on her new job the past few weeks, she hadn't asked Becca how she was doing after losing her baby. Although, judging from her enthusiasm tonight, she was just fine.

Becca handed her two small boxes.

"What are these?" Libby stared at them.

"Open them." Becca tucked a long curl behind her ear.

Libby lifted the lid off the first box. It was filled with business cards. She opened the second and found another set of cards with a different design. Libby's name, phone number, and e-mail address were printed on the cards along with "Interior Designer" and a website.

"I don't have a website." Libby glanced around the table.

"You do now. I know a guy." Becca peeked at Alex, who shook his head while smiling at her in adoration. "Well, Alex knows a guy. I'll give you his information. He's your web designer for the next year."

"This is too much, Bec. I haven't even decided if this is what I'm going to do."

"You're crazy not to," Becca said. "Alex will set everything up."

Libby peered at Alex, the only person who could talk Becca out of some of her schemes. Judging from the way he watched his wife, this wouldn't be one of those times.

"*If* I decide to do this, Alex will be my first phone call. But I need to make sure this is God's will and not a path I'm cutting on my own."

"I'll convince you it's his will while we're on vacation." Becca's response didn't surprise her. Once she made up her mind, everyone followed her lead.

Jack nudged her with his shoulder. "You should take some photos of the office and add them on the website. I can probably dig up some "before" photos."

"Oh." Becca sat up straighter, her interest in the idea apparent. "I want to see what you did."

"You're welcome to follow us back." Jack's offer came without hesitation.

A grin spread across Becca's face, and she turned to Alex. "Do we have time?"

"Sure. We're staying in town tonight." He inclined his head toward Chris. "What about you two?"

"We're here tonight as well." Chris winked at Callie sitting across the table from him. "Mom's keeping the girls tonight."

"Great!" Becca patted her husband on the back. "Alex, pay the waitress and let's get out of here."

"Yes, love." He settled his arm along the back of her chair, and she snuggled against him.

Libby had always liked Alex's endearment for Becca. He'd been in love with her for years before he admitted it to her. It fit. Becca was the love of his life.

Jack started to object when Alex asked the waitress to bring him the check. They could afford dinner for everyone, and Becca wouldn't appreciate Jack arguing about it. Libby grabbed his hand and gave a small shake of her head when he glanced at her. He clamped his lips together but didn't release her hand.

"Chris and I will stop and pick up some dessert on our way." Callie's eyes scanned the group and stopped on Libby. "Any requests?"

"I just want coffee," Becca said.

"We'll make some at the office." Libby leaned toward Callie and lowered her voice. "What about brownies?"

"I can do brownies. Anyone else?" When no one answered, she said, "Okay, brownies and whatever Chris and I want."

When Alex asked for the office address, Jack handed him a business card. The waitress returned with the bill, and Alex waved them away. Jack stood and pulled out her chair.

She'd have some explaining to do next week. Becca probably wouldn't let the plane leave the ground before she drilled Libby for more details about Jack. But tonight she didn't care. She hadn't enjoyed dinner with a man this much in a long time. Jack fit comfortably with her family and friends, which was important to her.

They strolled to the car, and he opened her door. Once they both buckled in, he grinned at her. "I had a great time tonight."

"Me too. Sorry about Becca. She comes on strong. I think she

223

was born with a big personality to make up for her small stature."

"I like her." Jack started the car. "At first, I assumed she was your other sister. You favor her."

"Weird, isn't it? I don't look like either of my sisters, but Becca and I have the same coloring. Except for the eyes. Aren't her blue eyes gorgeous? You'll have to meet Amy sometime." She babbled as he drove, nervousness crashing over her. Something changed during dinner, but she didn't want to be the one to bring it up. She took a deep breath to calm herself. "Are you sure you're okay with this, Jack? It might be a late night."

He shrugged. "Beats going home and going to bed early. I enjoy seeing you with your family. You needed this."

"I did. Thanks for coming along."

"It was my pleasure, Libby James."

She sat back in her seat and let the little thrill at the way he said her name run through her.

When everyone arrived at the office, Libby showed them around while Jack started the coffee. He had to be sick of people asking to see the rooms. Earlier today, he'd confided that his mom planned to come by and check out the changes soon.

The tour began in the lobby, and the group made their way around the office. The last stop was Libby's favorite. Aptly named, the small conference room held a round table surrounded by six chairs in the center. Libby had added a little cart in the corner with a black coffee service on top and the mugs on the lower shelf. All of the photographs she chose to use were black and white with at least one element in each colorized.

The picture of a bride and groom kissing with the wedding party standing around them revealed the purple roses in the bride's bouquet as well as in the boutonnieres and the bridesmaids' flowers. Another photo, probably an engagement portrait, captured a man and woman near a body of water. The man held a red umbrella over their heads as they stood wrapped in an embrace. The third wall held a framed picture of a four-tiered wedding cake. Delicate green calla lilies and yellow roses made from gum paste flowed from the top to the bottom of the cake covered with white fondant.

Two smaller portraits of children hung on the last wall. The first of a little girl, about two years old, lying on the ground with her chin in her hands staring at a field of yellow wildflowers. The other one was of a boy in a diaper holding a bunch of light blue helium balloons. It gave the impression the balloons held him up as he took his first steps.

Everyone complimented her work, and she thanked them. The men excused themselves, leaving her alone with Callie and Becca. She wondered if the two women had called each other on the way over and orchestrated this. It seemed Becca couldn't wait until Sunday for answers.

Callie stepped in front of her and studied her face. "Are you sure you're okay, Libby?"

"I am, Cal. I promise." If she wanted Callie to believe her, she needed to tell her everything. "Loud noises sometimes take me by surprise, and I'm anxious and a panicked in tight spaces, but I'm eating again and sleeping through the night. We've put some protocols in place to keep this from happening in the future. Kevin and Jack will make sure none of us gets caught in a situation like that again."

"What kind of protocols?" Callie squeezed her shoulder.

"None of us will leave an event room alone, and if anyone is bothering us, we'll tell one of the men about it." Libby narrowed her eyes at Callie. "The guys aren't giving Jack the third degree are they?"

Callie exchanged a glance with Becca.

Libby knew she'd guessed right. "Poor Jack!"

"It didn't look like *poor Jack* during dinner." Becca scooted closer and dropped her voice. "He drove you?"

"Not a big deal, Bec. It didn't make sense to take separate cars when we both left from here."

"What about the hand holding?"

Heat filled her face, and her eyes widened at Becca's question. She'd been certain no one could see them.

"I knew it!" Becca's grin was a mixture of excitement and smugness. "That answers my question. Your eyes always give you away, Libby. He *was* holding your hand."

"He was being supportive. Since Saturday, Jack's been protective of me."

"Why is that?" Callie asked.

"I have no idea." Until this evening, she thought he felt responsible for what happened. But had he held her hand out of guilt or was there more to it?

THIRTY-FOUR

"We can't thank you enough for taking care of Libby," Chris said and he and Alex joined Jack in the kitchen. "Thank you for saving her from a horrible situation."

Jack didn't think he deserved their thanks. If he'd paid closer attention, it wouldn't have happened in the first place. "I wish she'd mentioned something earlier. Emily said the guys hung around her at the ceremony and waited for them at the reception."

"Guys wanting to spend their time with Lib is not an uncommon occurrence." Chris clamped a large hand on Jack's shoulder. "You couldn't have predicted this."

Chris's assurance didn't ease Jack's guilt over the situation, or "the incident" as Libby called it.

"It's the same with Callie," Chris said. "Guys are drawn to the James sisters. We've never worried about Lib since most of the guys she hangs out with are from her church."

Jack cleared his throat. "We discussed putting some precautions into place." It had been the first item on yesterday's meeting agenda. He wouldn't allow this to happen to any of the women who worked for him again. After he explained what the group had discussed, he added, "I'm sure Logan will agree to look after Libby when he starts next month."

"Logan Griffin?" Chris glanced up from pulling the desserts out of the grocery bags.

"Yes. He's our new in-house photographer. Why do you ask?"

"I'm surprised to hear his name. Libby dated him for about a year during college. She's okay working with him?"

"She recommended him. Emily did tell me they'd dated, and I spoke with each of them to make sure their history wasn't going to cause any discomfort. I also asked Libby to let me know if things become strained."

"She won't say anything," Alex said. "Our women are stubborn."

Jack ignored the "our women" comment. Libby didn't belong to him. "That's why I asked Emily to tell me if Libby mentions anything to her."

The ladies entered the room, cutting their conversation short. Libby caught Jack's eye and mouthed *sorry*. He shrugged to indicate it didn't bother him. These people cared about her.

As soon as everyone had something to drink, they settled around the table. A plate of brownies and another of cannoli sat in the center. Libby took one of each.

Becca rolled her eyes. "Sometimes I hate you, Lib."

"Women say that to me all the time." Libby batted her eyelashes at her friend.

Chris, Callie, and Jack laughed. Alex whispered something in Becca's ear that made her blush. Jack watched how these men loved their wives. The way they interacted with the women proved their admiration. Had his father ever looked at his mother that way? Memories of hurtful, angry words and screaming matches overshadowed any recollection of love or affection.

"What are you doing next?" Becca waved her hand around the kitchen.

Evidently understanding her meaning, Libby said, "Kevin's office." She looked between her sister and brother-in-law. "I may need someone to build me a partition."

"You know we'll do it, Lib, but you should ask Dad." Callie wiped her hands on a napkin and turned to her sister. "He's a little hurt you haven't asked for his help yet, especially since Chris spent a day here."

"He volunteered, and you were already coming to town for your restoration project." Libby's tone was defensive. "I didn't want to ask Dad to make the drive."

"Since he's been cutting back hours at the R and R while he considers retirement, he won't mind."

Libby explained the abbreviation to Jack. "Dad runs a remodeling and renovation business. We shorten it—R and R." She focused on Callie. "He wants to retire?"

"Oh." Callie covered her mouth with her fingers. "I forgot they haven't told you yet. He and Mom want to travel and work on mission projects. I think they miss their time in Peru. Call him, Lib."

"I will." She paused. "Tomorrow."

The group sat and talked until Alex stretched and said they needed to get back to their kids. It was almost eleven, and everyone worked the next day, so the party broke up. When Libby offered to clean up, Jack refused, insisting she go home and rest. After a flurry of activity and a round of goodbyes, Jack stood in the now silent break room. Watching Libby with her friends and family encouraged him, but the confirmation he loved her did not.

He shouldn't have held her hand tonight. He'd spent the rest of the evening trying to find any excuse to do it again. When she mentioned another date with Brandon on Friday night, Jack was reminded he had no clue where he stood with her. She obviously considered him a friend, but was there a possibility of more? She'd held his hand tonight—twice. Jack blew out a long breath. He sounded like a woman with all of this inner turmoil.

Before he drove home, he sent Kevin a text and asked if they could meet before work. He needed to talk to a neutral party.

Kevin replied right away. *My place. 7:00. Coffee will be hot.*

After handing Jack a cup of coffee, Kevin settled on the chair across from him.

Jack stared at the dark liquid in his mug. "Where's Amber?"

"Garden. What's up? Did you call your dad?"

"No. He's leaving town tomorrow. I'm sure he'll disappear again."

Kevin set his cup on the coffee table in front of him. "Are you sure you want to let him leave without hearing him out?"

Jack jerked his head up. "Positive. He's getting a small taste of what I've dealt with for fourteen years."

"Careful, Jack." Kevin's eyebrows lifted. "Hurt and anger I can understand. Those are normal emotions in circumstances like this, but your words carry a lot of bitterness. You're making a conscious choice to hold on to that."

Jack shrugged. Sure he was bitter, but didn't he have the right? The man had left him and never looked back, never apologized. His own father didn't care about his family, only himself. It was selfish.

"If it's not about your dad, what did you want to talk about?"

Kevin rested his elbows on his knees.

Jack massaged the back of his neck to ease some of the tension. "I went to dinner last night with Libby, her sister, brother-in-law, and a couple of their friends."

"And?"

Time to say it out loud. "I'm in love with her."

Kevin chuckled. "About time you figured that out."

"I started to consider the possibility Saturday night. After spending the evening with her and her family, I'm certain."

"What are you going to do about it?"

"Nothing. We need her this summer, and she needs the job." He may as well talk about all of it. "She's dating some other guy, I have no idea how she feels about me, and she deserves someone willing to give her everything I can't."

"Why can't you give her everything?"

Why was Kevin answering everything with more questions? "I can't give her marriage."

"Can't or won't? Because I think you'd make a terrific husband. You've learned the hard way what kind of man you don't want to be. And we've done enough weddings that you know what love is. If you can't quote I Corinthians 13:4-8, I'll be disappointed."

Jack released a staccato laugh. "I don't think I'll ever forget it."

"Prove it," Kevin said. "Recite the verses."

Normally, he said the verses with disdain. The sentiment was nice; he just didn't believe anyone could attain the standard. He approached the verses differently today with Libby on his mind. He wished this for her.

"Love is patient, love is kind. It does not envy, it does not boast, it is not proud. It does not dishonor others, it is not self-seeking, it is not easily angered, it keeps no record of wrongs. Love does not delight in evil but rejoices with the truth. It always protects, always trusts, always hopes, always perseveres. Love never fails." He shrugged, a slight smile on his lips.

"That's the first time you've quoted that passage without sarcasm. You're starting to reconsider your stance on marriage, and it scares you to death."

"I won't hurt Libby the way my dad did Mom and me."

"You are not your dad." Kevin stood and walked to the window. He peered outside before glancing at Jack. "Libby's leaving for a couple of weeks, and you'll get some distance. Use the time to study Biblical marriage and pray about God's will in this."

"I like the way you think." He would gain some perspective without Libby's presence shading his judgment. "Thanks, Kev."

"And talk to your dad, Jack. You can't be the man she deserves until you tell him how he's hurt you."

Jack left Kevin's home with a mixture of hope and dread. He'd talk to his dad but not face-to-face. If he waited to call next week, his father would be out of town and unable to request a meeting in person. With that decision made, he committed to spending the next two weeks in prayer and study. Perhaps he would even call and make an appointment with one of the pastors at the church.

You're going to have to make this abundantly clear, Lord. My heart wants more with Libby, but my head doubts my decision. Give me the courage to speak with Dad and the patience to wait on your answer about a relationship.

THIRTY-FIVE

"Welcome home! How was Hawaii? We missed you. I have so much to tell you." Emily chatted as Libby threw her luggage in the back seat of her car.

Once the bags were loaded, she hopped in the passenger seat so they could leave the airport pick-up area. "Can we get dinner? I've been traveling all day, and those airline snacks do not fill you up."

Emily's head bobbed up and down. "I thought you might be hungry. I'm all yours tonight. You look gorgeous, by the way."

"Thanks." She ran a hand through her hair. "Becca treated us to a spa day that included manicures, pedicures, massages, and new hairstyles. I'm thrilled to have some of the blond back."

"You got a pretty fantastic tan too." Emily changed lanes and glanced at her. "I want to hear everything. Did you lose weight? Only you could lose weight on vacation. I bet you ate a ton too.

"Chasing the kids around kept me active." So did taking the stairs to the seventh floor every time she went to her room. The panic attacks in small spaces had gotten worse. When they arrived at the hotel, Libby struggled in the elevator despite her family surrounding her. She used the stairs the remainder of her stay.

"Where would you like to eat?"

233

"How about the Chinese place by the apartment?"

"The one with the buffet?"

Libby rested her hand on Emily's forearm. "I haven't eaten a real meal since breakfast, Em. The place with the buffet is the only choice."

As Emily drove, Libby shared the highlights of her trip. She'd spent quite a bit of time with the kids, but since the hotel offered a day camp for them, she also had plenty of free time. Alex and Chris took over childcare a couple evenings to allow the ladies to spend some time together.

Over the past two weeks, she'd observed Chris and Alex with their wives. The two men loved their families deeply. She had no doubt her parents loved each other, or that Amy's husband thought the world of her. Libby longed for someone who made her a better person simply by being with him, someone to cherish and protect her. By the end of her trip, her prayers revolved around one man in particular.

When Libby had gone to dinner with Brandon before her vacation, she agreed to meet him again when she returned. She'd keep the date, but after many discussions about both Brandon and Jack with Becca and Callie, she decided this would be their final one.

It wasn't fair to string Brandon along when she felt so strongly about Jack. Because these were the secret longings of her heart, and her friend would only argue in favor of Brandon, Libby didn't share any of this with Emily.

After piling food on her plate at the buffet, Libby returned to the booth. Emily shook her head. "Someday you're not going to be able to eat like this, Lib."

"All the more reason to enjoy it now." She folded her hands on the table. "I'll pray."

Her eyelids closed. "Thank you, Lord, for vacation and a season of rest. Thank you for friends who pick me up from the airport. Bless our evening and the food. Be with us this week. Amen."

"Amen." Emily picked up her fork.

"What's going on with you, Em? Did you and Adam go out last night?"

Emily beamed and bounced in her seat. "We did." She laid her left hand on the table.

Libby's stomach fell as the diamond on her friend's finger caught the light.

"He proposed last weekend." Emily squealed with excitement. "I'm getting married!"

"Isn't this kind of soon?"

She leaned back in her seat, folded her arms in front of her, and glared across the table. "Aren't you happy for me?"

"I am. Really." She forced a smile. "Adam's a great guy, and I guess you've known each other for a long time."

"We talked about how fast everything happened," Emily said. "I mean, we've dated less than two months, but we both believe we're with the person God's chosen for us. You just know when it's right sometimes. No guy treats me the way Adam does. He's my friend, Libby."

"Did he tell Chris?"

After thinking about it for a few seconds, she shook her head. "I don't think so. He hadn't even told his mom he planned to ask. We called her after."

"What about his dad?"

"Called him too. He's going to fly out for the wedding."

"You set a date?"

The radiant smile returned. "The first weekend in November. Will you be my maid of honor? You won't need to do much. Jack said he'd do everything at cost for me, and I already know which vendors I want to work with. But I want you to do the flowers."

"You told Jack before me? Why didn't you call?"

"You needed to hear this in person. And the only reason Jack knows is because he overheard me thanking Adam for the beautiful roses he sent. I may have told him I couldn't wait to marry him. You didn't answer my question yet. Will you be my maid of honor?"

"Of course I will." Libby grinned. A genuine one this time as she caught Emily's enthusiasm. "It will be an honor. And consider the flowers handled."

Silence filled the air as they resumed eating, and Libby processed the news. Her life kept changing. First a new job then Brandon and Jack. Now she was about to lose her best friend and roommate.

Libby gawked at Emily. "You're moving."

"That didn't take long," Emily said with compassion. "I'll move out of the apartment, but we're staying in Raleigh. I'm happy with my job. Adam's going to look for work here."

"Callie will hire him. New Life contracts enough projects in Raleigh, he wouldn't have to travel."

"I told him the same thing, but he wants to find something on his own. He loves Chris and Callie like family, but he's worked with Chris since high school and wants a new challenge. He does incredible woodwork. We're praying he finds something that allows him to use his talent."

"I know someone who might be interested. I'll call and check this week."

"Thanks. I hoped you'd have some suggestions. Adam and I are going to start looking for a house soon. Will you help decorate when we find a place?"

Libby waved her hand in dismissal. "You don't even have to ask."

"Will you be okay on your own? Financially? I talked to the apartment manager," Emily said. "He has a couple of one bedrooms opening up in October and will adjust the lease for you. Since we just signed a new one last month, I won't leave you in a bind."

"Don't worry about me." Libby took a sip of her drink. "Maybe I'll look for a new place or stay in our apartment and use your room as an office while I build my client base."

"You made a decision?" Emily straightened in her seat. "You're going to freelance?"

"I am. Becca convinced me this is the direction God's leading me." Libby smiled, excited about her new endeavor. "We discussed it a lot in Hawaii. I want to do this. Becca's already making a list of potential clients, and Alex offered to get me up and running."

"Will it cost a lot?" Emily's forehead creased.

"I'll take out a small business loan. Alex and Becca offered to invest. Becca said everything worked out with Callie and New Life Restorations, and she had no doubt another James sister will succeed."

"Good. With their support, you'll be set."

"I declined their offer. If I do this, I won't take any handouts."

"There's no shame in accepting assistance." Emily pushed her empty plate aside. "Alex and Becca's offer may seem like charity, but they believe in you. I believe in you. Don't stick your nose up at this because of some misguided notion they're trying to coddle you. Alex is serious about investing. If he didn't have faith in your success, he wouldn't let Becca talk him into giving you money."

Libby sighed. "I'll think about it. Becca said we'd talk about it next month. Whatever my final decision is about the finances, this is my future."

"This is exciting, Lib." Emily clapped her hands together. "You'll thrive on your own. You might even get some calls soon. We've gotten so many compliments on the changes to the office, Jack asked me to put your business cards out."

"That explains the voicemail I got yesterday." The call had confused her. "Someone called and asked me to redecorate their home office."

"Do it," Emily said. "Use your free time and get started."

"Not until September, Em. I made a commitment to Jack for the summer. He asked me to work on the rest of the office space."

"He told us during the staff meeting the Tuesday after you left." Her brows knit together. "He's been acting strangely. I'm not sure how to describe it. He almost seems…perky? No, that's not the right word."

She shook her head. "We had two wedding consults this week, and he didn't scowl once. He offered to take care of everything for my wedding before I asked."

"That was generous of him."

"Yes, and out of character. Do you think he met someone? A woman?"

Libby's heart missed a beat. She never considered the

possibility. "Wouldn't you know if he did?"

"Me?" Emily pressed a hand to her chest. "No. Kevin might, though. It's so weird."

"Has he had a girlfriend since you've worked for him?" She wasn't sure why she asked. Did she want to know the answer to that question?

Emily's paused to consider it. "There might have been someone when I first started working there. No one liked her, though. She was always hanging around and talking to Jack. I don't remember him taking her out. At the time, I figured he was being polite." She shrugged. "Wouldn't that be the craziest thing? If Jack, who's against marriage, ended up falling in love?"

Libby bit the inside of her cheek. Did she need everyone reminding her of Jack's opinion of marriage? "I'm going to get some more to eat," she said, attempting to get away from the conversation. "Can I get you anything else?"

"No. I'm good. Get whatever you want."

If only life was that simple.

Libby spent the morning shopping before making her way to the office. Her dad would come up next weekend and install the partition he'd been working on for her. Both of her parents were driving up to spend a couple days with her. They claimed they wanted to spend time with her before she got too busy with events, but she suspected they desired to make check on her state of mind after the incident. Getting away had been good for her.

Once she arrived at work, Libby's entire plan for the day was to finish painting Kevin's office. As she unlocked the back door, an older woman drove up beside her and rolled down her car window.

"What are you doing?" The woman leaned her head and shoulders out of the car.

Libby peered down at the keys in her hand then back at the woman. For some reason, the question confounded her and put her on the defensive. Why should she explain what she was doing? "I work here."

"You're Libby! The conference rooms and lobby are beautiful. I can't wait to see what else you come up with."

Unsure how to answer, she stared at the stranger, certain they'd never met. This woman was obviously familiar with the place, but Libby didn't feel comfortable inviting her inside.

As if sensing her unease, the woman said, "Oh, I'm sorry. We haven't officially met yet. I'm Rachel Price. Jack's mom."

Libby's heart rate returned to normal, and she smiled at the woman. With her concern ebbing, Libby saw the resemblance. Jack's brown eyes came from his mom. "I don't think he's in. His car's not here." It was the first thing she'd noticed when she pulled into the parking lot.

"Oh, I know. I just hung up with him. Since I'm in the area, he told me I could drop off a couple boxes for him. I cleaned out my garage this weekend."

"Let me unlock the door, and I'll help you carry them inside."

"Thank you, dear. Jack said you were kind, but he didn't mention how pretty you are."

Grateful her new tan hid most of her blush, Libby uttered a quiet "thank you."

"I'm only stating the truth. Go ahead and open the door while I park."

Libby and Jack's mom—Rachel—unloaded the boxes from her car and set them in a corner of Jack's office. They visited for an hour before Rachel left. Libby liked the woman. She talked about her son with a smile on her face and pride in her voice. After extracting a promise to join her for dinner sometime, Rachel left Libby to her painting.

Libby lost track of the time and rushed to clean up. Even if she got everything done in the next few minutes, she'd barely make it on time to meet Brandon. After picking up an armload of supplies and carrying them to the storage room, she set everything on the floor in order to organize as she put them away. The door clicked shut, and her movements stilled as she processed the sound.

No, no, no! She forgot to prop the door open. It locked automatically, and you couldn't open it from inside. Stupid ancient buildings. Libby dug for her cell phone. Emily would come let her out. She groaned when her fingers brushed the bottom of her empty pocket. Her phone was on Kevin's desk.

Her breathing became ragged in tandem with her increasing anxiety. It was after seven, and no one would come until tomorrow morning. She focused on inhaling long breaths and tried not to think about spending the night in the tiny space. Latching on to the door handle, she pulled with all her strength. It didn't budge.

She sank to the floor, pressed her back against the shelves, and hugged her knees to her chest. *I can't do this, Lord. Please help me.* Tears came as she rested her forehead on her knees.

THIRTY-SIX

I understand, Mom. I'm sorry, but you didn't warn me before today you planned to come by." Jack had been on the phone for an hour, and his mom kept bringing up the fact he'd been absent from the office when she stopped by.

He'd worked from home. Since Libby arrived back in town yesterday, he assumed she'd most likely go in. His mother confirmed his hunch when she told him all about meeting her. He missed Libby but hadn't come to a decision about their relationship. Avoiding the office—and her—was necessary.

When his cell phone beeped, he glanced at the screen as Emily's name and number flashed across. "Mom, I need to go. Emily's on the other line. I should make sure everything's okay."

"All right. Invite Libby to lunch on Sunday. I like her."

He held back a groan. His mother approved of every unattached female under the age of thirty. "Good night, Mom."

Emily had left a message, but he skipped the voicemail and called her back.

"Jack?"

"Yeah. What's up?"

"Was Libby at the office when you left?" Her voice strained as if trying to hold her emotions in check.

"I didn't go in today. What's wrong, Emily?" The muscles in his neck and shoulders tensed.

"Libby didn't show up for her date with Brandon. I know she remembered because she reminded me she'd be home late. Brandon tried to call her a few times. Since he doesn't have my number, he called Adam, who just now got the message and called me." Her words ran over each other.

"Did you try her cell?"

"Several times." Emily's volume increased. "She doesn't answer."

"What time was she meeting Brandon?"

"Seven."

Jack glanced at the clock, almost ten. Libby wouldn't show up three hours late for anything. Had those guys from the wedding tracked her down? He tried to focus on Emily's voice.

"He waited thirty minutes before he called her the first time. When she answered or called him back after an hour, he grew concerned and called Adam. I'm going to the office. Something's wrong."

"I'll go," he said. He wouldn't allow her to walk into a bad situation. "Stay at your place in case she comes home. Call if she shows up."

"Thank you, Jack. Call me back when you get there."

He grabbed his keys and wallet from the table and jogged to his car. He prayed while he drove, trying not to imagine every horrible scenario. As his headlights illuminated her car in the parking lot, he breathed a short sigh of relief, but his worry about what he might find inside didn't allow him to relax.

Not bothering with a parking spot, he threw the car into Park, shut it off, and jumped out. He unlocked the back door of the building and listened. A cell phone—Libby's?—rang.

"Libby?" He struggled to find a volume she could hear but wouldn't frighten her as he fought his own escalating panic. "Libby, you here?"

He peeked in her office. Empty. He checked Kevin's next. Her cell phone sat on his desk. After setting his phone and keys down, he went to search the other rooms. She wasn't anywhere.

At the door to his office, he called out again. "Libby? Are you in here?" *Please help me find her, Lord.* "Libby?"

"Who's there?" The muffled voice was faint.

He spoke louder. "Where are you, Libby?"

"Jack? I'm in here." Pounding on the storage room door revealed her location. "Jack, get me out of here."

"I left my keys in the other room. I'll be right back."

"Hurry, please."

Was she crying? He ran to Kevin's office and back. When he opened the door, Libby flew out of the closet, threw her arms around his waist, and buried her face against his chest. Her entire body trembled.

He wrapped his arms around her and held her close. "You're safe now."

"Thank you, Jack." She sniffed. "I wasn't going to make it in there all night."

"You would have managed. You're strong. What happened?" Despite the adrenaline coursing through him, despite her fear, he reveled in the weight of her in his arms, her nearness.

She rested her cheek on his shoulder. "I was in a hurry and forgot to prop the door open."

"I didn't realize you're claustrophobic."

"I never used to be until ..." She didn't finish, but he understood what had triggered her anxiety in tight spaces. Being trapped between a wall and a man had done its damage. If he ever saw those two again, he didn't know if he'd be able to restrain himself from causing them pain.

"I see." He loosened his arms around her, unwilling to remind her of that night. A locksmith would be coming to fix the door first thing tomorrow.

Libby tightened her. "Don't let go. Please."

"Whatever you need, Libby." He held her again, and dropped a kiss on top of her head, a head that held more blond than before and smelled of coconut.

"How did you know I was here?" She peered up at him through long lashes.

"Emily called. I guess your date tried to call you. When he couldn't reach you, he called Adam, who in turn called Emily."

"Oh no. Brandon must hate me."

"If he knows you at all, he doesn't hate you."

She tipped her head back further, and Jack got a close-up view as her eyes widened at his comment. "You have the most beautiful eyes. They're so expressive."

He felt, as much as heard, her breath hitch as he bent his head. His lips brushed hers in a feather light kiss. Not satisfied with that, Jack went back for more. Her smooth, soft lips responded.

"Jack?" she whispered when he broke the connection. Her

eyes shone, the gold strands more pronounced.

What was he thinking? He shouldn't have done that for so many reasons but couldn't bring himself to apologize. Given the opportunity to do it again, he'd take it.

"Call Emily and let her know you're okay." He pushed her away. "She's worried about you."

A shadow fell across Libby's face, and the brightness in her eyes faded. She nodded and left the room.

"Tell her I'm driving you home," he called after her and sank onto his desk. *What now, Lord? I don't want to scare her.* He spent the next several minutes in prayer.

"Can we talk about what just happened?" She leaned against the door and watched him.

"Sure." He stood. "You didn't get dinner. Let's talk while you eat."

She seemed to be arguing with herself. Apparently her hunger was as pressing as her desire to talk.

Jack bit back a chuckle. She was irresistible. "Come on. I can't promise anything fancy, but I'll buy you dinner."

"Let me get my bag."

He followed her across the lobby and frowned when she shivered. "Are you cold?"

"A little." She rubbed her hands up and down her arms. "I'll be okay."

"Where are the boxes my mom brought earlier?"

"In the back corner of your office."

"Hang on." He located them and dug in one until he found an old sweatshirt. When he returned to the front room, he handed it to Libby. "This'll warm you up."

She slipped it over her head. It swallowed her up, but he liked seeing her in his shirt. It was intimate somehow.

"Thanks." She rolled the sleeves to her wrists.

"You're welcome. Let's get out of here."

He drove down a main road with several restaurants and asked Libby what sounded good. She chose Wendy's. When they realized the dining room was closed, she suggested they use the drive-thru. He agreed and ordered her dinner and a drink for himself. His mouth had dried up in anticipation of the coming conversation. He wanted to be honest but didn't want his strong emotions to overwhelm her.

"Did you tell Emily we were stopping?" he asked.

"I texted and told her not to wait up." Libby giggled. "She thinks you have a girlfriend."

His head jerked toward her, and his jaw hung open. "What?"

"She said you've been in a good mood the past couple weeks and wondered whether you met someone."

"I wouldn't have kissed you if I had a girlfriend."

"I know. Too bad I can't say the same thing. But to be fair, I planned to end things with Brandon tonight." She let out a long huff of air. "I suppose that conversation will now take place over the phone."

Jack's heart rate kicked up. "You're breaking up with him?"

"Yes. I couldn't give him false hope when I'm interested in someone else." Her gaze landed on him. "Your turn, Jack."

"I'm not going to apologize, Libby. I've wanted to kiss you for a few weeks."

She smiled.

"But we can't do it again."

The smile fell. "I understand."

"No, I don't think you do." He shifted in his seat. "I like you, Libby James. More so than any woman I've met. When the summer's over, and you're no longer working for me, I'd like to take you on a proper date."

"I like you too, Jack." She set her food aside and laid her head back against the seat. "It's going to be a long summer."

"Yes, it will. And now I get to make things even more awkward. Mom wanted me to invite you to lunch this Sunday."

"My parents are coming this weekend."

"Mom will understand." He grasped her hand, ready to lay everything out in the open. "Look, Libby, this is going to be extremely difficult for me. All I want to do right now is kiss you again. We need to be careful not to put ourselves in situations where we're alone."

"Can't we keep it a secret?"

He ran his thumb across her knuckles. "I won't sneak around like we're doing something wrong. That's not fair to you. Besides, Emily would figure it out."

"In two seconds." Libby released his hand. "You better take me home."

THIRTY-SEVEN

Tuesday morning before work, Libby picked up her phone for the fourth time in fifteen minutes. This time, she refused to put it back down. Callie would be up, and Libby longed to talk with someone.

"Hi, Lib."

"Jack kissed me last night."

The silence on the other end of the phone stretched until Callie replied. "What?"

Libby smirked at her sister's shock. She recounted everything—beginning with her clumsy move of locking herself in the storage room and ending with the conversation in Jack's car.

"This may be a good thing," Callie said. "It gives you the opportunity to watch Jack interact with others. See if he's more agreeable at weddings. If he's still negative, you have your answer about whether he's changing his mind about marriage. You won't risk a relationship that won't go anywhere."

The only problem with that? Libby *wanted* a relationship with him. "I'll think about it."

"Pray about it," Callie said.

"I will."

"Chris and I are praying as well. If I need to send Chris to have a heart-to-heart with Jack, let me know."

249

Libby laughed. "That would drive him away for sure."

"How are you dealing with Emily's news?" Callie's tone grew serious again.

"It took me by surprise. Their engagement happened so fast, but she's happier than I've ever seen her. And Adam's a prince."

"He's thrilled. We're sad to lose him. He's family. I offered him a job on the Raleigh crew, but he turned me down."

"Em and I talked about that. Is he as good at woodworking as she says?"

"Better." Callie's instant answer left no doubt in Libby's mind. "His attention to detail is remarkable. Ask him to show you some of his carvings."

"I will. There aren't a lot of places interested in those skills, but I know a guy who might be. He creates custom furniture."

"Of course you do." Callie chuckled. "You remind me of Becca—always getting what you want."

"I'm not bossy, am I?"

"No. I didn't mean that. You're tenacious when you want something. Everyone already loves you. When you ask a favor, it's granted."

"Shut up, Callie. I should finish getting ready for work. I love you."

"Love you too. Call if you need anything. We'll be in the city most of the summer. Let's get lunch soon."

"Sounds good. I'll call you once I get back into the swing of things."

For the remainder of the week, Libby threw herself into decorating Kevin's space. With no assignments for the next two events, she'd focus on the office. Mid-month, she planned to take some responsibilities away from Emily. Jack requested she handle the décor and flowers for any events not yet contracted. And she'd double check on the existing contracts to avoid any last minute snags.

They were hosting a family reunion at a local park on Saturday. Per the family's request, An Affair to Remember had hired a caterer to serve a full southern barbecue meal. Complete with barbecue chicken, pulled pork, corn on the cob, macaroni and cheese, collard greens, and cornbread. Since there weren't decorations or flowers to worry about, she'd returned at a good time to ease back into a routine after her vacation.

When she got home Friday night, she met Adam in the parking lot.

"Thanks again for setting up that interview, Libby."

"You're welcome." She started up the stairs with him trailing behind her. "How'd it go?"

"I think it went well. He sure carried on about you." His footsteps clanged on the metal steps. "I don't know what it is about you and your sisters, but people love you."

"If you get the job, you'd better not change his opinion of me. He's my go-to person for unique pieces."

Adam's steps faltered. "I wouldn't dream of it."

Libby turned around and patted his shoulder. "I'm joking,

Adam. I checked your references before I made the recommendation."

"You mean Chris?"

"No. Callie. Between her praises and Em's, I had to make the call. You owe me one."

"Only if I get the job," he shot back as she opened the front door. "Emily mentioned all you're doing at her office. Let me know if I can help."

Adam's face lit up when he saw Emily waiting on the couch. His reaction reassured Libby he was the right man for Emily.

"Aren't you supposed to be offering to help me? My best friend's got you wrapped around her little finger before you even get here." Emily clucked her tongue.

He crossed the room and kissed her cheek. "But you hold my heart, Em. I love you."

"Good answer." She beamed at him and stood. "I love you too. Ready?"

They said goodbye to Libby and left. She took the seat Emily had just vacated on the couch and got lost in thought until her cell phone chimed. When she picked it up and read the text message, a grin stretched her cheeks. Jack.

JACK: I missed talking to you this week.

LIBBY: Me too.

JACK: What are you doing tonight?

LIBBY: Nothing. Emily and Adam just left for dinner.

As she waited for his response, her phone rang and she answered the call.

"I'd rather hear your voice," Jack said. "Is this okay?"

She smiled and settled into the corner of the couch. "More than okay."

They talked for two hours. Libby asked his opinion about the sketches she'd given him. They talked about work, her vacation, and their dreams for their careers. He said he would stay home on Mondays until she finished everything at the office. She asked him to make an exception this week since her parents would be with her. When he said it was getting late, she reluctantly agreed and said good night.

Libby's parents arrived early Sunday morning so they could attend church with her. When they got there, they found seats and settled in for the service. The church was larger than the one her parents went to, the one she went to as a teenager, but Libby enjoyed the teaching.

The service ended, and Jack came to greet them. Libby's dad invited him to lunch.

"I'd love to, but today's my monthly lunch date with my mom. Since the guest she hoped to join us isn't able to come, she's only got me to keep her company."

He studied Libby's face as if trying to memorize every detail. After several seconds, he turned to her parents. "Can I treat you to dinner tomorrow night to show my appreciation for your help with the office?"

"That sounds delightful." Libby's mom's gaze bounced between Jack and Libby.

They talked for a few more minutes until Jack excused himself, and they all left. The three members of the James family ate and visited before returning to Libby's apartment to change. They squeezed into the cab of her dad's truck and made a stop at The Home Depot before going to the office. They'd work all afternoon, pick up dinner on the way back to Libby's place, and relax that evening.

Libby pointed out several projects her dad could assist with before installing the partition tomorrow. Once he got started on the first chore, Libby and her mom moved to the kitchen.

"Jack seems like a nice man." Amanda James poured paint into a tray.

"He is." With her back to her mom, Libby smiled as she ran the roller against the wall. Her reaction to his name came automatically.

"I think he likes you."

"He does." An answer to her prayers.

"And you like him. I can tell you're smiling right now."

She spun around. Her family claimed her eyes gave away her emotions, and she wanted her mom to see her sincerity. "I do, Mom. It's crazy since we only met two months ago, but it's like I've known him my entire life. He's easy to talk to and he cares about me. He asks if I'm working too much and he's allowing me to redecorate the entire office."

Amanda smiled softly. "And he's your personal knight, come to your rescue."

"A couple times now." She explained locking herself in the closet last week, leaving out the part about their amazing kiss.

"Why hasn't he done anything about the way he feels, sweet girl?"

"Because he's my boss. He asked me on a date when the summer's over. We also agreed not to be in the office alone together. Neither of us wants the temptation."

"I'm glad he's considered that. Are you all right with waiting?"

"It will be hard. I enjoy talking to Jack and missed our conversations last week. He called Friday night, and we spoke over the phone. We decided to continue that once a week so we can learn more about each other."

"I suppose we'd better get to know this man." Amanda resumed painting. "Dinner tomorrow should be enlightening."

"Please don't say anything to Dad. Not yet."

"I won't. You talked to Callie?"

"Yeah. I called her Tuesday morning."

"I thought so. I'm glad you two are close. We worried about leaving you with her when we spent that time in Peru while you were in high school. God worked a few miracles that year."

"Yes, he did." Not only had she and her sisters grown closer, but Callie became a Christian and fell in love with Chris Graham. "Callie and Amy are my friends now instead of only bossy older sisters."

"I'm sorry you didn't have a sibling closer to your age like they did."

"That's not your fault. I couldn't ask for a better childhood." Her parents had always been available to her, and she never doubted their love. *Unlike Jack.* Her heart squeezed as she thought of how much his father missed out. Yet, he'd become a remarkable man even without a father's guidance.

THIRTY-EIGHT

Jack sat at his desk on Monday morning and grinned as Libby's laughter floated from the kitchen where she and her mom painted. He'd done a quick survey of their progress when he first arrived. They'd finish in the kitchen before the end of the day.

He again considered calling his dad. It was easy to get wrapped up in work and find reasons to delay the discussion. His plan to call the man while Libby was gone got pushed aside.

In truth, he didn't know if he could talk to him. He could think of nothing his dad might tell him that would excuse the man's absence. Forgiving him didn't seem possible.

David James walked past his office, and Jack latched onto the distraction. "Can I help you with anything, Mr. James?"

Libby's dad stopped in the doorway. "Please call me David. If you can spare a few minutes, I could use a hand."

"Sure." Jack followed him to Kevin's office and glanced around the room. "Wow, this doesn't even look the same."

"My Libby is talented." Pride shined on the older man's face.

"I agree. She said you made the partition." He walked around to the other side of a panel leaned against the desk and examined it. Shallow shelves were built into each side, an ingenious way to split the space and give both Kevin and Logan extra storage. The dark divider complemented the sage green walls.

"Libby came up with the concept and called with an explanation and measurements. This is the result. If you'll hold these while I anchor them, I'll install this beast."

Jack held the first panel while David attached it to the wall. He connected the second panel to the first. They repeated the process until all four panels split most of the office in half.

As Libby's dad walked around them, he tested their stability. "A little wobbly. I think it needs more support if they're going to use the shelves. Will you get Libby?"

Jack crossed to the kitchen and stopped at the door. Libby stood on the ladder and talked animatedly about her vacation. Last week had been absolute torture. Every night he'd dreamed of holding her in his arms again and replayed their kiss a thousand times. He cleared his throat, as much to distract himself as to alert the women of his presence.

When Libby twisted toward him, he said, "Your dad wants your opinion on the partition."

She set her paintbrush on the edge of the tray and climbed down. "I'll be right back."

"Take your time." Amanda James focused her gaze on him. "Jack can keep me company."

Libby's steps slowed at her mom's declaration. Her eyes locked on his. "Jack's working, Mom."

"I can take a break for a few minutes." He winked at her as she passed and turned his attention to Mrs. James. "I can't believe what a difference painting the walls makes in here."

"We never got the opportunity to thank you for coming to Libby's aid last month." She drove straight to the point.

"There's no need to thank me. I would have done the same for anyone." But somehow, he felt more responsible for this woman's daughter.

She searched his face for a long moment. "What do you think of Libby's work?"

He only had good things to say in this area. "She's excellent at everything she sets her mind to. I'm in awe of what she's able to accomplish. It will be difficult to let her go at the end of the summer."

"She said that was the arrangement you agreed to, but I wondered if you might try to talk her into staying once you realized how special she is."

If he hadn't fallen in love with her, he probably would have. Now he couldn't get her out of his employment fast enough. Waiting until the end of the summer to explore their mutual interest was its own kind of torture. "No, I won't hold her back from the plans she's making for her future."

"Good. No one should expect her to give up her dreams."

Was she implying he'd make her give those up? *Can you marry her, Jack?* He didn't have an answer yet. He held Amanda's gaze. "No one should ask her to give up anything she desires."

Libby returned and glanced at him before addressing her mother. "We're going to run out. Dad wants to find something to anchor the top of the partition to the ceiling. Do you want to come with us and get lunch or should we bring something back?"

"I'll stay here and keep working," she said. "You're almost as bad as Callie at those home improvement stores. Tell your dad to order lunch for me. He knows what I like."

"Okay." She peeked at Jack. "Will you eat with us?"

"Sure. Get me whatever you're having." He pulled out his wallet.

Libby waved him off. "You're buying dinner. This is my treat."

Letting her pay didn't sit well, but she could be stubborn. "I guess this means my break is over." They walked into the lobby together. "Text me when you get back if you need help carrying anything in."

"Okay."

"Be thinking about where you'd like to go for dinner."

"I'll ask Dad. This shouldn't take longer than an hour or so. Don't let my mom scare you. Callie's much worse than I am when it comes to shopping with Dad."

He raised his eyebrows and grinned at her. "You forget I've been to the craft store with you."

"You already know far too many of my secrets, Jack. How am I supposed to remain mysterious?"

"Get out of here, Libby." He placed his hand in the center of her back and gave her a slight push, no longer quelling the urge to touch her. "I also know you hope to finish Kevin's office today."

Jack glanced up at the tap at his door.

"We're done if you're about ready to wrap up for the day," Libby said.

"Did you finish the room?"

"Everything I can for now." She shrugged. "I'm meeting with Logan next week to choose some photographs to frame for the walls."

"How far did you get in the kitchen?"

"The painting's done. It will be a couple days before it dries enough for me to hang the border."

"Do you want me to put anything away for you?" A locksmith had replaced the handle, but he offered to put the supplies away for her whenever possible.

She stared at the door as a faint blush colored her cheeks. "I'll leave everything in the kitchen if it's okay with you."

"Of course. Where are we going for dinner?"

"Dad said Outback. Is that all right?"

Her hesitation caused him to pause in packing up his laptop. "That's fine." He studied her face. "Are you okay?"

"Did my mom say something to you?"

"Like what?"

"I don't know." She licked her lips, distracting him. "She asked me about you yesterday then wanted to talk to you today."

"She loves you and wants you to be happy. I respect that, and she didn't say anything out of line."

"You're too understanding, Jack."

"Not always." He snapped his briefcase shut. "Let's go eat."

When Amanda suggested Libby ride with Jack instead of squishing into the cab of the truck, a crease formed in the center of Libby's forehead. "I don't mind riding with them," she whispered to Jack.

"You can come with me." They couldn't get into too much trouble while driving.

"Are you sure?"

"Positive." He led her to the car, opened her door, and took a deep breath as she slid into the seat. She still smelled of coconuts. The scent would forever remind him of Libby.

He started the car and peeked at her. "I like spending time with you and your family. It's easy to see how important you are to each other."

"They keep me grounded. You haven't met my other sister or any of my nieces or nephews yet."

"How many do you have?"

"Three nieces and two nephews." She ticked their names off on her fingers.

"Maybe I'll meet them sometime."

"Not soon enough." She sighed.

"Only 117 more days," Jack said.

"Ugh! Three and a half months sounds better."

He gripped the steering wheel with his right hand as he drove. The urge to reach for her hand pushed at him, but he couldn't hold it again tomorrow, so he refrained. No sense starting anything tonight they'd have to put an end to after dinner.

Libby laid her head back on her seat and rolled it toward him. He could almost hear her thinking.

"What?"

"Will you tell me if you change your mind? If you decide you don't want to pursue this—us?"

"I doubt it will happen but yes, I'll be honest with you. What about you? You seem to have plenty of suitors."

"Maybe," she said, "but none of them compares to you."

THIRTY-NINE

May and June passed more quickly than Libby anticipated. They made it through both of their Fourth of July events and were gearing up for another formal wedding next Saturday. Libby had completed most of the redecorating as well. Only Jack's office remained. Working around each other's schedules proved a challenge, and she tried to stay out of his space as much as possible.

August promised to be even busier as Libby attempted a decorating job on the side. She also needed to call Amber and arrange a day at her house. If she planned it during one of her days off, Jack could work at the office.

Libby pulled into the office lot and released a heavy sigh as she parked next to the only other car in the lot—Jack's. Everyone else would arrive soon, but she just wanted to go inside and spend time with Jack. Was it even possible to fall in love with someone you didn't spend any time alone with?

Logan parked beside her and waved. She returned the gesture and exit her car. "Hi, Logan."

"Hey, Lib."

"How was your weekend?" She locked her car and swung her bag over her shoulder. Her foot hit a hole in the pavement at the same time she turned. Pain shot through her ankle as she fell to the ground.

"Are you okay?" Logan immediately knelt beside her. "What happened?"

"I think I sprained my ankle. Can you get me inside?"

He helped her stand. "Put your arm around me." She did as he asked, and they made their way to the back door. Logan dug his keys out of his pocket. "Can you put any weight on it?"

She shifted her stance but stopped when the throbbing intensified to a sharp pain. Tears pricked her eyes. She bit her lip and shook her head.

Logan unlocked the door, and they entered the building. Jack exited his office right as they entered the lobby. His eyes flashed, and his features tightened when he noticed Logan's arms around her.

Look at me, she silently pleaded.

His gaze moved to her face, his relief evident as his expression softened. "What happened?"

"She fell in the parking lot." Logan didn't let her answer. "She can't put any weight on her right foot without pain."

"If you get me to the break room, I can sit down," Libby said. "I'll be fine."

Jack was in front of her in four steps. He put one arm around her back, the other under her knees, and lifted her from the ground. She objected to him carrying her. "I'm too heavy, Jack. Put me down."

He ignored her complaints as his long stride took them to the kitchen. Since he wasn't listening to her, she took the opportunity to rest her head on his shoulder and inhale his clean scent. "What a horrible week for me to become a klutz."

"Shh," he whispered in her ear, and goosebumps covered her

from head to toe.

After he sat her in a chair, Jack marched to the freezer and yanked it open. "Let's put some ice on that ankle."

"Check the drawer to the left of the sink for a plastic bag." She pointed to the one she meant.

He dug around until he found one and filled it with ice.

Logan joined them and handed Libby her messenger bag. "What can I do?"

"Can you find something to wrap this bag of ice in?" Jack jerked his head toward the cabinets.

Since the only option in the kitchen was paper towels, which would get soggy, Libby shook her head. "There are some rags in the storage room. Thanks, Logan." She tried to counteract Jack's brusque demeanor.

When Logan left, Jack sat in the chair next to her, lifted her foot onto his thigh, and slid her sandal off. "Where does it hurt?" He wrapped a warm hand around her calf.

She sighed contentedly at his touch, and he looked up at her with eyes darker than normal.

"That doesn't hurt," she said.

He continued to work his way down her leg, causing her to sigh again as he moved slowly and gently.

When he reached the top of her ankle, she flinched and sucked air through her teeth.

His head jerked up at her reaction. "You need to see a doctor. Your ankle is swollen to twice its size."

"Em can take me after the meeting."

"I'd rather do it. This happened on company property."

She shook her head from side to side. "Don't you dare feel guilty about this, Jack."

"Why not? You—"

"Here you go." Logan returned with several rags and stopped to stare at Libby's foot resting on Jack's leg.

Jack slid from his seat and carefully set it on the chair. "She might have torn some tendons," Jack said as he took the rags from Logan and placed one over Libby's ankle. He wrapped another around the bag of ice and glanced at her. "This might hurt."

"Why do you think it's tendons?" She winced as icy chill.

"I've seen it before. A friend slid on some ice a few winters back. His ankle looked like this."

Julie and Emily entered the room and surveyed the scene. Emily spoke first. "Oh, no. What happened, Lib?"

Logan again explained the situation.

"You should get that looked at," Julie said.

"After the meeting." Libby reached for her messenger bag but couldn't quite get there.

Emily picked it up. "What do you need?"

"Aspirin."

She began digging through the oversized bag. "How do you find anything in here?" She came up with the bottle a few seconds later.

Jack set some water in front of Libby and winked at her. As she stared into his chocolate eyes, she forgot about the pain for a few seconds. He was so handsome. They'd been careful not to touch each other over the past couple months, so his nearness this morning had overloaded her system.

"How many, Lib?" Emily drew her focus from Jack.

She gauged the pain in her foot. "Three, and I should eat something."

Emily and Logan snickered.

"I'm glad it's not too bad." A smile twitched on Julie's lips.

Jack turned his back to the group as he got Libby the food she'd requested, his extra attention didn't go unnoticed by her.

"I can't take aspirin on an empty stomach," Libby said.

Kevin arrived and scanned the room. "What's going on?"

Libby groaned and dropped her head in her hands as the others recounted the story again. Jack rested a hand on her shoulder as he passed her the plate of food. She mouthed a thank you.

Once everyone else got their breakfast, Jack started the meeting. They discussed the upcoming wedding and made a backup plan in case Libby was out of commission for the week.

"I guess this is a good transition," Jack said. "Since Libby's leaving next month, I've lined up some interviews for her replacement. Libby's agreed to work with the new hire."

They'd discussed the decision over the phone the past few weeks. Thinking about leaving An Affair to Remember and her new friends made her sad. Whenever Jack tried to talk about finding her replacement, she agreed to whatever he suggested, unwilling to dwell on her departure.

"You can always call me if you find yourself in a bind," she said. When Jack frowned at her, she snapped her mouth shut. *Or not.*

His eyes shifted to Emily. "How do you feel about sharing your office with someone new?"

"If Adam will build me a partition like the one in the guys' office, I don't mind."

"That's fine with me," he said, even though Emily didn't ask for his permission.

"I'll design one for you, Em." Libby clasped her friend's hand. "If Adam can't build and install it, I'll get someone else to do it." She reached down and removed the ice pack from her numb ankle.

"Okay, let's wrap this up, so Libby can get to a doctor," Jack said suddenly.

They spent several more minutes discussing the calendar for the rest of the month and any concerns anyone had. When Jack dismissed the meeting, everyone but Emily, Jack, and Libby left the kitchen.

"Do you want me to drive you to the doctor, Lib?" Emily stood and gathered the remaining clutter on the table.

"I'll take her." Jack stood. "Since this happened at the office, I'll handle it."

Emily stared at him for several seconds before looking at Libby. "Call me if you need anything." She whirled around, dropped everything in the trash can, and rushed from the room.

Jack knelt beside Libby's chair. "You doing all right?"

"It's throbbing right now. If you help me up, I'll try to stand on it again."

He lifted her from the chair as if she weighed nothing and set her feet on the floor. Most of her weight remained in his arms as she balanced. "Okay, let go."

"Do I have to?" His husky voice reverberated through her.

"Jack."

He stepped back, and she shifted to her injured foot. When she cried out in pain, he snatched her up in an instant. "We're going, but I have to get my keys first."

She snuggled against his chest. "Do you hear me complaining?"

FORTY

How could he be so insensitive? Why couldn't he get his mind off kissing Libby? She was in pain, but at least she didn't object to him carrying her around. Jack would take whatever he could get.

Once she'd settled in the car, he hurried around to the other side. "Emergency room or walk-in clinic?"

"Walk-in clinic. The wait will be shorter." She halted him from starting the car with a light touch to his arm. "Will you go back inside and get my bag? I'll need my ID."

"You'll be okay here?"

Libby laughed. "Where am I going to go, Jack?"

"I'll be right back." He jogged inside and found her bag in the kitchen. Her cell phone rang as he grabbed it. What did she keep in there to make it so heavy?

Jack considered telling someone else they were leaving but decided he'd only get a lecture or cold shoulder from any of them. Emily could pass the information along.

He didn't have time to deal with either right now. After this morning, he suspected everyone in the office understood exactly how he felt about Libby James but he no longer cared.

"Thanks." Libby took her bag as he passed it across the car.

"Your phone was ringing."

"Who was it?"

"I have no idea. I'm not going to dig through your stuff."

She opened her bag, found her phone, and checked the display. "I forgot I asked to borrow Callie's truck this afternoon."

"Call her and explain what happened."

"No way. She'll get all overprotective and want to leave work. Sometimes I dislike the fact my sisters are so much older than me. I've got two extra moms who hover and worry."

"You can't ignore her."

"I don't intend to." Libby picked up her phone and made a call.

"Emily, you didn't call Callie, did you...Why, Em? She's going to show up at the apartment now...Not yet. We're on our way...Okay...Love you too." Libby groaned when she hung up.

Jack found a parking spot in front of the walk-in clinic and shut off the engine. "Would you like me to call her for you?"

"Let's find out how long the wait is. I'd prefer to know how bad it is before either of us calls anyone."

Libby scooted out of the car when he opened the door for her. After another heart-wrenching cry as her foot touched the ground, Jack swung her into his arms again. For as much as she ate, she was remarkably light. He hated to see her suffer but reveled in the way her softness sunk against his hard muscles. Her arms encircled his neck, and she rested her head against his shoulder. This almost made the two months since their kiss worth the wait. Almost.

Her hair brushed his chin as he carried her inside the small building and placed her on a chair. The three other people in the room stared at them. Jack approached the reception desk.

"Name?" The woman behind the counter typed Libby's name into the computer when he gave it.

"Fill these out." She handed him a clipboard with some forms attached. "We'll call you when one of the doctors is ready."

Libby took the clipboard from him and uncapped the pen before looking up at him. "Callie won't wait. Will you call her while I fill this out?"

"Sure. What's her number?"

"Use my phone."

"I'll go outside to talk." His hand lingered over hers as she gave him the phone. "Should I tell her anything specific?"

"Not to worry; I'm in good hands."

He chuckled. "I doubt it'll matter, but I'll tell her."

Once he walked outside, he located Callie's number in the missed calls. He tapped the screen to connect.

"Are you all right, Lib?"

"Callie, this is Jack Price. Libby asked me to call."

"How is she, Jack?"

"She's filling out the paperwork now. There are a few people ahead of her, so it may be a while before a doctor can examine her." He paced beside his SUV. "I think she may have torn some tendons in her right ankle since she can't put any weight on it without pain."

"Where are you?"

"At a walk-in clinic. She's okay, Callie. She said to tell you she's in good hands, not to worry about her."

"Like that's going to happen." She blew out a breath.

"We'll call you when we know more."

"I can leave work if she needs me to."

"I'll pass the message along." Jack glanced at the front door of the clinic as a mother and son walked out. "I won't leave her alone.

"Thank you for taking care of my sister. You should receive some kind of award for rescuing her again."

"Anyone would have done the same," he said. Libby was the only reward he cared about. "I should get back inside. Libby will call when she knows more."

He hung up and returned inside, but Libby was gone. The woman informed him she'd gone back with one of the doctors when he inquired. He sat in a hard plastic chair and prayed. *Lord, give Libby healing and comfort right now. Show me what the next step is for us. Our timetable got moved up this morning. Give me wisdom on how to approach the others.*

The longer he waited, the more his concern grew. He'd taken a couple calls and flipped through his fourth magazine when Libby hobbled out on crutches. A brace encased her ankle, and she struggled with her heavy bag. Jack stood and took it from her, sliding her phone in the front pocket.

A nurse approached them and handed Libby a piece of paper. "These are anti-inflammatory pills. They'll keep the swelling down. Aspirin or ibuprofen should help with any pain. Stay off the ankle as much as possible for the next five days and wear the brace whenever you move around for the next week."

She gave her another sheet of paper. "A week from today, you can do these exercises twice a day. Don't hesitate to continue using the brace if you feel any lingering pain or if you're on your feet for extended periods of time. If you're still experiencing pain in two weeks, come back and see us."

"Thank you." Libby handed Jack the papers.

The nurse glanced at him. "Is this your husband?"

"No, I'm her boss." He noticed Libby's shoulders stiffen at his immediate response.

"She'll need a few days off." The other woman smirked. "I can write a note if you'd like."

"That won't be necessary." He moved to settle the bill with the receptionist in order to get away from further scrutiny.

Libby pulled away from his touch once they were outside, claiming she wanted to get comfortable using the crutches.

"Why don't we drop off your prescription?" He took the crutches once she'd settled in and laid them across the backseat. "I'll buy you lunch, and we can swing by to pick it up afterward."

"You should go back to the office. Callie or Emily will babysit me."

He'd upset her somehow. "Callie did say she could leave work if you need her. And I'm sure Emily wouldn't complain about ending her day early, but we need to talk. Why don't you call your sister? We'll decide what to do after you talk to her."

She pulled her phone from her bag, pushed a couple of buttons, and twisted toward her window, away from him. "It's a severe sprain, Cal. The doctor said to stay off of it for five days…No, it's okay. Jack said he'd take me to lunch. I'm sure he can drive me home." She glanced at him for confirmation.

He nodded his assurance.

"He said yes…That's fine. I'm too wiped out to care…Love you too. See you in a while."

Libby ended the call. "Looks like you're stuck with me until two thirty, Jack. Sorry for all of the trouble this is causing."

"Would you stop apologizing? This wasn't your fault. It could've happened to anyone. Any requests for lunch?"

"There's a great Mexican place near my apartment." She told him the name and gave him directions.

Once they ordered their food, Jack spoke up. "I don't think we have to hide anything at the office any longer."

"You're probably right. Em said we need to talk." She rotated her glass of water in a slow circle on the table. "What does this mean for us, Jack?"

"I hope it means we don't have to wait six more weeks before our first date." He laid his hand, palm up, in the center of the table. "I'd like to cook for you soon. Kevin and Julie both called while you were in with the doctor. I'll talk to them this afternoon."

Libby placed her hand in his. "And I'll talk to Emily. If we have everyone's blessing, I'll talk to Logan."

"I'll do that."

"No." Libby squeezed his hand. "He'll take the news better from me."

They finished lunch and stopped by the drugstore for Libby's prescription. As she waited for the pharmacist, he gathered the few other items she'd written down.

Ten minutes later, he found a parking space in front of her building. "Give me your keys, and I'll take you up. You're not climbing to the third floor on crutches."

Libby dug them out of her bag and handed them over. He groaned when he picked her up, and she buried her face in his neck.

"Libby, stop."

She looked up at him in confusion.

He placed a chaste kiss on her forehead. "I can't concentrate when you do that, and I don't want to drop you."

Once they entered her apartment, he set her down. She leaned into him as she found her balance. He couldn't resist any longer.

The temptation had beckoned him all day. Supporting her with an arm around her back, he brushed her hair behind her ear and cupped his hand on her cheek as he kissed her. The intended peck turned heated as Libby slid her hands up his chest to the back of his neck and pulled him closer.

In a corner of his mind, her injury registered, and he broke away. His chest heaved. Libby's eyes shone, her cheeks flushed.

"You should get off your feet." He smoothed her hair back and kissed her forehead again before leading her to the couch. "I'll get your things out of the car. Do you need anything first?"

She bit her bottom lip. "No, I'm okay."

"I'll be right back." He ran down the stairs to his car. Arms filled with Libby's crutches, tote, and the bag from the drugstore, Jack shoved the door closed with his hip. A green truck whipped into the lot, and Callie jumped out. He stifled a growl. His plan to kiss her again was put on hold. Pasting on a smile, he greeted Chris and Callie Graham.

FORTY-ONE

After Jack left her apartment, Libby rested her head on the arm of the couch and traced her lips with her fingertips. His kiss lingered. She hoped when he returned, they could do that some more. She grinned when the front door opened.

"Libby, I'm here."

No, no, no. She opened her eyes as Callie entered the living room and rushed to her side. Chris stood behind her and gave Libby a sympathetic smile. Jack followed a minute later. He brought everything from the car over and set it beside the couch, his smile not quite reaching his eyes. Did the interruption disappoint him too? Her gaze remained on him as she tried to listen to what Callie said.

"I called everyone. I'll stay with you and Emily tonight. Chris will spend tomorrow with you."

That got her full attention. She glanced at her brother-in-law. "Will you bring the girls?"

"No," Callie answered for him. "They'll only get in the way."

"They won't, Cal. They'll provide distraction and entertainment."

"I can bring them along." Chris gave Callie a look that silenced any argument.

"You better watch them, Chris." Callie glared at him. "I don't want them bothering Libby."

"They never bother me." Libby grasped her sister's hand. "What's the rest of the plan?"

"Amy and Cindy will drive up Thursday morning and stay until Mom and Dad get here Friday afternoon. Aunt Maggie said she'll come next week if you need her."

"Amy's coming?" Their oldest sister rarely visited.

"She insisted."

Libby peeked at Jack again. "You can meet my other sister and oldest niece."

"Why don't I bring dinner for everyone on Thursday? You can introduce us, and I'll have an excuse to check in on you."

"You'll go broke feeding my family, Jack."

"I'm happy to do it, Libby." He straightened to his full height. "I should get back to the office. Call if you need anything." After saying good-bye to Callie and Chris, he left.

Libby's gaze followed him until he closed the door.

Callie went to the kitchen and rummaged through the fridge and cupboards. "Why is there so much junk food in here, Lib?" She didn't wait for an answer as she spoke to someone on the phone instead.

Chris sat in the chair next to the couch. "What can I do?"

"I'm supposed to elevate my ankle as often as possible. And we bought some ice packs when we picked up my prescription." She snatched the bag from the floor beside her and pulled everything out. "Can you put these in the freezer and bring me a glass of water?"

He took the bag from her and returned a few minutes later with the water. After arranging some throw pillows at the end of the couch, he tenderly placed her foot on them.

"Thanks, Chris. And thank you for bringing the girls tomorrow."

He winked at her. "I'll enjoy spending the day with them myself." His eyes twinkled. "It will be a treat for all of us to spend a day with you when you won't put us to work. Besides, they love spending time at your place."

Callie finished her conversation and joined them. "Amy says this should keep Libby stocked for the week." She handed Chris a piece of paper. "We only have to worry about dinner tonight and tomorrow."

"I'll take care of tomorrow, honey." Chris scanned the list. "Why don't you have something delivered tonight?"

Libby perked up. "We could order Chinese."

"Chinese it is." Chris stood. "I'll run to the store. Want anything special, Lib?"

"Ice cream?"

"Already on the list," Callie said before giving Chris a quick peck on the lips. "Thank you."

Libby opened her prescription and tapped out two pills.

"Did we interrupt something with Jack?" Callie sat in the chair Chris had vacated.

She choked on the water as she attempted to swallow.

"We did!"

Once Libby quit sputtering, she recounted her morning and the conversation she and Jack had at lunch. "I need to talk to Emily but I'm sure she's figured it out."

"When she gets home, I'll make an excuse and give you some privacy."

"Thanks, Cal. I appreciate you dropping everything to take care of me."

"You're more important than a couple hours of work." She brushed Libby's hair back from her forehead. "Get some rest. You look exhausted. I'll text Em and let her know we're ordering dinner."

"Let me get you money for the groceries." She should've offered before Chris left for the store.

"No, we want to do this. We enjoy helping you out, but you rarely accept."

Libby leveled a gaze at her sister. "You still refuse assistance from other people. Why do you expect anything different from me?"

Libby awoke to find Emily sitting in the chair and thumbing through a bridal magazine. "Hey, Em."

"Oh, good, you're up. Need anything?"

"Would you get me an icepack out of the freezer?" She must have slept hard. She hadn't heard Chris come back from the store or Emily get home from work. "What time is it?"

"Five thirty," Emily said from the kitchen. "Dinner should be here soon." She slammed the freezer shut. "What's with all the ice cream?"

Libby smiled. "Chris." The name was plenty explanation; he spoiled Libby.

"Enough said." Emily set a towel-wrapped ice pack on Libby's ankle. "How is it?"

"Not too bad, but I've been laying down for a few hours."

"Your family probably has everything worked out, but Adam's off Thursday and Friday. He offered to keep you company."

"I'm glad the job's working out."

"Me too. It's nice having him in town. We're going to look at more houses this weekend."

"I'm praying you find the perfect one. I'll let you know if Adam can help. Amy and Cindy might like a break. I hope you're prepared for the James family revolving door this week."

"I love your family. What's the plan?"

When Emily sat down again, Libby explained who would arrive and when.

"I'm off Sunday and Monday," Emily said. "Your parents don't have to stay all day."

"They'll insist. I'll sleep out here, so everyone can use my room."

Someone knocked at the door, and both girls stared at it.

"It's dinner." Callie laughed as she walked through the room to answer it.

Emily updated Callie on plans for her wedding while the three

of them ate. Libby's ankle started throbbing again, but she
wouldn't take more pills until she'd talked with Emily. The
medication had knocked her out earlier, and she needed to remain
alert for this conversation.

After dinner, Libby changed into pajamas and settled back on
the couch.

"I'm going to call Chris and the girls and say good night. I'll
check on you before I go to bed." She squeezed Libby's shoulder
and whispered, "Good luck."

Emily had cleaned up their dishes and put away the leftovers.
"Need anything else. Lib?"

"Water would be great."

She set the glass on the coffee table and plopped down in the
chair. "Ready to tell me what's going on between you and Jack?"

Libby wanted to find out what she'd figured out. "What makes
you think something's going on?"

"Give me a break, Lib." She rolled her eyes. "You and Jack
were all buddy-buddy before you left for vacation. When you got
back, the two of you acted as if you couldn't stand to be in the
same room together. And then today..."

"What about today?"

"Jack got overly protective, and you couldn't keep your eyes
off him. What's up?"

"He kissed me a couple months ago—the night I got locked in
the storage room."

"What?" Emily gawked at her, mouth agape. "And you didn't
say one word?"

"Jack and I talked about it and agreed to wait until the end of the summer to explore anything. Neither of us wanted to make things at the office uncomfortable. As much as I longed to tell you, the conversation had to be postponed."

"Exactly how do you feel about each other?"

"I like him, Em—more than any man I've dated. And he says he likes me. He didn't apologize for kissing me, said he'd wanted to do it for a while."

"What about his disdain for marriage? You're not going to change his mind, and I won't watch him break your heart."

"I know what I'm doing." She remembered how quickly he'd denied being her husband earlier. She'd liked the question. It amused her, but judging from his reaction, Jack took offense.

"I hope so, Libby. If he hurts you, I'll have to quit. And I love my job."

FORTY-TWO

I like working for you, Jack." Emily paced in front of his desk.

He'd expected this conversation. Libby sent him a text last night to warn him. When he returned to the office yesterday, he'd had a long discussion with Julie and Kevin.

Emily stopped suddenly and glared at him with fire in her eyes. "But if you hurt my best friend, I'm done. I won't stay."

"I understand, Emily. Libby's important to me. I'm not going to hurt her."

"You may not want to, but I'm afraid that's exactly what's going to happen."

"Do you remember the first day you brought Libby to work? You told me if I gave her a chance, I'd love her."

"I didn't mean literally!" She scoffed and threw her hands in the air before resuming her pacing. "For some reason, you make Lib happy, and I won't deny her that. You have my blessing." She shook her head when he grinned and held up her palm. "For now."

Jack raised his eyebrows. He'd expected more of a challenge. "Really?"

"Yes," she said with a sigh and plopped into a chair. "Don't make me regret this."

"Kevin and Julie asked me to find Libby's replacement before we move ahead with anything. They're concerned I'll distract her from work."

Emily stared at him. "She'd never allow it."

"My thoughts exactly, but I'll honor their request. I've scheduled three interviews this week. Can you sit in since Libby isn't here?"

"Sure. I should get a say in who I'll be sharing my office with."

"Yes you should, and I trust your judgment." Jack paused. "What should I tell Logan?"

"Let Libby deal with him. The guy's putty in her hands."

He's not the only one. "She said she'd talk to him. How's she doing?"

"She hates the extra attention and feels guilty about leaving us shorthanded."

"We've done this without her and Logan for the past three years." He'd tried to soothe Libby's conscience with the same argument yesterday.

"You're bringing dinner over tomorrow?"

"I am. Libby wants me to meet her other sister. Is this going to be too weird for you?"

"I think I'd better get used to it. It might be uncomfortable for you, though. Amy's the oldest and even more protective of Libby than Callie."

"Libby already warned me. What's your schedule like this week?"

"Not bad," Emily said. "My job's gotten easier with the limo contract, and Libby has everything on her end organized and ready. When's your first interview?"

"Tomorrow at ten and another at two. The third is Friday morning at nine. Want to look over the resumés?"

"Yes, please. I'll come prepared."

Jack handed her a stack of papers. "The three on top are the ones I called, but go through the others and see whether anyone else catches your eye. Those are copies. Take them home and get Libby's opinion as well."

"Okay. Thanks." She got up to leave but paused at the door. With her back to him, she added, "I hope you can give her what she wants, Jack."

"I'm working on it. Will you close the door behind you?"

As soon as it clicked shut, he called Libby.

"Jack? How'd it go?"

"Better than I thought. She gave us her blessing."

"Seriously? Emily?"

"Yes, but only because I make you happy." He couldn't resist teasing her.

"You do," she said with a smile in her voice.

"You make me happy too, Libby. How are you feeling?"

"I'm sick of sitting on the couch. I used to love this couch. At least Chris and the girls are here. We're about to watch *Tangled*." She sighed dramatically, causing Jack's grin to return. "Do you know how many times I've seen this movie, Jack?"

He laughed. "That many?"

"More."

"I gave Emily several resumés to look through. I'd like you to go through them as well. Maybe they'll make up for the movie. Do you need anything?"

"Other than my life back?"

"Soon, sweetheart." Silence greeted him. "Too soon?"

"No, but don't call me that at work."

He chuckled. "I won't. Call me tonight?"

"Absolutely. Have a good day, Jack."

Jack shifted the bags of food to one hand and knocked. Libby had called to place the takeout order, and he picked it up on his way over. Even confined, she managed to find ways to keep busy.

Emily swung open the door. "Come on in, Jack."

His eyes scanned the empty living room.

"She's in her room," Emily said. "She insisted on changing before you got here."

He was both elated and guilt-ridden she wanted to dress up for him. Guilt won out. "She shouldn't have gone to the trouble."

"We couldn't convince her otherwise. I figured it wouldn't hurt anything. She's been stuck on the couch for a few days and is going a little stir crazy. If you haven't noticed, Libby's usually in constant motion."

Oh, he'd noticed. A tall woman with strawberry blond hair came into the room and eyed him cautiously. Emily introduced her.

"It's a pleasure to meet you," Jack said. "Libby's told me quite a bit about you."

"Callie's told me about you," she said. "Libby's been too busy."

"Aims, you promised!" Libby entered the room on crutches and glared at her sister.

"Sorry, Lib." Amy spun around.

"I'm not the person who deserves an apology. Jack's the one you've got under the microscope."

Amy moved beside Libby and glanced at him. "I apologize, Jack. We've all been a little concerned about Libby this week."

"Apology accepted. I know how close your family is."

"What's Cindy doing?" Emily changed the subject. "Dinner's here."

"She better not be on the phone." Amy left the room, muttering under her breath.

Libby hobbled to the couch and leaned on the arm. "Sorry, Jack. She's the oldest," she said as if that explained her sister's actions. "Em, will you grab me an ice pack?"

Emily pulled one out of the freezer and handed it, along with a dishtowel, to Jack. He helped Libby get comfortable and placed the frozen bundle over her ankle. "It looks better."

"Feels better too." She stared up at him, searching his face.

"What are you looking at?"

"Nothing." She patted the chair beside her. "Have a seat."

Once he sat, he glanced around the room. All of his attention had been on Libby the last time he was in here. The place reflected her personality—warm and inviting. "You decorated this room." There was no question.

Her face lit up. "I did the entire apartment, but this is my favorite space."

"I can see why." He smiled when their eyes met. Man, he'd missed her the past two days.

Amy and her daughter joined them. Libby started to shift her foot off the couch, but her sister waved her off. "You're okay. We'll pull some chairs over from the table. Cindy, say hi to your Aunt Libby's friend. This is Jack."

"Hi." The girl didn't meet his eyes.

"It's a pleasure to meet you, Cindy."

Emily passed out the food, and Jack said a quick prayer. Amy questioned him while they ate. It felt a little like an interrogation. When Emily's phone chimed, she picked it up. "Adam says he'll be here at ten tomorrow, Lib."

"Perfect." She looked at Amy. "You and Cindy can go to lunch while you're out shopping."

"Are you sure?" she asked.

"I insist. You two should enjoy yourselves while you're here. No reason for you to be stuck in the house with me all day."

Once everyone finished with dinner, Amy offered to clean up and recruited her daughter to assist. Emily left to call her fiancé, leaving Jack and Libby alone in the living room.

With the kitchen a few feet away, they didn't have much

privacy. Jack leaned closer to Libby. "Want a change of scenery? We could go outside for a while."

She bit her bottom lip, peeked over her shoulder at her sister, then eyed her crutches.

"You don't need those," he whispered. "I'll take care of you."

"Jack and I are going outside, Amy."

"Cindy, why don't you go call your dad and say good night to him and the boys?" Amy turned to Libby as soon as the girl was out of the room. "Go ahead. Text me before you come back so I can make sure she's not out here."

Libby snorted. "It's not like she doesn't know about this stuff, Aims. You're married, and Evan's no slouch in this department."

"Callie and Chris are also married, but Cindy's been begging us to let her date on her own. If she knows about this," she waved her hand between Libby and Jack, "we'll never hear the end of it." Her voice took on a nasal quality that Jack considered an attempt to mimic her daughter. "But, Mom, Aunt Libby has a boyfriend."

"And you'll remind her I'm ten years older than her." Libby snickered and looked at him. "Let's go before she changes her mind."

He stood, lifted her up, and strode to the front door.

Once outside, Libby pointed to the left. "There are some benches two buildings down." She stared at his face as he followed her directions.

"You're making me self-conscious."

"I'm trying to memorize your face."

"Why?"

290

Her eyes focused everywhere but on him as she clamped her lips together.

"Are you worried about this?" He ducked his head closer until she looked at him. "About us?"

"No. Nothing like that."

"Then what?" He located the bench and put Libby down. When he took a seat beside her, he patted his thigh. "Put your foot up."

"It's a little embarrassing."

"The doctor told you to elevate it."

She chuckled and lifted her foot. "Not this. The answer to your question."

"You can tell me." He reached for her hand and laced their fingers together.

"I tried to draw you."

He peeked at her as she watched him with those gorgeous eyes. "I'd like to see that."

"I can't quite get it right. I'm can't figure out what I'm missing." With her free hand, she brushed her fingers over his brow, his cheeks, his lips.

"Libby," he murmured before his lips crashed over hers. She kissed him back with fervor and heat shot through him.

Suddenly, she gasped and jerked back. "Your hand, Jack."

He'd wrapped it around her injured ankle without realizing it. "Oh, sweetheart, I'm sorry."

"Don't be." She smirked. "It was worth a little pain."

They sat and talked, enjoying each other's company and the warm summer evening.

Libby sighed. "I'm sick of sitting. I'm ready to be mobile again."

"Enjoy the break while you have it." Jack squeezed her hand. "Maybe this is God's way of telling you to slow down."

FORTY-THREE

Two weeks after she'd hurt her ankle, Libby ran around as though she'd never sprained it. She was happy to be back at work, but miserable avoiding being in the office alone with Jack again. Her replacement started next Tuesday.

Emily had come home and gushed about the lady on the day of the interview. "You'll love her, Lib. Jack says she reminds him of you."

It was ridiculous to be jealous of a woman she'd never met, but Kelsey Bishop would spend every day with him. When she'd gone through the stack of resumés, Kelsey's stood out. Libby should be thrilled he'd found someone capable of replacing her so quickly.

"Do you have a few minutes?" Jack stood in the lobby when she arrived at work.

"Sure. Give me a minute?" At his nod, she went to drop everything at her desk. With butterflies in her stomach, from nerves or excitement she couldn't be sure, she crossed the lobby to Jack's office and sat in front of him.

"Is everything okay? You haven't been yourself this week."

"Yes," she lied.

He studied her face for several uncomfortable seconds as if trying to discern her every doubt. "Really?"

"It's nothing. I'll deal with it."

"Is it about us? I know we haven't talked much since you got back, but—"

"No, it's nothing like that." She reached her hand out to touch his arm but thought better of it at the last second. "Not directly."

"I wish you'd talk to me."

This was so petty. She didn't want to admit what she was wrestling with. She chewed on her bottom lip.

Jack sighed when she didn't respond. "Kelsey's coming by at ten thirty tomorrow. Will you be around to meet her?"

A surge of envy shot through her, and her words came out clipped. "Yes. I'll be here."

"I knew you were struggling with this." Jack leaned his elbows on the desk. "We discussed finding someone to come in and work with you, sweetheart. Why does it bother you?"

"I realize I'm being irrational, Jack. It makes no sense, but I'm jealous. Emily said she reminds you of me, and she'll spend every day here. With you."

"Libby, stop. I'll spend every day thinking about you, missing you," he said. "Kelsey reminds me of you because she's focused and driven. That's all. I'm not attracted to her."

"You weren't attracted to me at first either."

"That's not entirely true." He smirked. "I saw you for the first time right before Emily introduced us. You were sitting at a table with several guys. When you laughed, I decided I would at least learn your name."

His words soothed her. "Thank you for sharing that with me."

"I've also wanted to cook for you since that day. I'm making lunch at Mom's on Sunday. Will you join us?"

"You're not going to make her cook and try to pass it off as yours, are you?" Her eyebrows rose as she teased him in an effort to lighten her mood.

"Nope. I'm the better cook. You can even watch and keep me company as I do it. Mom might have other ideas, though. She's got a notion to redecorate the living room."

Libby glanced around his half-painted office. "I need to finish in here."

"Don't worry about this. It's not a big deal if you don't get it done." He held her gaze. "What about Sunday?"

Grinning, she said, "I never turn down free food. Will you sit with me during the church service beforehand?"

"It will be my pleasure, Libby James."

On Friday morning, Libby listened as Jack introduced Kelsey Bishop to Kevin and Logan and tried to prepare herself. She'd been praying about her jealousy but was hesitant to meet her.

"Emily's not here, but you've already talked to her." Jack's voice grew louder as they neared her office.

While sitting at her new desk, her back remained to the door. *Lord, help me remain cordial if not kind.*

"Libby's in here. You'll work directly with her for the next several weeks."

At the knock on her door, Libby stood and spun around to greet the newest employee.

Kelsey's short auburn hair framed a heart-shaped face. Cute wire-framed glasses magnified her brown eyes. In her mid-thirties, she had a friendly smile.

"It's nice to meet you, Kelsey. Your résumé listed some impressive credentials."

"Thank you, Ms. James. I'm excited to join the team."

"Please call me Libby. Do you have a few minutes to talk?"

Kelsey's smile widened. "Yes, I do."

Jack winked at Libby when her gaze shifted to him. "There's a fresh pot of coffee and some donuts in the kitchen." He turned to Kelsey. "I'll leave you in Libby's hands, and we'll see you next Tuesday."

When he left, Libby suggested they move to the kitchen. The women filled their coffee mugs and sat at the table. Libby pulled some paper plates from the cupboard. "Would you like a donut?"

"No, thank you. I can't eat gluten."

Libby stared at her. "Like bread?"

"Bread, cakes, cookies," she pointed at Libby's plate, "donuts."

"You poor thing." She couldn't imagine giving up most of the sweets she loved.

Kelsey shrugged. "I've learned to manage it."

They talked for an hour about the job and Kelsey's experience. She knew several people Libby didn't, who would become excellent contacts for Jack's company.

As they were wrapping up, Kelsey peered at Libby. "Do you mind if I ask why you're leaving?"

"Not at all. It's not a secret. This was a temporary arrangement from the beginning. I'm an interior designer and plan to freelance this fall."

"Jack mentioned you redid the whole place. It's stunning."

"Thank you. I've finished everything except his space. We're installing a partition in your office this weekend to give you and Emily a little privacy. I'll work out of the conference rooms or Julie's space while you settle in."

"You don't have to move out." Kelsey's expression revealed her anxiety over the idea.

"You and I will spend plenty of time together," Libby said. "We don't need to cram into the same space as well. Emily and I are roommates, so she'll enjoy getting a break from me during the day."

Kelsey stood and rinsed her coffee cup in the sink. "I can't wait to get started."

"Good." Libby followed her lead. "We'll see you Tuesday. I'm going to the floral wholesaler in the afternoon. You're welcome to come along."

"Oh, I've wanted to go in there for a few years but never had a reason."

"Now you do." She dried the mugs and put them away. "It's been a few weeks since I've been. Their flowers are beautiful, and the staff is pleasant and helpful. Do you arrange?"

"Not well, but I love flowers."

Once Kelsey's car disappeared around the corner, Libby breathed a sigh of relief. She liked the woman. Kelsey would be an asset to Jack's staff—even if there was still a tiny pinch of jealousy over her replacement.

"You okay?" Logan asked from behind her.

"I'm good." Libby spun around. "How are you doing?"

He stared at her for several seconds. "Can we go somewhere and talk?"

This was probably the best opportunity she'd get to tell him about Jack. She preferred to have that conversation outside the office. "Sure. Want to grab a quick lunch?"

"Okay. Give me ten minutes."

Libby knocked on Jack's open door. A grin spread across his face when he saw her. Her heart melted a little every time he looked at her like that.

"How did it go?"

"Really well," Libby said. "I like her. She's a good fit."

"I thought so. Can I interest you in some lunch?"

"I just told Logan I'd go with him." She lowered her voice. "He wants to talk."

A shadow crossed Jack's face. Seemed she wasn't the only one struggling with jealousy.

"I still need to tell him about us," she said.

"Be careful, Libby."

She chuckled. "It's Logan. I think I can handle him. I'll find you when we get back."

Logan drove to Wendy's. The one Jack brought her to that

night—the night everything changed between them.

When he attempted to pay for her lunch, she declined, not willing to encourage him in any way. They found an empty table and sat.

Logan glanced up. "Do you like Jack?"

The blunt question surprised her, mostly because Logan was usually laid back to the point of ignorance. She set her hamburger back down on the tray. May as well get this over with.

"I've wondered since the day you fell and hurt your foot," he continued. "Something was going on between you two."

This was the opening she'd prayed for. "Yes, I like him. We tried not to let our feelings for each other show at the office and had agreed to wait until September to start dating. But the day I got hurt, neither of us could hide it anymore."

"I thought so." His shoulders slumped. "You never looked at me the way you look at him."

"I'm sorry, Logan. You're a good friend but…"

"Nothing more." He finished the sentence for her. Finally, understanding what she'd tried to convince him of for years had sunk in.

"We're not going to allow our personal relationship to change anything at work. I don't want you to be uncomfortable."

"I'm not uncomfortable. Disappointed, but not uncomfortable. You won't be around much longer. Five more weeks, right?"

"Six. I'll stay through Labor Day weekend, but I'm positive Kelsey will make the transition seamless. Are you sure you're okay?"

"I'll get there." He shrugged in his carefree way. "Jack's a decent guy. If he makes you happy, I can't compete."

"He does. Make me happy, I mean." Thrilled. Ecstatic. But for Logan's sake, she wouldn't expound upon everything Jack made her feel.

FORTY-FOUR

Jack located Libby in the sanctuary on Sunday. After he slid into the seat beside her and said good morning, he leaned around her to talk to Emily. "Morning, Em. Adam's not here today?"

"He's parking the car." She twisted around and scanned the area behind them. "He probably stopped to talk to someone."

Libby slipped her hand in his, and he entwined their fingers together.

Adam joined them a few minutes later and sat on the other side of Emily. He leaned forward. "Hey, Lib. We still on for tomorrow morning?"

"Absolutely," she said. "I'd like to get the partition in before Kelsey starts Tuesday." She turned to Jack. "I hope to finish painting your office too, but if you planned to go in tomorrow, it can wait."

"I'll work from home in the morning and come in around one. Why don't I bring lunch for everyone?"

"You don't have to do that."

"I want to." He traced a circle on her wrist with his thumb. "I'll even paint afterward."

"Well, in that case..." She smiled at him.

Sitting beside Libby and sharing his Bible with her was

wonderful. Now that he'd hired Kelsey, he hoped to make this a part of his routine. The next six weeks promised to be bittersweet. While he now had the freedom to spend more time with Libby outside of work, the time was fast approaching when he wouldn't see her every day. Her laughter wouldn't carry to him from the lobby as he sat at his desk. He wouldn't get to look across the table during staff meetings and meet her bright eyes.

"You okay?" Libby whispered when the service ended.

"I'm great." He gave her hand a quick squeeze. "Want to ride to Mom's with me? I'll bring you back for your car afterward."

"You don't mind?"

"Not at all. I have to come back this way to get to my place, anyway."

When they were in his SUV, Jack took Libby's hand again and kissed the back of it. "I'm glad we don't have to wait any longer to do this. It's been difficult to restrain myself, especially over the past couple of weeks." Now that they'd decided to date, he was ready to get on with it.

"It's going to be weird not seeing you every day," Libby said. "I'm going to miss you."

"You'll be so busy you won't have time to miss me." He knew she already had two jobs lined up, and several more people on a waiting list.

"You're probably right." She sighed. "I'm a little anxious about doing everything on my own."

"You'll be amazing. We've gotten more compliments on the transformation at the office than I can count. You're going to be the most in-demand interior designer in the city."

Jack parked in front of his mom's house and shut off the ignition. "I should warn you about Mom. You're only the second woman I've brought to her house, and the first was a few years ago. She's probably going to ask you a million questions."

"I've met your mom before, remember?" Libby shifted in her seat to look at him. "We talked quite a bit, and I don't mind answering her questions. I might, however, need to hear more about this other woman." She smiled softly and shook her head. "But not today. Let's go inside. I'm hungry."

"There's a surprise." His dry reply coaxed a laugh from her. "I'll miss hearing you laugh the most."

She sighed and met his gaze. "Can we please not talk about when I'm gone and enjoy our time together today?"

"Agreed."

Jack made lunch while his mom and Libby visited at the kitchen table. When Libby asked for a tour of the house, his mom quickly complied.

Jack knew what she was up to. "Mom, it's Libby's day off. Don't put her to work."

"This doesn't concern you, Jack." Her voice held what Jack considered her 'don't mess with me, I'm your mother' tone.

"I don't mind." Libby's gaze collided with his. "How long until lunch is ready?"

"Thirty minutes. Do you need something to hold you over?"

"Very funny, Jack." Her eyes glistened with humor. "It better be worth the wait or I'll have to reconsider this relationship."

"It will be worth every minute." He'd win her over with dessert if lunch didn't do the trick.

Thanks again for lunch," Libby said for the fifth time. "And for the brownies. Emily's not going to be happy with you."

Jack pulled into the spot beside her car. "The grin you gave me when I told you to take them home was worth Emily's wrath." He rested his hand over hers. "Hang on. I'll get your door."

After he came around and opened it, he ducked his head to peer at her. "Did I pass?"

"Pass? You aced it." She stepped out of the SUV and patted his chest. "You're safe."

"I doubt that," he muttered as she unlocked her car and set the plate of brownies in the backseat. When she turned around, her bottom lip caught between her teeth, he let go of his restraint.

Their lips met, and her hands slid to the back of his neck, her fingers flicking through his hair. *Not safe at all.* He remembered they stood in the middle of the church parking lot and took a step back.

Libby's eyes remained closed, but her smile held pure delight. "Hmm. That gets better every time."

"You're so beautiful, Libby."

When her eyes snapped open, he held her gaze, willing her to believe that about herself.

The next month passed too quickly. Libby finished the redecorating, and Jack teased her, saying he wouldn't be able to quit thinking about her now. They had a small wedding followed by two company picnics over the Labor Day holiday on the schedule. After those three events, Libby was leaving.

Jack spent almost every evening with her. His mom had talked her into updating her living room, so they spent Sunday afternoons in the house he'd grown up in. Amber had also invited them to dinner a couple of times, and Jack had taken Libby out several evenings. Those nights were his favorite. The ones he got her to himself.

"Will someone help me with this?" Libby called from the front room.

He stood to go assist, but Kelsey beat him there before he moved around his desk.

"You shouldn't have carried this in one trip." Her tone held reproof.

"I know," Libby said. "It seemed manageable when I got it out of the car."

Jack went to find out what she was up to. Kelsey wrangled four grocery bags from her arms, leaving Libby with two cases of soda.

"What's all this?" He lifted the drinks out of her arms and headed to the kitchen.

She followed. "We're getting low on several things, so I thought I'd stock us back up."

"You're not even going to be here in another week." He regretted the comment the moment he saw tears build behind Libby's eyes. She was having a hard time coming to terms with leaving. Deciding distraction was his best option, he opened the fridge. "I'll help you put this away."

Kelsey spun from the counter where she'd set the bags. "I have a couple of calls to make." She hurried from the room, leaving him alone with Libby.

He shoved the drinks on a shelf and slammed the door shut. Pulling Libby into an embrace, he said, "I'm sorry, sweetheart. I shouldn't have mentioned it."

Her arms circled his waist, and she rested her forehead on his shoulder. "It's not like I won't ever see any of you. We're still planning to meet for our ladies' lunches every month, and Emily's wedding is only a couple months away."

He kissed the top of her head. "And I'll make time for you."

"Okay, I'm over it." She stepped out of his embrace and shook her hands at her side. "Let's put this stuff away."

He doubted it happened that quickly, but played along. They'd almost finished when the bell on the front door chimed. He remained where he was, listening for someone to greet the customer.

"Is Jack Price here?"

"In the kitchen," Kelsey said. "Through that door."

He and Libby both watched the entryway as the man approached.

"It's good to see you again, Jack."

He didn't agree. Jaw and fists clenched, he swept past him and strode to the front door without a word. Libby called after him, but anger drove him toward escape. He'd been too busy to call his dad. At least that's how he justified his procrastination in returning the phone calls. His dad hadn't attempted to contact him again since April, so why did he make an appearance now? When Jack was finally happy?

FORTY-FIVE

Libby stared after Jack in disbelief. She'd never seen him act so rudely, and he'd completely ignored her. Her instincts kicked in, and she tried to smooth things over with the man. "I'm sorry about that."

He shook his head. "I shouldn't have surprised him like this. He hasn't returned any of my messages, and I wanted to speak with him."

Tension strained her muscles. She guessed only one person's presence would cause this reaction from Jack, and the man's comment set off alarms in her mind. "Please have a seat." She waved her hand toward the table. "Would you like something to drink? We've got coffee, soda, or water. I'm Libby James, by the way."

The man looked at her with a small smile. One that didn't reach his eyes. "I'm Jonathan Price."

Libby stilled. Even though her thoughts had been running along that line, hearing it confirmed gave her pause. Jack's dad.

"Ah, he's mentioned me."

"Once or twice," she said. "He mostly said you weren't around."

Jonathan asked for coffee. Libby filled a mug and placed it on the table in front of him. Too nervous to drink anything herself, she sat across from Jack's father and visited with him.

When Jack still hadn't returned almost an hour later, Jonathan Price stood. "Thank you for keeping me company, Libby. I'm sure you're busy, so I won't keep you any longer. Would you tell Jack I'm back in town?"

"I will. It was a pleasure to meet you, Mr. Price." She'd enjoyed the conversation with the man despite all of Jack's misgivings.

As soon as Jonathan Price left, Libby locked herself in the small conference room. Jack's reaction to his father's appearance had smacked her with a cold dose of reality. If he was still this angry with his dad, could he give her what she desired most? Could he marry her? Give her a home and a family?

Oh, Lord, forgive me. I wanted a relationship with Jack selfishly and quit seeking your will where he was concerned. Give me the strength to do what I should have in the first place and let him go.

She'd quit praying for her future husband the day she injured her ankle, quit bringing their relationship to God because she enjoyed spending time with Jack. Emily had been right. Libby believed she could change his mind. But she'd obviously failed, hadn't even made a dent in his armor.

Several minutes after she sent Emily a text asking her to get Julie and come to the conference room, a knock sounded at the door. Libby took a breath and opened it.

"What happened?" Emily's voice and eyes expressed her concern.

Libby recounted the scene at Jonathan's arrival. "The man's been trying to talk to Jack since March, but evidently Jack's too hard-headed to return a phone call."

"What are you going to do?" Julie motioned to the table, and the women sat with her.

"I can't keep lying to myself," Libby said. "Jack needs to forgive his father. If he's not ready to do that, I can't continue with this relationship."

Emily slammed her palm on the table. "I warned him!"

"This is my decision, Em. I wanted to talk with you two because I can't stay. This will be difficult enough without spending the next two weeks around Jack. I'm going to call a few people who've expressed an interest in hiring me for interior design and line some jobs up for this month, but I'm sorry to leave you shorthanded again."

"We'll be fine." Julie laid her hand over Libby's. "Kelsey has everything under control, and the events are small. You do what's best for you."

Libby fixed her gaze on Emily. "Neither of you can quit. This decision is entirely mine, not Jack's."

"This is all Jack's fault. He's stubborn," Emily snapped then calmed with her next words. "Since you're asking, I won't leave, but I'm furious with him."

There was nothing Libby could do about that. "I'll talk to Jack when he gets back, then I'm going to spend the rest of the week with my family. I'll be back Monday in time for lunch. Even though I need space from Jack, I want to spend time with the rest of you."

"Good." Julie leaned over and hugged her. "We don't want to lose you because he's being an idiot."

Libby gave her a wobbly smile. "Thank you, Julie. You're a good friend. Please don't hold this against him. He needs encouragement right now."

"When's he coming back?" Emily asked before the other

woman could reply.

"I have no idea. He's been gone almost two hours and didn't take his keys or phone with him." She'd tried to call him after his dad left and heard the phone ringing in his office. When she went to check it out, his keys were lying on the desk beside his phone.

"It's four thirty," Emily said. "Kevin and Logan were on their way out when we came in here. We'll make sure Kelsey leaves with us so you'll have some privacy."

"Thanks, Em. I don't know what I'd do without you."

"Well, I'm here, so you don't have to find out. I'll be home. We can talk more if you need to, or I can pack a bag for you to grab and go straight to your parents' house."

"Put the bag together. If I can't talk tonight, I'll call you tomorrow."

"Okay." Emily pulled her into a crushing hug. "I love you, Lib."

She clung to her friend and blinked back tears, grateful for the support of friends. "Love you, too."

Twenty minutes later, the office stood silent and empty. Libby alternated between sorrow and anger. She phoned her mom, told her she was driving down tonight, and planned to stay until Monday. Callie called ten minutes later.

"I can't talk right now, Cal," Libby said when she answered her phone. "I'll come by tomorrow."

"No, stop on your way to Mom and Dad's. I'll wait up for you. Whatever happened, I'm praying. I love you."

Jack finally returned at a quarter after six. He knocked once and stuck his head in the room. "Thanks for waiting."

"Where were you?" Libby stood to face him.

"Walking around. Trying to clear my head."

"Your dad's been trying to contact you since March, and you never called him back?"

"Can we not talk about this, Libby?"

"Fine, Jack. If that's what you want." She hoisted her bag on her shoulder and brushed past him. "We don't have to talk about this, but you and I are through."

"Libby—"

She pivoted back toward him. "You know how important family is to me."

His face grew red. "Not everyone's family is perfect like yours."

The words stung. "My family is far from perfect. All your dad wants is an opportunity to apologize."

"How do you know that?" Jack glared at her.

"Because I bothered to talk to the man. He made a mistake and wants your forgiveness."

"The one thing I won't give him."

"And that's why I won't stay. I spoke with Julie and Emily, and they're prepared to cover for me. Kelsey's more than capable of handling anything else that comes up."

Jack stared at her in anguish. "Please don't do this, Libby. I lo—"

"Don't you dare, Jack! You don't get to say that to me." She let her anger loose so he wouldn't see her heart breaking. "I knew what I was getting into, knew how you felt about marriage. I thought I could be content spending time with you, but I need more. That's on me—ignoring the truth of the situation. Until you talk to your father, you can't give that to anyone, and I won't give my heart to someone who won't even try. I need a clean break. Please don't call or come by."

"Whatever you need, Libby." His words almost broke her resolve. They were the same ones he'd said to her the night of their first kiss.

"Good-bye, Jack. I'll pray you settle things with your dad." She secured her bag again and hurried outside. Once in her car, she allowed the tears to flow. The truth was, she'd already given her heart to Jack Price.

Libby sat in Alex and Becca's kitchen on Friday afternoon. Her mom and sisters were smothering her, and she had to get away from their constant attention and concern. When Alex suggested meeting at his house, he provided her with an escape, even if only for a few hours.

"How you doing, Lib?" Alex filled two mugs with coffee.

"Becca told you?" There were no secrets between Callie and Becca—or Becca and Alex, for that matter.

His shoulders lifted a fraction. "She cares about you."

"I'll live, Alex. Honestly, I'm tired of crying over it. I'm ready to focus on my future. Since I have several questions about my business, this was a good distraction, not to mention timely."

Alex sat across from her. "In that case, what's on your mind?"

"A few weeks ago, I ran into one of the ladies I used to work with. Taylor Designs filed for bankruptcy, and Linda closed the business, which releases all of us from our contracts. I want Stacy—and maybe a few more people—to work with me. I'm not sure where to begin."

"Sounds like you're interested in starting a company as opposed to self-employment."

Libby blew her bangs off her forehead. "Yes, but after doing some research, I'm more confused and overwhelmed than ever."

"I can help with a lot of this and put you in touch with someone who will take care of anything else. Let's start from scratch. Tell me what you envision for your business."

This was something Libby could talk about. She told Alex her dream of having three to five designers based out of a central office. They'd offer redecorating, staging, and organizing services. While she desired to use her design degree and experience, she preferred to have a team of people around her to share the workload. She thrived as part of a cohesive team where everyone was considered invaluable and treated as equals. Working for Jack had proven that.

"What about a name?" Alex asked. "Will you use yours?"

"No, it'll be easier for others to partner with me if my name isn't attached."

"Good. You're planning ahead. You'll need to come up with a name."

"I already have one. Comfort and Joy Designs."

Alex smiled. "I like it. We'll get Becca's opinion when we're done here. She'll want to update your website and business cards."

"I can do that. She shouldn't to go to the trouble."

"You try and convince her of that," he said.

Libby talked to Alex for another hour and grew more encouraged with her decision.

When he asked Becca to join them, Libby tested out the name. "What do you think of Comfort and Joy Designs?"

"I love it. It's perfect, Lib. I'll call Dan and have him update everything."

Alex raised his eyebrows at Libby in challenge.

She knew she couldn't dissuade Becca from something she'd set her mind to. "Thank you."

"Since we're all here," Alex said, "Becca and I want to discuss something else with you. We talked a little about this on vacation but never came back to it. We'd like to help you get off the ground."

"You both have done more than enough already."

"We love you, Lib," Becca said. "We've prayed and talked about this, so at least hear us out."

"Okay."

"It takes a lot of money to start a business." Alex removed his glasses and set them on the table. "We want to give you the money to get up and running. If you prefer, we'll call it a loan, and you can begin paying us back in five years. We'd rather give you this as a gift but realize you might be more comfortable accepting a loan."

"Wow, you guys. It's a generous offer and a huge decision. Can I pray about it?"

"Of course," Alex said. "You've got a couple of jobs lined up to get you through next month. There's no hurry. Talk to your family and friends about this too."

"Thank you for believing in me."

"It's not hard, Lib." Becca gave her a hug. "We love you."

FORTY-SIX

Twenty-seven days. Jack now measured time by how long ago Libby had walked out of the office and his life. The first week had been miserable, and almost a month later, he struggled to climb out of his despair. The night Libby left, Jack punched a hole in one of the walls in his office. His dad, who'd been absent for years, somehow managed to ruin his life. Again. The best thing to happen in Jack's life fell apart the moment his father made an appearance.

He threw himself into work, taking care of everything. His staff complained they didn't have enough to do. He scheduled every meeting possible offsite because every room inside the office suffocated him with constant memories and reminders of her.

After returning from a second meeting with a large local company interested in hiring them to handle their holiday party in December, Jack returned the extra brochures to the stand on the front table. He stopped by Emily's office.

"Hey, Jack. How'd it go?"

"Good. If they accept our bid, it'll give us a fantastic reference with the corporate community in town."

"That would be great." She resumed typing on the computer.

"What happened to Libby's business cards that were out front?"

"I removed them. Is that a problem?" Emily's anger showed in these little flashes. Since she hadn't quit on him, he allowed it.

He deserved much worse. The day after Libby left, he'd been convinced Emily was coming to resign every time she neared his office. Julie let him worry about it the entire day before explaining Libby asked them they stay.

Shaking his head to clear the memories, he focused on Emily. "Why? I don't mind if they're out."

"She asked me to get rid of them since she's not doing that anymore."

"What? Why isn't she decorating?" Had he crushed more of her dreams? The thought brought a sharp twist to his heart, and he rubbed his hand over it. Libby loved her work, and despite everything, Jack wished her every happiness in life.

"I'm not going to talk to you about Libby, Jack." It wasn't the first time she'd warned him away from the topic over the past month.

"I understand." His shoulders sagged under the knowledge he'd hurt the woman he loved even further.

Kevin followed him into his office and shut the door. "Why haven't you called him yet?"

"Because he destroyed my life again." He didn't need to ask who Kevin meant.

"No, you did that all on your own." He crossed his arms over his chest. "She asked you to do one thing, Jack. If you truly love her, you'll make the call."

"Did my mom call you?"

"No, but if she's telling you the same thing, then you know what you need to do. Call your dad."

Kevin walked out of the office, leaving Jack alone with his thoughts once again. The truth of his friend's words sunk deep. His own complacency pushed Libby away. His dad made a convenient scapegoat, but Jack had held so tightly to his bitterness, he refused to acknowledge his father's requests. He picked up his phone and dialed the number he'd saved in his missed calls.

"Hello?"

"I'm ready to talk."

"Jack?"

"Yes, it's me."

"Can I buy you dinner? Or coffee, if that's too much."

"Dinner's fine. Are you still in town?"

"I am. When are you available? Is tonight too soon?" Hopefulness dripped from the man's voice.

"Tonight's fine." He should get this over with as soon as possible.

"Thank you, Jack. I can't express how much this means. Where would you like to go, and what time? I'll meet you anywhere."

Jack sat across from the man who was more a stranger than a father after fourteen years of separation. *Lord, I'm not sure what to do here. I need you tonight. Help me see this through and honor Libby's request. Open my mind and heart to what Dad has to say.*

They made small talk until their food arrived, and his dad

surprised him when he asked to pray. When he finished blessing the food, he glanced at Jack. "I enjoyed meeting your young lady."

He stared at the man, trying to figure out who he meant.

"Libby? She visited with me the afternoon I came by your office."

"She quit. I haven't seen her since that night." Jack wanted to make certain his dad was aware of the pain he'd caused.

His expression reflected regret. "I'm sorry, Jack. I didn't mean to create problems for you."

"I blamed you for a while, but I'm the one at fault. She deserved more than I was willing to give her at the time."

"Your mom mentioned your sour outlook on marriage. I'm sorry you had such a skewed view of it growing up. I'd like to explain more about why I left. Your mom kept a lot of the details from you. It's time you hear the whole story. I never expected her to protect my reputation."

His dad proceeded to tell him about his addiction. He'd been a closet drinker, hiding the evidence from Jack and his mother. When Jack was twelve, his mom figured out what was going on, and the fighting began. It continued for two years until she couldn't deal with the constant concern for her son's safety around his father.

"I agreed not to drink at the house but kept several bottles hidden," his dad continued. "When your mom kicked me out, I drank constantly. I lost my job and moved from place to place, finding temporary work whenever I needed my next fix.

"Three years ago, I hit rock bottom. I was living on the streets and begging for money. Your mom and I crossed paths once. It took several minutes, but she recognized me beneath the grime and filth. After she gave me some money and told me to get a hot meal, she said she prayed for me every day and would continue to do so.

319

"I couldn't believe she prayed for the man who'd abandoned both her and her son. She was beautiful, more beautiful than I remembered." He met Jack's eyes. "Your mom's the only woman I'll ever love. I'm grateful she's speaking to me again."

Jack's mom had mentioned talking with him over the phone, but this sounded like more than one conversation. How long had they been speaking, and about what?

Jonathan Price continued to share his story. He spent that night at a homeless shelter. The next day, he showered and shaved. When a man mentioned he needed some part-time help, Jonathan volunteered. In exchange for working at the man's small antiques shop, he provided a room and three meals a day. Jonathan also earned a small percentage of whatever he sold.

After a couple of weeks, the man invited Jonathan to go to church with him. He agreed, unaware his new employer was the guest speaker. The man talked about his addiction to alcohol and how it had destroyed his life.

He went out for a drink one night, which turned into six. When he returned home, his house was on fire, his wife and son asleep when it started. Help came too late, and they both died of smoke inhalation.

"Our stories were so similar, it was almost eerie." Jonathan stared at his empty plate. "I could have lost my family permanently. Luke attended AA meetings with me for a year and encouraged me to connect with you and your mother again. I put it off, ashamed of my failure as a husband and father.

"One day a young lady and her father came into the store." He looked up with a small smile. "Your Libby reminds me of her. As I watched them, the desire to make amends with you almost brought me to my knees. I know we'll never be as close as that father and daughter, but I want to apologize.

"I'm sorry I didn't teach you how to drive or shave. I didn't attend your high school or college graduations. Or help you get ready for your first date. Even before I left, I missed so many important events in your life. I can't make up for them, but I'd like to get to know you again. If you're open to it."

Jack stared at the man, speechless. How had he missed his dad's drinking? Sure, he'd been sullen and moody most of the time, but Jack always assumed it was related to his job. And he'd never considered his father might be suffering.

"I also wanted to make you aware of the predisposition you may have toward alcoholism," his dad said.

"I don't drink." There was a reason Jack made that decision, and now he understood his mom's reaction that day. "Mom caught me with a beer when I was sixteen or seventeen. She didn't say a word but cried for two days. I never touched the stuff again."

Jonathan's smile held no joy. "Your mother's an astounding woman."

"Yes, she is." Jack loved her more after hearing the choice she'd made in order to protect him. "So, where do we go from here?"

"It's up to you." His dad leaned back in his seat as if to give him space. "If you want to continue to talk, I'm happy to meet once a week. I realize you're busy, so I'll work around your schedule. Your mom wants to have a Sunday dinner together. When you're ready, of course."

"Where are you living?" Jack knew nothing about his dad's life, but after hearing his story, his heart began to soften toward the man. Despite all of his past protests, he wanted a relationship with his father, no matter how small. "You said something about leaving town last spring."

"I live in Raleigh. The man who took me in passed away last April. He requested to be buried with his wife and son in Charlotte, so I went to make sure it happened."

"That was kind of you."

"A small way I could repay him for everything he did for me. He introduced me to the Lord and encouraged me to make amends with my family. He even left his house and the antiques store to me since he didn't have anyone else."

"Libby will love that." The words escaped before he thought them through.

Resting his elbows on the table, his dad leaned forward. "Fight for her, Jack. Take the advice of a man with years of regret behind him. When you have something good in this life, fight for it with all your might."

"She doesn't want to see me."

"Are you positive?"

"Yes, I am. I need to make some changes before she'll believe I love her. Today was a step in the right direction." And getting to know his dad again was something he found himself looking forward to. "I'll call Mom about lunch. What are you doing this Sunday?"

FORTY-SEVEN

As the day of Emily's wedding approached, Libby grew more nervous. Only a few days now, and she'd see Jack again. To make matters more awkward, Brandon was Adam's best man and Emily pushed them together every chance she got. And the wedding provided plenty of opportunities.

The past two months had kept Libby running ragged. She worked on the four jobs she'd scheduled for September while Alex, Stacy, and she set everything up for Comfort and Joy Designs. Working with Stacy again reassured Libby she'd made the right decision with her business. In two weeks, they'd officially open their doors.

After much prayer and discussion with her family and a few friends, Libby accepted the startup money from Alex and Becca. It was a difficult decision, one she still wrestled with, but she understood they'd offered it in love. She'd swallowed her pride and promised herself she wouldn't waste this gift. Alex found an office, and when both Libby and Stacy approved, they signed a lease. Once in possession of the keys, the two of them worked furiously to decorate the space for their grand opening.

"Are you all right? You seem a little stressed." Stacy sat on the floor in the center of Libby's future office with several swatches of material spread around her.

"I'm nervous about Emily's wedding." She needed to wrap things up for the day and pick up the rest of the vases and adornments for Emily's flowers. She'd drive to her parents' house early the next morning.

"I can help with the flowers if you need me, but you're better at arrangements."

Libby hadn't told Stacy about Jack. She'd become Libby's safe place—the one person who didn't treat her like she might break or ask how she was doing with a note of pity. "It's not the flowers. There's a strong probability I'll run into someone at the wedding. And I'm not sure I'm ready."

Emily's ceremony would be held in the church they'd attended as teenagers. Jack would be in the places she considered home— *her* church, surrounded by *her* family and friends. She missed him so much her heart hurt. If she didn't have a task to occupy her mind, it wandered to memories of him.

It was embarrassing how often she pulled out the sweatshirt he'd given her. The few times Libby tried to return it, he'd managed to leave it behind. Her new business venture took a lot of time and attention. The project allowed her space to begin healing. She worried seeing him again would set her back to the days immediately after she quit. The nights she'd cried herself to sleep.

"You mean Jack?" Stacy's question pulled her back to the present.

Libby's head whipped around, and she gaped at the woman. How did she know about him?

She shrugged. "When we were working out of your place, Emily said under no circumstance should I pass along any messages from Jack Price."

"Thank you for not asking about him." Libby shoved past her annoyance with Emily for interfering. It was bad enough her family sometimes treated her like a child, but her best friend too?

"It's none of my business." Stacy glanced up from the swatches she sorted through. "He came by once."

Libby's heart betrayed her by beating double time at the news. "When?"

Stacy's mouth twisted as she tried to remember. "About a month ago. You were finishing up at the Hale house. I asked if he wanted to leave a message, but he said no. Emily said not to mention it. I hope I did the right thing."

"You did, Stace. Em was watching out for me." But Libby had a few things to discuss with her best friend when she called tonight. She was sick of others trying to control her life.

On Thursday afternoon, Libby sat in her parents' kitchen with her mom, Emily's mom, and Leah Graham. The four of them worked on the centerpieces and bouquets for the wedding.

"Thanks for helping today, Leah," Mrs. Duncan said.

"Believe me, it's my pleasure. I don't get out of the house without the kids often. Mark insisted I come. He'll pick the kids up from school and take them to Chris's house for dinner."

Libby smirked. Hopefully, Callie wasn't feeding everyone.

"I saw that, Libby." Leah's eyes twinkled with mirth. "Chris promised he'll take care of dinner. Callie's working late."

"Do you miss teaching?" Libby asked. Leah taught high school English when they'd first met, but quit when she was pregnant with her second child.

"Sometimes. I'm grateful I could stay home with the kids. Mark and I have discussed the possibility of my going back when the twins are a little older. What I really miss is working with the teens at the church." Leah glanced at Libby. "Those were special times."

She nodded, remembering the simpler times. "Watching you and Mark fall in love was eye-opening."

"Do you still pray for your future husband?" Leah asked.

"Have you been talking to my sisters?"

"Amy shared a little."

Libby looked at the three women seated around the table, each one an example of a godly wife. They loved their husbands and families wholeheartedly. These women wouldn't judge her. She could share her struggles, and they'd offer advice and prayers. "I prayed for my future husband every single night since we talked about it at camp." She peeked at Leah. "That was what, twelve years ago?"

Leah smiled. "A while ago."

"And then in July, I stopped."

Mrs. Duncan glanced up from the ribbon she wrapped around the stems of the flowers of the bouquet and focused on Libby. "What happened in July?"

"Jack and I agreed to date. I quit praying for my future husband because I wanted to be with him." She released a bitter laugh. "I was convinced if he'd spend time with me, he'd change his mind about marriage. I didn't pray about our relationship because I didn't want God to tell me Jack wasn't the right man." Her vision blurred through her tears. "I failed to protect my heart, and now it's broken."

Leah set her flowers on the table and hugged her. "I'm sorry, honey. It's hard to watch one of my girls hurting like this, but I want you to remember something." She pulled back and held Libby's gaze. "God makes beauty from ashes."

326

"I said something similar to Jack once." Libby swiped at her eyes with the back of her hand. Her mom passed her some napkins from the counter, and Libby dabbed at her tears. "Not about God, but taking someone's junk and turning it into something special—a treasure."

"Exactly," Leah said. "You'll understand this better than most. Read Isaiah 61 tonight. I think you'll find comfort in it. And remember this: Even if you veered from the course God originally planned for you, he hasn't forgotten you. Your grief is his, and he'll forge a new path for you."

"Thank you, Leah. I needed to hear that." Libby exhaled and gave her a tenuous smile.

"Emily's worried seeing Jack again will prove too difficult for you," Mrs. Duncan said.

Libby nodded. "She's been asking how I'm doing more often the past couple of weeks. There's no way my feelings for Jack Price will ruin her day. I doubt we'll even talk. He'll be working while I'm busy taking care of the bride."

"If you need a buffer, find me." Mrs. Duncan squeezed her hand before returning her attention to the flowers.

She wasn't the first person to offer. Probably wouldn't be the last, either.

Libby awoke early the following morning. Last night had been late, but she finished all the flower arrangements. Emily had reserved the church and reception hall for the afternoon to allow Libby to set up the flowers before Jack's group arrived. During their phone call last night, Emily assured her again no one from An

Affair to Remember would arrive before six.

"Well, Julie and Kelsey might come early," Emily amended.

"Oh, I'd love to see them since I missed lunch last month."

"I'll text Julie. They're excited to see the flowers, and I can put them to work."

"Be sure and tell them I agreed to this."

Now, Libby rolled onto her side and noticed her Bible lying on the nightstand. She hadn't gotten a moment to read the passage Leah mentioned yesterday.

She opened her Bible to Isaiah 61. The first three verses resonated with her. *The Spirit of the Sovereign Lord is on me, because the Lord has anointed me to proclaim good news to the poor. He has sent me to bind up the brokenhearted, to proclaim freedom for the captives and release from darkness the prisoners, to proclaim the year of the Lord's favor and the day of vengeance of our God, to comfort all who mourn, and to provide for those who grieve in Zion—to bestow on them a crown of beauty instead of ashes, the oil of joy instead of mourning, and a garment of praise instead of despair. They will be called oaks of righteousness, a planting of the Lord for the display of his splendor.*

Libby whispered a prayer. "Thank you for your promises, God, and for friends who share them. Give me wisdom and strength this weekend. My love for Jack weakens my resolve to stand firm. Bring healing to the relationship between him and his father. Bless Emily and Adam in their marriage. Thank you for bringing her love.

She pulled back the covers and rolled out of bed, ready to face the day. Perhaps she could face Jack Price as well.

FORTY-EIGHT

Jack stopped in front of the antiques store at five on the dot. Jonathan Price had agreed to come to Emily's wedding and offer some much needed moral support. Hopefully, Libby would see the progress he'd made with his father.

Emily was the ideal client. Libby handled the flowers, a block of hotel rooms at the reception site had been reserved for out of town guests, and they could get into both venue sites the day before the wedding.

Julie and Kelsey had left for Emily's hometown earlier that morning. They told him they wanted to help Emily, but he overheard Julie on the phone telling someone they were meeting Libby. When Kevin stopped by an hour later to tell him Amber wanted to leave earlier than planned, Jack had a pretty good guess as to who'd been on the other end of Julie's conversation.

Jonathan laid his suit and bag in the backseat before he slid into the passenger seat. "How are you doing, Jack?"

"Fluctuating between scared, nervous, hopeful, and anxious." And he might have an ulcer.

His dad chuckled. "Be thankful for this opportunity. I'm praying for you."

"Thanks, Dad. I hope I get a chance to talk to her."

"You will." His dad's answer held more confidence than Jack felt.

Jack had formed a tentative friendship with his father over the past month. After dinner at his mom's house that first Sunday, they'd continued to meet twice a week. A few days ago, his dad suggested studying the Bible together.

"I would like to do the Bible study," Jack said while he was thinking about it. "I didn't spend a lot of time in God's word over the summer, but it's been comforting during the past two months."

"I'm glad, son. Anything in particular you want to study?"

"This might not be something you're interested in, and if not, we can find something else. I'd like to learn more about becoming a Godly husband."

Jonathan clamped a hand on Jack's shoulder. "You'll make a wonderful husband. You've already learned what not to do."

"I forgave you." He glanced over at his father. "It's time you forgive yourself." Once he'd let go of his bitterness, his opinion and attitude toward his father had undergone a complete transformation.

"I know." The man sighed. "It's hard sometimes."

"I love you, Dad." He hadn't said the words in more than fourteen years, but Jack realized he spoke the truth. He loved his father.

Thank you for healing this relationship, Lord. Continue to bless us, and please give me an opportunity to mend my relationship with Libby. I love her and don't want to lose her.

From the moment Jack entered the reception room at the hotel, thoughts of Libby assaulted him. The women had accomplished a lot. Large centerpieces on each table spilled over with white and red flowers and greenery. He knew only one person with the talent to create those magnificent floral arrangements.

Julie updated him on what still needed to be done at the hotel. The ladies had already finished at the church.

He scanned the room again. "How long ago did she leave?"

Julie held his gaze for a long moment. "An hour ago. She had to get ready for the rehearsal dinner before Brandon picked her up."

A vise tightened around his chest. Had Libby already moved on? She'd never said she loved him or cared for him. Sure, she admitted to liking him, but was it enough? She liked everyone. When she left that day, she said she wouldn't give her heart to him. She was angry, yes, but there was also sadness in her eyes. Or was it disappointment? Had he projected his emotions onto her?

They spent the next hour working. Once everything was in place, the group decided to turn in for the night. They had an early start and a busy day ahead of them tomorrow.

After an hour of tossing and turning, Jack gave up any hope of falling asleep. His dad snored softly on the other bed. Unable to lie still with his thoughts running circles around his head, Jack slid out of bed. He quietly got dressed and crammed his feet into his running shoes. He needed some air and space to move.

He crept out the door and stepped into the elevator. When the doors slid open to the lobby, he saw Chris Graham standing near the front doors talking with Emily's fiancé. Jack knew Libby's family would be at the wedding, and he'd most likely receive a cold reception from them. Quickly considering his options, he pushed the button to call the elevator back.

Before it arrived, Chris glanced up and waved. Jack decided to get the first encounter over with and approached the two men.

"The girls wanted to see how everything looked after dinner." Chris inclined his head down toward the hallway leading to the reception area.

Jack glanced that way. Was Libby here now?

"They left a few minutes ago." Adam answered the unvoiced question. "I should do the same. Tomorrow's a big day, and I need to get some sleep."

"Good luck." Chris clapped the younger man on the back. "I'm thrilled for you and Emily. Call if you need anything. Anytime."

"Thanks, Chris. I can't express my appreciation enough for everything you've done for me." He took a step back to include Jack. "Good night."

"Night, Adam." Jack shoved his hands in his pockets and addressed Chris once Adam was outside. "Your family seems to adopt everyone."

"You have no idea." Chris chuckled. "It's the James's influence. Callie's dad took me under his wing when I was sixteen. If you have time, I'll buy you a cup of coffee and tell you the story."

"Sounds great. I have nothing but time."

"Let me text Callie and tell her where I am."

Ten minutes later, the two men slid into a booth at a local diner. "It's not Starbucks," Chris's gaze flitted around the room, "but the place is open all night, and the coffee's decent."

Chris shared his story. His father had passed away when he was ten, and he lost his sister only four years later. When his brother moved away for college, Chris struggled with feelings of abandonment. The year he turned sixteen, he spent a summer working for Libby's dad. "If David hadn't taken an interest in me,

I probably would've left town and never come back, never strengthened my relationship with my brother, or reconnected with Callie." Chris chuckled. "We had a rough start, but that's a tale for another day. What about you, Jack?"

"I'm not sure what you mean."

"Libby mentioned your father left when you were younger. Did anyone fill the void in your life?"

"My mom did what she could."

Chris's head bobbed. "It's not the same, is it?"

"It's become more apparent this past month as I've spent some time with my dad. We're talking, repairing our relationship."

"I'm glad to hear it. We've been praying for both of you since Libby..." Chris snapped his lips together.

"It's okay," Jack said. "It's been rough, but she did what she thought was best. I blamed Dad for a while. When I admitted to myself my actions—or more precisely inactions—were the reasons she left, I called him. Honoring her request is important to me."

"It's nice to hear one of our prayers was answered."

The two of them sat lost in their thoughts, the whirring and clanking of the dishwasher in the kitchen their soundtrack.

After a couple minutes, Chris spoke again. "Okay, Jack, I need to say this. Libby is my wife's little sister, and since she doesn't have any brothers, this falls on me. I want the best for her and watching her hurting is painful for all of us. She thinks she's hiding her broken heart, but it's evident she's in love with you. If you're not willing to do something about that, stay away tomorrow. I'm sure your people can take care of everything without you."

Jack nodded. "They can, Chris, but I'll be at the wedding. I love Libby and want to talk to her, at least tell her about Dad."

"Good. If you hurt her again, we'll introduce you to Amy's husband."

Jack grimaced, imagining what kind of man had married Libby's oldest sister.

Chris laughed at his expression. "You'll like Evan. He's the complete opposite of his wife. And speaking of wives, I should get home to mine. I hope we'll see you tomorrow."

"Definitely." After this conversation, he was more determined to speak with Libby.

FORTY-NINE

Libby stretched her arms over her head and kicked the comforter off her legs with a grin. Today was Emily's wedding. Spending the afternoon with her, Julie, and Kelsey yesterday had been a blast. Amber even joined them at the hotel. Libby missed her friends. Everyone tiptoed around the topic of Jack as if they didn't know what to say.

The doorbell rang, and Libby hurried to the living room before her parents woke. She swung open the door to find her sisters and Becca standing on the porch.

"Good, you're up." Becca pushed her way inside. "Get your shoes and a jacket. We're going to breakfast."

This couldn't be good. She hadn't been ambushed like this in years. "I've got a lot—"

"Don't even, Lib," Amy interrupted. "I talked to Emily, and she said she doesn't need you until one. You finished decorating yesterday, so there are no more excuses. Hurry up." She waved her hands in a shooing motion.

Libby shuffled to her room, pulled on a pair of jeans and her boots, and grabbed her jacket. This should be interesting.

When she returned to the living room, the other three eyed her warily. Libby sighed. They wanted to discuss Jack. "Where are we going?" She made sure her tone reflected her lack of enthusiasm.

"Where do you want to eat?" Callie matched her tone.

"Is the place with the breakfast buffet still open?"

Callie and Becca exchanged smiles.

"It is. Let's go," Becca ushered the group outside. "I'm starving."

"Hey, that's my line." Everyone laughed at Libby's comment as they piled into the minivan.

At the restaurant, they filled their plates at the buffet and sat down to eat. After twenty minutes of small talk, Callie got to the point. "Okay, Lib. Tell us the truth. Do you love Jack?"

These three women had cared for Libby since she was born. They were the women she admired most—her mentors and confidantes. They already knew the answer. "Yes, I do."

"Is it going to be too hard to see him today?" Amy set her fork on her plate. "We'll keep him away from you."

Libby narrowed her eyes at her sister. "Don't you dare, Amy. This is Jack's career. Don't make him regret doing Emily a favor."

"Okay, we won't interfere." Amy returned to her breakfast.

Libby knew these women too well to let the subject drop so easily. Her gaze connected with each of theirs. "You can also pass the message along to Dad and your husbands. None of them needs to get all overprotective of me around Jack."

"Too late." Callie grinned. "Chris ran into him last night."

"What?" Libby's stomach churned. "Callie, please tell me he didn't make Jack regret coming."

"We're talking about Chris. He doesn't have it in him." Callie leaned forward and lowered her voice. "Jack told him he's been talking to his father."

The news encouraged her. "That's fabulous. How are things going?"

"No idea. Chris said he mentioned they're working on their relationship but didn't elaborate."

"It's a start and an answer to my prayers." Libby glanced down at her empty plate. "I'm going to get some more to eat. Anyone else coming?"

"Sure." Becca's smile reached from one ear to the other as the group stared at her. "What? I'm eating for two, and this little one is already taking after her Aunt Libby, always hungry."

"Her?" Callie asked.

Defying all logic, the grin on Becca's face widened. "*She's* due in March."

After her miscarriage last spring, Libby had wondered whether Becca and Alex would give up on having another baby. But Becca wanted another daughter, and what Becca wanted, she got. The women talked about the baby, the pregnancy, and life in general for the next hour.

It was after eleven when Libby returned to her parents' house. She took a shower and put a bag together to take to the church. Emily's wedding started at four, but the hair and makeup people were scheduled to arrive at one. Before she left, she found her mom and dad in the kitchen.

"You're going to be beautiful, sweet girl." Her mom crushed her in a hug.

"Emily's the one who's supposed to be beautiful, Mom. Not really a challenge for her."

Amanda's hands rested on her daughter's shoulders. "Libby, you've never believed you were worth that compliment. Quit comparing yourself to Emily. You're both beautiful, vivacious, and talented young ladies."

"Someone made me believe it once."

Her mom smiled with understanding. She knew Libby's heart. Neither of them needed to say his name.

"We love you, Libby." Her dad looked up from the paper he was reading at the table.

She gave him a quick peck on the cheek. "I love you too. My family is my blessing. I have to go. Em will kill me if I'm late."

Libby located her friend in the Sunday school room they'd use as a dressing room. Emily's eyes sparkled with excitement. "I'm getting married today!"

"You sure are, Em." Libby beamed and hugged her friend. "I'm going to miss you, but I'm happy for you to start your new life. Adam's the man God chose for you."

"Thank you. And we'll see each other all the time. You're still going to help with the house, right?"

"Of course I am." She'd make time for Emily.

The bride breathed a sigh of relief. "I hoped you weren't too busy with the new business."

"I'm never too busy for you." Libby circled the room and surveyed the walls. It seemed as if the only things that had changed in this room were the Bible story coloring pages hanging on the cork bulletin boards. "Does it feel weird to be back here?"

"A little, but some of my favorite memories are from this

place."

"Mine too." She squeezed Emily in another tight embrace. "This is where I met my best friend."

The hair and makeup people arrived and spent the next hour pampering the two friends. When they left the girls to dress, Mrs. Duncan entered the room, tears already flowing down her cheeks.

"Mom, don't get me started," Emily scolded.

"I've prayed for this day since you were a little girl." Emily's mom wrung her hands together. "My baby's getting married."

Emily's eyes shimmered with unshed tears.

Libby stepped between them, blocking her friend's view of her mother. "Mrs. Duncan, can you find one of my sisters or my mom? I could use their support right now." She hid her smirk. Her breakup with Jack provided her with a necessary distraction.

The woman left the room, and Emily shuddered. "Thanks. She was starting to get to me."

Someone knocked a few minutes later. Libby cracked open the door then swung it wide to let Kelsey and Julie inside.

"Mrs. Duncan said you needed help." Julie glanced between them.

"Em needed a breather from the emotions. If you two can keep her away, that would be great. We can't have the bride crying before she sees her groom."

"On it," Kelsey said. "I'll find her a project."

"I'm glad she's working out," Libby watched Kelsey scurry from the room.

Julie grasped Libby's hand and squeezed. "She's not you, but she's probably the closest we'll get."

"Is everyone coming?" Emily turned from the mirror. "We wrote our vows."

Libby held her breath, and Julie peeked at her before answering the question. "Everyone but Jack is here already."

"Figures." Emily huffed. "I specifically asked him to come to the ceremony."

The brittle pieces of Libby's heart that had begun to heal fractured. Jack still didn't believe in marriage. She'd held on to a single thread of hope that talking to his dad would change his opinion. The thread snapped at Julie's admission.

"Are you all right?" she whispered.

Libby bit the inside of her cheek, blinked rapidly, and nodded. Today was about Emily. She wouldn't ruin it by crying over Jack Price. "Let's get the bride into her wedding dress."

They spent the next thirty minutes helping Emily. Her dark skin and hair contrasted beautifully with the snow white wedding gown. Libby's eyes watered. "You're gorgeous, Em, but you don't need any help from the dress. You're glowing."

Emily beamed. "I can't wait to see yours. Hurry up and change."

Julie assisted with the red, floor-length chiffon dress with diamond bead work around the empire waist. Wide straps hugged the top of Libby's shoulders. She and Emily had discussed at length whether the dress was appropriate for a November wedding. In the end, it was the one both of them liked best.

"Wow, you look beautiful." Julie fussed with the skirt of the gown. "You won't lack dance partners tonight."

Libby frowned. "I hate dancing."

"I love it." Emily's soft, dreamy voice flitted to them as she swayed from side to side. "Adam and I will dance together all night."

"Keep telling yourself that." Julie exchanged a smile with Libby. They'd done enough weddings to know the bride and groom were often separated during the reception. Julie gave Libby a light hug, so she didn't mess up the dress. "If you need to get away, find me or Kelsey. We'll let you hide out in our room."

"Just make sure you dance with Brandon." Emily's forehead scrunched. "And don't disappear all night."

"I'm going to let you get away with that because it's your wedding day." Libby shook her finger at Emily like a parent who'd caught their child in an act of disobedience. "Don't expect to boss me around after today."

Mrs. Duncan returned. "Everyone's seated. Your dad's waiting for you."

"So is Adam," Libby whispered in her ear.

FIFTY

Jack was late. Since Emily made a point of asking him to come, skipping the ceremony wasn't an option. Once he'd parked the car, he peered over at his dad.

"Quaint," the man said while studying the church.

"No words of advice? No pep talk?"

His dad chuckled. "You're a big boy, Jack. You'll figure this out. I'm praying for you, though."

They hurried inside and located Kevin and Amber among the other guests. Jack took the seat beside Kevin, and his dad slid into the pew after him.

"Glad you made it," Kevin whispered. "I'm not sure Emily would forgive you if you missed her wedding."

Jack rolled his eyes. "Tell me about it. She's finally eased up after what happened with Libby."

"Are you going to talk to her?" Kevin shifted in his seat.

"I want to."

Julie and Kelsey joined them and sat on the other side of Amber, cutting their conversation short.

Jack glanced around the sanctuary. The women had done a beautiful job decorating. The floral arrangements at the front of the church held a combination of white Calla lilies, yellow roses, and a red flower Emily had called amaryllis. Yellow and red candles sat on the altar, and bunches of red flowers tied with yellow bows hung on every pew lining the center aisle. Perhaps Jack should put the ladies in charge of decorating venues from here on out. His employees would welcome more responsibility.

Adam's parents entered and sat up front. A tall, blond guy ushered Emily's mom to her seat.

"That's Brandon?" Amber asked.

"Yeah," Julie whispered back. "Libby introduced him to us yesterday. He stopped by the church with some snacks and asked if we needed anything. And by we, I mean Libby. It was kind of sweet."

Jack studied Brandon. He couldn't picture Libby with the guy, but he didn't want to think of her with anyone other than himself.

Once the parents were seated, Brandon and Adam made their way to the front of the church. Jack's heart pounded against his chest in anticipation. A few more minutes, and he'd set his eyes on his beautiful Libby once more. Glad he came, Jack would get to watch her while she focused on Emily and the wedding. Due to the time crunch between the wedding and the reception, he'd wait until the reception to find an opportunity to speak with her.

The music over the sound system stopped. The pianist began to play, and Emily's flower girl shuffled up the aisle, dropping one flower petal at a time. Libby followed. Jack's heart crawled up into his throat. She looked radiant with her hair down, curling at the top of her shoulder blades. The red dress was stunning on her.

Her gaze remained toward the front of the church. Jack couldn't tell whether she was looking at Adam or Brandon. *Stop it! Chris said she loves you, not Brandon. Don't create something that's not there. You have enough to deal with.*

Libby took her place on stage and smiled at Adam. The music

changed, and everyone stood as Emily entered. Jack glanced at her and immediately turned back to the front of the church to watch Libby. She grinned at the bride with joy.

The pastor announced Emily and Adam had written their vows. It didn't surprise him. Emily made no secret this was her favorite part of the wedding events they hosted.

Adam spoke first. "Emily, God placed some men in my life who showed me what loving someone with your whole heart entails. They treat the women in their lives like their most precious possessions and put their needs first. I didn't truly understand what that meant until you agreed to go to one dinner with me. From our first date, I wanted to both protect and display you. You're beautiful, inside and out, and I will spend the rest of my life treating you like the gift you are. I can't promise I'll always do everything right, but I do promise always to try my best. I'll stand by your side for the rest of our lives. I love you to the moon and back."

Both Emily and Libby swiped at their eyes before Libby handed a piece of paper to the bride.

"In case I forget." She sniffled and took a deep breath, but her eyes never left Adam's face. "When Libby and I were teenagers, we got lost in Raleigh one summer. We were in the middle of this big city with thousands of people around us, uncertain and scared. When Chris found us, we knew we were safe." She smiled at the man sitting behind Adam's parents. "He's been our hero ever since." Her gaze returned to her groom. "The first time you said you loved me, I felt that way again—like everything was exactly where it was supposed to be. I found my home. You saw past my appearance. Not only do you hold my dreams in your heart, but my insecurities and my fears as well. I'm grateful it's you, Adam Nichols. I'm thankful God brought us together. We were friends as teenagers, but you've become the man God created to love me, the man I've prayed for. You've become my hero."

Jack smiled. Emily deserved a hero, and Adam would bring

her happiness. He prayed he could be that kind of man for Libby, ready to give her everything her heart desired. It was easy to envision spending his life with her. She'd tell him about her day as he made dinner. He'd wake up every morning and stare into her hazel eyes. She'd decorate their house and leave reminders of herself everywhere like she'd done at his office.

When the ceremony ended, Adam and Emily led the recessional. Libby's hand rested in the crook of Brandon's elbow as they followed the bride and groom. Her gaze locked with Jack's, and her smile fell. His stomach twisted at her expression. Was he too late?

The guests filed out, and Jack's group huddled as the wedding party posed for pictures. While Logan finished the photographs, Kelsey and Julie would clean up at the church. As much as Jack desired to stay, it wasn't the most efficient plan. Since the women decorated yesterday, they knew where everything belonged. Amber volunteered to stay and help, so they had an extra set of hands. Jack, his dad, and Kevin would take the gifts to the hotel and welcome guests as they arrived at the reception.

Once they'd loaded the SUV, Jack scooted behind the steering wheel and said a quick prayer. He glanced at his dad before backing out of the parking spot. "Did you see her face when she saw me? She's not going to make this easy."

"You surprised her, but she recovered quickly. Your Libby's a pretty young lady."

"She's beautiful." Pretty didn't begin to describe her.

Jonathan smiled. "Seeing her again was good for you. Now you need to talk to her. Don't make assumptions, Jack. Speak with her tonight."

"I'll try." His confidence from an hour ago faltered. But he had to know if he had any chance of a future with Libby James.

FIFTY-ONE

Libby's heart missed a beat when her eyes met Jack's. For two months, she'd dreamed about him and drawn his face in her sketchpad. The images in her memory and on her paper didn't do him justice.

Focusing on Logan as he took the pictures outside became more difficult. Libby longed to run and find Jack, to hear his voice. Was he still here or had he left? What mattered most was that he'd come.

"Libby!" Logan huffed with exasperation. "I need you to stand over here with Brandon."

"Sorry." She moved to the spot he indicated and shaded her eyes from the sun. He was losing patience with her, so she needed to concentrate. The sooner they wrapped up the photographs, the sooner she could see Jack.

When they finally finished, Libby went back inside. She found Julie in the sanctuary and asked if she could help since they were short staffed.

"I'm done in here." Julie removed a bouquet from the last pew and placed it in a box filled with flowers. She stood and surveyed the room. "You can check on Kelsey and Amber while I carry this to the car. They're in the dressing rooms."

Libby hurried down a short hallway and found Amber stuffing trash into a large garbage bag. "How's it going?"

"This is the last of it." Amber arched her back. "I can't believe how many decorations were here. Hopefully there's room in Kelsey's car for me."

"You can ride with me." Libby wanted to talk about Jack, and Amber knew him well.

After Julie made a final check of the rest of the church and declared it good, the four women walked outside to their cars.

Libby pulled off her heels and dug through the bag she'd packed earlier. "Don't mind me. Emily picked out these shoes, and I didn't have time to break them in. My feet are killing me. I'm wearing my ballet flats until we get to the reception." She grimaced. "Dancing's going to be painful."

Amber stood beside her as she swapped her shoes. "Your dress is long. You could leave the flats on during the reception."

Libby peered at her feet. The dress covered all but her toes, and the shoes were black. "Maybe I will."

Once they were on the road, Libby broached the subject most pressing on her mind. "Jack came to the wedding."

"He sure did. Are you disappointed? You didn't seem pleased to see him."

"No, not at all." She peeked at the other woman out of the corner of her eye. "He surprised me. Julie told us he wasn't there when we were getting dressed, so I assumed he wasn't coming."

"I don't think he realized the church was so far out of town. He's changed over the past month, Libby. He's forgiven his dad and spending time with him. They even meet a couple of times a week. He misses you, though. Kevin says he doesn't stay in the office and schedules meetings offsite whenever possible. You realize he's in love with you, right?"

"He tried to tell me the evening I quit." Libby swallowed, her mouth and throat dry. "I was angry and told him he didn't get to say those words to me."

"Libby, he told Kevin he loved you last April. Before you went to Hawaii."

She jerked her head toward Amber, her mouth slack. How? "He'd just met me."

"Sometimes when you meet the right person, you just know." Amber shrugged. "It's as if they've always been a part of your life, and you're missing a piece of yourself when they aren't around."

"I'm not sure what to do, Amber. I love him but I dream of what Emily had today—a wedding followed by marriage. A life without family doesn't interest me."

Amber patted her leg. "Give Jack a chance, okay? He's changed his mind about his dad; he'll change it about making you his wife."

"What if he doesn't? What if I give him another chance, and he breaks my heart again?"

"What if he does? Don't allow fear of the past repeating itself to cause you to miss out on something wonderful."

Libby dropped into a chair at the table where most of her family sat. The reception had been going strong for a couple of hours with no sign of winding down. Her ankle throbbed, and she was exhausted.

"You sure are popular tonight," Amy said.

She rolled her eyes and grimaced at her sisters and Becca.

"Would you please tell your husbands they can quit asking me to dance? I need a break."

Leah slid an empty chair beside her and sat. "Your Jack sure is handsome."

"You talked to him?" Libby jolted in her seat and turned to stare at Leah.

"No, but he hasn't taken his eyes off you all night." Leah leaned closer and lowered her voice like she was about to share a secret. "It wasn't difficult to figure out."

Over the past couple of hours, Libby had felt him watching her but couldn't bring herself to look at him. Amber's earlier words had her mind and emotions spinning.

"You've got another suitor, Lib." Becca smiled at someone, and Libby twisted around.

"May I have this dance?" Jack's father held out a hand.

"Absolutely." She placed her hand in his, and they strolled to the dance floor.

The music began, and Jonathan Price moved into position. "I understand you're to thank for my son's change of heart."

"I'm glad you're talking to each other." Libby placed her hand in his, and he twirled her around the dance floor.

"It came at a pretty steep price for him. He admitted it took a while to get in touch because he blamed me for you leaving."

She sucked in a breath. "I'm sorry. I never thought Jack would be upset with you. It's what I needed to do. He held so strongly to his bitterness, and my family is the most important thing in my life. I didn't want Jack to turn his back on his own."

"That day at Jack's office wasn't the first time I've seen you. I wasn't positive until you danced with your dad." Jonathan tilted his head toward where her parents were dancing. "You both came into my store at the beginning of the year, and I watched you. Seeing your love for each other and how close you were made me realize how much I missed my family. Your visit convinced me to reconnect with Jack and his mom."

"Wow." Sometimes God surprised her. "What store was it?"

"Laura's Legacy."

Libby's eyes widened when she looked at him. "I love that place. You're the owner?"

"I am now. A good friend left it to me when he passed away."

"Oh, I'm sorry for your loss."

Jonathan offered a sad smile. "He's in a better place and spending eternity with his wife and son. I miss him, but I'm building new relationships."

As the final chorus played over the speakers, Jonathan held Libby's gaze. "Please give my son another chance, Libby. Consider the advice of an old man who's lived with regret for the past fifteen years. Talk to Jack."

The song ended, and Jonathan returned her to her family's table. "Think about what I said," he whispered.

"I will." She smiled then turned to face her sisters. "I'm going to get out of here for a little bit. Julie offered the use of her room, and I'm going to take her up on it."

"Do you want some company?" Callie scooted her chair back as if she'd go immediately.

"No. I want some time alone." She'd waited all night for Jack to say something to her. Even though he was working, she'd hoped he would ask her to dance.

350

Libby found Julie and got her keycard. Before she left the room, her gaze landed on Jack as he danced with Emily. Her friend's head was tilted back, and she spoke quickly as if arguing with him about something, but Libby had never envied her friend more. She rushed through the doors.

Once she reached Julie's room, she sank onto the bed closest to the door and poured her heart out. *Lord, I love him. I need to know if he's changed, if there's any chance of a future with him. Please give me wisdom in this. Don't let my desires overshadow your will.*

FIFTY-TWO

Emily asked him to dance and proceeded to vent her frustration with him when the music started. She called him a coward for not fighting for Libby. When he pointed out she'd asked him not to contact her, Emily told him to quit making excuses. Oddly, her angry words encouraged him.

When the final note of the song filled the air, Jack went in search of Libby, unwilling to wait any longer. Forty minutes later, he hadn't found her and wondered if she'd left. No, she wouldn't leave her best friend's wedding early. Did something happen to her? Deciding to approach her family, he'd made it halfway across the room when she returned. She stopped to chat with people as she strolled to her table.

"Ask her to dance." His dad stepped beside him and placed a hand on his shoulder.

"She just sat down."

"Jack, quit procrastinating."

He shook his head. "One dance isn't enough time for everything I want to say."

"But it's a place to begin."

"Yes, it is." Jack inhaled, filling his lungs with air before releasing it slowly. "Wish me luck."

His dad chuckled and squeezed his shoulder. "You don't need

it, son. That girl loves you."

Jack continued across the room to her table and waited for a break in the conversation. Callie smiled at him, and Libby twisted around to see who was behind her. When her gaze landed on him, her expression remained neutral.

"May I have this dance?"

She studied him as if weighing whether or not to accept.

"Good grief, Lib." Amy clucked her tongue. "You've danced with every other guy here. Give the poor man a break."

Libby glared at her oldest sister before standing. "Sure, Jack."

He itched to hold her hand, to weave his fingers with hers. Since he thought she might push him away, he walked alongside her instead. When the song began, Jack said a silent prayer of thanks it was a slow one. He placed one hand on Libby's waist and grasped her hand with the other. She lifted her free hand to his shoulder, her touch so light, he checked to make sure it was there.

As she stared at his tie, he longed to see her eyes, and what emotions they held. "I miss you."

"Me too."

"I wish I were worthy of you, Libby. It's selfish of me, but I won't let you go without a fight." He felt the slight release of tension in her body. "You captured my heart like no other woman. I'm ready to give you everything your heart desires."

Her head tilted back to reveal bright gold flecks in her eyes. He allowed himself to hope more than he had in two months.

"Everything?" she whispered.

He moved his mouth to her ear and said, "Everything and more. I love you, Libby James." He glanced at her family and straightened when he realized all of them were watching. "We have a lot to discuss, and this isn't the most ideal place. Will you meet me for lunch tomorrow?"

"I can't, Jack." Her words dashed his hopes. Until she smiled. "My family's getting together after church. You're welcome to join us."

Jack's own grin appeared. "Thank you. Is it okay if Dad tags along?"

Libby's eyes narrowed, and she cocked her head to the side. "What were you going to do if I'd agreed to lunch tomorrow?"

"Send him home with Logan or Kevin."

She laughed. Man, how he'd missed that sound.

"Bring him," she said. "I'd like to talk to him some more."

He slid his hand to her back and pulled her closer. This was exactly where she belonged—in his arms. "You're always beautiful, Libby, but exceptionally so tonight."

"Thank you." Her head rested on his shoulder. The song ended, and she stared at him. "Is it over already?"

He brushed his knuckles down her cheek. "Unfortunately. I'd ask for the next dance, but Emily and Adam are getting ready to leave."

Libby twisted in his arms and watched her friends with a long sigh. "Duty calls. Come to church with us. Service starts at ten thirty."

"We'll be there." He reluctantly released her hand. "Go say good-bye to Emily. We'll talk tomorrow."

After church the next morning, Jack followed Libby to Chris and Callie's house. She'd explained they had the most room, and Becca lived next door if they needed more space.

The house was bursting with people. Libby introduced him and his dad to Chris's brother and sister-in-law, Chris's mother, and Libby's aunt and uncle—who weren't related to her at all. Jack's head spun as he attempted to keep track of everyone. Becca and Alex arrived next, and the kids almost outnumbered the adults. Somehow the women managed to keep track of them.

Jack and his dad sat in the living room. Everyone included them in the conversation as if they'd been coming to lunch for years.

David James sat beside him. "If this is too overwhelming, we can go out back. It takes some getting used to."

"It's definitely a different experience for me." He tried to engage in the conversation, but thoughts of Libby distracted him. She hadn't said she loved him. He shouldn't expect it so soon. He needed to prove he meant what he'd told her the night before.

The men visited and joked around with each other until Callie announced lunch. The conversation continued throughout the meal and clean up.

When the group began to disburse later that afternoon, Jack overheard people telling Libby they'd see her in two weeks. He wanted to ask about it. He also wanted to ask her why she'd decided not to pursue her interior design plans.

"Are you driving home today, Lib?" Callie approached from the back of the house.

"Yeah. Stacy and I plan to finish up at the office in the morning." She gave Callie a hug. "It was great to see you, but I should get going."

Jack panicked. They hadn't talked yet. Maybe he could ask her to dinner.

"I don't like the idea of you driving home by yourself." Amanda James stood from her seat on the couch and joined them. "You had a full day yesterday and were up late the past few nights."

Libby rolled her eyes. "It's an hour, Mom. I'll be fine."

"I'd feel better if you had some company." Libby's mom raised an eyebrow at Jack.

"I'll ride with you." He could take a hint. "Dad can drive my car back."

"You've been busy too," Libby said, but her smile indicated she wouldn't object for long.

"I'm fine." Jack looked toward his dad for backup.

"I slept well and didn't work yesterday." Jonathan winked at Libby. "I'm sure Jack prefers your company to mine."

"All right." She gave in.

"Why don't you let Jack drive?" Callie suggested.

He fought a smile. It seemed Libby's family was rooting for him.

Libby peered at him through her eyelashes. "Do you mind?"

"Not at all."

They said good-bye, and Libby gave everyone a hug. Her

mom held on to her. "We'll see you in two weeks, sweet girl. Dad and I want to treat everyone to dinner to celebrate. We're proud of you."

"Thanks, Mom. You better make reservations."

"We'll reserve a room." She gave Jack a hug. "Drive safe and take care of my girl."

"I will." He heard the deeper meaning behind the words.

Libby handed him the keys and slid into the passenger seat. Silence filled the air as they drove out of town. She broke it first. "You came by my apartment."

The comment took him by surprise. He hadn't left his name or a message and didn't recognize the woman who'd answered the door. "You knew?"

"I only found out last week. When Stacy described you to Emily, Em told her not to say anything to me. Why did you stop by?"

"Emily said you weren't decorating anymore, and I was concerned." Not to mention desperate to see her.

"Why would she say that?"

The question was posed to herself, but Jack answered. "I asked her why she removed your business cards, and she said you weren't doing that anymore."

"Oh, Jack." Libby giggled. "Emily was mad at you so she didn't explain. I decided not to do everything on my own. The grand opening of my design firm is two weeks from tomorrow."

He reached over and grasped her hand. "That's incredible, Libby! Your company will be a tremendous success."

"Thanks for the vote of confidence. I'll be satisfied with a handful of clients. It's just Stacy and me right now, but we're interviewing candidates for intern positions this week. Alex also suggested I hire a human resources manager. It's exciting, nerve-wracking, and exhausting all at the same time."

"You have nothing to worry about."

"I hope Emily didn't make your life too miserable." Libby shifted the topic from herself. "At least the wedding distracted her."

"I deserved much worse. Thank you for asking her to stay."

"She loves her job. I didn't want her to leave because of my decision, and you couldn't lose both of us."

"Losing you almost broke me. I was so angry at my dad that blaming him was easier than admitting my own failure."

"But you called him." Libby squeezed his hand.

"After Kevin knocked some sense into me."

"Everything worked out in the end."

He nodded. "For the most part. I enjoy spending time with Dad. He shared his side of the story, and I realized how little I know about his life. He encouraged me to talk to you, to tell you I love you."

"How long have you loved me, Jack?"

Why did she ask? Did she need reassurance because she was uncertain of her own feelings? "I admitted it to myself the week before you went on vacation.

"Did I mention how much I missed you those two weeks? Several times I found myself wanting to share something with you. I wasn't planning to say or do anything to indicate how I felt, but the first time I saw you when you returned, those plans flew out the window. When I opened that door to the storage room, you held on to me like I was your lifeline. Then you looked up at me."

"You told me my eyes are beautiful," Libby said, "that you could read my emotions in them. You're the only person, other than my family and close friends, who's noticed."

"I don't believe you." Jack was incredulous. "It's so obvious."

"Only because you're paying attention."

"From the first day I met you, you've been the only woman in the room, Libby James."

FIFTY-THREE

The morning of the open house, Libby's nervous energy kept her flitting around the office making certain every detail was perfect. Hopefully, the turnout would include potential clients in addition to her friends and family. And Jack. She smiled when his name came to mind.

Over the past two weeks, they'd talked about their future. He even mentioned marriage and shared his concerns about being the husband she deserved. She had no doubt he'd be wonderful, but he needed to believe it for himself. They committed their relationship to prayer daily, both as a couple and individually.

Jack had visited her new office a few times. Libby enjoyed teasing him about neglecting his own business, but passing on more responsibility to his senior staff gave him more freedom. Even when their schedule remained full with events through the end of the year. Libby's pride in his success was genuine. She'd be thrilled if her own business did half as well.

Her two interns officially started next week, but they both planned to come in today to help. The girls' designs lined up with Libby's vision for her company, and their references had given glowing recommendations. Jack had sat next to her on the couch and gone through the applications with her. When she got stressed, he remained a calming presence. Her anchor. A reminder of what was most important.

Even though the open house wouldn't begin until two, Libby arrived at seven. Stacy showed up at nine as scheduled. Libby had already walked through the office once, but she and Stacy did so again. It never hurt to be thorough, and perhaps the other woman might see something she'd missed.

When they returned to the lobby, Libby caught a glimpse of movement outside. She edged closer to the door and saw Jack talking to someone on the phone. What was he doing here already?

He hung up, noticed her standing inside, and grinned. Shifting a large paper sack to his left hand, he pulled open the glass door. "Happy grand opening." He passed her the bag.

She peeked inside. Laughing, she showed Stacy the contents. "My favorite kind of bouquet. One made of candy bars."

"I know better than to bring you flowers." He gave her a quick peck on the temple.

Stacy snickered. "She's trained you well."

Libby squinted her eyes at him. "I never told you not to buy me flowers."

"You didn't have to, sweetheart. If you want flowers, you'll buy and arrange them yourself." His forehead creased. "I suppose I could have taken you to pick some out."

"This is perfect." She kissed his jaw. "Thank you."

"You're welcome. I wanted to commemorate this day somehow."

"I love you, Jack." She blurted it out.

His eyes darkened. He'd said the words a few times since Emily's wedding, but this was the first time she had. They felt good—right.

"Can I talk to you?" His voice turned husky.

"Always." She glanced at the bag he'd taken back and winked at him. "Bring the candy."

He chuckled and followed her. Once they entered her office, he shut the door. "I planned to do this when your family arrived, but I don't want to wait that long."

After the teasing out front, his serious tone and expression bothered her. "Is something wrong? You can't stay, can you? That's why you're here now, isn't it?"

"I'm all yours today." Grasping her hand, he led her to the loveseat. They sat beside each other, and he took her other hand in his. "Nothing's wrong. Everything's perfect. You came into my life and turned it upside down. I'm a better man with you by my side. Let's make it permanent. I love you, Libby James. Will you marry me?"

Everything in her stilled as she searched his eyes and saw only love reflected back. A grin split her face. "Of course I'll marry you. I love you."

He smiled and leaned over for a kiss that made her dizzy, and the rest of the world fell away. When he pulled away, he grew serious again. "Sorry I don't have your ring with me. They called a few minutes ago and said it's ready, but you'd seen me by then."

Libby's response came immediately. "There's nothing more to do here but worry. Can we pick it up now? I'd really like to have that ring on my finger when my family shows up."

Jack laughed and scooped her in her arms. "Whatever you want, Libby." The variation on the statement that changed their relationship had her instigating another smooch.

"Why don't you tell Stacy we're going out?" He nudged her toward the door. "We'll stop by the jewelry store before I take my fiancée to lunch."

Libby gaped at the building in front of her. The specialty jewelry store was known for creating unique pieces. Had Jack gotten her a one-of-a-kind engagement ring?

"Libby?"

Positive her expression reflected her awe, she turned to him. "What did you do, Jack?"

"Let's go inside and find out."

The man at the counter asked for a name before exiting through a door in the back. He returned a few minutes later with a small box. Jack took it and knelt in front of Libby. "Marry me?"

"Yes!"

After lifting the lid, he pinched the ring out and slipped it on her finger. A simple one, yet unique and pretty. Perfect in every way. The platinum band, etched with a leaf pattern, was topped with a small teardrop diamond.

"It's beautiful." She wiggled her fingers and stared at the diamond as it caught the light and glinted off the glass counter in front of her.

"Yes, she is," Jack said.

Libby pulled her gaze from her ring to find his eyes on her.

He winked at her before standing. "Where would you like to celebrate?"

"Let's pick something up and take it to the office. Stacy may want to get out for a while."

"Give her a call. We'll bring her something."

Libby sent a text and got an instant reply. "She says thanks, but she'd rather get out for a few minutes."

Once they were back at the office, Jack parked the car and rushed around the front to let her out. He shook his head at the greasy brown paper bag she carried like precious cargo. "Of all the places we could have stopped, you request burgers and fries."

"Don't forget the milkshake." She shook her drink in front of his face and nestled into his side as they strolled to the front door. "Mom and Dad are buying us a fancy dinner tonight. Besides, you're going to feed me for the rest of our lives. Be grateful I asked for something quick and easy."

"I plan to cook more when we're married. Someone should make sure you're eating balanced meals."

She giggled. Between the grand opening, his proposal, and now obtaining a personal chef, she'd never forget this day. Her heart overflowed with joy. "As long as by balanced, you mean dessert's included."

"I think you agreed to marry me for the benefits." Jack held the front door open and she slipped past him.

"Don't forget the kisses," Libby peeked at him over her shoulder. "Wait, those are another benefit, aren't they?"

"I consider them one." Jack pulled her closer.

A few minutes later, Libby went to relieve Stacy. When she reached the kitchen, Jack had set the food out but stood in the center of the room studying the wall.

She watched him for a minute, admiring his physique. At his plaintive sigh, she grew concerned. "What's wrong?"

He spun around. "We have a lot to think about, to plan. I

should warn you about something. I have zero decorating skills. It's the main reason I haven't ever invited you over to my place."

"I'm sure your house is fine, Jack."

"No. It's sparse. There's nothing on the walls, sweetheart."

"You'll have to show me sometime. Preferably before we decide where we're going to live."

"My place is a definite fixer-upper."

Libby shrugged. From the state of his office last spring, she'd guessed that about him. "I might know a few people who can help with that." She raised an eyebrow in challenge. "Any more excuses?"

The corners of his lips tipped up. "No. Will you do me the honor of joining me for dinner at my house tomorrow night?"

"I thought you'd never ask."

Jack laughed.

"What about the wedding?" Unable to resist any longer, she popped a French fry in her mouth.

"I might know a few people who could help with that." He unsuccessfully tried to squelch his grin as he parroted her words.

Libby snickered. "Not what I meant. When do you want to get married?"

"Tomorrow?" He chuckled at what she hoped was a joke and shook his head. "You pick the day, and I'll make it work."

"I always dreamed of an outdoor wedding, so sometime in the spring." She gave Jack a coy smile. "I'm kind of partial to the first of May."

Her sisters arrived at two, but neither commented on the ring. Libby and Jack agreed not to say anything and enjoy their secret as long as possible. Thirty minutes later, Emily and Adam came in. Libby gave them a tour while the interns welcomed guests and Stacy answered questions. When they'd gone around the office, Emily grabbed Libby's arm.

"What's wrong?"

"Do you have a minute?" Emily's gaze flitted to Libby's hand. "We need to talk."

"Sure." She barely contained her excitement as she led the way to a small office. Calming herself as she closed the door, she strove to keep a neutral expression on her face when she looked at her friend. "What's up, Em?"

"Don't 'what's up' me. What is that on your finger, Libby James? And, more importantly, why didn't you call me immediately?"

Libby's cheeks ached from all the grinning. Words bubbled out of her. "You noticed! My family hasn't yet. Jack proposed this morning, so we haven't said anything. Will you be my matron of honor?"

Emily bounced on her toes, stopping short of hopping up and down. "You bet I will. I'm glad Jack came to his senses."

"Were you pushing Brandon and me together before your wedding to make Jack jealous?" Emily's guilty smile was all the answer she needed. "Emily! You've been horrible to Jack."

"He hurt you, Lib, and I had to watch you suffer. I could hear you crying at night, and it fueled my irritation. I love you too much not to respond when someone breaks your heart."

She hugged her friend. "I love you too, Em. Are you and Adam coming to dinner?"

"We wouldn't miss it."

"Good. Jack plans to announce our engagement if no one else figures it out before then. I'm glad you're the first to know."

Becca and Alex arrived at the same time the friends returned to the lobby. When Libby hugged Alex, Becca's eyes locked on her hand. She glanced behind Libby and marched out of the room.

Libby turned around to see concern etched on Jack's face. "She thinks Callie kept a secret from her. They'll be back."

Alex's forehead wrinkled. "What secret?"

Libby lifted her left hand and wiggled her fingers.

"Oh boy," he muttered as he drew Libby into another embrace. "Congratulations, kiddo."

Becca returned with Callie and Amy in tow.

"Seriously, Lib? We've been here over an hour, and you didn't say a word?" Callie grasped Libby's left hand and lifted it.

"What a beautiful ring! It suits you, Lib." Amy smiled at Jack. "Excellent job."

"Thanks. I wanted something as unique as she is."

"Congratulations." Chris leaned against the wall with his arms folded over his chest, eying the group of women. "I wondered who'd figure it out first."

"You knew?" Callie stalked toward him.

He held his hands out in surrender. "They've been staring starry-eyed at each other all afternoon. It wasn't that long ago you were that enamored with me."

Becca rolled her eyes when Callie kissed Chris and returned her attention to Libby. "When?"

"This morning," Libby answered.

Another round of hugs and congratulations broke out as Libby's parents, aunt, and uncle arrived.

"Sorry we're late." Her mom hugged the person closest to her, Amy. "Did we miss anything?"

Libby's and Jack's eyes met, and they burst into laughter. He wrapped an arm around her shoulders. "We're getting married."

"I've prayed for this." She patted Libby's cheek. "Beauty from ashes, my sweet girl. It's your promise."

Libby thought about the past year. The decision to quit her job had been a difficult and scary one. But she'd been blessed with more than she could've imagined when she trusted God and took a step of faith. Today she stood in the building where her company was housed with the man she loved. God had taken the ashes from her unfulfilling job as well as Jack's severed relationship with his father and formed them into something beautiful, something she'd cherish for life. It was, indeed, her promise.

EPILOGUE

Tomorrow Libby James would become his wife. Both his and Libby's staffs worked diligently in preparation.

This wasn't the first time they'd combined their resources for an event. Libby and her employees had been invaluable to Jack last Christmas. The décor at his corporate events had garnered so much praise, the newspaper sent a reporter to one of their holiday parties. The article ran the following Sunday in the Lifestyle section and mentioned both An Affair to Remember and Comfort and Joy Designs. Since Libby's group took care of the decorations and flowers, his staff focused on caterers, desserts, transportation, photography and any special requests. Sharing the spotlight with her pleased him. They'd begun discussing the possibility of combining the two businesses in the future. The prospect of spending every day with Libby was a major incentive to make it happen soon.

This week, everyone poured their energy into his wedding. Libby had booked the Landmark Hall and Gardens. The ceremony would take place outside, so preparation was minimal. Most of the work took place in the hall where the reception would be held.

Jack missed his fiancée. Over the past week, they'd spoken on the phone every night, but he hadn't laid eyes on her since Sunday. With their rehearsal and family dinner tonight, he counted down the minutes until he'd pick her up.

At this time last year, his attitude about marriage left a lot to be desired, but Libby swept into his life and stole his heart. Tomorrow, she'd take his name, and Jack was one hundred percent positive God's hand guided their relationship.

As he drove, he took a moment to thank God for bringing her into his life and changing his heart. In addition to his upcoming marriage, his relationship with his dad had grown stronger.

He grinned when he parked in Libby's driveway. Their driveway. When they discussed where they would live and weighed all their options, they agreed to find a new place—a new start. They'd sell Jack's house after the wedding. Once they'd purchased this home in January, they immediately began working on it. Libby's family made the structural changes she requested, and once those were completed, she decorated their home. She moved in at the end of March. With the exception of the past week, Jack spent most evenings here, returning to his house only when he needed a change of clothes, a shower, or sleep.

In his excitement to see his bride-to-be, he jogged to the front door. Libby swung it open before he raised his hand to knock. Her eyes glistening, she beamed at him. "This is my last night as Libby James!"

"I was thinking the same thing earlier. He took his time admiring her dark red blouse, black skirt, and heels. "You look beautiful." He didn't think it was possible, but her grin grew wider.

"You're the only person who's ever made me believe that about myself. Thank you, Jack. I love you."

"I love you more." He kissed her, lingering to savor the moment. If it were possible, he'd stay right here all evening. But it wasn't. People were waiting on them. "We should get going. Can't be late to our own rehearsal."

The night passed both too fast and too slow. He wanted to enjoy this time with Libby but couldn't wait until tomorrow.

At the end of the evening, he dropped her off. They stood on the front porch, and he rested his forehead against hers. "I won't have to leave you here by yourself tomorrow. Sweet dreams, beautiful Libby."

She hugged him tighter. "Until tomorrow, Jack."

David James walked his daughter down the aisle. Jack barely registered the fact the man swiped at his cheeks before his gaze locked on his bride. She took his breath away. Her hair had grown long over the past six months and now fell in dark blonde waves to the center of her back. She wore a simple strapless dress of satin and tulle with pearl beading on the bodice and around her small waist.

Libby's dad hugged her and kissed her on the cheek before placing her hand in Jack's. Her gold-flecked eyes shone with love. Jack hardly heard the pastor but he must have said everything he was supposed to because all of a sudden he was kissing his bride. His wife.

As Logan posed the members of the wedding party on the bridge, there was no doubt Jack's wife was in charge. He'd never get tired of those two words. His wife. Had he stopped grinning at all today?

Libby told Logan what she wanted then arranged everyone for the shot. Jack sensed his photographer was nearing the end of his patience. They'd been taking pictures for almost an hour.

"You've got your hands full with that one," his dad said with amusement. "I'm proud of you, son."

"Thanks, Dad. And thank you for standing up with me today."

"I'm honored you asked. I hope you'll do the same for me."

Jack pulled his gaze from Libby. She'd told him she thought his parents still loved each other. Since Christmas, they'd prayed for his parents' relationship as well as their own. "You asked her?"

He peered at Jack's mom, involved in conversation with Emily, and shook his head. "Not yet. I didn't want to take away from your day. But soon."

"Jack!" Libby's voice stole his attention. "Get over here."

"Coming, sweetheart." He grinned at his dad, and followed Libby's orders. His dad's laughter followed him.

As soon as Logan assured her he'd gotten the shot—for the fourth time—Jack swung her up in his arms.

"What are you doing?" Her giggles thwarted her attempt at sternness.

"Are we done with the photographs yet, sweetheart? Our guests are waiting." He'd insisted on a sit-down dinner so she'd get to eat.

She circled her arms around his neck and nuzzled the spot where his it met his shoulder. "The last time you carried me, you told that nurse you weren't my husband."

"Temporary insanity." He set her feet on the ground and realized the rest of the wedding party had disappeared. After making a mental note to thank them later, he wrapped his arms around his bride and stared into her eyes. "I love you, Libby Price." Two more words he'd never tire of hearing. Libby Price.

"I love you too, Jack Price." She lifted on her toes.

As Jack kissed her, astounded this beautiful woman was now

his wife, he wondered what God had planned for them next. He was certain of this: life with Libby was an adventure worth taking.

Suzie Waltner

Dear Readers:

The past two years have been an interesting journey for me. Who knew when my friend encouraged me to join in the fun for NaNoWriMo (National Novel Writer's Month), it would spark my passion for writing again.

Since November 2013, I've learned a lot and hope to someday go back to *Remembrance* and implement everything I've learned to make that story even better. I hope you've noted my growth as an author through this first series.

I'm happy to report I'm already well into the next series. The first three books are written, and I'm currently working on a novella to start everything off.

Thank you to all of those who have bought my books, sent words of encouragement, or passed the word along. It's word of mouth that pulls in new readers, and I appreciate each and every one of you.

Suzie Waltner

Suzie Waltner

Did you enjoy Jack and Libby's story? Learn how some of the other couples in the book met and fell in love. Turn the page for more information about the first three books of the *Remembrance* series.

Remembrance

Leah Waters enjoys her career as a high school teacher. For the most part she loves her students and spending her time with them but she misses having close relationships with family and friends. When she stumbles upon the Graham family and their church, she starts to build the relationships she's longed for and maybe more.

Mark Graham is hurting from wounds from his past when Leah shows up at his mother's house. After a rocky start, he finds they have a lot in common and they become friends. Can he let go of his past enough for more?

Pursued

After twelve years away, Callie James agrees to return home. Taking care of her dad's construction business and her younger sister proves to be more of a challenge than she anticipated. As she struggles to balance business and family, she also struggles with the end of a relationship. Callie is thrown one more curveball when Chris Graham, a guy she's disliked since she was sixteen, turns up. Can she let go of her independence enough to trust God with her struggles and her future?

Chris Graham has been surrounded by couples since the marriage of his brother three years ago. He often feels like he's the only single guy around. His interest is piqued when he learns Callie is back in town. He never understood why the girl disliked him so much when they were young. When his brother and sister-in-law decide they would like more room and hire Callie to build an addition to their place, Chris begins to spend more time with her. The more he learns about her, the more enamored he becomes. Can he get past the walls she's erected around herself and her heart?

Enduring Love

Becca Jackson loves the quiet life she has built for herself. She remains hidden from the public eye despite her father's wealth and success. She loves her friends and her job. When her brother shows up at her house asking for money, Becca's life becomes immersed in turmoil. Between Brad's arrival and her shifting emotions toward her boss, she struggles to find peace. When Becca is shoved into the spotlight, memories of the past overwhelm her and she runs. Can she let go and trust God to take care of her?

When his best friend leaves and refuses to speak to him, Alex Newsome regrets not sharing his true feelings with her. He has loved Becca for years but never acted on it. When the threats toward her take a turn for the worse, Becca's decision to move leaves Alex hurting and helpless. He promises he'll wait for her but wonders if she'll ever be able to trust him enough to share a life with him.

ABOUT THE AUTHOR

Suzie Waltner graduated from the University of Idaho and decided to make the move to Nashville, Tennessee. After seventeen years, she now claims Nashville as home. She loves all things Jane Austen, reading, movies, and cheering the Nashville Predators to victory. While she hasn't found her true love, she hasn't given up on him. *Beauty from Ashes* is her fourth novel.

Follow me on Facebook: www.facebook.com/remembranceseries
Follow me on Twitter: www.twitter.com/nashpredsfan
Find me on Goodreads
Check out what I'm reading and find periodic updates with my books on my blog: www.remembrancy.com

Reviews are always appreciated on Amazon and Goodreads.

65369331R00219